THE GOLDEN DYNASTY

THE FANTASYLAND SERIES

BOOK TWO

KRISTEN ASHLEY

A LOVE IS EVERYTHING SAGA BY

KRISTEN

NEW YORK TIMES BESTSELLING AUTHOR

ASHLEY

FANTASYLAND BOOK TWO

THE GOLDEN DYNASTY

The Golden Dynasty

Cover Image: Pixel Mischief Designs

AUTHOR'S NOTE

The Golden Dynasty
Kristen Ashley

The land you're about to be introduced to has its own language. In order not to disturb the look and flow of the book, I have not italicized this fictional foreign tongue. I have, however, translated within the narrative, or if not, the dialogue is annotated, and the translation is included at the end of the section or chapter. For your reference, I have included a Korwahk dictionary at the end of the book. This dictionary is also available for download on my website on the Fantasyland series page. It includes definitions of Korwahk words as well as explanations of the different countries, regions and seas of my fictional alternate universe.

In order to move the story along, I also took liberties with the amount of time it takes our heroine to learn the new tongue and our hero to learn hers. Our Circe is a clever girl, and our Lahn is fabulous, but no one is that clever and fabulous...except in a fantasy.

Welcome to Korwahk. I hope you enjoy spending time there.

Author's Caution

This book is a deep exploration of the theme of compromise. The story takes place in a land in a fictional parallel universe that does not have an evolved attitude toward women. As such, there may be scenes that are disturbing for some readers. Please read cautiously.

And if you have issues around these themes, I hope you have someone, or find someone to provide help and support.

PROLOGUE
RUNNING

I was running.

Running on those stupid, flimsy little sandals.

Running for my life.

He was on his horse, I could hear the beast's hooves pounding behind me, hear this mingled with my own panting, ragged, panicked breaths—and those hooves were getting closer.

I was covered in blood. Not mine. It was still warm from spurting from that man's body.

I didn't know where I was or how I got there. I wasn't certain what was happening. I went to sleep in my bed in a world I understood, and I woke up here in a world that was entirely foreign to me, everything about it, and not one thing about it was good.

And now I was running for my life.

The horse's hooves got closer. I knew they were almost upon me. Frantic, I glanced back and saw I was right. Not only were they close, the man—the rider, so huge he seemed giant—had leaned so deeply to the side, his body was in line with the horse's middle.

And his long arm was stretched out.

I faced forward and tried to run faster.

But I couldn't go any faster and I certainly couldn't go faster than a horse.

I cried out when the arm hooked me at the waist, closed around and lifted me clean off my feet before my ass was planted on the horse in front of him.

Without thinking, I screamed bloody murder, twisted on the horse and prepared—instead of running for my life—to fight for it.

I

THE PARADE

One hour earlier...

I WAS IN A PEN, a kind of corral.

Yes, a *corral*. Like you keep animals in. Except basic. Not modern. Primitive—tall, thin but sturdy-looking stakes woven with leather bands all around.

There were enormous, extremely muscled men standing guard every four feet around the corral wearing nothing but pants made of hide, their upper bodies painted with black and white streaks. And the inside of the pen was filled with women dressed like me.

Flimsy sandals and wisps of thin silky material of all shades curved around our bodies and held together at two ends at a kind of ring-like necklace at our necks.

Their faces were made up to extremes. Heavy kohl eyeliner. Pink, purple, green and blue eye shadow. Penciled in brows. Rouge. Deep red, pink or berry lips.

And everyone had lots of hair. Lots and lots of it. Out to *there*.

I suspected I looked the same.

Truthfully, if I hadn't been in that corral wearing a light blue wisp of material and a silver ring-like necklace, I would have thought they looked cool. Whoever did their hair and makeup was a master. It was phenomenal.

But I was too terrified to think anything was cool.

There were people milling around the corral, looking in but not getting too close. They were not getting too close because the guards weren't letting them get too close. We girls in the pen were off-limits, it was clear. They could look but they couldn't touch, nor could they speak to us.

Some of these onlookers wore weird clothing.

The men, hide pants like the guards but some had loose vests on top or wide leather bands around their chests (only the guards had the black and white paint, however).

Some women wore what looked like sarongs at the bottom attached to and apparently held up by belts mostly made of woven material or leather or some were made of metal—silver or copper—but there weren't many of those. Up top they wore bandeau-style or halter bikini tops, some a folded piece of material that went straight across the tops of their breasts, the bottom coming down to a point.

There were other men looking in too, these men dressed in old-fashioned clothes, breeches, boots, flowy shirts, vests, wide-brimmed hats with feathers.

There were no women wearing old-fashioned clothes. Just the men peering in.

It was clear there were two types of people there. There were those, like the warriors, with deep-tanned skin, dark-toned eyes and black hair. These were the women in their sarongs and the men in the hide pants.

They looked at us with curiosity.

The men wearing old-fashioned clothes were different. They had all-colored hair and eyes.

All of them were looking in with curiosity too, but this wasn't benign or indifferent. It was lewd.

And it scared me.

Outside the pen, beyond the onlookers, I saw big, round tents and torches. Beyond that, it was dark because it was night, but it appeared the ground was dirt or sand and stone broken by intermittent thrusts of dark brush. It looked like a set from *Gilligan's Island* but not fake and therefore definitely unfunny.

I had woken up there not an hour ago, panicked and freaked way the fuck out mainly because I was not in my bed in my townhome in Seattle, which would freak anyone out but waking up *here* meant I was freaked way *the fuck* out.

This caused a minor sensation when I surged to my feet and started to act exactly what I was—scared out of my brain, panicked and freaked way the fuck out. This was not looked upon favorably by the painted, muscled guards. In fact, they made it very clear my freaked-out, panicked behavior was highly unwelcome. Luckily, an unknown sense of self-preservation kicked in and I quieted immediately, sat on my behind, pulled my shit together and decided to get my bearings.

At first, I thought it was a dream. In fact, I decided it *had* to be a dream. This kind of shit didn't happen to people, right?

But unfortunately, after repeatedly pinching myself and coming to the understanding that in dreams you didn't think you were in a dream, I realized it was not.

It was something else.

And that something was *way* bad.

So, as I surveyed my surroundings, I decided that I had to get out of that something bad, but I was in a pen, for goodness sakes, being leered at by icky men and looked over by people who appeared to be natives of some weird, foreign fantasyland.

And furthermore, to get out I had to know what I was *in*.

At this point, I began to pay attention and took in my surroundings.

The thing I noticed, outside what was going on at the outskirts of our pen, was that there were different kinds of women *in* the pen.

There were those with black hair, dark eyes and tanned skin—in fact, this was the vast majority of the women. And they did not seem panicked or scared. They seemed content, some chatting to others in a language I didn't understand, others holding themselves separate and eyeing their compatriots in a guarded or even calculating way (and it made matters worse that a lot of these kinds of looks were aimed at me). Some even preening for the onlookers.

Then there were others who were not like them.

Not many. I counted three.

These women looked scared out of their brains.

These women were like me.

And once I made this realization, I decided what I was going to do first. I had no clue what I was going to do second but at least I knew what I was going to do first.

And that was find out what the fuck was going on.

It appeared we had freedom to walk around and talk, so I decided my target, got up and started to move her way.

This was a mistake. The guards hadn't forgotten my minor freakout and dark, forbidding eyes came to me. Also, onlookers who had witnessed my freakout turned their attention to me, likely because they were keen to see what happened next. And further, nearly every black-haired, dark-eyed woman in the corral pinned her eyes on me and they did it in a way that didn't feel all that great.

Um...*yikes.*

Cautiously, I persevered and walked across the pen to a woman with pale skin, light-brown hair and light-colored eyes.

She didn't look panicked, as such. On closer inspection, she didn't even really look scared. She looked resigned and she looked wired. Like something was about to happen and she was mentally preparing for whatever that was in a way that took all of her concentration.

I made my way across the pen and jumped when one of the black-haired women reached out and pinched me hard on the sensitive skin behind my arm.

"Ouch!" I snapped, my hand going to the skin, my eyes going to her.

She leaned forward and hissed at me from between her teeth, sounding like a snake.

I jumped further and scuttled away.

Jeez, what was that all about?

Bee-yatch.

I glared at her as I backed away, and when I was out of her reach, I turned back to my target. I saw she'd stopped concentrating on whatever she was concentrating on and had her eyes on me.

"Hey," I said quietly when I got to her.

Her brows drew slightly together, her head tipped a bit to the side, and she replied hesitantly, "Erm...hey."

"Do you, um...mind talking?" I asked.

"No," she said softly.

Awesome, she spoke English.

Then I watched a small, weird smile play at her lips. "Especially not since you're the first person I've talked to from Hawkvale since I was taken."

Oh no.

Taken?

Oh no part two.

Hawkvale?

I was getting the distinct impression she had not woken here from a dream. Not like me.

Her hand came out and captured mine, holding strong. Her eyes searching mine, she whispered, "It'll be good knowing, once we're claimed, someone close will be from home."

Um.

On no again.

Claimed?

She'd spoken two sentences and we already had a lot of ground to cover, so I prioritized.

"I'm not from Hawkvale," I told her, and her head tipped further to the side.

"Bellebryn?" she asked.

Okay, there it was again. I was thinking she wasn't like me.

"Um...no, listen—"

Her face changed before she cut me off to say with some surprise, "Middleland?"

"No, I'm from Seattle."

This time, her brows shot together, and she asked, "Where is that? Is that across the Green Sea?"

"Yes," I lied swiftly in order to move things on. Then I asked, "Where are we?"

Her body started and her face went slack. She stared at me a moment, her hand in mine squeezed and she pulled me closer to her.

When I was near, she took my other hand and got nearer to me, declaring, "You were sheltered."

"Sheltered?" I asked, and she nodded.

"My father traveled, my mother died when I was a child, so he took me with him. He shared with me many things..." She got even closer, and her voice dropped to a whisper, "Including tales of Korwahk." On that, she looked around and squeezed my hands.

"Korwahk?" I prompted and her attention came back to me.

"Where we are now."

Korwahk.

It could not be said I was a geography whiz, but I was thinking I had no freaking clue where Korwahk was. Or Hawkvale, Bellebryn, Middleland or the Green Sea.

What I knew was none of them were home.

I already had a feeling I was screwed, seeing I was in sacrificial virgin attire and in a corral. But now I was thinking I was *way* screwed.

My attention focused back on her when she went on to say in a dire tone, "The Wife Hunt."

Uh-oh.

"The what?" I asked, my voice breathy.

She dropped a hand, kept the other one and slid an arm around my waist so we were even closer before she asked, "What's your name, my lovely?"

"Circe," I answered.

She gave me her small, weird smile and whispered, "Circe...that's pretty."

"What's yours?" I asked.

"Narinda. I'm named after my great aunt who, they said, looked like me. Though, I wouldn't know because I never met her."

"That's pretty too," I told her and her arm at my waist gave a squeeze.

She continued in a gentle voice, "So, the tales of the Korwahk Horde were kept from you."

"You could put it like that," I replied, and she nodded with understanding.

"Many girls, my father told me, were sheltered from this information. It's understandable. I spent my life mostly on ships with men. I was loved." Again with the small, weird smile. "But not sheltered."

I knew what that was like.

"So you know where we are, why we're in this pen?" I asked.

"Indeed," she whispered, but before I could ask more, a strange, expectant vibe stole through the crowd, most of the girls in the enclosure came alert and suddenly there were drums. The steady, deep, thumping beat of very loud drums.

Oh crap.

I did not get a good feeling about that.

"The parade," Narinda breathed.

Oh crap!

"What parade?" I asked, but her eyes weren't on me though she kept her hands on me. She was looking outside the corral, so I shook her hand. "What parade, Narinda?"

Her gaze came to me, and she said urgently, "We'll walk together and we'll talk. Stay close to me. We'll try to hide you. You do not want the Dax to see your hair."

"What?" I whispered, but the girls were moving, pushing in toward a swing of the stakes that was being opened by a guard.

Narinda moved me with the girls, keeping me close, her hands on me, her eyes scanning.

"We will not be able to hide you from the warriors. They'll see you. The Dax, though, I hear does not leave his podium and gives scant attention to the parade. It is said he is prepared each Hunt to claim his bride, should he see something he likes, but he has never seen something he likes. We should try to keep it that way."

We moved through the opening and out being jostled by some of the girls who clearly could not wait to start the parade.

Very weird.

"They don't seem scared," I whispered to Narinda as she kept us moving ever forward, a line of onlookers forming at both our sides.

"They are Korwahk," Narinda explained. "Some, daughters of The Horde, others from the villages and settlements of Korwahk. They feel this is a great honor, to be chosen for the Hunt. They grow up wanting nothing more than to be chosen, paraded, hunted, claimed and taken as wife by a Korwahk warrior."

There were a lot of words I didn't like in that statement, but I didn't dwell. We were walking through tents and moving toward an area that was much better lit. I didn't have time to dwell.

"And you and me?"

"Scouts sent out to faraway lands. I don't know this Seattle where they found you. I did not know they traveled beyond the Green Sea. I have heard they scouted in Hawkvale but rarely. King Ludlum is not a big fan of this and will, if a scout is captured, deal with them harshly. Thus, they usually find women like you and me who are traveling. I was with my father on a ship on the Marhac Sea. We'd anchored at a Korwahk port. Father left me with two guards who were overwhelmed, and I was taken."

"Kidnapped?" I hissed in shock.

Her eyes came to me. She didn't smile her small, weird smile. She just looked in my eyes, kept us steadily moving forward and nodded.

Oh crap.

This had not been pleasant. Even in the torchlight dancing, which did not exactly illuminate the space like a football field, I could see this had not been pleasant.

"I'm sorry, Narinda," I whispered on a squeeze of her waist. "So sorry."

"It has happened, it is past. I must look forward. Father taught me that. What has been has been but what will be is what *you* make of it."

Well, that was a positive way to look at it.

Still.

"I just hope the warrior who chooses me is kind," she said softly, her eyes were now peering at the sidelines from under her brows.

I did too.

"And I hope we can keep the Dax from seeing you," she continued.

"Why do you keep saying that?" I asked.

"You are fair," she replied. "You are the only fair woman in the parade. You stand out."

Oh no.

"And you have great beauty," she went on.

That was nice. Or it would have been nice at any other time in my life.

Not this one, obviously.

"Does he like blondes?" I asked and she shrugged.

"I do not know. What I do know is that they do not have any females who are fair in the Southlands, Korwahk or anywhere. You will stand out."

She wasn't wrong. Glancing at the girls, I definitely stood out.

"Who is the Dax anyway?" I asked, moving my gaze to the sidelines then back to the girls around us, some preening, smiling at the onlookers, nearly skipping with excitement. The few, like us, dragging their heels and moving forward warily.

"King Lahn," she answered, and I looked at her. "They do not use our language. In Korwahk, 'king' is 'dax,'" she explained then shivered before going on. "He is a savage. Tales of his exploits have spread wide. Very cruel. Heartless."

I didn't have a good feeling about that either, considering we were walking through a village of tents and torchlight, people wearing hides and wisps of material. I figured they were all relatively primitive. "Savage," "cruel" and "heartless" upped that ante by quite a bit and were not words I liked.

She looked forward and suddenly her manner became urgent, her hand slid from mine up to my forearm where she grasped it and pulled me closer even as we kept walking.

"We are about to enter the avenue of warriors, so you must listen," she said swiftly, sounding just as urgent as she was acting, and a thrill raced up my spine and it was *not* a good one. "The Wife Hunt is what its name says it is. The warriors of Korwahk are strong and fierce. They are respected. To be a warrior, you must train from a little boy and endure many trials. Only the most powerful men will be allowed into the Korwahk Horde. To give your life to this training and then go out on raids and make war with the Dax, you are promised riches, booty from pillaging and war and also participation in the Wife Hunt, which offers you the opportunity to claim a great beauty as your bride."

Okay, it was safe to say that things were not getting better.

Narinda continued.

"As you can see, we are being paraded through the Daxshee—or the Dax's village—his camp where he lives with his warriors. We will be paraded in front of his warriors. They will look us over, decide who to take as wife. Once the parade is finished, they will mount their horses while we are taken outside the Daxshee. There, we will be set free. And there, they will hunt us."

Oh.

My.

Fucking.

God!

"*What?*" I cried and she shook my forearm.

"Circe, quiet! Listen," she hissed. "This is important."

I was trembling and I was listening. Hard. So hard my ears hurt.

Narinda carried on, "They will hunt us, and they will claim us." Her fingers gripped my forearm, and she pressed closer. "They will claim us like any husband claims his wife on their wedding night."

Oh shit. Oh God. Oh shit. OhGodohshitohGod.

She kept at it. "They will bring us back to the village, naked and claimed."

OhshitohGodohshit.

"And then the wedding rite will be held before the Dax."

I didn't want to know. I really didn't.

But I asked, "What's that?"

"Settle, my lovely," she said softly, hearing and reading my tone even over the loud beat of the drums. "It is whatever the warrior wants it to be. Mostly, they just present the Dax with their bride. Then there is dancing, drinking, eating and revelry."

"Do we...?" I swallowed. "Do we get to put clothes on for this, uh...revelry?"

She nodded. "After presentation to their king, we will be clothed in clothing our warrior provides us."

That was good.

But I wasn't going to get to that part.

Not me.

No way.

I was going to run. I was going to hide. I was going to fight. I was going to do whatever I could do to get away, find out what in *the fuck* I was doing in this crazy, freaking place and get my ass home.

"I see you are frightened," Narinda called my attention to her, and my gaze snapped to hers.

"Well...*yeah*," I bit out.

"Do not, Circe, listen to me now, do not do anything foolish," she said quickly, her eyes again scanning the crowd. The lit space getting closer, I could see the urgency on her face.

"And foolish would be?"

"Do not fight the claiming. Don't. It is their tradition. They don't see anything wrong with it and look at the Korwahk women. Circe, look at them. They can't wait."

I looked at the Korwahk women. It was true. It was insane, but it was true.

They obviously couldn't wait.

Narinda went on to advise, "Take your warrior and endure the claiming and hope, *hope*, my lovely, with all your heart, that you get a warrior who is soft under all that hardness."

I was trembling head to toe, and I wanted to bolt. I wanted to run.

But it was too late.

We were entering the avenue of the warriors.

I knew this because the onlookers had disappeared. The only thing left were two lines on either side of us shoulder to shoulder of men wearing nothing but hide pants, their glistening, brown-skinned bodies painted. Some had painted white streaks in addition to black, not many, a few. More had red. About the same amount had a deep blue. Some had a combination of all of these colors. But there were some only painted in black even though those painted solely in black were nowhere near the majority.

And it was scary. *They* were scary.

This was because they were *huge*. Not big, not tall. *Huge*. They were all lean and muscled, not a little bit, *a lot*. Some had scars. Some had seriously nasty scars. All of them had black hair, all of it long and pulled back from their painted faces. All of them were wearing what looked like a long, looped chain that was wound around their waists. All had massive swords in scabbards at slants on their backs and all had two knives in sheathes at either side of their waists.

They looked like warriors, and they looked like savages.

The place was lit with tons of torches and some big fires. The drums were still beating—louder now—the sound pummeling my skin.

I walked in front of the warriors, and I became glad the Korwahk women wanted these men. I was glad because they also knew I would draw attention because I was blonde and *they* wanted that attention. Warrior eyes came to me, but the minute they did, a Korwahk woman moved to get in front of me, catch their eyes. They leaned in to show their faces, leaned back to show their bodies, pressed their arms together to push out their breasts.

Thank *God*.

"Circe, close to me, duck your head without looking like you're doing it. We approach the Dax," Narinda warned under her breath but over the drums, and I moved even closer to her and tried to duck my head without looking like I was ducking my head.

And come to the Dax we did. The drums were so loud they were all I could hear. Each beat felt like it was hammered against my body. And the Korwahk women around us became frenzied. They flooded the area to our left side and did everything to put themselves on display.

I leaned forward and peered through the undulating bodies trying to see but all I caught were scraps. Nevertheless, those scraps were not good.

A vast, wide dais, some ten steps up. On it what looked like a huge throne made almost entirely out of colossal, black, curling horns that shot up and rounded in an array at the back, the same for the armrests and seat. The feet, though, looked like elephant feet.

Um...not nice.

Behind the dais there was what looked like a stream of fire that danced the length, illuminating it. To either side of the throne, massive fire pits then huge drums that were at least the height of two grown men, and the men banging the drums had to run toward it and hurl their mallet with the flying weight of their whole body, drop to their feet, run away and then run back again. They were glistening with sweat for their efforts.

That was all I caught. No man was sitting on the throne. There was no one there.

No one.

Until I saw him.

Standing at one side and up toward the edge of the dais looking down was a giant of a man. A *beast* of a man. Taller than any of the extremely tall warriors on the sides of the parade, broader, more muscled, *more savage.*

He was looking down the dais not at the parade but at a man in robes who was gesturing up to him. His strapping arms were crossed on his brawny chest, his chest and face painted in streaks of black, one going clean across his eyes. He wore no other colors.

And he appeared bored.

That was all I saw before frenzied Korwahk girls, calling out in their strange language, closed in front of me, jumping up and down like they were at their favorite boy band concert.

"He doesn't intend to take a wife this Hunt, thank the Gods," Narinda breathed at my side, and her relief was so great, it communicated itself to me. I relaxed and she moved us forward hurriedly, but I could tell she was trying to make it not look hurried.

At this point, I did something stupid. I don't know why I did, but I did.

When we were past the dais and the girls started to circle me again to deflect the attention the warriors were giving me, I looked back at the savage Korwahk king.

And when I did, I looked right into his dark, painted eyes.

Oh fuck!

I twisted back around swiftly and sucked in breath.

"Circe?" Narinda called, hearing my breath even over the drums.

"He saw me," I whispered.

"What?" she asked.

"He saw me!" I cried. "The Dax!"

Her eyes got big, and she cried in return, "Oh no!"

I shut my eyes tight.

"All right, all right, my lovely, maybe he didn't. Maybe he—" she tried, clutching my arm.

"He did," I whispered as we moved beyond the avenue of warriors into another sea of onlookers.

She gripped my arm. "Maybe he didn't."

I nodded. "Maybe he didn't," I said softly.

But he did.

2

THE CLAIMING

One warrior slashed out with his enormous sword, cutting open the warrior who had chained himself to my necklace.

The warm spurt of blood splashed across my front, I screamed and jumped away as the warrior attached to me dropped lifeless to the ground.

Narinda had not told me about the Hunt. She had not told me that the warriors would fight each other for their brides. You could hear the grunts of men everywhere, the clash of steel, the howls of pain, the roars of victory.

You could also hear the cries of women, most were in surprise, some fear, some distress, some were in ecstasy mingled with the groans of men finding sexual release.

All of it coming at me from every direction in the dark night.

It was a nightmare. It was a nightmare's nightmare.

This was the third time I'd been caught, tackled to the hard ground by a warrior who threw himself off a horse to do it. He then took the end of the chain around his waist and hooked it to my necklace, and he started wrestling me. Fights I knew I'd lose because all of them were inhumanly strong and stinking *men*, I might add, so already stronger than me.

Not long after, they'd be challenged by another warrior (once two). They'd battle, sword against sword, knife against knife, fists against flesh, and the only thing I had to be thankful for was that the chain was long and every warrior who hooked it to me shoved me well out of the fray.

The others had given up though, by batting the victorious warrior on the head, seeming not all that bothered. They'd just unchain my chain, remount their steed and take off into the night.

This warrior had killed the man chained to me.

I backed up, trying to drag the massive, inert warrior I was attached to with me as the new warrior stalked toward me, his eyes intense, his body scarred more than most, his face—even only lit by the moonlight and the faraway torchlight of the Daxshee—ferocious and *mean*. I knew instantly, as I panted and yanked at my chain, dragging the motionless warrior with me as the new one prowled toward me, that although I didn't want any of them, *this* one I *really* didn't want.

Suddenly, he tossed his sword to the side and rushed me. Before I could get my feet to turn my body, his heavy weight was flying through the air. It hit me and I went down to my back, the wind knocked out of me, his weight now on top of me.

I struggled for breath and thrashed beneath him as he unhooked the chain at my neck and hooked his own, completely immune to my flailing.

Once he had his chain connected to me, his head turned to me.

I stilled a second at the cruelty easily read in his eyes. His hand went between us, he shoved one of my legs aside and I shrieked in his face. I bucked with everything I had, and by some miracle he went up, and I pushed him over. I scuttled from under the rest of his body, made it to my feet, my hands going to the chain at my neck to try and unhook it.

And I *ran*.

I got four steps before my chain was yanked viciously. I flew back and landed hard and painfully, ass to stone.

Whipping around on my behind, one of my hands going to the hook at my necklace and fumbling with it, the other going to the chain to hold on and give myself some slack as he yanked it again, pain piercing through my neck where the necklace dug in and my bottom was dragged across the rock toward him.

God, he was reeling me in like an animal.

What the fuck did I *do* to get transported to this *hellhole*?

"*No!*" I shrieked, tugging hard at the chain.

And then we both heard hoof beats.

My head turned, my heart clenched, my stomach dropped, and I stared at the Dax astride a huge, dark-colored horse bearing down on us.

Fuck, fuck, fuck, fuck, *fuck*!

The warrior chained to me roared in fury, pulled both knives from the sheathes at his waist and took a battle stance. But the horse kept coming. It came fast, so very, *flipping* fast, and the rider clearly wasn't going to dismount.

He didn't.

At the last instant, his muscular arm came up. He tore the sword out of the scabbard across his back, and with an almighty downward strike—the second his horse jumped the chain connecting me to the warrior, with a spark and hiss of steel against steel—the chain was severed and I flew back, again on my *fucking* ass.

The other warrior again roared his fury. This time, if it was possible, it was clear his fury was seriously *furious* as the Dax instantly rounded his horse in a tight circle and charged the standing warrior.

Oh shit.

Forget this crap.

I was *out of there.*

I got to my feet and I freaking *hauled ass.*

I had no idea where I was going. I had no idea where I was. I had no idea what was out there.

And I didn't care.

I just headed away from the lights of the Daxshee into the bright, moonlit stone and dark brush of what appeared to be mostly wasteland around it.

I had no plan. I had nothing on my mind.

Except escape.

My side hurt. My feet hurt. My neck hurt. My ass hurt. I needed a fucking *bra.*

But I didn't care. I just ran.

And ran.

And freaking *ran.*

I heard the hoofbeats behind me, steady, fast, pounding into the rock, and I knew the Dax had triumphed against scary, huge, cruel warrior.

I didn't have to look.

The Dax was coming after me.

I knew it.

I ran faster, sprinting, the pain in my side agonizing but I kept going as fast as I could.

The horse's hooves got closer. I knew they were almost upon me.

Frantic, I glanced back and saw I was right. Not only were they close, the man—the rider, so huge he seemed giant—had leaned so deeply to the side, his body was in line with the horse's middle.

And his long arm was stretched out.

I faced forward and tried to run faster.

But I couldn't go any faster and I certainly couldn't go faster than a horse.

I cried out when the arm hooked me at the waist, closed around and lifted me clean off my feet before my ass was planted on the horse in front of him.

Without thinking, I screamed bloody murder, twisted on the still running horse and prepared—instead of running for my life—to fight for it.

He had an arm around me, the other hand dropped the reins, and he went for the chain at his waist.

I lifted my hands, nails bared, and went for his eyes.

I caught the flash of surprise that slashed across his dark, painted features before he abandoned the chain and his hold on my waist. He reared back and caught my wrists before my nails reached their target.

I took that opportunity to slide off the slowing horse.

Doing this, he was forced to let go or come down with me. I hit feet first, pain shooting through my ankles and up my calves, and I dropped because of it, rolled, found my feet again and started to run.

The horse came back at me, but this time I was prepared. When I glanced back and saw him *this close,* I ducked under his arm. Him and his horse shot past me, and I instantly changed directions and ran the other way.

I seemed to be making some headway and I heard no horse but was stopped when a steely arm wrapped around my waist, lifted me off my feet and whirled me around.

Shit, he was off his horse.

And shit again, he could run *without sound.*

I bucked violently then kicked my feet out even more violently.

His arm loosened, my feet hit stone, and I tried to run but he caught me again. I whirled in his hold and lunged in the small space. Bracing against a foot I planted behind me, I shoved with all my weight.

His torso rocked back, his arm loosened again, I took three quick giant steps back then *he* lunged. There was more of him than me and it was more powerful. He tackled me and I landed on my back, him on top of me.

Grunting, straining and struggling, I fought, pushed, kicked, scratched and bit.

I was no match.

Not even close.

Subduing me with his body, one arm and his heavy legs, his other hand came up and he hooked his chain to my necklace.

Damn it all to hell, I knew what *that* meant.

My back arched and I screamed with all my might the frustrated rage that surged through my system.

But even chained to him, knowing it was a fight I'd never win, I didn't give up.

My hand went to his waist. I found the hilt of the knife and pulled it free, whipping it back. But he disarmed me before I could take that first slash. Then his own hand went to the other knife, pulled it out and tossed it away.

Damn.

I still didn't give up. I kept fighting.

Nails, teeth, screams, punches, bucking, kicking...nothing worked.

He succeeded in positioning himself, hips between my legs. He then yanked the edges of the material covering me aside so roughly, both sides tore away from my necklace, leaving me fully exposed.

My back arched again as I screeched, "*No!*" right in his face and didn't give up.

His hands caught my wrists, tugging them over my head. One hand transferring both of my wrists to be imprisoned in just one of his big hands, his other went down between our bodies.

"Please, no!" I cried as I kept struggling. His hand worked at his hides, and I knew what he was doing. I felt him hard against me. "Please, please, please, no."

His head came up, his eyes caught mine, the whites so white against the black of his paint, his hand at my wrists squeezed hard, causing pain, my back to the stone causing more, I gave him the only fight I had left.

I glared at him.

He held my glare for long moments.

Then, his eyes never leaving mine, he whispered, "Lahnahsahna."

And he bent his head, shoved his face in my neck, and he violated me.

THE SECOND HE ENTERED ME, I didn't see it, my eyes had squeezed closed, but a flash of lightning rent the dark night.

3
THE RITE

I was bloody and naked before him on the massive steed, his arm around me, his big, hard, heated body all I could feel at my back, the horse moving all I could feel under me.

But I felt something else.

I felt the aches in my muscles, the pains on my skin, both seemed to cover every inch of my body, inside and out.

And I felt something else, something so hideous I refused to feel it.

So I didn't. I blanked out everything as I watched the lights, fires and tents of the Daxshee get ever closer and I concentrated on whatever horrors that were next for me.

He was going to parade me naked through his village, through his people, through his warriors, through those awful *spectators*—hunted, beaten, naked and shamed.

I closed my eyes.

How was I going to bear it?

The long way back his horse had walked, not trotted, not cantered, not galloped.

Walked.

It took forever and he'd said not a word. He also didn't hold me with tenderness or triumph. It was like I was a bundle he had to deliver safely. Nothing more.

Nothing more.

I was his wife now.

Jeez. *His wife.*

Oh God.

I needed to get home.

The horse slowed then stopped.

My eyes opened and my body started.

Five women were rushing to us carrying a variety of things I couldn't really make out in the dark. I looked beyond them to see we were well outside the outskirts of the Daxshee. It was visible but still a ways away.

Why were we stopped?

He dismounted and his hands came up, closed around my waist, and he pulled me off the horse.

I tried to hold it back, but I couldn't stifle the moan of pain. He set me in front of him but did not let go of my waist or move away.

I looked up into his painted eyes to see he was observing me like a specimen under glass. There wasn't a lot of light, but I could see his face and it was blank and uninterested.

God, I hated him.

His hand lifted, and he unhooked the chain from my necklace. He turned his head and barked something at the women then stepped away from me. The minute he did, one of them rushed forward. Gently taking my hand, she guided me away from the horse to the other women.

And that's when, weirdness of all weird, they fawned and cooed over me, talking in their foreign tongue in soft voices as they wet rags from big jugs and carefully, soothingly wiped away the blood and dirt on my body. While they were doing this, one of them divested me of the silver ring around my neck.

What on earth?

I started to move away, not thinking to run, that monster would catch me, but to get away from the women. My body was twisting this way and that as their soft rags worked at me, but one woman stayed close and held me firmly but kindly while the others cleansed me. The whole time the woman who held me murmured gently in my ear.

Once I was washed head to toe, the woman holding me said something quietly. The others nodded, rushed away, bent to some trunk that was about five feet away and then they rushed back carrying things that sparkled in the moonlight.

Oh please, God, let it be clothes.

My prayers were answered, sort of.

First came what looked like gold chain links. Tinkling over my head, they pulled it down, fastened it and I saw it was a halter top exposing as much as it covered.

Not great but at least not nothing.

A short skirt of the same links was wrapped low around my hips.

Okay, still not great but not nothing.

Then a wide, low-hanging, very heavy, battered gold necklace was pulled over my head. It was so wide and hung so low, it covered my breasts almost completely, just some flesh at the sides and bottoms showing.

All right, this was getting better.

After that a *very* heavy, very wide belt made entirely of gold disks, more dangling from the bottom, was attached around my hips, hiding my sex, but I could feel not entirely covering the cheeks of my ass.

It wasn't enough, it didn't make me comfortable, all that gold was damned heavy, but I was not going to quibble.

Gold bands were pushed up my arms to my biceps on both sides, the same with very wide cuffs wrapped around that nearly covered me from wrists to elbows.

Well, I would have preferred that amount of coverage elsewhere, but again I was not going to complain.

And then, a thin band of golden feathers—so golden, they glinted in the moonlight like they had glitter on them—was wrapped around my head at my forehead and tied at the back.

Finally, moving quickly, they coated my body in a thin layer of oil so that it glistened.

Totally weird.

This was clearly the finishing touch, for the minute they were done with the oil, they all moved, stepping backward and bowing while the woman who held me murmured something to the Dax.

Before I knew it, me and all my heavy gold were swooped up in a powerful arm and planted on the horse. The second my ass hit the horse the Dax swung up behind me.

But we didn't move and one of the women rushed forward. She took one of my ankles in her hand, pushed up and made as if to swing my leg around the beast's neck.

She was telling me I was meant to ride straddling, not as I had been, side saddle.

I didn't demur. I didn't have it in me to demur. Any demurring was left on a stone some ways back. I swung my leg around. She nodded in approval, smiled at me and started to step back, bowing.

The Dax made a noise of tongue against teeth and the horse moved forward even before the woman fully cleared the animal.

Okay, so, the bad news was, I was in another world, I had no idea how I got there, and that other world was absolutely no way a place I wanted to be. I'd been paraded before warriors and hunted. I watched a man die for me, a man who did not even know me. I'd been pursued through a wasteland and forced to receive the attentions of a savage king. I'd then endured the humiliating ride back wearing nothing but a necklace, chained to a brute. I had no way of knowing when this would end, *if* it would end, and if I would ever get back home.

But at least I wasn't going to be paraded through a primitive village naked. The gold was heavy, the chain links weren't exactly the finest silk, the whole ensemble didn't entirely cover me.

But I decided I'd look on that as the good news.

People started flooding toward us as the horse became visible outside the Daxshee and the Dax changed our positions on the horse. This change was minute but significant. His arm around my waist slid up so the swells of my breasts rested on it, and it tightened so I was held snug to his big body. This said I was not a bundle to be delivered safely. This was more intimate.

This said I was claimed.

His mouth came to my ear, and he said the first words since he took me.

I didn't understand a one of them, but I recognized the last one, and even if I didn't, I wouldn't forget it.

The last word he said in his deep, scary, rough voice was a forceful, "*Lahnahsahna.*"

Okay, whatever the hell that meant, it meant something to him. Therefore, I needed to find out what it meant. And I was figuring I needed to find that out fast.

With the old-fashioned attired men holding back but their eyes still on us, his native people rushed the horse, took one look at me in my golden outfit and started cheering, smiling, laughing, jumping in joy, holding their hands up and waving them. Some of them chanting as we rode through them. Flowers were thrown, just petals, but the deeper we got into the Daxshee, the more people there were, the more petals drifted around us until they were all I could see.

It sucked, but I had to admit their softness felt nice floating and gliding against my hot, scraped, aching flesh. And if this was a joyous occasion, like a real wedding of people uniting in love (which it was *not*), those light petals drifting through the torchlit night would be beautiful.

The Dax said not a word as he rode through the crowd and his horse didn't miss a beat but kept his slow, steady walk through the throng.

The people and their petal throwing stopped when we reached the dais area. They hung back but their cheers and chants carried on as the horse took us to the center of a wide semi-circle of stone that bowed out from the dais. This semi-circle was created by warriors astride horses, their claimed women in front of them on the horse, straddling it, wearing nothing but their necklaces with the warrior's chain hooked to it.

At this, I was realizing it might be good to be queen.

None of them, including—I looked and found Narinda—had a stitch of clothing on.

When I caught her eyes, I tipped my head to the side and gave her what I knew had to be a small, weird smile.

Her face grew soft, and she returned it.

I looked at the other warriors and their women. Some women appeared thrilled beyond belief. Some disappointed. Some frightened (and these were even the native women, apparently having men fight to the death for you then being raped in a barren wasteland was not all it was cracked up to be).

The Dax stopped us at the foot of the steps to the dais and didn't hesitate in dismounting or pulling me off the horse.

I tried (and failed) not to think of my ass cheeks showing as he took my hand and walked up the dais toward the thrones at the top.

Yes, *thrones.*

Now there were two of them. The massive black one was now accompanied by another, smaller one. The same style but the horns were white, and the feet were not elephant feet but some other animal's feet. Maybe deer. Maybe gazelles.

Serious gross.

The black throne had no pad, as it had none before and obviously this was meant to show that seasoned, badass warriors didn't need sissy things like cushions for their asses. But the white throne had a fluffy, gold silk covered pad on the seat and another one on its end resting against the back.

Okay, more good news. I got pads. I could use pads. My ass was freaking *killing* me.

We made it to the top and he turned us to the crowd. I could see beyond the large, wide arc of what had to be at least a hundred warriors, it could actually be more, their brides and their horses, that the crowd had closed in.

The Dax stood there, holding my hand, his gaze moving over the gathering. Someone had taken his horse away so at the immediate bottom of the dais there was nothing but a vast open space, torchlight dancing on the smooth, cream stone.

He did not speak. He just surveyed the crowd with his frightening, painted eyes. They did not cheer or chant. They just stayed silent and watched us.

This, by the way, was not fun, but I'd had less fun that night so I just took it and stood there.

He started shouting so suddenly my body jerked. I had no clue what he was saying but whatever it was, he *meant* it, like, *a lot*. And this was proved to be true when, twice, he banged his mighty fist on his muscled, painted chest.

He shouted for a while then suddenly he tugged my hand. He bent as my body fell into his and his other arm tagged me behind the knees. He let my hand go, his arm going around my waist, and he swung me up with such force, my legs went flying and my arms automatically circled his neck so I wouldn't be sent soaring through the air.

Once he had me in his hold, he roared, "*Kah Lahnahsahna!*"

A deafening cheer tore through the crowd, so fierce, the wall of sound hit me like a physical thing.

But he didn't bask in whatever glory he was receiving. He turned toward the chairs, and when he did, my eyes tipped to his just as his bearded chin (he had a full, black beard; it was long at the chin and held at the point with a gold band) and his eyes locked with mine.

His arms squeezed me so tight, I thought he'd break bones.

Then he whispered fiercely, "*Kah* Lahnahsahna."

Before I could say a word, he deposited me on my throne and then sat in his.

Okay, I *seriously* needed to find out what that meant.

I looked over at him to see him tip his head at the first warrior in the arc. More drums started sounding, not the booming sound, these were smaller, made less noise, but it wasn't music. It was just a beat and the wedding rite (I guessed) started.

Each warrior rode his horse right before us to the foot of the steps to the dais, stopped, dismounted, pulled down his bride and walked her up the steps to us. This happened one after another. All of the men jerked their chin up to the Dax then their eyes came to me, and they bowed their head slightly. Some of the women bowed to the king and to me.

After the jerking chin, bowing thing, one of the warriors pulled his bride in front of him, wrapped his arms around her, one at her chest so he could lift his hand to cup her jaw and he grinned at his king.

Clearly, he was pretty pleased with his bride, and in spite of myself I had to admit it was kind of cute. And I allowed myself to admit this mainly because the girl looked a little tentative but also a little pleased too.

I glanced at the Dax who had no visible response. He might have thought it was cute or he might have been fighting a roll of his eyes. But his face gave away nothing.

Still smiling, that warrior walked away with his arm around his naked bride's shoulders.

A few couples later, Narinda came up with her warrior. She had blood on her too. Clearly, he'd fought for her because he had a minor wound at his shoulder. The chin jerks and bows went on while I leaned forward and caught her eyes.

"I'm all right," she mouthed before she hesitantly tipped her head back to her (handsome, I was pleased to see, very handsome but also hopefully soft under all that muscle) warrior.

I was equally pleased to see him slide his arm along her waist in a way that looked kind of tender before he guided her down the steps.

Okay.

Shoo.

Maybe Narinda was going to be okay.

More warriors, more brides, more drums, more chin jerks and bowing and then, almost to the end, I was shocked to see the cruel warrior who got his chain on me before the Dax had severed it was striding up the steps dragging an extremely beautiful native girl behind him.

He, too, was wounded, one eye swelling, a cheekbone too and he was bleeding profusely from his nose and shallow but nasty gashes on his chest.

But it wasn't his wounds that freaked me out. It was his eyes.

His eyes were burning, and this burn came from his soul, that soul was filled with hate and his eyes were locked on his king.

Oh man, *that* did not bode well.

His bride stumbled on the steps, but he didn't even slow. He dragged her on her knees to the top of them. This caused me to take in a sharp breath and I felt it.

Something coming from the Dax.

Something not good.

I tore my eyes away from the bleeding, vile warrior whose new wife was on her knees by his side, his blood—and probably others, considering her beauty—all over her naked body, and I looked at the Dax.

He gave nothing away. His expression had not changed, and his body was held loose and relaxed. And somehow, I knew his not giving this man anything was taking away what that man most wanted. He wanted the Dax to look angry or alert to the obvious threat he posed.

But the Dax wasn't giving him even that.

Still, my new husband did not like this guy. I could sense it.

My attention snapped back to the warrior when I heard his bride cry out in pain.

I froze in horror when I saw he was pulling her up by her hair.

Unless I missed it, he didn't give the Dax a chin jerk or me a bow.

Instead, he positioned his new bride in front of his body, kicked her legs apart with his foot, his arm circled her as his other hand stayed clenched in her hair, clearly in a painful way for both her hands had wrapped around his wrist and her stunning face was twisted in distress. His torso bent low, his hand moving from her waist, to her belly, down, over her sex, curling in...

My eyes shot to the Dax as I heard her whimper.

He did not look at me. His face was set to blank, and his gaze was glued to the warrior. That gaze was up, not down, not watching what he was doing but locked on the warrior's face.

Then I watched his lip curl.

But I didn't feel the warrior move away, though I heard his woman keep whimpering.

He was still hurting her.

I couldn't allow it. After what had happened to me that night, to Narinda, to all those frightened girls out there who had been claimed on rough rocks by savage warriors, I couldn't allow it. Not this. What we'd endured was humiliating. *This* was beyond that.

I had to do something.

"Stop him," I whispered to the Dax, but he didn't tear his eyes from the warrior. "Stop him," I repeated, but he ignored me. Hesitantly, not wanting to do it, never wanting to touch him but spurred on by the girl's whimpers and fresh memories of my own nightmare, I reached out a hand and wrapped my fingers around his wrist. "Stop him," I implored.

At my touch, the Dax's head turned, his dark eyes dropped to my hand then they lifted to my face. I saw them move over my features, but he gave me nothing. I didn't know what he was thinking. I had no clue.

When the whimpers continued, I moved my hand to his, curled my fingers around, shook it, leaned in and begged, "Please, *please,* stop him."

The Dax stared at me.

God, he had no idea what I was saying.

Or worse, he didn't care.

Suddenly, his head turned to the warrior, and he said something to him in a low voice that included two words I knew, "Kah Lahnahsahna" and one that struck me, "Dahksahna."

"Tooyo!" was the response spit from the warrior, and that got a reaction.

The Dax's face went hard.

Uh-oh.

My hand slid away.

He was freaking scary normally, but when his face went hard like that...

Yikes.

"Tooyo?" he asked softly.

"Tooyo!" the warrior repeated.

I pulled my eyes away from the Dax and wished I didn't.

The warrior was working the girl with his fingers, right there, right in front of us and for all who could see. She was not enjoying it, not even a little bit, her face stained with tears, her body twisting madly to get away.

The instant my gaze took it in, I didn't even attempt to hold it back.

I tensed and shouted, *"Stop it!"*

The warrior's eyes sliced to me, and he smiled a cruel smile, but he did... not...stop.

I jumped from my seat and screamed, *"Stop it!"*

"Tooyo!" he shot back at me.

And that was it.

The Dax was out of his seat, the woman ripped from his hands and thrown at me. I caught her in my arms as the Dax moved on the warrior. The warrior shifted to deflect him, but without any apparent effort and so fast the warrior didn't even begin to defend himself, the Dax rammed his hand palm first, fingers wrapping around, into the man's throat. He lifted the huge guy right off his feet, took two long strides and threw him down all ten steps, the man flying through the air to land on his back at the base of the dais.

That's right...*threw him*. He *threw* an enormous, grown man *through the air* down ten steps.

Holy *crap*!

The Dax stood at the top step looking down and then his rough voice rumbled through the drum filled night when he called, "Kah Dahksahna me ahnoo."

The warrior scrambled to his feet. The Dax's body tensed to alert. The crying woman in my arms shoved closer into my body, my arms tightened around her, but other than that, I stood stock-still.

They went into staredown and this lasted awhile before the warrior spit on the steps and stalked away.

The Dax turned, and without looking at me or the girl, he moved back to his throne and sat. Two women bustled up the steps and laid gentle hands on the girl, pulling her away from me to the side of the dais. They ducked into the crowd after they reached the bottom of the steps.

"Kah Dahksahna." I heard the Dax say from behind me.

I turned and caught his painted eyes.

They were burning into mine. Then they looked at my throne and back at me.

Guess it was time for me to sit back down.

I took in a shuddering breath and slowly lowered myself to the pad under the Dax's black gaze. Once my ass was to the pad, he turned away and jerked his chin at the next warrior.

And then the wedding rite continued like nothing happened.

No joke.

Like nothing happened.

God, I had to get out of this place.

4
THE GOLDEN DYNASTY

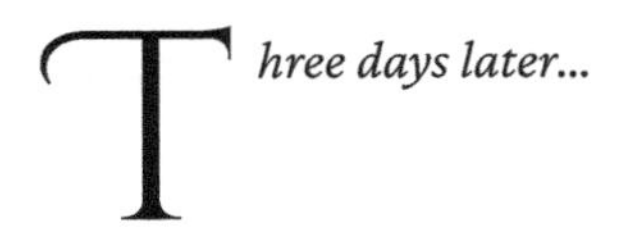*hree days later...*

"Kah Dahksahna, shalah dahnay," the woman implored, her hand resting light on my hip over the silk sheet.

My head was to a pile of silk pillows. My eyes were open and unseeing. I could feel the soft hides under my body. The light silk sheet was down around my waist, but I was covering my naked breasts with my arm.

And I wanted to die.

Every day, I didn't wake up at home. Three nights of sleep, three days of waking up, and I wasn't going home.

Three days of waking up to the attentions of the king.

Three nights of being woken to more attention when he arrived back at the tent.

There were no murmured words of tenderness, even ones I didn't understand. There was no attempt at foreplay. No cuddling afterward. He didn't hold me in his sleep. He just turned me to my belly, yanked me up to my knees, used me, pulled out, dropped down beside me and fell asleep (or, in the mornings, after he took me, he got up, dosed himself with water from a jug, pulled on his hides without even toweling off and prowled out).

He didn't share meals with me (not that I got up to eat, I didn't get up at all, except to use the pot at the back of the tent). He didn't visit with me.

He didn't even know my name.

At least he was gone during the days.

And he had just left, and like every day when he left, the five women who'd seen to me after the claiming rushed in and bustled around his tent with great activity. The one with dark skin (clearly the leader of the group) as usual coming to me, talking gently but increasingly anxiously using words I didn't understand. But her hand was always light on me, the shakes she'd give my body always gentle, and I got the message—she wanted me to get up.

I didn't get up and eventually they gave up and stole out.

I barely looked at them.

I needed to get home. I needed to get *the fuck* out of there.

I needed to do it, but I had no clue, not that first stinking clue, *how* to do that.

And my nightmare rolled on.

The hand left my hip and I felt her get up from the bed. Then I heard her speaking softly but urgently to the other women.

I shoved my hand under the pile of soft pillows at my head and kept staring across the tent, seeing nothing, still feeling him between my legs, knowing he'd be back.

What could have been five minutes or five hours later, I heard the tent flap slap back. My body tensed, my mind searched the tent to see if it could feel if it was *him* who had returned (it would be a first, it was still daylight), and I didn't feel his raw, brutal energy filling the space.

I relaxed.

I then felt a presence seat itself behind me and another light hand on my hip.

"Kah Dahksahna, my dear, you must rise. You must eat. You must show yourself to The Horde."

I blinked and turned to my back, my arm moving to cover my breasts as I stared up at a very pretty woman with dark-brown hair, hazel eyes and a gentle expression. She was wearing the clothing of the natives and speaking my language.

"You speak English?" My voice was scratchy because I hadn't used it in three days.

Her head tipped to the side. "English?"

Great. She didn't know what English was. She wasn't here from a dream either.

I stared at her and guessed she was maybe in her early forties and aging very well. I also knew in their desperation the women who tended me went out and found a woman who spoke my language.

Well, interesting to know that there was another person in that vile place who spoke my language but not interesting enough for me to care.

I turned to my side again and resumed my contemplation of nothing.

Her hand shook my hip gently. "Kah Dahksahna, please, you must rise. There are whispers."

"I don't care," I stated, though it was more that I didn't understand. But I didn't care enough to understand either.

"I see you were sheltered," she muttered to herself, her fingers giving me a kindly squeeze.

No.

I wasn't sheltered.

Like Narinda, my mom died when I was young. It happened when I was ten. A freak incident, the kind you never heard of unless it was on TV or in a movie. Mom going to the bank, a robbery in progress. The robber flipped out when Mom walked in, he turned and shot her. She died in the ambulance. She was doing something simple, making a deposit and then...no more Mom.

My father owned a moving company and was not loaded by a long shot. Therefore, he couldn't afford to pay for babysitters or childcare, but also, with what happened to Mom, I thought it was about him keeping me close and around people he trusted. So I grew up in his office around his men who looked after me, took care of me, were cool about it, and I loved them. They did their best to be appropriate around me, but they were guys. Shit happened. I heard things. It was the way of the world.

And I grew up in that office until I started managing that office at fifteen. Now, at thirty-five, I still managed that office, and the men didn't do their best to be appropriate around me. I was older, I'd been around awhile, so I was one of the guys.

Though one of the guys with tits and ass that I caught some of them staring at on more than one occasion.

But I wasn't sheltered.

That said, I'd definitely been sheltered from *this*. Then again, Pop didn't know *this* existed. If he did, though, he'd have sheltered me from it. He'd take a slash from a warrior's sword to protect me from it, as would any one of his boys. I knew it.

I wondered what he was thinking, being at home, me not there. He was probably going out of his mind.

"I know this is strange for you," the woman said.

Right. *Strange.*

Yeah, she hit that on the head.

Strange.

Though, I might use another word for it.

Or several.

"But you *must* care, kah Dahksahna," she whispered on another squeeze.

"My name is Circe," I told her quietly.

"Pardon, my dear?"

I sighed then repeated, "My name is Circe, not kah Dahksahna."

"Circe, lovely," she murmured. "But Dahksahna isn't your name, it is just you. It means 'queen' and you are our queen."

I decided not to reply. That had been working with the other women—no reply, eventually they'd go away.

Her fingers gave me another squeeze and I felt her bend closer.

"I remember feeling much the same as you. Seerim, my warrior husband, was different than the Dax, of course, but I remember this feeling, my dear. I know it is not a good feeling. But you will come to understand it is their way."

"It sucks," I muttered, forgetting about not responding.

"Sucks?" she asked, sounding confused.

"It sucks. It stinks. It's for the birds," I explained, rolling to my back again with my arm over my breasts, and I locked eyes with her. "It's hideous, foul, vile, detestable...it *sucks*."

Her eyes got soft, and she said quietly, "It is their way."

"Their way *sucks*," I returned and rolled again to my side.

Her voice came back to me.

"I understand you see it that way. But they know of our way, of wooing and falling in love and waiting to claim your mate after your wedding celebration, not the peasants doing that but soldiers doing it, *warriors*, and *they* think *that* is strange. Laughable. Silly. They think it is ridiculous, not to face a challenge, best your brothers in order to earn a beautiful wife. You don't believe me now, but I promise, as unbelievable as it seems, you will come to understand their way. I have seen now ten Wife Hunts since my own. There are girls like you, girls who settle in and enjoy their lives with The Horde. You will too. You just need to get up and face it, learn their ways, be amongst—"

I cut her off. "I'm not getting up."

"You must."

"Well, I'm not."

I felt her get close, her mouth at my ear. "You *must* Dahksahna Circe. For your slaves, for your Dax, for The Horde and...for *you*."

My body got tight, and my head turned to her. "My...*slaves*?"

I watched her nod. "The women who have been seeing to you. Those are your slaves. The Dax has given them to you. It is very generous. Most warrior brides receive a slave, at most two. I have been with my warrior over twenty years and I only have three."

I blinked then repeated, "*Slaves?*"

Her face flooded with understanding but still she stated, "The Horde takes slaves. It, too, is their way. In fact, this is the way throughout the Southlands."

Jeez, these guys *were* savages.

"That's insane," I whispered.

"It is their way," she replied, and I had to admit, I was tired of her saying that.

"It's insane," I repeated.

"It is their way, Dahksahna Circe," she returned firmly. "And if you do not get up, the Dax will be forced to intervene."

Uh-oh, I did not like the sound of *that*.

I stared at her.

She went on but she did it looking like she really didn't want to.

"He has bragged greatly about you. The Lahnahsahna, a *true* warrior's wife."

Is that what Lahnahsahna meant?

And...

He *bragged* about me?

She kept talking.

"He told his people he did not claim you. He told his people he *battled* you before he won you. He told his people you challenged him. The warrior king's bride fought like a warrior. She did not lay back and accept her fate. She stood strong and shouted in the face of a king. She fought and did not give up. Even knowing she'd taste defeat, she fought on, like a true warrior. He told his people you are not his queen. You are his *warrior* queen."

I stared at her not knowing what to say.

She took this as her cue to keep going.

"He clothed you in gold before the rite. This is not their way, Dahksahna Circe. A warrior, king or not, never but *never* covers the bride they claimed before the rite is performed. It is important to them to display their triumph in *all* its beauty. Dax Lahn clothing you in gold was an announcement to his people that you are more than his Dahksahna, you are the golden queen, the warrior bride. This is not a simple declaration to make. A Dax would not do this unless he believed into his soul that he had claimed the golden queen."

"Wh-what," I stammered, "is the golden queen?"

She gave me a gentle smile before saying, "It is the Korwahk people's belief that the mightiest Dax in their history will find the golden queen, a warrior bride, fair of hair, kind of heart, fierce of spirit. This story has been told for centuries, millennia...the mighty Dax and his golden Dahksahna would unite, and the Golden Dynasty would begin, bringing the Korwahk nation great wealth, abundant crops, fruitful women. Magic would descend upon the land and the Korwahk people would be safe under the strength of their king and the enchantments of their queen."

"That's...that's...that's *whacked*," I told her, pushing up to sitting, pulling the sheet over my breasts, and when her face grew confused, I explained quickly, "Insane. Crazy."

She shook her head and sat back, smiling at me.

"They do not think it's crazy. They believe it's true. Every generation prays that the mighty king and golden queen will reign during their time on this earth. And they believe when the mighty Dax finds his golden queen, he will clothe her in gold before the rite and install her at his side. This is what the Dax did. And this is not something he would do unless he *believed* he had found his golden queen and..." she leaned forward, "*this is what he did*. And in so doing, he brought great joy to his people. But you do not show yourself. You do not walk amongst them. You hide in your tent and there are whispers. Whispers that you are not what he said you were. Whispers that the Dax lied to them, bragged with falsehood, claimed a Dynasty that was not his to claim. And this is very dangerous, these whispers, dangerous for him and *for you*."

I stared at her knowing my eyes were wide.

"Why?" I asked on a breath.

"Because, my dear, there is no dynasty amongst the Korwahk now. A Dax becomes a Dax through challenge. He does not inherit a kingdom. He *seizes* it," she whispered.

Oh boy.

She kept speaking.

"The Dax only stays the Dax as long as he can defeat any challenge. If he is killed, his reign transfers to the warrior who defeated him, or, when he knows he can no longer stand up to a challenge, he and his queen go into exile, and they do not live with The Horde of the Daxshee. But by claiming you his golden queen, he claimed the reign for himself until his death and then his son and so on until the Golden Dynasty falls, if it ever does. This is *not* a trivial claim to make. It challenges their way of life. There will be those who will wish to prove it wrong. There will be challenges to the Dynasty, and you hiding in your tent and not showing them you are their golden warrior queen is putting our Dax in jeopardy."

That I didn't care about.

No freaking way.

"And?" I asked sharply, and she blinked.

Then she said softly, "And, if the Dax decides he has been mistaken, he will need to make that known amongst his people prior to any challenges being thrown. And he will do this, my dear. He will renounce you and he will do it in a way you will *not* like."

Shit.

She kept talking.

"But, if a challenge is thrown before he does this and the Dax falls, *you* fall. They will kill him, my dear, but *you* they will not kill."

That didn't sound bad.

Or at least the words didn't, the way she said them did.

"And?" I asked a lot less sharply and a lot more hesitantly.

She studied me.

She then said carefully, "And...they will burn your tent, they will murder your slaves...after enjoying them," she eyed me, "*repeatedly*.

I sucked in breath, and she kept going.

"They will loot your belongings, and you...you, my dear, they will mutilate in ways and in places no woman wants to be mutilated. Then they will share you. Share you amongst all the warriors until they lose interest in you. After you endure that, you will be cast out and it will be known that if anyone provides you aid, they will be punished. You will die of thirst or malnutrition, burning in the sun. They will not kill you, but you will die. But before you die, you'll *want* to die. No death is pleasant, Dahksahna Circe. But *that* death would be far more unpleasant than most."

Dear God, she had *that* right.

Seriously, this...place...*sucked*.

I stared into her eyes. Then I looked beyond her at the five women who'd been serving me and caring for me in kind ways for three days and had been so gentle with me that awful night. They were standing in a huddle just inside the flap to the tent.

They looked more than anxious.

They looked freaking scared.

I looked back into her eyes.

Then I whispered, "What's your name?"

"Diandra, my queen."

"All right, Diandra," I said softly, making my decision. "Let me get up. I've got some people who need to see me."

Diandra kept hold of my gaze for a long moment before, slowly, she smiled.

5
GETTING A FEW THINGS STRAIGHT

I sat cross-legged in the middle of the bed waiting for my king to come home.

I had spent most of the day with Diandra.

That morning, I had gotten out of bed and Diandra had called for my robe, or my lornya as they called it. It was long, had slits up the side, was sleeveless and was made of the finest light-blue silk I'd ever seen.

While I ate (creamy yogurt, sweet, dried fruit and some kind of grain all mixed together, it was actually quite tasty) and drank coffee (the only good thing so far—the savages had coffee, though the milk they had to put in it tasted slightly tangy), Diandra chatted to me.

She told me about Seerim, her three sons (all, she bragged openly, in training to be warriors; her first, she bragged scarily, had already made his "first kill") and her one daughter ("He would deny it, he is proud of his warrior sons, but Sheena is Seerim's favorite," she said).

She did this as my women (I refused to call them slaves) carted in a big, oval copper tub with one side swayed back and filled it with buckets of steaming water. They poured some milky substance in it, some oil, swirled it around and dropped flower petals on top.

After I was finished eating, three of them guided me to the warm, fragrant bath and Diandra went to some trunks in the corner with the dark-skinned woman. Teetru was her name, and Diandra confirmed that, since she once had the charge of a Maroo princess (Maroo being Teetru's homeland), she therefore had experience with serving "royalty" and she was their boss of sorts.

I tried to protest, but they refused to accept as they bathed me and washed my hair in a bath that smelled vaguely of spice, vaguely of musk and not-so-vaguely of orange blossoms.

I had to admit, it was nice.

It was weird, but it was nice.

Once bathed, they clothed me in an outfit Teetru and Diandra chose. A sarong woven with gold thread shot with white and turquoise blue with a hint of silver. This was attached to a wide, braided belt of thick turquoise, white and gold threads with thin gold chains plaited through. My breasts were wrapped in a turquoise bandeau bikini top. Added to this were gold bands at my biceps, a necklace that was a fall of intricate gold chains with tiny blinking aquamarine stones and chandelier earrings of the same.

Best of all, they gave me a pair of turquoise silk underwear. Actual *underwear*. They fit snug in the ass and the silk had no give, but I didn't care. I wanted to do cartwheels because I...had...*underwear*.

And, okay, it sucked to admit, but there was no way around it. The outfit was freaking *great*. Everything about it was *amazing*. The material, the colors, the jewels—they freaking *rocked*.

And since I had nothing (so far) but coffee to be happy about, I was not going to berate myself for being happy about my cool-as-shit clothes.

I had to hang on to something, didn't I?

They sat me down and put eye shadow and kohl on my eyes and a gooey, tasty stuff tinted pink on my lips.

They also brushed out my hair, dipping their fingers in a clay pot with more goo and gliding it through my hair, twisting it in long coils then securing it back from my face with a succession of little gold pins with aquamarine stones at the end (almost but not quite like bobby pins) that went from ear, over the top of my head, to ear.

Diandra took one look at me when I was done and smiled with happy approval, stating, "Your king showers great bounty on you. This is very good."

I stared at her.

Bounty. Right.

Whatever.

Once I was all done up, out we went into the camp.

And it was—mostly—a camp.

A bunch of tents with firepits out front, some had tables at the side of the tent with primitive-looking cooking stuff on it, big buckets resting beside them and other tools like axes and hatchets and the like. Some had smaller tents around them, which Diandra told me were where slaves slept or where food and supplies were kept and meals prepared (around my tent, we had one of both).

There were a lot of torches stuck in the ground on the pathways, which I knew from the night of the parade but also from seeing it hit the side of the king's tent that they were lit at night.

The only official area, as it were, was the dais, which I noticed now was roughly carved from a huge, wide, long, cream slab of stone. The area in front of it deep and sweeping, made up of the same stone. A firepit did indeed run the length of the back with two pits at the top, though while we wandered the camp these were not lit, mostly, I guessed, because it was sunny, and, I knew, it was stinking hot. The drums, incidentally (the big ones and small ones), were still set up.

There were also people. Lots of them. All of them looked at me and many of them smiled, many of them nodded, many of them appeared happy to see me. Some of them, however, looked at me with interest or intensity, not exactly happy—cautious, and I figured undecided. A few avoided my eyes.

This, I didn't get.

I also didn't dwell. I had enough to dwell on.

Diandra chattered on and she tucked my hand in her elbow and kept me close as we walked. She informed me this was only a camp, not a settlement. The Horde was nomadic. They came to this location for the Wife Hunt every two years and the warrior selections, three times a year. They had homes, of sorts, in some Korwahk city, but they visited them infrequently during their roaming. Although, she explained, they did settle in them for two months over the winter.

She told me tents were called *chams*. She told me *shahsha* was thank you. She told me *poyah* was hello.

"What does *me ahnoo* mean?" I asked after the words the king had spoken to the cruel warrior, and she looked at me, her brows up.

"Me ahnoo?" she asked back.

"The king said, 'Kah Dahksahna me ahnoo,' to that warrior he threw off the dais during the wedding rite. What does that mean?"

She patted my hand in the crook of her elbow, looked forward and smiled. "It means, my dear, 'my queen does not like.'"

"What?" I asked.

She looked back at me.

"He told Dortak that you do not like...in other words, you did not like what he was doing to his bride. And, I will add, not many of us did. Definitely not the peasants, merchants, slaves or wives, and I'm certain, many of the warriors." She bobbed her head at me. "You made that clear. Even though you do not speak their tongue, it was plain for all to see you didn't like what he was doing. He was challenging you by continuing to do it even though you told him not to. It is, in truth, not a woman's place to command a warrior, even if that woman is queen."

She looked forward and I got the sense she was avoiding my eyes when she went on.

"Sometimes," she paused, "I will admit, the wedding rite can get lewd, the warriors get wound up. If a battle is mightily fought to claim a bride, they need to expend some energy and sometimes do so in..." she paused again then finished cautiously, "*unsavory* ways."

Fabulous.

Diandra carried on after looking at me again.

"But *you* are not just any queen. You are King Lahn's Lahnahsahna. But more, you are the Dax's golden warrior queen. You made a command. It went unheeded. The king acted to make Dortak adhere to your command." Her fingers squeezed mine. "It was a bold statement. This is not done. In saying simply that you do not like, but in punishing Dortak before all, he was telling his people you rule at his side." She grinned at me. "It was very sweet and *very* uncharacteristic...of a warrior, of a king, but *especially* of Dax Lahn. He, my dear, is not normally sweet. Seerim was even shocked." She looked away and muttered, "A sight to see. A good one."

I looked forward too as these words moved through me. I wasn't certain I believed he was sweet, that would take a lot of convincing. But she had told me he'd bragged about me to his people, and he had acted on my wishes to stop that girl from continuing to be defiled publicly.

Not to mention, he made it clear I ruled at his side.

I supposed that was nice.

"That warrior's name is Dortak?" I asked because I needed a change of subject, pronto.

She nodded, didn't look at me but her face lost its friendliness. I still saw it, even in profile.

"Dortak. A bad seed. As was his father before him, and, as Seerim's father tells me, *his* father before *him*. He covets the throne of horns. They all did. He will challenge the Dax."

My body started at this pronouncement.

"But King Lahn tossed him bodily down a flight of steps," I reminded her.

She looked back at me.

"I said he was a bad seed, Dahksahna Circe." She leaned in and grinned. "But I did not say he was a *clever* bad seed."

I knew what she was saying.

"The king will defeat him," I whispered.

She looked forward again murmuring, "Without doubt."

"This Dortak tried to claim me. The Dax severed his chain and—" I stopped talking when she abruptly halted us, and her attention snapped to my face.

"He severed his chain?" she whispered.

"Uh...yeah," I confirmed.

"Oh my," she breathed.

"What?" I asked.

"Oh my," she breathed again, and her eyes had a faraway look in them.

I shook her arm and hissed, "What, Diandra?" and her eyes focused on me.

"Warriors battle for their brides, as you know, my dear, and there are very few rules with anything to do with any fight, indeed anything to do with The Horde *or* the Korwahk nation. But the warriors of The Horde *do* honor their brothers. Although it is not unheard of for things to get out of hand and one warrior kill another for his bride, or perhaps deliver a wound that will eventually kill or one that festers and brings the warrior low. But this is very infrequent. Because of this, there are other whispers around the Daxshee, not just those about you. These other whispers are about Dortak and the Hunt. It is known that Dortak took the life of a warrior for the bride he was claiming. I just did not know it was you. *Was* it you?"

I nodded and whispered, "It was me."

Her eyes went soft as she realized what I witnessed then she carried on.

"This has not been taken positively as the warrior he brought low was well-liked and Dortak is not. Although the kill was not witnessed, because of his reputation, many believe that it was not due to both warriors descending into bloodlust as the battle raged on but that he did not give the fallen warrior the opportunity to surrender before he delivered his killing blow."

I didn't know if this was true or not. I hadn't been paying that much attention, mainly because I was freaked right the fuck out.

"I'm sorry, I don't know enough about this stuff to know if he gave that guy an opportunity to give up or not. And, I have to say, I honestly wasn't taking much in. I had other things on my mind," I told her.

She gave me an understanding smile and said softly, "Of course not, my dear." Then she took in a deep breath and went on, "That said, although there are few rules, like I mentioned, there is also honor and you do *not* sever a chain. *Never.* It's a slap in the face. An insult. It says you hold no respect for the other warrior. If a warrior has attached their chain to you, the other warrior battles until that warrior is beaten, surrenders or has fallen. Only *then* can they detach their chain and hook their own to their chosen bride. To sever the chain is to say you feel the battle will be won before it is even started. It's actually *worse* than a slap in the face. It's akin to spitting in it."

She looked away and started us walking again.

"Another bold statement," she kept talking quietly. "King Lahn is forcing a challenge, I see. He grows impatient with Dortak. He wants him defeated."

"But, if that's true, why didn't he kill him when he challenged him for me?" I asked.

"Because, my dear," she patted my hand again and kept walking, "that would bear no witnesses. He will wait for Dortak's challenge so he can humiliate him before all. He wants that shame to be the last thing he feels before the Dax takes his head."

Oh God.

Takes his head?

Oh God!

At that, I decided I was done talking.

Diandra didn't and chattered away as we walked through the encampment before she walked me back to my tent.

She spoke to my women who hurried off to do whatever it was they did. Not long after, bunches of large, square pillows, some with fringe all around, some with tassels at the four ends, some with no adornment, all silk, satin or brocade and all in rich colors, were arranged on some thick hides on the dusty stone around our tent. We reclined in the cool(ish) shade of the tent as the women brought us flat bread, strong cheese, dried spiced meat, almonds and crisp, fresh, deliciously *cold* (if it can be believed) fruit juice.

I couldn't say I was comfortable being waited on while lounging and five women rushed to answer my every unspoken whim.

What I could say was that that particular conversation with the Dax was for some future time, *if* I was still around at that time (which, God, I hoped I was not). And *if* I ever decided I intended to try to speak to the brute.

A lot of people passed our tent as Diandra babbled at me and I part listened but mostly I tried to figure out what to do next. After a while, it occurred to me that it was unlikely that many people passed the Dax's tent on a normal day, and it was much more likely that they'd come to check me out.

This made me feel weird, on show, and I didn't like it. But then again, I didn't like a lot of things, so I kept my peace, kept my lounge and listened to Diandra talk.

In late afternoon, promising to come back the next day and take me to the marketplace bringing her daughter Sheena with her, Diandra left me.

When she did, I realized I'd forgotten to ask after Narinda and the evil (and apparently stupid) Dortak's unlucky bride.

After she left, I lay on the pillows noting that my women were busy bustling around doing whatever they were doing. But whatever they were doing, they were doing it no longer looking anxious, but instead happy, smiling at each other while working and chattering.

I watched them and smiled whenever they caught my eye.

They smiled back.

They seemed like nice ladies.

Shit, if I didn't wake up home soon, I was probably going to have to get to know them and figure out what to do about them. But one thing I knew, whatever this world was or my place in it, I was not going to own slaves.

On that thought, I sighed, fiddled with the tassel of a pillow, tried to sort my head out and smiled at anyone who passed by who smiled at me. I also nodded to anyone who caught my eye. And I took the lovely pink flower from a little girl who dashed up and handed it to me, murmuring, "Shahsha, honey," as I took it. She giggled and rushed back to her beaming mother.

It was after a dinner of roasted spiced meat, more flat bread and potatoes cooked in onions that I took at the table in the tent when I decided what I was going to do.

And it was after my women—Jacanda (petite, chubby and seemingly outgoing), Packa (also petite, not chubby and somewhat shy), Gaal (tall, thin and quiet, but not in a shy way, in a careful, watchful one that made me slightly uneasy) and Beetus (tall, skinny, the youngest I was guessing, mostly because she looked it but was also extremely giggly in a way I almost, *almost* found infectious)—washed my face, slathered it with heavenly smelling stuff they gouged out of clay bowl (stuff that made my skin feel divine), took off my jewels and clothes and ran their fingers through my hair to pull out the gunked up twists.

All that done, they helped me don an actual nightgown made of pale pink satin. No joke, *a nightgown*. It, like the robe, had slits up the side, thin straps, the skirt to the ankle. It fit snug at the boobs and hips, but, like the outfit I wore that day, it was *awesome*.

They tried to take my turquoise undies, but I flatly refused, and after a brief verbal tussle that made no sense to any of us, they gave in, murmured words that I took as goodnight and left me alone.

I climbed in the bed, sat cross-legged in the middle of it, pulled the silk sheet up to my lap and waited for my warrior king to come home so I could carry forth my plan to get a few very important things straight.

And I waited.

Night had fallen and I was usually asleep by the time he returned, so after I waited for a while I figured I was in for a long one.

At this juncture, I looked around the tent.

Having been in it for days, I was seeing it for the first time.

The bed was smack in the middle on a painted blue wooden platform that was probably one foot tall. There was a mattress, I knew. What it was made of, I didn't know, but it was thick, tall and soft. It was covered in heavy hides that were also soft, warm and comfy (the day was hot, the sun shone brightly, but when it dropped, it got cold). This was covered in a heavy, light-blue silk sheet (which didn't do much to ward off the cold, I had discovered, so it was lucky we slept on the fluffy hides).

The pillows didn't have cases. They were square or rectangular, and like the big cushions the girls had set outside for Diandra and me, they were silk, satin and brocade, no tassels or fringe and not in rich colors but in pastels.

There were heavy-looking trunks lining the circular tent on one side. All wood, all carved, all with latches with strong-looking locks hanging from them. Some of them were inlaid with what looked like mother of pearl. Some of them surrounded by sturdy-looking black iron.

On the other side of the tent, a narrow, rectangular wood table, also carved, two chairs at each end, ladderback, cushions on the seats with tassels. There were silver and copper candlesticks with candles (now burning) of all shapes, sizes and widths that scattered the top.

And against that side of the tent beyond the table, two short, square chests with latticework doors and brass latches. In one, I could see a variety of small to medium-sized clay pots, and in the other, there was what looked like pottery or enameled clay plates, bowls and jugs plus silverware that I already knew was used at the table.

At the back of the tent, there was a three-panel screen made of wood with a light-green gauze hiding what was behind it from view. This was where the chamber pot was.

Close to the entrance flaps, a small bed of hides that was at least three feet tall, one hide stacked on top of the other, a bunch of cushions at its head, a squat, carved, small round table also at its head and also covered in candlesticks of all shapes and sizes. A place maybe to read (if they had books in this hellhole) or lounge.

There were more tall candleholders, dozens of them. These were wrought iron, scrolled, all holding thick candles and dotted around the room, all lit. A number of them circled the bed, not close, not far and at what seemed like random places.

The stone ground was covered with thick woven rugs with rough designs on them. They were, I'd experienced, slightly abrasive on your feet, but they were a heckuva lot better than the stone.

I studied the space.

With night having fallen, the candlelight dancing, the silks and satins gleaming, the torchlight from outside glowing against the sides of the tent, I noted that in my world, this would be an exotic and romantic setting. Comfortable. Inviting you to relax, lounge, and if you were lucky enough to be with someone who mattered, engage in other activities that were a little more energetic and a lot more fun.

So it sucked that for me this tent—this whole *world*—was my torture chamber.

On that thought, the flap to the tent slapped back.

I jumped and my determination to get a few things straight slipped as I watched the Dax bend low and enter the tent.

I sucked in breath.

He straightened, walked in two steps and stopped, his dark eyes on me.

Gone was the paint. He hadn't painted himself since that night.

But still, he scared the shit out of me. I forgot how dark he was, how sinister, how savage and how *huge*. It couldn't be said the tent was enormous, but it was the biggest tent I'd ever seen and there was room to move, room to breathe.

With him standing in it, his forceful energy invading, his huge, powerful body on display, his brown skin gleaming in the candlelight, the tent seemed tiny.

Another direct hit to my determination.

He moved toward the foot of the bed, and as he made it there, I threw up a hand and stated firmly, "Stop."

He stopped. He hadn't taken his eyes off me as he moved, and he didn't then, not even to look at my hand.

"You and me..." I went on. Pulling up the courage to speak to him, the first words I'd said to him since that awful night, I gestured between his big body and my own. "We need to talk."

He stared at me.

I pointed between us again then lifted my hand and flapped my fingers in lame sign language to indicate talking. "Talk. You and I are going to talk."

He looked at my hand then back at me, but he didn't speak nor did his impassive expression change.

All right, moving on.

I pointed to myself. "My name is Circe."

Nothing.

I leaned in and repeated slowly and phonetically, "Sir...see."

More nothing.

I pointed to him. "You are King Lahn. *Dax* Lahn." I pointed to myself. "I am Queen Circe. *Dahksahna* Circe."

His hands went to his hips, and I tensed, but they just rested there. He still did not speak, nor did he tear his dark-brown eyes from mine.

Hmm.

I had to assume he got that and sally forth.

"We," I gestured between him and myself again, "have to get a few things straight." I had no gesture for that and knew he would have no way of knowing what that meant. Then I pointed to the bed. "Here and..." I pointed to the flaps of the tent, "out there, you and I have to sort our shit out."

His hands moved at his hips, my eyes dropped there, and I saw he had yanked some hide ties loose.

Oh shit.

My body tensed and my gaze flew to his.

"You and me," more gesturing, "need to find a way to come together." I clasped my hands together in front of me.

His hands moved lower down the sides of his hips, and he pulled more ties so his hides loosened at his waist.

Shit!

"Okay," I said softly, scooting back. "*This* is *exactly* what we have to get straight."

Another set of ties loosened, and his hides fell to the ground.

He was already ready to take me.

Shit!

I scooted back to the pillows at the head of the bed and lifted a hand up toward him. "Before we...carry on, we have to find a way to talk. *Understand* each other."

His eyes dropped to where I was kneeling on the pillows then he turned, stepped free of his hides and calmly strode around the bed.

Fuck. Fuck.

Shit!

He made it nearly to the corner of the bed at the head, completely casual about his erect nudity—something which I was *not* casual about because the man was *huge,* and this meant *all of him*—and I was not liking where any of this was going.

I scuttled to the foot of the bed and kept trying.

"Please stop, sit and try to listen to me." I pointed at him then cupped my hand at my ear and then pointed at myself.

He changed directions and strode back around the bed.

I scampered to the middle of it, my arm out, palm up to him.

"Please," I begged on a whisper.

Mistake.

Colossal mistake.

His hand snaked out so fast it was a blur. His fingers wrapped around my wrist, and with a forceful tug that wrenched my shoulder and made me cry out, I was across the bed and up, my torso plastered to his, my legs dangling, feet skimming the bed and his arms were around me, caging me in.

I tipped my head back to look in dark eyes that were gazing down at me. I curled my fingers into the hard, warm muscle at his shoulders, exerting enough pressure hopefully to make my point, and I whispered over my hammering heart, "Please, Lahn, listen to me."

He didn't listen to me.

Oh no.

He didn't do that.

He shifted his torso so my legs swung to the side then he fell forward, his mammoth weight landing on me.

I was winded, but I was not beaten.

That, that right there, was why we needed to get things *straight*.

I arched my back, shoved at his shoulders and shouted, "Seriously, big guy, we need...to get...a few things...*straight*!"

His hand trailed my side then went between our bodies.

I lost it.

On a frustrated, furious cry, I struggled.

This surprisingly worked. I managed to push him back, slide out from under him and nearly gain the side of the bed before I was caught at the waist and pulled back.

I whirled and fought.

I managed to use my nails to score his skin, opening up two thin, short streaks that beaded instantly with blood just under his shoulder.

That shoulder rocked back as I froze in shock that I'd managed to wound him.

He gave me his full weight, tipped his head down to look at the scratches, and, fuck me, when he looked back at me there was something in his eyes I did not like and whatever that something was made him grin like he was supremely pleased.

Shit!

I unfroze and again gave it my all, just like that heinous night, grunting with the effort.

The problem was, even with the bastard knowing he was bigger than me, stronger than me, he gave it his all too, and it became clear that if I wasn't smart, and fast, he'd break bones if he had to.

God, I hated him.

And when he'd maneuvered me to my knees, my back to him, my wrists held in one of his fists pinned unmoving to my chest and I knew what was next, I reared back my head and shouted it.

"God, *I hate you*!"

His free hand slid along the silk at my belly and his mouth went to my neck.

"Kah Lahnahsahna," he muttered.

I jerked (to no avail) in his arms and screamed, "*Stop calling me that!*"

His fingers curled in, fisting the material at my belly, bunching it up, and when he had it all up, his hand moved down.

I froze.

"Kah Dahksahna," he whispered against my neck.

"Fuck you! I'm not your queen!" I snapped, my hips finally moving to avoid the path of his hand.

"Kah rahna Dahksahna," he murmured, and his hand slid into my panties.

My hips stopped moving.

"God," I whispered on a jerk of my arms that did nothing to loosen his hold. "I freaking *hate you*."

His fingers glided between my legs.

And that was when it hit me his touch wasn't clinical. It wasn't removed. He wasn't shoving me face first into the bed and taking me from behind like I was nothing but a warm vessel to receive his seed.

His touch was gentle, light, soft.

Oh shit.

His finger glided light as a whisper over my clit.

Oh shit!

"Lahn," I whispered.

"Lahn," he repeated, pushing his hips into my back as his finger started to circle in what was very clearly a caress.

And, dear God, I couldn't believe it but it was a nice one. It was a sweet one. And my body, damn it all, recognized it as such.

What on earth was happening?

"Please." I kept whispering.

"Please," he repeated after me again, still circling his finger with a gentle touch.

"Don't," I begged.

"Don't," he repeated, and my eyes closed slowly.

God, was this happening to me? After all he'd done, was this really happening to me?

His finger asserted just a wee bit more pressure.

My head automatically fell back to his shoulder as a tiny spiral of pleasure unfurled in my belly.

Yep, this was happening to me.

I jerked my hands again, whispering, "I won't."

"I won't," he whispered back and his deep, rumbling whisper spiraled through me too.

His finger started circling faster, a little harder, a lot better.

God.

I turned my head, his lifted, and I pressed my forehead into his neck. I fought against that spiral of pleasure that was unfurling. But I didn't win. It unfurled, then it grew, then it spread.

"Lahn," I breathed as the continued workings of his fingers forced the last bits of tension from my body.

"Lahn," he murmured and circled faster.

Oh, that felt nice.

"Circe," I whispered.

His hand at my wrists tightened, pulling them into me as his finger pressed deeper.

"Circe," he whispered, and my hips bucked.

Yes. I liked that.

"Circe," I said again, and he pressed his hardness into my back and circled even faster.

"Circe," he repeated softly, and I whimpered as that spiral in my belly whirled out of control.

"Yes," I breathed.

I felt his lips a whisper from mine.

"Yes," he murmured.

Oh God.

My hips moved with his hand, grinding down, seeking more from his finger, and he didn't keep it from me. He gave it to me, and I took it, I reached for it, and it started coming.

My eyes flew open, and when they did, his dark ones, *not* looking detached, *not* blank, *not* impassive, but heated and turned on, and God, could it be?

Totally freaking sexy.

His finger pressed deeper and circled faster.

Oh yes.

I gasped, "Lahn!"

"Circe," he whispered against my lips.

I drew in a ragged breath and moaned against his as I came.

Hard.

And while I was doing this, he let me go and shoved me down into the bed, ass in the air. He pulled the panel of my nightgown up, ripped my panties away, separated my legs with his knees and drove inside.

My head flew back.

Oh yeah.

Hell yeah.

"Yes," I breathed.

Without a thought, my body thinking for me, I reared back into his thrusts.

He leaned forward, reached around and cupped my breast in a rough hand as he pounded into me, jerking my hips back with his other hand.

"Kah Lahnahsahna," he growled.

"Oh yeah," I moaned.

His fingers found my nipple and tugged, that hard tug slashing through me like a hot knife, trailing fire. "*Kah* Lahnahsahna."

"Kah Lahnahsahna," I whimpered, pushing back, meeting him thrust for thrust.

His hand left my breast, and both spanned my hips, hauling me back, giving me all of him, and I took it, invited it, stretched for it.

Amazing.

So amazing, my head flew back again, and my arms reached out straight.

He saw it and reached forward. His hand circling my throat, he pulled me up to my hands and kept driving into me, his fingers gliding up to cup me under my jaw.

The hold was gentle, tender even.

And it was possessive, claiming.

King Lahn was fucking his queen.

Oh shit, fuck me, but I liked that too. All of it, every inch of him pounding into me, his hand at my jaw, me on my hands and knees before him.

I liked it so much, my back arched, my head tilted further back, and I came again. Harder. Crying out loudly, it was that fucking good.

I heard him growl then his hands went to my ribs, yanking me back, pounding savagely now, he kept at me until he drove in deep, and his groan of release was nearly as loud as mine.

Shit. Holy shit.

Shit!

He moved slowly, in and out, as his hand slid around my ribs. He kept moving, leaning forward, his hands moving up, cupping my breasts. Then carefully, he lifted my torso so I was up straight, impaled on his cock. He was so long my knees didn't hit the bed, only his cock and hands supported me.

Dear God.

One hand crossed over to the other breast and held on while his other hand went to our connection where his fingers slid in, his palm cupping my sex.

Then his mouth was at my ear.

"Circe, *kah* rahna Dahksahna. Circe, *kah* Lahnahsahna," he growled in my ear, his voice a fierce rumble, his words a declaration.

"Um..." I whispered. "Okay."

Shit! What else could I do?

He emitted another growl that slithered across my skin like silk then I felt his tongue move from the back of my ear, down my neck to my shoulder.

At this, my body trembled in a full-on shiver.

He lifted me off him, turned me roughly, shoved me to my back in the bed and then he came down on top of me.

I barely got a chance to adjust to my new position before he twisted, reached down, yanked the sheet up to our waists then came back to me. He hauled me nearly fully under him, tangled his heavy legs with mine, his arm curving almost fully around my body, his face at the side of my head, his mouth at my temple.

I felt his weight settle into mine and I lay immobile, waiting.

Um. I wasn't sure.

Did we get things straight?

When he said nothing and his breath evened out, I called, "Lahn?"

His arm gave me a powerful squeeze.

"Trahyoo," he ordered firmly but softly.

Definitely an order, though I had no idea what he said.

"Uh...okay," I whispered and got another arm squeeze that took the breath from me.

Time to be quiet.

I stared into the candlelit tent.

All right, did that just happen?

I felt his breath stir the hair at my temple, his heavy weight, his body's warmth.

Yep, it just happened.

I needed to go somewhere and think. I needed to figure out how in *the hell* I let a man I didn't know, a man who had raped me seven times (essentially), a man I didn't like, make me come twice.

I needed to get away from him.

His weight settled more firmly into mine at the same time his arm tightened.

He was asleep.

His arm tightened around me in his sleep.

Damn.

Okay, I wasn't going to get away from him.

So, I needed to wake him up and find some way to communicate there was no way I was going to be able to fall asleep with his weight on me.

I figured he wasn't going to like being woken.

And I was figuring that the second before my eyes drifted closed and I fell asleep with his weight on me.

6
The Marketplace

Our mouths were close, my fingers were wrapped around the side of his neck and the fingers of my other hand had slid into his hair at his scalp under his long ponytail.

His head was tipped back, his breath mingling with mine, one of his arms was wrapped tight around my waist, the other hand curled around the back of my neck.

I was riding my king and I was doing it hard. I wasn't going fast. I liked the feel of him too much. So much, I wanted to savor it.

But when I rammed down, I did it hard because I liked that too.

"Mayoo," he growled an order I didn't understand.

"I don't understand you, baby," I whispered breathily into his mouth.

His arm squeezed, jerking up and slamming down.

"*Mayoo,*" he stated fiercely, and I got him.

"Okay," I whispered, going faster.

My eyes closed, his fingers at my neck tensed, and my eyes opened.

"Linas," he demanded.

I took a wild guess and stared into his eyes, going faster, driving down on him, my fingers tightened into his neck, I tried to hold his gaze, but I couldn't.

My head tipped back, my lips parted, and I gasped softly as I came.

He kept me moving with his arm around my waist, and after my sweet orgasm swept through me, I focused and took over again. Watching him as

I kept moving on top of him, I saw the burn deepen in his eyes, felt the pressure of his fingers increase on my neck, his arm around my waist got so tight I couldn't breathe, and on a downward stroke he held me so I was full of him, tipped his face forward and groaned into my chest.

I closed my eyes.

There it was.

I did it again.

I had no choice. He woke me with his hands, they were gentle but effective, and I was primed before I was conscious, so I gave it up again.

Gladly.

Shit.

What was happening to me?

His head tilted back.

I looked down at him and it was like I saw him for the first time.

And seeing him looking up at me, his eyes still warm on my face, his cock deep inside me, God, no joke, as insane as it was, I thought he was the most unbelievably handsome man I'd ever beheld—in a dark, savage, totally hot way, of course.

I was about to inform him of this (not that I could do that), when suddenly I was in the air then flat on my back. He loomed over me on a hand in the bed and his other hand cupped me roughly between my legs, his long middle finger invading.

His elbow bent, his torso dipped, and his face was in mine.

He shoved his finger up higher and I gasped.

"Kah Lahnahsahna?" he asked.

I stared and his finger shoved deeper. So much deeper, my entire body jolted upward. I couldn't say it hurt, in fact, it didn't. I was still sensitive, and it felt freaking great, but...

What the fuck?

"What?" I whispered, his finger slid out then thrust right back in.

"Kah Lahnahsahna," he growled.

"Kah...uh, Lahnahsahna," I whispered, taking a stab at what he was demanding from me.

He glared down at me.

Jeez, what did I do?

His hand slid from between my legs, trailing his and my wetness up my belly. It cupped my breast forcefully, the pads of his fingers digging in before they tweaked my nipple so hard my body jerked (and not, I had to admit, in an entirely bad way) and his torso twisted. His mouth captured my other nipple, he sucked in hard and that also made my body jerk in a *definitely* not bad way.

Then his face was in mine, his lips a breath away, his eyes all I could see, and they were burning with a different light. One that made me catch my breath as his hand went back between my legs and his finger thrust back into me.

"Lahnahsahna Circe lapoo meera kah liros anah," he declared forcefully, and I blinked.

"Uh...okay," I whispered, thinking maybe agreement was the best way to go, and he continued to stare in my eyes.

The fire died out of his and he whispered back, "Okay."

His finger glided gently over my clit, my body jerked, lightly this time as his hand trailed up to my belly at the same time his eyes disappeared because his head moved so his tongue could glide across my throat.

Then without looking at me, he exited the bed.

I watched his naked body move toward the flaps.

Okay.

What was *that* all about?

He slapped open one of the flaps, again totally not heeding his nudity, and he barked something through them. He moved away from them, not looking at me in the bed, and he prowled to the trunks at the corner.

The flaps went back and in came Teetru followed by Packa, both of them carrying big, earthenware jugs. I quickly reached down and pulled the sheet up to hide my nakedness (not that they hadn't seen it, repeatedly) as Lahn moved away from the trunks and threw a new pair of hides on the ground. He yanked the jug out of Teetru's hands and tipped it over his head, the water splashing all over the rugs and all over his new hides. He used his big hand to swipe the water around his body then he jerked the jug back to Teetru. She took it and he yanked the one out of Packa's hands and did the same.

After he did all that, without toweling off, he hauled up his new hides, tied the laces tight at the hips and prowled out of the tent, his attention not coming to me once.

I stared at the flaps of the tent.

Okay, maybe I was wrong.

Language and a killer freaking culture gap were standing between us, but outside of that last bit, I thought Lahn and me got a few things straight last night and, um...this morning. We'd shared words (kind of), he'd grinned at me (of course, this was after I'd drawn blood, but still he did it), his touch had changed, he held me while we slept, his arm tightened around me while *he* slept, and he put a fair amount of effort into giving me three really freaking great orgasms.

I guess I thought wrong.

Teetru came to the bed, bending over it, tugging at the sheet, speaking quietly to me but the edge of excitement in her voice made my eyes move from the tent flaps to her.

And I saw she *was* excited. Her eyes were shining with it. She was happy. Something good was happening and it wasn't just me getting up and getting dressed.

"Please," I whispered, reaching out and taking her hand. "Get me Diandra."

She looked in my eyes. Then she nodded. She turned her head and said something to Jacanda who was dragging in the tub. Jacanda looked at me, looked at Teetru, nodded, left the tub where it was and dashed out of the tent.

I fell down to my back and stared at the top of the tent.

"Another day in paradise," I whispered, my voice sounding defeated.

This was because it was and that was because *I* was.

I allowed myself to feel this for approximately two minutes.

Done with that, I pulled my shit together and hauled myself out of the bed to face whatever next was to come at me that day.

THE MARKETPLACE WAS a short way away from the encampment, through a small stand of weird, thin, green-stalked trees that looked a bit like bamboo but weren't.

And the marketplace, unlike the encampment, was a fixture. There were tents but there were also buildings, not sturdy by a long shot, but buildings nonetheless.

And they had, I discovered, everything for sale there.

Everything.

Diandra, her pretty dark-haired, dark-almond-eyed, twelve-year-old daughter, Sheena (who spoke enough English to make herself understood in a broken and charming way, mostly because she spoke it smiling a sweet smile and giggling after practically every word) and I caused quite a sensation when we arrived.

And this sensation, I figured, was not entirely due to my new kickass outfit—ice-blue halter bikini top that hooked to a golden chain around my neck and was also fastened with a chain around my back. Ice-blue skirt with shafts of gold and hints of white and silver. Wide belt made of gold and silver disks. No bands at my biceps but so many gold and silver skinny bangles on my wrists it took Gaal five minutes to push them up my hands, and they covered me from wrists to mid-forearm and tinkled every time I moved my arms (which was, I noted for the first time in my life, a lot). Gold earrings, again chandelier but dripping with rough, seed pearls. And pearl pins affixed to the coils, twists and braids in my hair *everywhere*.

The queen had come calling.

With a chatty Diandra and a giggling, smiling, brokenly chatty Sheena, I wandered the marketplace looking over the wares.

Earthenware jugs, bowls and vases of all shapes and sizes. Bolts of materials of everything from burlap to silk in every color you could imagine. Dried, cured meats. Hard, salami-type sausages. Cheeses. Vats of yogurt. Dried fruits. Fresh fruits and vegetables. Nuts, both with shells and without. Sacks of various grains. Pottery. Enameled bowls. Knives and spoons (no forks, I noted, as I'd noted none were at Lahn's table) made of silver or pewter and even wood. Trinkets, bangles, chains and hair bobs. Yarn of every color. Thread of every color. Looms both big and small. Rugs, again, both big and small. Casks of wine. Candles.

You name it, they had it.

The place was huge, it was bustling, and from the horses (with rickety, primitive wagons and without) and what looked like oxen (not that I'd ever seen oxen, I was guessing) tied to basic wooden fences outside the marketplace, it wasn't just there for whenever the Daxshee set up at the dais. Instead, it stood there always, and people came from other places to purchase what they needed.

I was wandering and taking it all in, but I was also in my head.

This was because I was wondering about Diandra. She seemed kind. She seemed friendly. She seemed to want to be my friend, to want to help.

And I needed help.

Like, *a lot* of it.

I just didn't know where to start.

"The whispers are fading, Dahksahna Circe," she told me, lifting a bolt of silver fabric shot with crimson and violet.

I stopped fingering a heavy cream silk and looked at her. "Sorry?"

She turned to me and dropped her hand. "The whispers are fading." Her grin turned wicked and knowing. "The warrior king and his warrior queen battled on last night, I hear." She leaned in and raised her brows as I sucked in breath. "I also heard...*he* won."

"What?" I breathed, and she laughed softly, getting closer.

"Something else you need to get used to, my dear." She bumped me with her hip then looked down at the fabric, her lips twitching. "The walls of tents are thin. And, especially with the Dax, people *listen*."

Oh my *God*.

"People heard us?" I breathed (yes, again!).

"You *were* shouting," she answered on another wicked grin.

Oh my God!

"Then you were moaning and crying out." She chuckled as I stared at her in mortification. "The spoils of victory for King Lahn, I'm sure."

"Oh my God," I whispered.

She threw back her head and laughed then she wrapped an arm around my waist and guided me away from the fabric stall still chuckling as I noticed Sheena grinning unabashedly at me.

She knew too.

And *she* was *twelve*!

The horror!

"Settle, my dear," Diandra urged on a squeeze of my waist when the look of mortification stayed rooted on my face. "This is good." Her face dipped to mine. "*Very* good. His people could not know his words of the wedding rite were true. But last night, you proved them true. Shouting at a king?" She shook her head in mock disapproval all the while tsk-tsking, and I knew it was mock because she was grinning the whole time. "That's not done, Dahksahna Circe. Only the bravest heart and fiercest spirit in the soul of a woman would risk challenging a mighty warrior king." She gave me another squeeze, looked away and murmured, "Well done, my dear."

Okay, shit.

I was in trouble.

"Um...Diandra?" I called as she moved us to a trinket stand filled with bangles, earrings, delicate chain bracelets, necklaces, and all sorts of cool shit for hair, Sheena trailing and stopping around the side of the table where the wares were laid out.

Diandra fingered a silver hair pin with what looked like a garnet in it and murmured, "Mm?"

"What does *trahyoo* mean?" I asked and her eyes came to me.

"It means, *sleep*, in the imperative. As in *ahnoo*, which is imperative, *ahnay* would be used if you were to say," she picked up the pin, "'I like this,' or in Korwahk, 'Kay ahnay sah.' But if you were to want to put emphasis on it, say, if you were a king...or a queen, where you expect your merest whim obeyed, you would say, 'I *like* this.' Or 'Kay *ahnoo* sah.' Therefore, if you are ordering someone to sleep, you wouldn't say, '*trahyay.*' You would *order*, '*trahyoo.*'"

"Oh," I whispered, and she put the pin down. Then I asked softly, "And *mayoo*?"

I watched her profile smile a smile I knew was knowing even getting only half of it. "An order again. *Faster*."

Shit.

Well, I was right about that one.

"You would say *mayay* if you were not commanding it," she explained further.

"Right," I said softly then I mumbled, "Um..." I picked up a set of gold bangles inlaid with tiny seed pearls and continued, "And, uh...what does... lapah meer-something kah lira anahl mean?"

I felt her eyes on me. "Lapah meer...kah lira anahl?"

I looked to her. "Um...I think so."

Her head tipped to the side in confusion and Sheena piped up to suggest, "Lapoo meera kah liros anah. Anah, Loolah. *Anah*," she finished with emphasis.

My eyes swung back to Diandra, and I saw light had dawned.

"Yes, lapoo meera kah liros anah. This means 'is between my legs tonight,'" Diandra explained, and I felt the blood rush to my cheeks as my stomach clenched.

Diandra saw the pink instantly, smiled gently and got close.

"Not what you're thinking," she said softly. "The men gather tonight. Tomorrow, the Dax is choosing his new warriors. Tonight, the men will celebrate as only men can—being loud, drinking a lot and watching warriors beat each other half to death."

I felt the blood that rushed to my face drain away and Diandra caught that too, so she shook her head.

"No, Dahksahna Circe, it isn't like that. It's sport. Or they think it is. It's harmless. That isn't to say warriors don't get beaten bloody, but they *want* it and *like* it. They train for it. A test of strength, endurance. They like to show off and it helps to settle the order of things. Who is strongest, who needs to get stronger, who is faster, who needs to get faster, who is more tactical, who needs to learn strategy. And the others who do not participate enjoy it with much enthusiasm. That said, Seerim has long since stopped taking me. I, on the other hand, don't enjoy it. The warrior wives don't."

She got closer and kept explaining.

"And, my dear, the good thing is, not many men allow their women in, wanting their wives to be with them while they commune with their brethren." Her eyes got bright. "And it is very rare, indeed *so* rare I have never heard of it, that a new warrior husband would honor his bride with wanting her attendance. It usually takes months, even years and sometimes doesn't happen at all." My heart skipped a beat but then it stopped altogether when she finished, "And when you attend, you sit on the ground between his legs."

I stared at her.

Great.

Just great.

"I sit on the *ground*?" I asked and she nodded. "Between his *legs*?" I went on to clarify and she smiled.

"It isn't what you think," she told me, and I looked to the bangles.

"Oh yes it is," I mumbled, and her hand came to my chin, pulling it up so I would look into her understanding eyes.

"It is for some of the warriors, my dear, just what you think," she said quietly. "For others, it is a way of being close to a loved one while enjoying something he likes very much." She leaned in. "For a king and his long-awaited bride, taking her to the games just five short days after he claimed her, my guess is, it's the latter."

I stared at her again and breathed, "He doesn't love me."

Her head tipped to the side and her lips tipped up.

"It is said, throughout history, that many a great warrior, in fact the strongest and fiercest have fallen in love with their brides simply by gazing upon them in the parade." Her hand slid over my cheek as she suggested, "Perhaps this has happened to you."

I thought about that morning. I thought about the last four days.

I thought she was very wrong.

Then I stated, "I don't think so."

Her hand dropped, she stepped away and turned back to the trinkets.

Then she said to the trinkets, "Many a Wife Hunt has gone by where King Lahn has watched the parade and let it pass him by. His people have waited for years for him to claim his bride. A warrior, any warrior, but a warrior like King Lahn especially, has not developed a vast array of feelings. They war. They pillage. They plunder. They fight. They train. They do not form close alliances with their brethren for there are many opportunities for them to fall. They are rarely, in some cases *never* touched by kindness, a soft hand, a warm gaze and most certainly not before they're wed." Her eyes turned to me and locked on mine. "Many humans do not need that, can live their entire lives without it, but some cannot and fewer still of those are warriors." She paused. "But they exist."

At that, to cover how what she said made me feel, I blurted, "What does Lahnahsahna mean?"

She smiled. "It means 'tigress,' my dear."

"Tigress?"

She nodded and went on, "And 'Lahn' means 'tiger.' He was named 'tiger' by his warrior father, who was, incidentally, also a Dax. Before he challenged and bested the Dax who bested his father, and even now, King Lahn was and is known as The Tiger because he is ferocious, clever and strong in battle. He declared *you* at the wedding rite as his *tigress.* Obviously, the perfect mate for the tiger, and I will say, it seemed quite clear with the way he said it that it meant little to him that you were claimed as his Dahksahna, even his rahna Dahksahna. But far, *far* more that he claimed you as his Lahnahsahna. He was not always the Dax, but he was born The Tiger. It is who he is. It is who he will always be."

Okay, I had to admit she was right. It definitely was clear that meant a lot to him. More than a lot. *A lot,* a lot.

"And *kah* Lahnahsahna?" I asked quietly.

"*My* tigress," she answered quietly.

Oh my.

I looked away and changed the subject quickly before my heart could beat out of control.

"And rahna Dahksahna? What does 'rahna' mean?"

"Golden."

"So *kah* rahna Dahksahna...?" I trailed off.

"*My* golden queen," she answered.

"Mm-hmm," I muttered, still fingering the pearl bangles, and I heard her chuckle.

The vendor said something eagerly to me. My head lifted and I saw his excited eyes go from me to the bangles and back again.

"Oh no, sorry. I don't have any money," I told him, smiling at the same time shaking my head and putting the bangles down.

His face fell.

"Take them," Diandra urged, and my gaze shot around to look at her.

"I don't have any—" I started, and she shook her head.

"He will send a messenger to the Dax. The Dax will give him coin or bestow a favor on him. If you want them, take them." She grinned at the vendor then back at me. "You do, you do him a great honor. The queen has visited many stalls but has not offered her custom. They are all hoping you will shine your golden light on them, so take them."

"I'm not sure I want Lahn to—"

"My dear, he has much coin. The proof is covering you head to toe. *Take them.* He won't blink. He will *expect* you to take your custom to his vendors. It keeps them happy. It feeds their coffers, puts food in their bellies, and he needs their allegiance. Take them. Trust me."

I studied her and she tipped her chin at me encouragingly.

"Take them, Dahksahna Circe," Sheena urged then tipped her head and smiled a white smile. "Pretty!" After she said that, she giggled.

I looked at the bangles, picked them up and turned them in my hands. They were roughly made but they *were* pretty. There were five of them and they'd go great with my outfit. Heck, those pearls would go great with *any* outfit.

I slid them on my wrist.

"Ah! Suh rahna Dahksahna fahnay ta kay! Rah fahnay ta kay! Shahsha, kah Dahksahna, shahsha! Shahsha!" the vendor cried, ending with his hands in prayer position, smiling at me like a lunatic and bowing repeatedly.

"He says the golden queen smiles on him. Thank you," Diandra translated, grinning.

"How do I say, 'you're welcome?'" I asked.

"Nahrahka," she answered.

I turned to the vendor, bowed my head and smiled.

"Nahrahka," I said to him.

"Suh rahna Dahksahna lapay sahna! Shahsha fahnay ta kay. Shahsha, kah Dahksahna!" he yelled.

I laughed and looked at Diandra.

"He says the golden queen is beautiful. Thank you for smiling at him," she explained, and I nodded to her, to him and smiled again.

"Shahsha, uh...good sir," I muttered.

He bowed, shaking his clasped hands in front of him then turned to the next stall and shouted, "Suh rahna Dahksahna fahnay ta kay! *Fahnay ta kay!*" Then he bent his torso back, looked to the clear blue sky and shook his clasped hands at the heavens.

"Well," I muttered to Diandra as we moved from his stall. "You were right. He seems pretty honored."

After I was done speaking both she and her daughter laughed and it felt really, really good to join in and laugh with them.

We moved through the marketplace, and it wasn't near the same as going to a mall (what could I say? I was a shopper) with my friends from home (something I wasn't thinking about, I already missed my pop and was worried about him, I didn't even want to think about my friends). But it was just as much fun...in a different way.

I liked Diandra and the more I was around her friendly, helpful chatter, the more I liked her. And Sheena was a sweetheart and proved, while shopping (and begging her mother for this treat or that trinket) that twelve-year-old girls were universal—no matter what universe you happened to exist in.

We'd drunk some juice that tasted of mangos we got from another vendor who was pleased beyond rationality that I partook of her cool beverage, and this was when I saw them.

A pen in which...

I stopped and stared...

In which there looked to be pure white baby *tigers*.

"Oh my God," I whispered and rushed forward to the pen. "They're so cute!" I cried and looked at the man standing beside the pen. "They're *gorgeous*! Unbelievable! Are they for sale?" I felt Diandra and Sheena get close, and I turned instantly to Diandra. "Do you think they're for sale?"

Diandra was eyeing the tiger cubs. "Erm...Dahksahna Circe..." she started, but I shot around her on a beeline to the man by the pen.

"I want one," I declared when I was standing in front of him. "They're white!" I whirled to Diandra. "I've never seen a white tiger! I didn't even know they existed!" I whirled back to the man. "Do they change color?" He blinked down at me, and I kept talking. "I hope not. I want to name mine Ghost. No!" I cried. "Casper!" I shook my head. "No, I think Ghost is better." I whirled to Diandra again. "What do you think? Casper or Ghost?"

"I think, my dear," she moved closer, "that you should discuss this with your king."

"Why?" I asked and her brows knit.

"Why?"

"Yes, why? He's The Tiger, he's got to like a baby one," I stated.

"Dahksahna Circe," she said softly and took my hand. "He is The Tiger, and you are his Tigress, but you are introducing a pet into your family. Not a cat or a dog or a bird but a dangerous *carnivorous animal.* You don't even know how to speak to your new husband in his language. I think, perhaps, you should settle into—"

"Look at them!" I exclaimed, throwing an arm out to the pen of cute, cavorting baby tigers. "They're adorable. They're not carnivorous animals."

"Even now, my dear, I suspect they eat meat, but even if they don't, they will," she replied rationally.

"So?" I replied irrationally, as I had done, all my life, before my mother died and after, anytime I saw something I wanted, and I wanted that something bad. "*I* eat meat too." I returned irrationally.

"You don't kill it and chew it raw off the bone," she retorted.

This was true.

I bit my lip and looked at the animals.

One of them loped to the side of the pen, sat on its behind, looked up at me and made a noise I swear, I *swear,* I understood as "Loolah," which I had learned from Sheena that day, in Korwahk meant "Mama."

My body went still, and I stared at the creature.

"Oh dear," Diandra muttered.

I looked at her and I knew she heard it to.

"Did that...did that...?" I swallowed, looked at the cub and back at Diandra. "Did that baby tiger just—?"

Another mew from the tiger cub which I understood again as Loolah.

I took a step back.

Holy moly, the animal was *speaking to me.*

Diandra sighed, reached out, grabbed a boy running by and spoke swiftly to him. The boy peered up at me and dashed away, darting through the crowds.

I paid little attention to this. I was staring at the cub.

"That creature called me Loolah," I whispered.

Another noise, which meant another Loolah then another noise that I heard as "gahsee," and Diandra spoke to the man which meant she heard it too. He moved, bent, opened the lid on something that was sunk into the ground and came out with a bottle made of wavy glass with a weird kind of nipple on the end, and that bottle was definitely filled with milk.

"Gahsee," Diandra whispered to me, "means hungry."

The creature *was* speaking to me!

I could hear baby tigers talk to me in this world!

How bizarrely, amazingly, fantastically *cool*!

The man came back to us, bent over the pen, scooped up the tiger cub, turned, and without hesitation, dumped her in my arms. I automatically held on as he jerked the bottle to me.

"Oh dear," Diandra muttered again as I looked down at the baby tiger in my arms.

All I felt was the soft, thick fur of the cub, the pads of its cute fluffy paws. All I saw was her proud nose and rounded ears and beautiful pale-blue eyes looking up at me with complete trust.

Oh shit.

I was in love.

I turned the cub in my arms, took the bottle from the man and offered it to the baby tiger.

Her big pink tongue lashed at the nipple then she started to feed.

Yep.

Totally in love.

I turned shining eyes to Diandra.

"Honey, I'm so freaking totally in love," I whispered.

Her gaze moved over my face then she looked at Sheena and whispered, "Oh...*dear*."

Sheena giggled.

I dropped my head back to the cub, cradled her and rocked slightly side to side.

"Casper?" I called experimentally and the cub just sucked, eyes closed. "Ghost?" I called, and the cub's eyes opened then slowly closed again. "There it is then," I decided in a quiet voice. "You're my Ghost."

Five minutes later, when the bottle was nearly drained dry, I heard hoof beats. My head came up and I belatedly felt that the vibe in the marketplace changed.

I turned my head and knew why.

Lahn was galloping our way on his big bay stallion complete with a glossy black mane and tail and black around all four hooves and partly up his legs.

I took a step back as he galloped toward me and reined the horse in at the last minute, jerking him to the side so Lahn could get close, turn his head and stare down his nose at me.

I looked up at my husband in the broad daylight, a sight I'd never seen.

He had a fabulous chest. It was huge but it was well-defined, and I could see my nail marks had scabbed over under his shoulder. Ditto in regard to the huge, well-defined and fabulous parts when it came to his shoulders. The muscles of his thighs could be seen through his hides.

Gorgeous brown skin everywhere. Thick, black facial hair with pointy beard at the chin held by a gold band that was strange, but it was also cool. Hair pulled back in a thick braid that probably went nearly to his waist but was now dangling over his massive shoulder, also held by a gold band. Strong brow that jutted attractively over his eyes. Heavy, black eyebrows. Fabulous cheekbones. Deep-set, piercing, dark-brown eyes. Full, grooved lips surrounded by his beard.

Totally hot.

And the look he was giving me was totally ferocious.

It was clear to see he was not best pleased he'd been interrupted in whatever kings of savage hordes did during the day and called to the marketplace because his new bride had fallen in love with a baby tiger.

I took another step back.

Then I remembered who I was.

In my world, I was Circe Kaye Quinn, the office manager of her father's moving company, unlucky at love (something I tried, twice, had long-term relationships with guys I thought were the ones that ended (twice) so I knew I was unlucky in love) but beloved by family and friends.

Here, I was not an office manager. I was the Golden Warrior Queen and The Tigress, and I was wearing a kickass outfit.

So I needed to suck it up and not be so scared of this guy. He could hurt me—he already had, more than once—and I survived.

So...fuck it.

I pulled in a deep breath and lifted my chin at the same time I lifted up the cub an inch.

"This is Ghost," I introduced her. "She's our new pet."

Lahn scowled at me.

"Erm," Diandra stepped forward then said a bunch of stuff I didn't understand, but my guess was she was interpreting for me.

His eyes didn't leave my face and his glower didn't leave his.

"I'm bringing her home. You'll need to give this man some...um, coin," I jerked my head back to indicate the tiger man.

Diandra spoke again and Lahn kept scowling.

"She's sleeping in bed with us," I declared.

Diandra translated (haltingly this time) and the scowl grew dark or, I should say, *darker*.

I endured his scowl for a long time. Then I sucked in another breath, felt the thick fur and warm body of the cub growing heavier in my arms as she drifted to sleep.

Jeez oh Pete, a *white* baby *tiger* was sleeping *in my arms*, and she called me *Mama* and I *heard her*.

I stepped closer to Lahn, reached out from under the cub, curled my fingers around his hard thigh and tipped my head way back to look in his fierce eyes.

"Please?" I whispered.

He glared at me, and he did this for another long time.

So I squeezed his thigh.

He glared another second then he jerked the reins of his beast. It side-stepped twice, Lahn reached way down, scooped me *and* Ghost in his arm and swung us up, planting my ass in front of him on the horse.

Was he…?

He barked something at the tiger man. The tiger man smiled and bowed his head, then Lahn wheeled the horse around and we were galloping back through the marketplace.

He was! He was letting me have the tiger!

Yippee!

I turned, and peering around his big body, I carefully waved at Diandra and Sheena as best I could while still keeping tight hold on my new baby.

They waved back. Both were smiling and both smiles were *huge*.

I straightened and looked up at Lahn who was staring impassively into the distance. He must have felt my gaze for his dropped to me and he pinned me with a glower.

I smiled at him.

His glower deepened when his eyes narrowed on my mouth.

I turned to face forward, settled on the horse and cradled Ghost.

He wanted to be in a bad mood, so be it.

Whatever.

I had a new baby tiger who could *talk to me* and thought I was her Loolah!

Not to mention some fun new bangles.

Yippee!

7

THE GAMES

The tent flaps slapped open.

I jumped. Ghost's head came up. Teetru, Jacanda, Packa, Gaal and Beetus (who, every last one, even the reserved Teetru, squealed in delight at the vision of me and Ghost earlier when we rode up with Lahn to the tent, he dismounted, yanked me down and then remounted without a word or look and rode off), all surrounding me on the bed and playing with Ghost who also jumped and looked to the tent opening where Lahn was bending low to enter.

He stepped a step inside. Ghost jumped off the bed and scampered over to him, all furry white body and big paws. The baby tiger made it to her new daddy, jumped up with two paws and clawed his hides.

Lahn stared down at the creature, crossed his arms on his chest, lifted his head and skewered me with a glare.

Oh hell.

"Vayoo," he growled at me.

I had no idea what that meant but Teetru and Jacanda started to push me off the bed.

It was night. I'd had dinner and I was guessing it was time for the games.

I got off the bed, sauntered over to my husband and bent to pick up Ghost who was now clawing at the rugs. She was heavy so I lugged her up and got eye to eye with her.

"Be good," I warned.

She shoved forward, rubbed my jaw with her head, made a purry noise I knew was Loolah, and I laughed and brought her close to give her a hug.

Then she was pulled from my hands and my head turned to Lahn to see him drop her on the ground.

"Lahn!" I snapped but his big hand came out and engulfed mine.

"Vayoo, Lahnahsahna Circe, boh," he bit out, pulling me toward the tent flaps.

"Oh, all right," I muttered then turned to the girls and called while waving, "Goodnight, ladies. Take care of Ghost." I pointed at the cub and got a bunch of smiles with waves and nods.

The tent flap slapped back, and I followed Lahn through it. Or, more accurately, was hauled through it.

"I'm coming, I'm coming, slow down," I called as I raced to keep up with his long strides.

"Mayoo," he replied.

"I can't *mayoo*, Lahn. Jeez, you're like, six foot seven. You've got a whole foot on me. Every stride you take is two of mine at least," I said to his back.

He stopped abruptly and I nearly slammed into him.

He turned and glared down at me then said a bunch of stuff I didn't understand. But I'd been around guys long enough to know that when the end of what he said went up in a question, he was likely asking me something about females that even if I *could* understand him, and he me, I could never explain.

So I put my hand to his chest, leaned slightly into him, tilted my head way back and said softly, "That's just the way it is, big guy, so," I took my hand off him and pressed it palm flat toward the ground, "*slow down*."

His eyes were riveted to my hand, and he looked beyond unhappy. He looked weirdly pissed off.

Uh-oh.

Okay, maybe I was reading there were times to be The Tigress, but when The Tiger was eager to watch a bunch of warriors beating the shit out each other, I should just hurry and keep up.

When he kept looking at my hand in that angry way, I took a precautionary step back. His eyes cut to mine then he moved fast, his arm shooting out and his fingers wrapped around my wrist. They tugged me hard and I fell into him just as he pressed my hand flat on his chest exactly where I'd placed it moments before.

I stared at him as his eyes stared at my hand just under the scratches at his chest and I felt my heart start to hammer.

Then he looked at me.

"Kay ahnay see," he murmured and pressed my hand deeper into his chest.

I knew what that meant.

He was saying he liked it.

Oh my.

"Uh..." I mumbled. "Good."

"Good," he muttered.

I tipped my head to the side and smiled tentatively at him. "Yeah...good."

His gaze dropped to my mouth and his other hand came up. His calloused skin rough at my jaw, his thumb pressed hard against my lips.

"Kay ahnay see," he repeated quietly, and my breath stuck in my throat.

Oh.

Wow.

He liked my smile.

Wow.

He liked my smile!

I stared up at my warrior husband.

His neck was bent deep so he could look at me, his skin was firm and warm under my hand, his body the same against mine and his face...

God...he was gorgeous.

Without thinking, I leaned deeper into him, my hand gliding up his chest, taking his with it. It went up, up, up to curl around his neck. His hand dropped and started to curve around my waist, the other one already there as I tipped my head far back, my eyes closing slowly as his lips got closer...

And then we heard, "Poyah, Dax Lahn! Poyah, rahna Dahksahna!"

Damn it all to hell!

My eyes opened to see his head, still close, was turned, but he had not straightened away from me. I looked in the direction he was glaring and saw a warrior approaching.

It was the grinning one from the wedding rite who was so pleased with his bride. He was grinning now too, looking no less pleased, in fact, infinitely more so.

Someone was getting himself some and he liked what he was getting.

My body tensed when I felt Lahn straighten and he snarled a bunch of not happy words at the warrior. Although clearly not happy—as in *way* not happy—the warrior didn't miss a step nor did his grin falter. In fact, it got bigger and then he threw his head back and roared with hearty laughter.

He stopped laughing and shook his head as he made it to us, said a bunch of stuff, and while doing it, once gestured to me with his head.

Lahn returned his volley and also gestured to me with his head.

The other warrior's eyebrows went up in disbelief and then he said something that sounded disbelieving, but if I wasn't wrong, it was a kind of "you the man" disbelieving. I was pretty sure I was proved right when his eyes came to me, and he looked me up and down then turned to Lahn and nodded his approval.

Totally *you the man.*

Um.

Was my husband bragging about his escapades with me *right in front of me*?

I stepped out of his arms and planted my hands on my hips.

"Uh...baby," I called, and both men turned to me, both looked at my face, clearly both read my face and before I could say more, Lahn did—not to me, to the warrior.

And I didn't speak Korwahk, but it was clearly, "See what I mean?" and whatever he meant made the warrior roar with laughter again.

The thing was, Lahn did it with him.

I stood there staring.

I'd never kissed my husband and I'd never seen him laugh.

Until then.

Jeez, how weird was that?

He had a great laugh and he looked good doing it.

And he had very white teeth.

They stopped laughing and the other warrior said something and tipped his head to me.

Lahn nodded, smiling and then suddenly he grabbed my bicep, and my body was in motion. I had no idea how he did it, but he swung me up on his back so my arm was around his neck and my thighs were at his hips. His big hands came to my ass, and he started walking while talking to the other warrior who fell in step at his side, all the while carrying me on his back.

I curved my legs fully around him to hold on, my other arm going around his chest, and there was something about this, something sweet, something intimate, something I liked.

Oh man.

We walked through the encampment and drew every eye from every person we passed. I noticed Lahn didn't smile or nod his head. I noticed Lahn had his hands on my ass, me on his back and a warrior at his side and that was his whole focus. The people we passed did not exist. He didn't acknowledge them in any way.

So I did, smiling and nodding at anyone who caught my eye. And there were a lot of those too.

Lahn's fingers tensed into my flesh, and he turned his head and said something to me.

I didn't understand, obviously, so I dropped my chin to his shoulder and whispered, "I don't understand you, baby."

His dark eyes caught mine and he said quietly, "Lahnahsahna Circe...okay?"

Oh man.

Yeah, I was okay. Okay with Lahn attempting to communicate with me in my own language.

Yeah, totally okay.

I closed my eyes and squeezed my arms then nodded, opened my eyes and whispered, "Okay."

That got me another squeeze on my ass as Lahn looked forward again and his warrior said something to him.

I looked forward too, sighed, held tight and enjoyed the ride.

Okay, it was safe to say the minute we entered the ginormous tent where the games were held, I knew I wasn't going to like it.

This was because there were a lot of beefy men sitting around on benches, it smelled like man and booze and there were two men beating the crap out of each other in the middle of the circle of benches. And by that I mean, sweaty, bloody, grunting *beating the crap out of each other.*

Very few eyes came to us such was the attention on the match. But an entire bench was open at one side. The other warrior broke off from us and Lahn walked right to it, swung me off his back—jarring my shoulder as he did (the big guy was rough, but I was getting the feeling he didn't know it). He deposited me, feet to the ground, sat, opened his legs wide and grabbed my hand. He tugged it so hard it jarred my shoulder again and my knees gave out. With no choice, I sank to the stone ground.

He hauled me between his legs. I did my best to get comfortable and looked around.

Lots of warriors—though I couldn't find the one who claimed Narinda, not that I was sure I would remember what he looked like. There were no women except the two scurrying around with jugs and filling the leather covered cups the men were guzzling from. One scurried to Lahn, he took the full cup she offered, put it to his lips, gulped back a huge swallow then righted himself and his eyes locked on the fighters.

No beverage was offered to me before the woman scurried off.

Hmm.

Apparently, women weren't provided with refreshments.

Figured.

To get comfortable, I scooted close between his legs and draped an arm on Lahn's thigh. I didn't know if that was all right, but I figured if it wasn't, I'd find out soon enough.

He didn't remove it, so I leaned into it and looked at the shouting, cheering, stamping warriors.

Man, they were eating this shit up. Nearly frenzied.

I turned to the fighters. One looked about to drop. This was good and bad. Good for me because it meant this match was nearly over. Bad for him because it was clear there were no technical knockouts in this game, and he looked like he could use one.

I was right. Five minutes later he was down and out.

One minute later he was dragged unceremoniously across the stone ground as the other fighter beat his chest, threw out his ripped arms, stamped his tree trunk legs and shouted his triumph. Then he tore a leather cup from a passing waitress-type person, downed most of it in one gulp and poured the rest of it over his body, shaking his big head, blood, sweat and booze flying everywhere, and he shouted again.

Yikes.

"Lahnahsahna Circe." I heard Lahn call my name and I leaned back to look up at him.

"Yeah?"

He brought the cup to my lips.

"Gingoo," he ordered, and it didn't take a linguistics master to know he meant drink.

I parted my lips. He tipped the cup, and I noticed as he did, he was watching with intense interest.

I expected a beer-like substance, seeing as we were at a sporting event.

It wasn't a beer-like substance. It was a straight, raw spirit and it burned my throat, but it didn't taste all that bad.

He took the cup away and I grinned at him.

"Kay ahnay see," I said.

He stared at me a second, his bearded chin jerking back in surprise, and then his entire head tilted back as he roared with laughter.

I didn't know what was so funny.

His head tipped down, his eyes moved through the tent and his fist crashed against his chest before he shouted, "Kah Lahnahsahna ahnay see!"

He lifted the cup and spirit splashed out. I heard a roar of cheers and turned my head to see, belatedly, that all the warriors had their eyes on me. Some were stamping their feet. Some were clapping. All were smiling.

"Lahnahsahna hahla!" one warrior yelled, and they all cheered again.

I felt Lahn touch the back of my head. I looked up at him again and he held the cup to my lips.

"Gingoo, kah fauna," he ordered gently, then he tipped the cup, and I took another drink. When the cup came away from my mouth, the warriors again cheered, and Lahn grinned down at me. "Hahla," he muttered, still grinning.

"Hahla," I repeated, not having the first clue what I said but happy to say anything to keep him grinning at me like that.

I got what I wanted but he gave me better. The grin broadened to a blinding white smile.

Then his head went back to the action as two more fighters came out.

I smiled to myself and turned back too, thinking, *okay, this wasn't so bad.*

Without any ado whatsoever, they went at each other. I noticed immediately this was not like a boxing match from home. Not that I watched much boxing at home, but these guys didn't have gloves, for one thing. For another, there were no referees. And also, I didn't think boxers were allowed to part wrestle, kick, aim at (and sometimes connect with) the groin and the like.

It wasn't brutal.

It was *brutal.*

And in this match, I instantly had a favorite. I didn't know why, I just liked him. Maybe because the other guy kept trying to kick or punch him in the groin, so I didn't think that was fighting fair.

So, when my guy started to look like he was winning, I got excited.

And therefore, not thinking, I cheered. And, as the battle wore on, I cheered *loud,* and I cheered *hard.*

When the bad guy went down, my arms went straight up.

I bounced on my behind between Lahn's legs and I screamed, "*Woo hoo!* You decked him! Way to go! You *rock*!"

The victor did not stamp, shout, beat his chest or down a half cup of raw spirit.

His eyes came to me.

Then I felt that all eyes had come to me as the warriors' bellows petered out.

My arms dropped.

Uh-oh.

I'd fucked up.

Lahn's huge hand curled tight around the back of my neck.

Uh-oh!

The triumphant fighter took two steps toward me, I tensed, and he stopped.

Then he leaned into me, I reared back, and he boomed, "*Suh Rahna Dahksahna!*"

"*Suh Rahna Dahksahna!*" Another shout rang out.

The stamping began as they stood, stomped their feet, punched the air with their fists and chanted, "*Rahna Dahksahna! Rahna Dahksahna! Rahna Dahksahna! Rahna Dahksahna!*"

Okay, um...it appeared crisis malfunction. Apparently, these boys liked it when their women cheered during blood sports.

Good to know.

I smiled uncertainly at the boys and then felt pressure on my neck. I tipped back my head to see Lahn looking down on me, his face expressionless.

I bit my lip, his gaze dropped to my mouth then his eyes lifted and locked on mine.

Then he muttered, "Good."

I felt my face melt into a smile.

He shook his head, his lips tipped up and he brought the cup to my lips. I took another big drink, and he took the cup away and squeezed my neck before took his hand away. His attention went back to the center and mine followed.

The boys calmed down, new combatants entered the circle and the games resumed.

~

I KNEW things were not going to be good when Dortak came in dragging his terrified-looking, cowed, eyes-sunken-in, arms-covered-in-bruises new bride.

Unlike when Lahn and I arrived, the minute Dortak hauled his woman into the tent, attention went to him, and the vibe changed. There was still cheering, stamping and the fighters didn't miss an opportunity at landing a blow, but a lethal undercurrent slithered low through the tent, and it did not feel good.

When I saw her, without thought my hand moved swiftly, searching until it found Lahn's, and I curled mine into his. He didn't give me a reassuring squeeze. He moved my hand to his thigh and curved my fingers around the firm muscle then his hand left mine.

Okay, I didn't know how to read that. Maybe he just wasn't the kind of guy who held hands during knockdown, drag-out warrior fights. But I was guessing it was an indication that I was his kickass rahna Dahksahna and I needed to suck it up. This was their world, and I was in it.

And suddenly, that sucked.

The night had been kind of fun. I knew I was more than slightly tipsy on the spirit Lahn kept giving me and I was feeling loose and truly happy for the first time since I got to this world (again, I was more than slightly tipsy...but still).

Now, the night was not fun, and as hard as I tried, I could not take my eyes off Dortak and his bride.

Something there had to give. She was clearly miserable, and he was clearly mistreating her. It wasn't only the bruises. It was the defeated look on her face.

I was going to have to have a word with my husband. The problem was, he understood, at my count, two of my words, and I didn't understand much more of his.

I laid my cheek against my hand on his thigh and stared without interest at the fighters. But my gaze kept drifting back to Dortak and I caught it when one warrior leaned over to Dortak, jerked his head at me, telling him something while smiling. Something Dortak didn't think was worthy of a smile if the ferocious frown he aimed my way was anything to go by. Therefore, I knew my cheering and drinking had been recounted and Dortak would not have been amongst those shouting my title in approval.

I pulled in a steadying breath to stop myself from having a visible reaction to the hate coming my way and my attention went back to the fighters.

Minutes later, I heard a cry from his direction, and it wasn't from a warrior. My eyes moved there, and my torso shot straight.

Dortak had his hand in his wife's hair, he was yanking her head this way and that at the same time pulling his sex out of his hides.

No, he wasn't going to...

He pushed her face into his lap, forcing himself into her mouth.

I surged to my feet and took a flying step forward, but two iron arms clamped around me, one at my belly, one at my chest and Lahn's mouth came to my ear. He spoke quietly, even gently, but I didn't hear a word he said (regardless of the fact I probably wouldn't understand them) as I stared in shock and tried to get venom to spew out of my eyes and fly with precision at Dortak who held my angry stare and used his meaty fist in his wife's hair to force her mouth back and forth on his shaft.

"Stop him," I whispered as Lahn pulled me back then sat, not pushing me to the ground but settling me in his lap. "Stop him," I repeated louder, and he turned me in his arms and shoved my face in his neck so I could no longer see. "Kay me ahnoo!" I snapped into his neck.

"Rayloo, kah fauna," Lahn murmured and kept my face in his neck with his hand cupped on my head and my body in his lap with his strong arm clamped around it.

I lifted a hand and curled it around the other side of his neck.

"Kay me ahnoo," I told him, and his arm gave me a squeeze. "Kay me ahnoo," I repeated on a whisper, but he didn't do anything except for the fact that he didn't let me go.

I knew it was over when his hand loosened on my head and dropped down to become an arm wrapped around my body.

He still didn't let me go and he didn't shove me off his lap and force me between his legs. He just kept me where I was, holding me in his lap. I carefully took my face out of his neck and looked at his profile. He was silently watching the fighters. Then I chanced a look at Dortak. His bride was still between his legs, body facing the fighters, but her head was bent, her cheeks flaming, and her eyes were directed to the ground.

I turned back and shoved my face in Lahn's neck.

I felt his chest expand with a big breath that he let out very slowly.

I didn't want to be there anymore, and I curled into him and tried to shut everything out, hoping it would be over soon.

This became impossible when I heard taunting, loud words hurled in what seemed to be our direction. I lifted my face out of Lahn's neck, turned my head and saw Dortak standing before us, jeering at Lahn, spittle coming out of his mouth, his face red and his fist beating his chest.

My eyes darted to his wife who was where he left her on the ground but now curled into herself, arms tight around her legs, eyes peeking from behind her knees.

Lahn said something calmly and I glanced at him to see he appeared as calm as his voice. Swiftly I looked to Dortak who had not taken to Lahn's calm very well. He was red in the face and the veins in his neck were standing out as he continued to shout.

What was going on?

Lahn asked him a question to which Dortak spat out a, "Meena!"

Lahn nodded. Then he stood, me in his arms. He set my ass on the bench and his eyes coasted across mine before he straightened and turned.

The instant he did, the warriors all rose from their seats, arms up, shouts deafening, and they were saying only one word.

"*Dax!*"

Oh fuck.

Was Lahn going to fight this guy?

Dortak immediately swung a punch, connecting with Lahn's jaw.

I rose to my feet.

Lahn took two steps back, pointed at me, his finger moved to the bench, and he clipped out, "Lutoo! Boh!"

Dortak closed in and connected again, this time with Lahn's ribs.

I sat, not wanting to divert his attention again, but I sat on the edge of the bench, and how I stayed on the bench I had no clue since I was shaking like a leaf.

Dortak connected, again, again, again, a quick succession of blows that Lahn didn't appear even to try to deflect.

Then another one to the face so brutal Lahn's torso swung around and down, his hand going to the blood that was now dripping from his mouth.

Dortak charged to attack, but Lahn lifted an elbow, connecting with Dortak's nose not only with the strength of his arm but Dortak's momentum. Dortak stumbled back and Lahn went in, palm to throat. He lifted Dortak clean off his feet and slammed him flat on his back on the stone, the crack of his skull hitting the stone sounding with a sickening thud that made my stomach to turn.

The warriors went wild.

Lahn had gone down on a knee to take Dortak to his back and he swiftly moved one leg to put his knee to Dortak's arm in order to incapacitate it, the other calf he shoved in Dortak's neck as he twisted the rest of his body to Dortak's legs. He caught a flailing ankle, yanked the man's hides back and then he pulled a small knife out of a sheath.

All cheering silenced instantly, and I rose again to my feet, the fingers of both hands coming to my mouth.

None of the other fighters had weapons. They used their fists, their feet, their wits...not steel.

Lahn removed his legs from Dortak but swiftly turned and kept him down, one hand wrapped around his throat, the other hand holding the knifepoint aimed half an inch from his eye.

He growled something in his face.

Dortak's only response was to choke. Lahn was strangling him. Dortak's face was turning purple and veins were popping out along his temple.

Lahn repeated what he'd growled earlier.

Dortak kept gasping for breath, his hands pushing ineffectually at Lahn's arm, his legs kicking out.

Lahn repeated what he'd growled.

Dortak made gurgling noises.

Then, quick as a flash, the knife moved and blood covered Dortak's face as he howled.

I gasped, stepped back and hit bench, so I stopped.

Lahn pushed off him and up to his feet, tossing the knife down so it landed on Dortak's chest, bounced off and clattered to the stone ground.

Lahn stared down at him then spit in his direction, the spittle landing on Dortak's shoulder.

After delivering that, he turned and started to me.

I watched him move, my body shaking, then I saw Dortak get up, still choking, and my body froze as I saw Lahn had carved a deep, gaping, curving gash from temple over cheekbone partially through his lip and across his jaw.

"Lahn," I whispered. Dortak bent, snatched the knife off the ground, straightened, and I shouted, "Lahn!"

Dortak charged and Lahn turned like I hadn't shouted his name to indicate imminent danger, but like I'd suggested he might want to look over his shoulder and observe the flight of a pretty butterfly.

His arm came up, he caught Dortak's wrist that was connected to the hand that was carrying the knife, used it to swing him around and caught him around the throat with his other forearm. Lahn then twisted Dortak to facing this bride and he used the knife still in Dortak's hand to slash another curving, deep gash down the length of Dortak's chest, down, down nearly to his groin, and then he moved Dortak's hand and sunk the blade in Dortak's side.

Dortak grunted in pain and my knees buckled.

Lahn pulled out the knife and let Dortak go. He dropped to his knees, hands to his wound, and Lahn wiped Dortak's blood off the knife against his hides.

He tossed the knife well away.

Then he turned and stalked to me.

I tried to step back but nearly stumbled over the bench as he came at me, and I tried to come to terms with the violent justice I just witnessed my husband dish out.

Perhaps it was justified but it still freaked me out.

His long legs had him to me in seconds. He grasped my bicep, turned his back to me, swung me up, my legs automatically curled around his hips as he wrapped my arm around his neck and stalked out of the tent.

Welp. Guess that meant the games were over.

Yikes!

~

"Hold still," I snapped at Lahn, who was sitting on one of the chairs in our tent, and he kept jerking his head out of the way when I tried dabbing his cut lip with the wet, soapy rag I'd managed to explain to Teetru I needed.

My eyes moved from his annoyed ones, and I tried to dab at the blood again.

He jerked his head away.

"Lahn!" I hissed. "Hold still!"

He didn't hold still. He tore the rag from my hand, tossed it on the table and came out of the chair with his shoulder in my belly.

I let out a gust of air as I went up then I went down as he threw me on the bed. I let out another gust of air when he landed on top of me.

"Lahn, we need to clean your cut lip." On a wheeze I told him something he wouldn't understand and clearly had no intention of sitting around and allowing me to do. It was a miracle I got him to sit in the first place. It only happened five minutes ago, and I still didn't know how I managed it.

His hand went between us, and he yanked one panel of my sarong aside.

I knew where this was going.

"Lahn—"

"Rayloo," he growled.

"Lahn! Your lip!"

That bloody lip (and his not bloody one, they luckily came in pairs) came to mine. "Rayloo, Circe."

I glared into his eyes as his hand glided up the skin of my side.

Shit, that felt nice.

"All right, *rayloo*. I'll *rayloo*, whatever the hell that means," I grumbled.

His eyes went soft, and his hand went away from my side.

It came up to my face where the pad of his thumb put pressure on my chin and his fingers put pressure on my lips.

"Rayloo," he said quietly.

Ah.

Rayloo.

His hand left my mouth.

"Quiet," I whispered.

"Quiet," he repeated.

"Rayloo," I tried it out.

He shook his head like he didn't know what to do with me (as, perhaps, he would, considering he'd told me to be quiet and I kept talking) but affirmed, "Rayloo."

"Okay," I said softly.

His hand slid down my arm, took mine in his and then it pulled mine between his legs and moved it down inside his hides.

His fingers curled mine around his hard cock.

Wow. Nice.

I bit my lip and squirmed under him.

He shook his head like he didn't know what to do with me again, his hand left mine around his cock and his went into my panties.

Okay, I was wrong. He knew what to do with me.

So I shut up and let him do it.

8

New Warriors

I felt the thump of something heavy and soft and my eyes opened.

The minute they did, I saw a furry paw and then felt the gentle thump of it against my cheek.

"Loolah," Ghost mewed.

I smiled at my baby, captured her in my arms and gave her a snuggle.

She squirmed free and then bounced and rolled around the bed, a bit on the mattress, mostly on me.

I looked to the other side of the bed.

Lahn was gone.

This was the first time I'd woken up in this world without him.

No, strike that.

This was the first time *he* had not woken *me*.

And, again, I had woken up in this world.

I rolled to my back, pulled the covers up to my chest and stared at the ceiling as Ghost jumped around, clawing and playing, and anytime I could get my hands on her, I scratched or stroked but she was not having that and kept bouncing around.

My mind was bouncing around too.

One, I kept waking up in this world. Two, I had no idea how I got here. Three, I had no idea when I'd be sent home. Four, I had no idea *if* I'd be sent home. Five, I now had no idea how I felt about that.

Two days ago, I would have begged, borrowed, stole or killed to get home. No joke. Anything to get away from this place.

But now, I'd spent time with Diandra, Sheena and my girls. I had Ghost, a white baby tiger who freaking called me Loolah. The marketplace was interesting. My clothes were kickass. The warriors approved of me. I was a queen which, seriously, had its perks.

And then there was Lahn.

As freaking crazy as it sounded, the man was getting to me—smiling at me, carrying me around on his back in that sweet way, letting me have Ghost, being everything he had *not* been in bed those first three days and, in fact, being the best lover by far I'd ever had *in my life*.

Not to mention he was beautiful.

And I was starting to feel a weird connection to him that didn't make sense, but I knew it was there. I felt it, that connection, a fierce pull. And it scared me because I didn't get it. It made no sense, so I decided to bury it, deep.

At the same time, I watched him carve into a man without blinking, then stick him with a blade. He'd hunted me. He'd had no problems raping me and then taking me repeatedly when he knew I did not want it and was nowhere near ready to receive him.

He still scared me at the same time he fascinated me, drew me in.

And I had seen my husband smile. I had seen him laugh. And both looked good.

I *had* a husband, which in itself was bizarre.

But my husband had still not (even last night) kissed me.

And bizarrest of the bizarre, I really wanted my husband to kiss me. I wanted that intimacy. I wanted it a lot, too much. So much, I freaking ached for it.

Totally...*whacked*!

And lying there in our bed, waking up without him for the first time, I had to admit, I was disappointed he wasn't there.

Crap.

I didn't want to be stuck in this world. It frightened me. Not only the culture I'd been thrown into but whatever power might be out there that took me to it.

I had to admit some parts of it were interesting and some parts even cool.

But the rest scared the shit out of me.

And I worried about my pop. I worried that he was frantic, wondering where I was.

Pop lost a wife and now his daughter had gone missing. He'd loved Mom. He'd told me time and again they were the perfect match, made for each other. He'd dated—he was a good-looking guy—but he never got even close to serious with any of the women he'd had in his life. No one could replace Mom, I knew. He'd never said that, but I knew it.

And he loved me, totally and completely, and he'd be sick with worry that I'd disappeared.

I also worried about my friends who I knew would worry about me. And I worried about the state of the office because, Lord knew, those guys didn't know where anything was. They'd mess everything up and they'd do it in a way where it would take me a year to get it back the way I liked it.

I didn't know what to do, but even so, I felt guilt that I wasn't doing anything. And more guilt that I had laughed here, cheered here, smiled here, had sex I enjoyed with a man here and got myself a freaking pet.

"What am I doing?" I whispered to the tent, and Ghost jumped up, all four paws landing on my chest and belly. I grunted, then giggled and wrapped my arms around Ghost who squirmed, when I heard the tent flap slap back.

I looked to see the girls streaming through, Teetru coming straight to me, Jacanda dragging the tub, Gaal, Beetus and Packa all following her with buckets of steaming water. Their faces were smiling but their manner was urgent.

Oh well.

One step at a time.

Teetru came to me, snatched Ghost off my chest and dropped her on her feet on the ground. She tugged at the sheet once, smiled at me and scurried off, coming back in seconds with my robe.

First step, get up.

I was sitting at the table taking my next step, which was eating the breakfast Teetru served of passionfruit and grain mixed with a thick, velvety, sweetened cream cheese (totally delicious) and coffee, when I heard a call of, "Poyah!"

The tent flap slapped back and Diandra and Sheena were there, dressed, for the Korwahks, to the nines.

"Hey," I smiled at them, taking in their cool-as-shit fancy duds.

"You will not believe what's happened, Dahksahna Circe!" Diandra cried then didn't wait for me to respond, she clapped her hands together in front of her and semi-yelled, "The Dax sent word to Seerim! He wants me to act as your translator! Isn't that *wonderful*?"

I stared at her.

Sheena grinned with pleasure for her mom and then Diandra grabbed her daughter's hand and dashed over to the trunks, all the while babbling.

"We must hurry. The ceremony is fast approaching and there is much to do to prepare you." She straightened from the trunks and whirled to me, eyes bright. "And *I* get to stand on the *dais* next to *my queen* and translate!" She clapped her hands again and whirled back to the trunks, dropping to her knees where Sheena already was digging through. "I must tell you, Dahksahna Circe, this pleases me greatly. For years, my boys have been gone, in training. And Sheena, she's not a baby anymore. She's off and about with her friends, at her studies. Seerim is busy with training his warriors, so I rarely see him. I'm alone a lot, too much, and sometimes it's difficult to find things *to do*." Her head twisted to me. "And now I have something *to do*, and it is an *important* something being interpreter to *our queen*!"

She smiled and I smiled back at her. I couldn't help it.

Her excitement was catching.

Jacanda came forward, took my hand and pulled gently. I stood, grabbing my coffee cup and taking the last sip before I put the cup down and allowed her to lead me to the bath.

"Uh..." I started as I moved through the tent. "Speaking of interpreting. Some things happened last night."

"Oh, I know!" Diandra cried, still digging through the trunks, Sheena at her side holding a sarong up and studying it. "It's all over the camp. Well done you *again*!"

"Well done me?" I asked, allowing Jacanda to take away my robe, and I quickly stepped into the warm, milky, fragrant bath.

"More proof you are the rahna Dahksahna," Diandra answered, slipping the sarong Sheena was holding from her fingers then carrying a bunch of stuff in her arms to the bed and dumping it there. She turned to me and put her hands to her hips, and I was pleased the milky water and floating flower blossoms covered me up to my chest. "How did you do it?"

"Do what?" I asked as I tipped my head back and Gaal poured fragrant, warm water over my hair.

"Consume the zakah?" she asked.

I blinked water out of my eyes and turned to Diandra.

"Zakah?" I asked back.

"The distilled spirit they drink." Her face twisted. "I do not know a woman who can abide it. It's a man's drink, and not even that, it's so strong and foul, it's a *warrior's* drink. Tales sweeping the camp say you didn't even make a face."

"Uh...in my, um...*land*, we drink shots like that all the time. Not that raw but—"

"Unusual," she muttered, interrupting me, and whirled back to the bed where Sheena was separating clothing. "Well, even young warriors cannot drink it for the first time without gasping for breath or spitting it out. Learning to consume it in vast quantities is part of being a warrior."

There it was.

Guys were guys in this world, my world, probably *every* world.

"You honored a warrior with your accolades too," she went on. "It is said you watched with avid interest. Another thing wives do not do. They were deeply impressed."

I definitely got that.

"Diandra?" I called and changed the subject, "Lahn and Dortak fought last night—"

She turned to me and announced, "This, too, is sweeping the camp."

I had no doubt.

"It was..." I made a face but didn't go on.

"Not less than he deserved," she declared, her expression going slightly hard. "Seerim told me he dishonored the games. Unlike in my land, or I am sensing, in yours, these acts amongst men and women are not as guarded, they do not happen always behind cham flaps. If there is a celebration or the men come back from war or plunder, it often gets quite," she paused to search for a word, "*sordid*, as we would see it in our lands. And, I will say, there are other times too. They do not hide these things. But the games are a gathering of warriors. It is about men, strength, fortitude, cunning. It was not looked upon positively he did that to his bride. It was not looked upon positively that he even brought her, considering it is clear he carries no feelings for her. And it was even less agreeable that he challenged the Dax to a match and did it armed. You do not fight in the games armed. That is *not* done."

I got that last night too.

Gaal lathered my hair as I caught Diandra's eyes and whispered, "But that's not what I'm talking about. I'm talking about Lahn killing him."

She waved a hand in front of her face and breathed out, "Oh posh! He left his mark on him and Seerim told me it was a short blade. A flesh wound. Dortak, unfortunately, will be up and about in a few days. Dax Lahn knew what he was doing. Dortak is attended by healers, and he'll be just fine." She leaned toward me. "But he'll carry the Dax's marks for all to see until he's foolish enough to extend the true challenge and his headless body will burn carrying the marks of the Dax. *This* was the Dax's intention. *This* was his punishment for dishonoring the games, a punishment I heard the Dax seemed not to intend to carry out, likely because you were in attendance, but Dortak in all his wisdom essentially *asked* for it. And the Dax, given the opportunity, as you witnessed last night, does not hesitate in meting out punishment."

Oh yes. I witnessed that last night.

Gaal whispered something to me. I'd heard it before, it included the word *linas*, which I'd figured out was eyes, so I closed my eyes, and she rinsed my hair with another jug of warm water.

Diandra said something to Sheena, and I opened my eyes, wiped the water from them and Gaal massaged what I suspected was a kind of conditioner in my hair for this was what she did the last two mornings. It didn't lather, but when my hair was dry, it left it shiny and soft. Or maybe the gunk they put into it did that. I saw Sheena move to Teetru who was sorting through the smaller trunks that held my jewelry. Sheena smiled at Teetru, and they carried on digging through the trunks.

My eyes went to Diandra to see her pouring herself a cup of coffee.

"Diandra?" I called.

"Yes, my dear," she replied, dripping some milk in her cup.

"What does *hahla* mean?"

She turned to me and sipped, smiling as Jacanda rinsed the soap from one of my arms. "It means 'true,' 'pure.' The word means both. This, too," her voice had dropped, "is sweeping the camp. After last night at the games, you are no longer rahna Dahksahna or Lahnahsahna but rahna Dahksahna *hahla* and Lahnahsahna *hahla*. This means, Dahksahna Circe, the warriors believe you are the true golden warrior queen, a pure tigress." Her smile got bigger. "This is good."

No.

No. It was bad for they believed this, and they believed the Dax was the mighty warrior of legend, and from what I'd seen, *that* could be true.

But I was a girl from Seattle. And I was likely a girl who would go back to Seattle. Not a queen who, with her king, legend tells begins a dynasty.

Shit.

I shook that off, and after Gaal rinsed my hair again, I asked Diandra, "What does kah fauna mean?"

Her body gave a start causing her head to jerk. Then she stared at me. Finally, her eyes warmed, her face got soft, and her lips smiled big.

"Kah fauna?" she whispered, her warm eyes beginning to light.

"Uh..." I stared into her eyes, feeling my stomach dip and my heart beat faster. "Yes, kah fauna."

"Did your king call you that?" Diandra asked and I felt that it wasn't only Diandra's gaze but every female's gaze in that tent was on me.

A quick glance proved this to be true.

I swallowed and looked back at Diandra.

"Yes, uh, twice," I whispered.

Diandra's eyes closed slowly. She opened them, turned her head to her daughter and lifted up two fingers.

Sheena beamed.

"What?" I asked and Diandra looked back at me, still grinning. "*What?*" I asked more urgently.

"It means, Dahksahna Circe, 'my doe' or, as we might say it in my land, 'my sweet' or 'my love' or 'my darling.'"

She moved toward me carrying her cup and her eyes didn't leave mine as I sat in the warm, fragrant tub with flower blossoms floating around and stared at her in shock at the same time my belly didn't dip.

It warmed...as did my heart.

Shit!

"Warriors do not speak like this." She shook her head. "No, this isn't true, they do. But it is rare and when it comes, it is precious." She was speaking softly, standing by the tub looking down at me. "My Seerim has called me *kah fauna* ten times in the twenty-two years he has been my husband. I have counted. I remember each time. And each time was a treasure."

I blinked up at her.

Oh. My. *God.*

"It is true," she whispered. "The mightiest, strongest warriors *can* fall in love upon gazing at their bride in the parade."

Oh shit.

"Diandra—"

"A blessing," she cut me off, still whispering. "For our Dax, for his people and *for you.*"

Oh shit!

"Diandra—"

The tent flaps slapped open.

I jumped, water sloshed, Diandra turned, and my eyes went there to see Lahn bending low to enter.

My heart warmed again, and other places warmed too.

Shit!

His eyes swept the tent going clean through me before he looked at Teetru and barked something. She rushed to a chest, and he turned to Diandra and barked something else. She nodded, bowed slightly and murmured something back.

Teetru rushed to him with a largish clay pot that had a lid. He seized it from her fingers, barked something else at her and jerked his head at me. She nodded, he turned, and without a word to me or another glance, he stalked to the tent flaps and was gone.

I stared at the tent flaps.

Then my gaze went to Diandra who was smiling at the tent flaps.

"Uh...Diandra, I don't think that's love," I pointed out the obvious. "He barely looked at me. I haven't seen him this morning and he said not one word to me."

She waved her hand in front of her face and replied, "He's a warrior," like that explained it all.

"He's my husband who *you're* convinced loves me," I returned, and her gaze came down to me.

"He's a husband, he's a king, he's a man, but above all, my queen, always remember, above all, he...is...*a warrior*."

I didn't know what that meant but I knew it was important. And I didn't get the chance to ask either because Gaal touched my shoulder in the way she did to indicate it was time to get out of the bath.

Diandra saw it and turned her back to give me privacy. Sheena's attention went back to the jewelry trunk and Diandra muttered on her return to the table, "We haven't much time and there's much to do. No more chitter chatter. We need to prepare you for the selection."

I rose from the tub. Packa instantly curved a thick, soft, absorbent cloth around me, and I stepped out.

Once I was out of the tub, I decided that was my last step. My next one was to be Lahn's queen for whatever was happening today.

The step after that, we would see.

Then all seven women helped me prepare to sit at my king's side at the warrior selection.

~

We were moving through the encampment, and I knew by the hustle and bustle of people hurrying around us that the selection was close, and this was a big event they didn't want to miss.

I was getting a lot of looks and this was not surprising. They had no mirrors here that I knew of but there was no doubt about it.

I looked *awesome* and I looked like *a queen.*

A golden one.

They'd chosen a silk sarong for me, its color gold shot with pure white. My bandeau top was also pure white.

I was wearing a latticework necklace of delicate gold chains that covered nearly my whole chest and matching earrings that hung so low, they swept my shoulders. I had on the gold wristlets that went from wrist to nearly elbow and the gold bands at my biceps, both I'd worn the night of the rite.

I also had on the wide, heavy gold belt made thick with discs and more discs that hung down and jangled as I moved.

The leather of my flimsy, strappy, low-heeled sandals was also colored gold.

I had gold eye shadow on my lids, dark gold pencil around my eyes, gold dust arcing along my cheekbones and up to my temples and peach-tinted gloss on my lips.

I further had gold dust in my twisted, curled hair, making it sparkle and glitter. And if that wasn't enough, lightweight gold clips, dozens of them, adorned my hair making it, too, a golden latticework of twists and curls.

And I wore the golden feathers around my forehead.

I was right that first night when Teetru had fastened it around my head. The feathers were shiny, brilliant, so much so they shimmered in the sun. It was thin but each feather was perfection, pure beauty. It was the absolute coolest thing I'd ever seen in my life.

It was, Diandra explained when Teetru set it against my forehead, wove the ends through my hair and fastened it at the back, my Korwahk queen crown.

And it was a good one. A huge, jeweled affair would not in any way be better than those feathers.

No way.

In my killer outfit, I felt ready to face the Korwahk people. But even if I didn't have that sweet outfit, that feather band alone would have done the trick.

We were being escorted by warriors, two at front, two at back. They'd come to the cham, slapped back the flaps and grunted, "Vayay, boh," which Diandra told me meant, "come, now" (though I'd already figured that out).

And off we went, Diandra and I, followed by Sheena, guards in front and rear, moving swiftly through the encampment toward the dais.

"I forgot to ask, and before I forget again," I told her, "I need to find a new bride named Narinda."

Her head turned to me and her hand on mine in the crook of her elbow squeezed. "Pardon, my dear?"

"I need to find a bride named Narinda. She helped me. We were in the Hunt together. I haven't seen her since. I want to make sure she's all right. Check up on her," I explained and Diandra nodded.

"I will ask Seerim to see if he can find your Narinda."

"Thank you," I replied. "Or, I mean, shahsha."

She smiled her approval then her eyes flitted over my shoulder, and they narrowed.

I looked over my shoulder to see a man, not a native, but one with blond hair, a hat on his head, blue eyes and old-fashioned clothing, white shirt with laces at the top (that kind of needed to be washed), tan breeches, brown boots. And he wore a low-slung belt on his hips with a nasty looking knife attached to it.

His gaze sifted through the guards at our front then Diandra and it hit me he was walking at our sides, and he was doing it with something on his mind.

"Dahksahna," he mumbled when his attention came to me.

Yep, he was walking at our sides with something on his mind.

"Veeyoo," a guard behind us grunted.

The man looked over his shoulder and said something conciliatory to the guard. I felt Diandra's hand tighten on mine then he turned back to me.

"I am a man from your land," he told me.

I blinked and my step faltered.

"You're from Seattle?" I asked, my heart in my throat, but he blinked back.

"Erm...no, Middleland," he replied.

"*Veeyoo,*" the guard behind us grunted again, this time a little more impatiently and a lot more scarily, and the man quickly glanced at the guard and his manner became urgent.

"The Dax will not like you speaking to his bride," Diandra warned him. "She is not of your land. She is of another land, but now she is Korwahk. She is queen. I advise you step away."

He ignored Diandra, something I didn't like all that much, and kept his eyes on me.

"It is said you are having difficulty adjusting," he remarked.

"She is fine," Diandra snapped.

He ignored her again and spoke to me.

"You fight with your king," he stated.

"I—" I started, but Diandra talked over me.

"She is the warrior queen. The warrior queen has a fierce spirit. It is legend. Step away."

The dais was coming up. His eyes went in that direction, a slash of fear he couldn't quite hide marked his features, the warrior grunted again, "*Veeyoo!*" and the man's focus swiftly came back to me.

"My name is Geoffrey, Dahksahna, and remember, I am a friend," he stated urgently, his eyes peering deep in mine.

I felt my brows draw together and suddenly there was no hustle and bustle around us because we were out of the throng and walking into the stone clearing before the dais.

I looked away from Geoffrey and up to the dais.

Then I sucked in a sharp breath.

The firepits were burning at both sides and behind.

And Lahn was there.

He was painted again, the thick black streak across his eyes, three thin ones sweeping his cheekbones, one wide one going from collarbone down the middle of his chest all the way into the top of his hides, thinner ones sweeping arcs from it over his shoulders, across his pectorals, ribs and abs. Black stripes circling his bulging biceps and muscular forearms. He was wearing a belt of huge gold discs that hung low on his hips.

And his hair was free, no ponytail, no braid, the long thickness of it waved and curled down his back, over his shoulders and next to his face.

I felt my lungs start burning.

Holy freaking moly...my husband was *hot*!

His head had come up when we entered the space, and even though he wasn't close, I saw it go hard with what could only be described as wrath and it looked like his gaze was pointed at Geoffrey.

Uh-oh.

We had continued moving across the clearing and I looked over my shoulder to my right to see Geoffrey had slowed then he turned, and I watched Geoffrey quickly move back across the clearing and fade into the crowd.

I turned back when Diandra's hand squeezed mine.

"We will speak of him later," she muttered to me.

I nodded and the warriors led us to Lahn.

We walked up the steps. The warriors peeled off and Diandra stepped away when I was presented to their king. His eyes swept me head to toe, but they showed no reaction, which kind of sucked because it took seven women a lot of time to get me all gussied up. I didn't often feel I looked hot, but I felt it then and it would have been nice for him to give me something. A lip twitch. His eyes warming. A wink. *Something.*

But I didn't get something. I got absolutely nothing. He looked beyond me, barked something then sat on his throne of horns, leaning forward on a forearm at his knee. He also leaned to the side, looking around me stating clearly I was in his goddamned way.

Jeez, I hated it when he got like this and I shared this with him by glaring at his head with its flowing, freaking gorgeous, black hair.

He didn't even look at me.

Diandra caught my arm, scuttled me to the side, took me to my white throne and touched my shoulder, indicating I should sit.

I turned and sat on my gold pad as Diandra moved to my left side, and the instant my ass touched pad, Lahn barked something loudly and the men started beating at the small drums.

I looked at him to see he was still leaned forward on his arm, his eyes off into the distance, and I wondered what the point was of me being there if he wasn't even going to look at me.

The man I'd seen the night of the rite wearing black robes and having his hair cut short (even the non-warriors wore their hair long) hurried forward and stopped at the dais.

Lahn barked another order at him.

The man bowed his head and hurried away.

It was at this point that I realized the sun was blazing as were the firepits all around us and it was freaking hot. I was going to get roasted out here, in more ways than one.

"That is The Eunuch," Diandra whispered in my ear, and I turned my head to see her bent to me.

"Sorry?"

She tipped her chin in the direction of where the man in the robes was and repeated, "The Eunuch. He has charge of the scouts who search for the wives for the Hunt. He has charge of the Hunt and its celebrations. He has charge of the warrior selections, and once the warriors are selected, he chooses who will be trained by whom then, once they are of an age, who will be assigned to whom. The warriors spend years as what we would consider squires, serving at the same time training before they are sent out to make their first kill. And when we ride, once the Dax chooses camp, The Eunuch has charge of organizing the chams, making sure livestock and horses are kept downwind, refuse is disposed of correctly, things the Dax has little interest in."

I was stuck on something she said previously.

"He's a eunuch?"

She nodded. "The Dax before King Lahn did the deed himself. I watched it. Everyone did. It happened on this very dais."

Oh my God!

I stared at her then breathed, "Why?"

She shook her head. "There are those who..." she paused, "*prefer* their, erm..." she hesitated again, "*own kind.*"

"He's a homosexual?" I asked, aghast at where this was going.

"A what?" Diandra asked back.

"He likes men as in, having relations with them," I explained.

She nodded and muttered, "He did."

Yikes!

"They don't..." It was my turn to pause, "They don't allow homosexuality and they—?"

Diandra shook her head. "No, Dax Lahn does. He does not seem to care. He only punishes those who force it on others who do not wish it. The other Dax though..." She trailed off then whispered, "It was unpleasant."

I bet it was.

It was also unacceptable. So unacceptable, it was hideous.

I pressed my lips together and looked forward.

"He was cast out, Dahksahna Circe." Diandra kept talking to me. "But Dax Lahn remembered he was a fine warrior under his father's reign. He remembered he had a sharp mind. He sent scouts to find him and gave him this role. It is a high honor."

I nodded, feeling slightly better about that (*slightly*) and even better that Lahn would do that, but my mind had turned because I was watching the clearing, and something was happening.

Then it happened.

"This can't be," I whispered to Diandra.

I was staring at the little boys lining up in front of us on the slab of stone at the foot of the dais.

A quick glance to the side showed that Lahn was sitting in his black throne next to me, still leaned forward, elbow to knee, eyes to the boys.

I looked back at the boys and saw that each had a belt in which they carried two knives at the sides, and each had a leather strap across their little boy chests that held a sheath and small sword at a slant at their back, like adult warriors. I also saw that the knives and swords were made of wood.

And last, I saw that these boys had to be no more than four or five years old.

What was going on?

"Diandra," I whispered, my voice trembling.

"It is their way," she whispered back, lips close to my ear, and I twisted my head and caught her eyes.

"They're little boys!" I hissed.

"My queen, it is their way."

"But—"

She cut me off firmly. "Sit, watch, listen, but do not disgrace yourself or your king. Do not. There is a time where you can defy your king. There is a time when you can make your preferences known. He has made this clear. But, Dahksahna Circe, this is a crucial ceremony to the Korwahk, it guarantees the future of The Horde so this is *not one of those times.*"

I stared into her eyes, and she held my stare.

Then I pulled in a deep breath.

I turned to face forward just as Lahn barked an order and the little boys immediately flew into action fighting each other with their wooden swords, knives, and in some cases, fists and feet.

Oh man.

I did not like this. I did not like this because it was not play. There were little boy grunts of effort *and* pain.

"The Dax must see their promise for them to be chosen," Diandra said in my ear as the boys fought before me. "Their fathers spend much time preparing them for the selection and then their parents bring them here *hoping*, even *praying* they will be chosen warriors."

"And if chosen, they leave their homes and train?" I asked, not prying my eyes from the proceedings.

"Indeed, never to go home again until after their first kill, which is usually when they reach seventeen, eighteen years of age."

God, it was insane.

By that time, they wouldn't even know who their parents were!

I watched as the man in black robes started wandering through the fray, holding his hands over struggling boys' heads, his eyes going up to Lahn on the dais.

I turned to look at Lahn and saw him jerk his chin up then not a second later, shake his head sharply in a no.

I looked back at the fray to see the robed man continue through it, holding his hands over heads then yanking at boys' arms, sending some to one side where they sheathed their weapons (if they still had them) and huddled together and others he tossed (yes, *tossed*) away, indicating they were not selected. These boys scurried quickly out of the area and to the sidelines, melting into the crowds, probably to find their parents.

This took a while, there were a great many boys, and I watched in the blazing sun and roasting heat of the fires as the last two boys were separated from fighting. One was actually bloody, and he was tossed aside. The other one was pushed toward the huddle.

The robed man shouted an order and the boys lined up at the foot up the steps. I felt Lahn move at my side, looked and saw him rise then slowly stride down the steps.

Once he was two steps above them, he walked in front of the boys, his head tipped down. All I could see was his muscular back, which also had a line of paint down the spine, arcs of it shooting out from the line and I wondered distractedly who had painted his back.

He moved slowly down the entire line then he moved back.

Instantly, he turned and started moving again. In front of each boy, his hand up, fingers raised, palm out, he would either flick his fingers to the side or press his hand down. Those who got the flick were weeded out, those who got the palm press grinned and dropped to a knee, head bowed.

When he was done and the last flicked boy scuttled away and disappeared into the crowd, the drums stopped, and Lahn started shouting.

Diandra's voice was at my ear, and she translated as, sauntering back and forth in front of the boys, he bellowed words these young boys couldn't possibly fully understand.

"You are now Korwahk warriors. You serve *me*," she said just after Lahn thumped his chest. "You serve your golden queen," she said after Lahn, not looking back, swung a muscular arm and pointed my way before dropping it. "You know nothing now but horseflesh between your legs, steel in your grip, blood on your tongue, victory your only focus. There is no other path. You have no mother. You have no father. You have no brothers except those who wear the paint. You have only The Horde. You *are* The Horde. You serve me, your queen, your Horde. You will seize bounty. You will claim your bride. You will grunt and sweat and bury your seed to create warriors. You do not own your flesh. The *Horde* owns your flesh. You sink your blade into flesh, you do it for The Horde. You will wake up a warrior, you will sleep a warrior and you will *die* a warrior."

Okay, this selection freaked me out, but I had to admit that was a freaking cool speech.

Diandra had not finished translating before a rousing cheer burst forth from the crowd and then there was a commotion, an avenue in the crowd quickly parted and warriors, all painted, galloped on their horses straight into the clearing, circling, reining, reeling, horses going up on their hind legs, front hooves striking the hot air as warriors roared, pounded their chests and some unsheathed their swords at their backs and crashed them against others.

It was pandemonium, loud, out of control, horses bumping into horses, hooves slashing against warrior thighs, steel against steel piercing the warrior cries.

The little boys had all risen and turned around, and I had to admit, as they watched the adult warriors and smiled big white smiles, they looked excited.

Lahn barked a loud order and it all stopped instantly. The warriors cut their reins and formed a semi-circle around the dais, the horses backing up, shoving back the crowd to make room for their large number.

Okay, that was executed so smoothly and without even a bit of disorder, I had to admit that was freaking cool too.

The second they were in formation, Lahn shouted, "*Suh Tunak!*" and Diandra translated, "The Horde."

All the warriors *and* the crowd, shouted back, "*Suh Tunak!*"

When that died away, Lahn shouted again, turned his back on the boys, started up the steps and Diandra said in my ear, "Now we feast."

The crowd was cheering, the robed man was hurrying the boys away and the warriors were circling their steeds to exit the area as the drums struck up again, a pounding beat, faster and people rushed into the clearing. They were laughing, cheering and more cries of *Suh Tunak* could be heard. All of a sudden, they were stamping their feet, knees high, jerking their bodies, and it hit me they were dancing.

Lahn made his casual way up the steps, turned, sat and surveyed the burgeoning revelry again without a word or glance at me.

Therefore, I figured my role was complete and I could get out of the hot sun and back to my cool tent to play with my baby tiger and decide what to do about my crazy life.

I turned to Diandra and asked, "Can I go now?"

Her head tipped to the side and her brows drew together. "Go?"

"Home, um...back to the cham."

"But no, my queen, of course not. We eat. We drink. We dance. The celebration will last into the night."

Was she kidding? It was barely noon.

"I can't sit out in this sun until it sets, Diandra. I'll be a lobster."

"A lobster?"

"My skin will burn red," I explained, and she smiled.

"Ah, I see, a lobster after it is cooked. Clever, Dahksahna Circe."

I wasn't trying to be clever. I was trying to save myself from third degree burns.

"Diandra, I'm serious."

She stared at me, the smile died out of her eyes, and she looked uncertainly at the king.

Then she muttered, "I see this job will have its downfalls," before she called out to Lahn.

I looked to him and saw his head turn to her. He watched her as she spoke then his eyes dropped to my arm for a fraction of a second before they sliced back to her.

"Me," he grunted and looked away.

"He says no," Diandra told me.

She had to be kidding. *He* had to be kidding.

"But I'll fry out here!" I cried.

She bit her lip, and I heard Lahn speak.

I looked to him and back to Diandra when she interpreted.

"The golden queen sits at her king's side."

I turned to Lahn. "Seriously, Lahn, this sun is hot, the fires are hot, and my skin isn't like yours. It's not—"

Diandra was talking with me, and Lahn cut us both off with, "Me."

"Lahn!" I snapped, he leaned into me, and his eyes were scary.

"*Me*, Circe. *Me*."

He looked away and that was it.

No.

Okay, one good thing about that was that my dilemma was solved as to how I felt about being in this world and how I felt about my savage king.

And that solution was that I was done.

I needed to find a way out.

As soon as fucking possible.

9
THE CELEBRATION

Night had fallen, torches had been lit and I knew by the tightness of my skin that I was burned to a crisp.

Diandra wasn't wrong, the celebration lasted into the night and things could get sordid.

This was, I was guessing, because this culture was whacked.

It was also because, like any people, primitive savage cultures or not, you pass the booze around freely, shit happens.

It all started merry. Drumming, dancing, jugs were produced and shared, casks were set up. The latter two, people partook of liberally as in, the Korwahk knew how to party, and they did it *hard*.

Women threaded through the throngs weighed down by huge wooden platters groaning with food. There was a lot of laughter, lots of random cheers of *Suh Tunak!* and the constant din of happy party conversation under the equally constant banging of the drums.

Throughout this, I sat on my white throne, and often people would approach—children, adults, the elderly—and all of them had flowers or petals. Their eyes would go to their Dax, they'd receive his consent (an arrogant jerk of the chin, by the by) and these flowers or petals would be tossed at my feet or in my lap or anywhere around my chair so that now I had a pile of them around me everywhere.

I had flowers but no conversation. The Dax allowed them to bestow their blossoms on me, but they were not allowed to come close or speak, and outside of his arrogant jerk of the chin, they ceased to exist for him too.

Weird.

Shortly after the celebration began, a woman moved to Lahn with a silver chalice that she handed to him, filled from a jug, and then she backed away while I stared at her thinking it didn't surprise me *I* didn't get a chalice, but it would become clear why very quickly.

I was to be watered and fed by my king.

No joke.

If he wanted me to have a drink, he turned to me and offered the chalice, which at first was filled with what tasted like orange juice mixed with pineapple and then later, water, and finally wine.

If a woman (and there were a great number of them) advanced with a tray of roasted meat, roasted vegetables, slabs of spiced meat, cut fruit, flat breads slathered with what looked and tasted like herbed hummus or a white yogurt sauce with cucumber, onion and garlic or even pieces of candy that looked like creamy white sugar bark doused liberally with nuts and candied fruit, Lahn would make my selections for me. He would then turn to me, lean in, his hand held out and I'd have to take it *not* with my hand (I learned that with a quick, clipped, bark of "*me*" from Lahn at the beginning) but with *my mouth*.

Annoying and, might I add, *insane*.

But I played the role of the golden queen, took food and drink from my king's fingers at his command, listened to the drums, watched the dancers and revelry, listened to the shouts of laughter and cheers and searched the crowd hoping to see Narinda.

I did not see Narinda.

I saw Sheena dancing a couple of times, but no Narinda.

I also saw the vendor who I got the bangles from. He was talking to some people and pointing at me, so I waved at him. This caused him to smile a smile so big it had to hurt his face, jump up and down and clasp his hands toward the heavens again which made me laugh the only laugh I'd laughed since getting to the selection.

Shortly after the ceremony was over and the celebration began, with a terse order, Lahn relieved Diandra of her duties.

She gave me an encouraging smile, moved quickly down the steps and disappeared in the revelers. This meant I didn't even have my new friend to talk to.

If I was truthful, there was a lot of it that was interesting. The fruit juice, food and even wine were all delicious. The dancing was manic and strange but fun to watch. And clearly Lahn's people were having a good time.

This was my first celebration where I had it in me to pay attention, so I didn't know the normal vibe, but it seemed everyone was very happy, joyous even. And a lot of those types of looks were thrown in Lahn and my direction indicating a great many people believed the legend of the Golden Dynasty was coming true, and a future of promise lay before them.

And, I had to admit, it didn't feel crap in the slightest that people rained flowers on me.

That said, I was not wrong, and I knew I was scorching under that hot sun, and although Lahn often got up to wander the top of the dais, chat with the man in robes, warriors who came forward or other men who approached, I was not allowed to do so. And since my husband could not communicate with me and since he was in warrior king mode he didn't try, so a lot of the time I was bored out of my freaking mind.

The sun had long since set and I was glad for it. Lahn had just offered me wine and it was the third sip in a row he allowed me to refuse. After that heat, and it being hours since I had any water, I needed alcohol like I needed a hole in the head. I had been sitting all day, but I was exhausted.

I needed to get to the cham, figure out how to communicate to the girls I needed a cool bath and then I needed to figure out how to get the fuck out of this place.

I lifted my heels to the seat, wrapped my arms around my legs and pressed my cheek to my knees, doing all of this carefully so as not to aggravate the tightness of my skin but doing it because night had fallen, a chill had hit the air, and against my burning skin, that chill was freaking chilly.

I turned my unseeing eyes at the dancers.

They blinked as what my eyes were encountering penetrated my distraction and my head came up. Then it turned away because I had seen a painted warrior with a woman who was wearing a short sarong, not a long one like mine and all of the other women I had seen while in that world. The back of her sarong was at her waist, she was bent forward, he was behind her, she had nothing but his hands pounding her hips into his groin to keep her up and they were fornicating.

Fornicating!

On the dance floor!

Diandra called it sordid?

I'll say sordid.

Good God!

My eyes swept the scene, and I noticed something I hadn't noticed before. Most of the crowd had moved the revelry amongst the tents. The front of the dais was taken up now by painted warriors and a lot of women the type I'd never noticed before. Skimpy bandeau or halter tops (if they had any on at all!) and short sarongs, bare feet, very painted faces, wild hair.

And I knew that the celebration had changed. This part was for the warriors and these women were not wives or brides.

They were something else.

And there were a lot of warriors, enough that at least *some* of them had to have wives.

Seriously, I needed to get the fuck out of there.

"Kah Lahnahsahna," Lahn called, and I turned my head to him. "Vayoo ansha," he ordered, his voice quiet, his head tipping to his lap.

I stared at him, my heart lurching.

"What?"

"Vayoo ansha," he repeated with another dip of his head to his lap.

Oh God.

I didn't move, just stared.

He leaned toward me. His fingers curled around my elbow, gliding down to my wrist at the same time pulling my arm away from my legs. Once he had it extended to him, he lifted it high and repeated, "Vayoo ansha, Circe."

Fuck. He wanted me to come there.

My concern was...*why*?

Hesitantly, I slid my heels off the throne, let my legs go and got up. Lahn didn't let go of my hand and kept it lifted high until I was standing in front of him. His hand released mine, both of his came to my hips and he pulled me forward. Not so I was sitting in his lap but so my knees were in his throne at either side of his hips, and I was straddling him.

Shit, shit, shit.

Luckily, I'd been able to use my sarong to shield my legs from the sun, but my current position still wasn't comfortable because his horns had no pads and they were hard and rounded, digging into my shins.

He tilted his hips down and reclined against the back of the throne so my privates were resting on his and his hands slid from my hips, up my back, pulling my torso closer.

Shit!

When his hands were between my shoulder blades and my face was close to his, he spoke to me softly saying something I didn't understand.

"You know," I replied, "I don't understand a word you're saying."

He tipped his head to the side, his mouth twitched then he spoke some more.

When he stopped, I informed him on a shake of my head, "Nope, didn't get any of that either, big guy."

"Big guy," he muttered, his mouth twitching again.

That was appealing, I had to admit, but not so appealing I could forget he was a huge dick.

I looked over his shoulder.

"Circe," he called, one hand gliding down my back, the other one going up to curve around my neck, and I looked at him again.

"Yes?"

He said something else. It was soft. It was gentle. It went up at the end in a question, and if that didn't do it, his brows went up too.

But all I felt was his hand that had lowered to cup my ass.

Dear Lord, I hoped he didn't think I would engage in what was happening all around us.

"Lahn," I replied, squirming a little with discomfort in his lap.

He repeated what he'd asked, but this time, his hand at my neck moved around, and when he finished his question, it had curled around my jaw and his thumb and forefinger moved the sides of my mouth up in a smile.

I guessed at his question and answered, "No, I'm not happy."

His hand drifted down my neck, my chest, over my breast and I sucked in breath when it stopped, holding me there.

This wasn't getting better.

"Good?" he asked.

"No, not good," I answered, shaking my head and wondering what would happen if I pulled away.

"Okay?" he went on and I shook my head.

"No, *not* okay," I stated and lifted a hand to curl it tight around his wrist at my breast, making my point.

His fingers tensed at my bottom.

"Not okay," he muttered, his painted eyes moving over my face.

"Nope," I affirmed.

"Me sah," he stated, his fingers giving my breast a light squeeze then he took them away and lifted his hand, touching his finger to my chest, "*Sah.*"

Not this, he said, *this.*

In other words, he wasn't asking if I was okay with him touching me but if I was just okay.

"No, Lahn, I'm not okay. My skin is burned. My ass hurts from sitting for hours. I don't like what's happening out there." I swung my arm behind me but kept his eyes at the same time I shook my head. "And I'm tired. I want to go back to the tent." I pointed at me and then said, "Cham."

His fingers moved to trail lightly along the top of my bandeau as he said something in a quiet voice.

"Whatever," I muttered, looking over his shoulder.

I heard him call out and I looked back at him to see his head turned. I turned mine in that direction and saw a woman with a tray headed our way. She nodded, bowed, turned and scuttled away. I looked back at Lahn when he started talking and the only word I understood was cham.

I hoped this meant I was released from my duties and going home.

Then his hand lifted. Going around my back, he pulled my hair off one side of my neck and his hand wrapped around the back of my neck. He drew me closer and to the side until his mouth was at my ear. He whispered something there as his other hand left my bottom and started to stroke my back.

I had a feeling this meant I had the sweet Lahn back, but too little too late. My skin was fried, I'd been bored out of my brain and people were fornicating on the dance floor, something he had to know was not of my culture but definitely knew I didn't like.

He didn't give one shit about me. He could be sweet, but when he wasn't, he *really* wasn't and there were far more of those times than the sweet ones.

His fingers tensing at my neck pulled me back and positioned me until his face was all I could see, and his hand kept stroking my back in a light, sweet way (the brute!) when he spoke again.

"Me Geoffrey, na kuvoo?" he asked, his face serious but not hard.

"No Geoffrey," I stated, and he nodded once.

"No Geoffrey, Circe. Nahna Dax tahnoo tee, na kuvoo?"*

He shouldn't have dismissed Diandra. I had pretty much no clue. The only thing I could do was nod.

"Dohno," he muttered, his hand left my neck, his eyes moved to it, and I watched his face go soft when he stared at it.

That look was appealing too, the asshole.

Then he moved his hand to his chest and wiped it all around. Even in the firelight I saw he was rubbing my gold dust on his skin.

"Na loot kay. Rah loot quaxi. Dax loot Dahksahna." His hand moved around my neck again and he jerked me gently forward so my face was in his. "*Lahn* loot *Lahnahsahna*. Nahna rah lapay loh kah luna boh. *Kah* quaxi lapan loh *nahna* luna anah, kah Circe."**

Seriously, he shouldn't have dismissed Diandra.

"I get that whatever you said you meant it, big guy, but I...don't...*understand*...you," I told him.

He smiled and he knew I didn't understand him. But he totally didn't care.

"Kah Dax?" We heard and both our heads turned to the side to see a painted warrior coming our way.

My eyes moved to the steps to see another warrior striding up, eyes on us.

Lahn started communicating his orders before he got up, both his hands on my ass, holding me to him, and my hands went to his shoulders to steady myself so I wouldn't take a header backwards down a killer flight of stone steps.

He kept talking as his fingers gave my bottom a squeeze then he moved me slightly away indicating I should drop my legs. I did.

He set me on my feet, and I heard the name "Geoffrey" in whatever he was saying before he finished saying it.

The warrior nodded and his eyes cut to me. Then he extended his arm to the steps.

"Cham, kah Circe," Lahn said softly, his hand again at my neck. He gave me a squeeze, my eyes went to his face and then he tipped his head to the warrior.

Another honor guard. I nodded, got another squeeze, Lahn let me go and his eyes went back to the open space.

I followed the warrior, the other one moving in behind, and they escorted me to my cham, and once they made sure the cham was safe for me, the flaps closed behind them.

My skin must have looked as bad as it felt, for when the girls came in and Teetru and Jacanda took one look at me, Jacanda scurried out and Teetru started giving orders. Jacanda and Beetus drew me a cool bath with some kind of additive that I could have kissed them for because it took the sting out of the burn. Then Packa and Gaal came in with huge, spiked pieces of an aloe vera plant.

"Shahsha, my beautiful ladies," I breathed when I saw the aloe vera. "Shahsha."

They looked at each other, lots of brows raised or knit but this went along with smiles, and they kept busy.

Once I was out of the bath, all five of them and myself pressed the moisture out of the aloe vera and swiped it carefully on the burned parts of my skin.

God. Heaven.

That done, I put on a lightweight, short nightie made of sky-blue satin. Teetru and Jacanda set jugs of water on the table with soft cloths, Teetru making motions to me to communicate I was to use the jugs if I needed cool compresses.

I smiled at her, pressed my hand against my mouth and extended it to her, to Jacanda and to Packa, Beetus and Gaal standing at the cham flaps.

"Thank you," I breathed.

They nodded and Beetus even hesitantly gave my gesture back to me.

It was cute so I winked at her. She, being Beetus, giggled and winked back.

Ghost jumped up on the bed. I winced when she got to me and her paw grazed my skin before Teetru rushed forward, confiscated the cub and said soothing words to me (and Ghost, who she was taking with her) on her way out.

The minute the flaps closed behind them, I collapsed on the silk sheet and stared at the ceiling of the tent.

One day down.

Tomorrow, hopefully I would wake up at home and this sunburn would be a memory of the coma I was kind of hoping in a sick way I was in.

If not, I'd tackle the next day, again one step at a time.

**Translation:* "No Geoffrey, Circe. The King commands it, you understand?"

***Translation:* "You and me. Gold and paint. King and Queen. *Tiger* and *Tigress*. Your gold is on my body now. *My* paint will be on *your* body tonight, my Circe."

I WOKE when my thighs were gently pushed apart. My eyes opened, my body started and then I felt Lahn's mouth between my legs.

Oh man, he hadn't done this before.

"Lahn," I whispered, scooting up to get away from him but his big hands shoved under my ass, his long fingers curled around at my hips, and he held me to him. "Lahn," I called but he made no noise, just kept working me.

I twisted my hips, but he held on and then what he was doing penetrated.

God.

I didn't want it to feel good, but fuck me, he wasn't good at this. He was *great* at it.

"God, Lahn," I breathed as my body melted and it did this against my will.

He lifted me at the hips and sucked my clit hard and any will I had against what he was doing evaporated. My hips jerked. Then they started rubbing against his mouth, I couldn't stop it, I didn't try. It felt that good. So good I didn't want it to stop.

No, I wanted more.

So I rubbed harder, more demanding and my hands went into his thick, soft, long hair to hold him to me.

But he wasn't going anywhere, and he gave it to me harder. He didn't stop, his mouth worked me until he got what he was working for, and in getting it, he gave me fireworks.

"Lahn!" I cried as he made me come against his mouth and I was still coming when he surged over me, pulling the nightgown with him. Over my head it went and then it was away and a second later, Lahn was inside me, filling me and damn, but I loved taking his cock.

My eyes opened after I came down and I saw he had both hands in the bed beside me, none of his weight on me, just his hips moving, slow, steady, delicious, between my legs. His head was bent, and his eyes were on me.

I looked up at the painted warrior fucking me, and as I did, I thought he was the most beautiful thing I'd ever seen. Fascinated by his streaks, I lifted a hand and trailed it down the paint at the center of his chest, down his abs and to the hair between his legs.

"Kah quaxi, nahna quaxi,"*** he grunted, his hips rotating as he slid back in and my neck arched as my eyes closed.

Wow, whatever that was he did with his hips felt *good.*

"Kah quaxi, Lahnahsahna Circe, nahna quaxi," he grunted, his hips rotated the other way, that felt better, and he kept taking me, slow and sweet.

My eyes opened and my hand slid back up his belly to his chest as I breathed, "Baby."

That must have been what he was looking for because he lowered his body to mine and I took his heat on my fevered, burning skin and didn't care. I simply wound my limbs around him, pulling him closer.

"Ruhnoo kah quaxi, Circe, ruhnoo kah xac,"****

"Yes," I whispered as his hips rotated again and his thrusts got marginally faster. "Mayoo, Lahn."

"Me," he denied. "Ruhnoo kah quaxi."

"Okay," I breathed as the slow burn built.

"Ruhnoo kah xac, kah Lahnahsahna," he growled.

"Yes," I repeated, lifting my hips to receive all of him and he gave it to me, slow, slow, then faster and faster until we were both breathing heavily. I knew I was close again and the whole time his painted black eyes never left mine.

"Lahn," I whispered when it started, my limbs getting tighter, my hands, which had been roaming his back, his ass, his shoulders, his arms, clenched him to me.

"Ruhnoo kay," he grunted, putting power behind his thrusts, my frame jerking with them and that was it.

My body arced from the small of my back to my head, pressing into his as an orgasm as slow and sweet as his lovemaking swept through me.

Then I kept taking him, his face now in my neck, his driving cock jerking me with every thrust, his grunts sounding against my skin until he pounded in slow, his hips rotating with each thrust, again and again and again as he groaned in my neck.

He stayed still for long moments before he pulled out and slid off, his slick skin gliding against mine.

He was on his side, head in hand, elbow in the pillows, one leg cocked with his foot in the bed, the other leg the length of mine (and longer). He watched in the candlelight as his hand slid through the black paint he'd transferred to me, over my chest, between my breasts, down, down, between my legs then his finger slid over my clit, making my hips jerk lightly and a noise escaped my throat.

His sexy, sated eyes came to mine and his hand moved back up, now trailing our combined wetness through the paint on my skin to come to rest light on my belly.

"Kah quaxi, nahna quaxi," he whispered, and I had no idea what that meant but whatever it was, it was important to him.

"Okay," I said softly.

"No," he whispered back and leaned an inch into me. "*Good.*"

I wished he wouldn't be like this, for instance, great in bed and sometimes so damned sweet.

"Right," I muttered. "Good."

He grinned at me, bent his head and ran his tongue along my shoulder. Then he settled down on his side but not on me like the last two nights, just beside me. He grabbed my hand, cocked my arm and held it against his chest but that was it.

He was minding the burn.

Shit, *shit*, he could be sweet.

Damn.

Then again, I reminded myself, I wouldn't have the burn if it wasn't for him.

I turned my head to look at him.

"Trahyoo, kah fauna," he whispered, his hand pressing mine to his chest.

There it was again, *kah fauna.* His doe. Now I had three. Not knowing what it meant, it felt nice. Knowing what it meant, it felt freaking great.

Damn.

"All right, Lahn," I whispered back, he tipped his chin back and closed his eyes.

I looked at the ceiling and closed my eyes.

And I decided one of my steps if I woke up here tomorrow was going to be avoiding my king. And I'd keep taking that step until I figured out some way to get myself home.

Because if I didn't, I knew all would be lost.

****Translation:* "My paint, your paint."

*****Translation:* "Take my paint, Circe, take my cock."

10

SUNSTROKE

My body's uncontrollable shaking woke me, and about a second later, it woke Lahn.

"Circe?" he called, getting up on an elbow in the bed and looking down at me, his hand still holding mine at his chest.

Sunstroke.

My skin was chill at the same time it was burning. It was tight and it hurt like hell.

I turned my head to look at him and saw his face awash with concern.

My body was shaking so hard the bed was moving with it and I felt shit but neither of those took away from the fact that that look made him more beautiful than ever.

"Sunstroke, baby," I whispered.

"Sunstroke?" he asked and seriously, feeling crap and needing to explain why, was *not* a good time not to be able to communicate.

I looked to the tent flaps to see weak sun washing through. It was nearly dawn.

I looked back at Lahn.

"Diandra," I whispered as the shaking turned to quaking and my teeth started chattering.

He noticed, his brows drew together under narrow eyes, and he growled, "Circe."

I clenched his hand.

"Sunstroke, it's just sunstroke, Lahn. I need water." He glared at me with no comprehension. "Shit!" I snapped in frustration and the tremors gliding over my skin didn't feel nice. "Baby, get Diandra for me so she can translate."

He looked at my body, mumbled something, let my hand go and then instantly jerked the silk sheet out from under me. He threw it over me, and its coolness felt nice and tortuous at the same time.

He rolled off the bed on the other side and I chattered, "W-water," to him.

He didn't go to the jugs.

He went to the tent flaps, slapped one back and thundered, "*Teetru!*"

"Lahn! Water, honey, please," I begged as he walked to the pile of hides, tossed aside the pillows so forcefully they flew across the tent, then he seized the top hide and came to me.

I was holding on to the top of the sheet and shaking my head as he stalked to me and carefully draped the hide over my body.

"No, too much weight, too much heat," I whispered but his focus turned to the tent flaps as Teetru stuck her head in and he paid no attention to me.

He barked orders at her. Her eyes came to me then she rushed out of the tent she hadn't fully entered.

Luckily, in his orders I heard Diandra's husband's name.

He turned and scowled down at me. I'd moved an arm outside the hide and was trying to shove it off.

"Too heavy, baby, too hot," I semi-repeated, but he wrapped his fingers around my wrist, gently pushed my arm back under the hides and my eyes flew to him. "No, Lahn."

"Yes, Circe," he growled.

Okay, I'd give up on that.

I heard the tent flaps open and Jacanda, Beetus and Packa came in, wearing worried looks.

"Water," I said, tipping my head to the jugs. Jacanda caught it and hurried to the water. "Yes," I whispered and kept quaking.

Jacanda poured water and rushed to me but didn't make it. Lahn snatched the cup out of her hand, sat on the bed beside me, wrapped his other hand around the back of my neck, gently lifting me, and put the cup to my lips.

I drank.

Hydration good.

He kept tipping it to my lips until my eyes lifted to his indicating I was done, and he took it away, lowering me back to the pillows.

Then he growled something at me and the only word I understood was my name at the end.

"I'll be okay," I assured him.

"*Not* okay," he fired back and kept scowling.

I bit my lip then I dropped my gaze and realized he was buck naked.

"Lahn," I said when my eyes returned to his dark ones that were still painted. "Put some pants on."

He started his next sentence with "Lahnahsahna Circe..." but the rest of it I had no clue except it had the exact cadence of me telling him I didn't understand what he was saying.

I gave him a shaky smile, pulled my arm from under the hides and ran my fingertips up his naked thigh to his also naked hip.

"Pants, hides, you need to put something on," I said quietly.

He kept scowling then he surged up, stalked to the table and slammed the cup on it. He then went to his hides and yanked them on.

Okay, that went better.

The tent flaps opened, Gaal rushed through followed by a small, round woman with lots of dark hair mixed with gray and she was carrying a small trunk. She looked like she'd had fun that night and had been interrupted in sleeping it off. I guessed this because her complexion was gray and she was wearing what I would assume was a Korwahk-style nightshirt, short, off-white gauze, strapless, shapeless, held up over her breasts by a drawstring tied tight at the front.

Um...that wasn't Diandra.

Lahn bit some words off at her. She nodded and rushed to me.

"Hey," I greeted after she bent and put the trunk on the ground by the bed and turned to me.

"Kah rahna Dahksahna hahla," she muttered, her eyes moving over my face, my shoulders. She carefully lifted the hide and sheet and peered under them then she just as carefully dropped them, turned to Lahn and started talking.

He was standing with his arms crossed on his chest, feet planted wide and eyes piercing her with ferocity, and whatever she was saying made his dark glower darker.

She kept talking and he kept glowering.

The tent flaps opened and Diandra rushed through followed by a large, older warrior who, like Lahn, had to bend to enter. Teetru followed them.

"Dahksahna Circe!" Diandra cried, seeing me quaking. "What on earth?"

"Too much sun, Diandra, sunstroke. It's nothing. I just need water and I'll be fine. Tell Lahn," I informed her.

She nodded, turned and spoke to Lahn.

He spoke back in clipped tones, and she nodded and looked at me.

"He has never heard of this, my dear."

I shook my head. "Well, he wouldn't. You all live in the sun. Where I come from, we *do not*. My skin isn't used to that kind of sun. My *entire system* isn't used to it. I tried to tell him, but—"

She cut me off by turning to Lahn and speaking.

His glower got even darker.

Then he barked something at the woman standing by the bed. She said something in return and Diandra spoke to me.

"He's told the healer to fix you. She's going to give you something that will dull the pain and help you sleep. She understands what this is and says there's nothing for it but time."

Lahn was still snarling at the healer and the healer was replying.

"She's right," I said to Diandra, but Diandra lifted a hand to me and I was quiet. She was listening.

Then she looked from Lahn to me and started talking and I could tell she was summing it up for Lahn, and the healer said far more words than she translated. "He wants you fixed. She says she can't. The Dax isn't happy, my queen."

Well, anyone could see *that*.

"Tell him it'll be all right. I've had this before. I got too much sun during a vacation in Mexico, and I just need to sleep and stay out of the sun a couple of days."

Her brows knit at my words, but she nodded, turned to Lahn and spoke. He spoke back and then snarled something at the healer who instantly bent to her box.

"What?" I asked Diandra and she looked at me.

She shrugged. "He wants you fixed."

"I will be...*in time*," I replied. "Please explain that to him."

"He doesn't care, my queen," she returned.

"But—"

She stepped forward. "Dahksahna Circe, the Dax did this to you. He knows it. He feels guilt. This is not a feeling he understands or knows how to cope with. He might not even understand what it *is*. Let the healer put you to sleep. The quaking will stop, he will think it's fixed. Just let him think he found a cure for you."

I stared at her a moment before I whispered, "Oh, all right."

The healer was at the table, pouring water and tapping some white powder into it from a folded piece of paper. Then she set that aside, picked up a squat, bulbous bottle and tapped some other powder into the cup. She swirled the cup in her hand as she brought it to me.

Again, she didn't make it. Lahn was there, taking the cup, more gently this time, sitting beside me, doing the hand around my neck lifting thing again, and he held the cup to my lips. He removed it at intervals for me to swallow, then back and again until I drank it all. The liquid was bitter and didn't taste good at all, but I forced it down.

"Shahsha, Lahn," I whispered when he took the cup away for good and lowered me back to the pillows.

"Nahrahka, kah Lahnahsahna," Lahn whispered back, and my eyes slid to Diandra.

"What did she give me?" I asked.

"A sleeping draft mixed with something to dull the pain. It's from nature, my dear, not witchcraft. I've had it before. It works fast and it's safe. I promise."

I nodded and clutched the hides around me in an effort to control the shaking.

Lahn handed the glass to the healer and barked more orders. The man with Diandra, who I was assuming was her husband, Seerim, put his arm around her and guided her away after she and I exchanged nods. My girls drifted out after I gave them reassuring smiles. The healer said a few words to Lahn, left the squat, green, corked bottle filled with white powder on the table, grabbed her trunk and hurried out.

Lahn took his hides off and slid under the sheet at the other side of the bed. Moving toward me, he turned me to him and gathered my still shaking body in his arms.

I pressed my hands to his chest and whispered, "I'll be all right, Lahn. I'll be okay."

"Yes, okay, Circe," he agreed on a light squeeze.

I nodded my head against the pillows. "Yes, honey, okay."

"Honey," he repeated on another squeeze.

I sighed.

Okay, Lahn could be a dick, a *big* one. But when you were sick, he didn't like that, and he didn't fuck around in finding a way to make you better.

Shit.

About five minutes later, my lids got heavy, and the quaking turned to mild tremors.

"Okay, Circe, good," Lahn muttered, drawing me nearer.

I forced my eyes open, tipped my head back, saw his bearded chin was dipped down and his painted eyes were on my face.

"Yes, baby, good," I mumbled back and fell asleep cradled in a warrior king's strong arms.

11
SWEET

"Kah Circe." I heard Lahn call softly, my eyes drifted open, and I saw him looming over me, one arm across my body, hand in the bed, his torso close, his eyes on mine.

"Hey," I whispered, and one side of his mouth twitched.

"Hey," he replied then he straightened, his hand in the bed slid around my neck and he lifted me up as his other hand came toward me, carrying a cup. He put it to my lips and ordered quietly, "Gingoo, Lahnahsahna."

I drank the bitter liquid and knew he'd prepared another dose of medicine.

Yeah, damn.

He could be sweet.

When I was done, he took the cup away, set it on the ground by the bed and came back to me. His eyes roamed my face, and his hand smoothed my hair back, his fingers sifting through it as he did.

It felt nice, him doing that, really nice.

Oh shit, yeah. He could be sweet.

And that sucked.

"You know what sucks?" I whispered to him, doing it because I knew he would have no clue as to a word I was saying. "It sucks that you can be sweet, and when you're sweet, you're *really* sweet. That sucks."

He didn't stop tenderly stroking my hair as I spoke, but his eyes dropped to my mouth, and when I was done, they came back to mine.

Then my heart squeezed when he whispered back, "I don't understand you, baby."

There it was again.

Sweet.

I lifted a hand and placed it on his chest. He looked down at it, but his gaze came back to mine when I spoke.

"Out there, King Lahn is a fierce warrior, but in here, *my* Lahn...*kah* Lahn is sweet."

His eyes changed, intensity shifting in when he murmured, "Fierce warrior, sweet."

I grinned at him. "You've sort of got it."

"Fierce warrior, sweet," he muttered again.

"Yes," I replied, and his hand came up to mine at his chest, his long fingers curling around, swallowing mine when they did and they held tight, keeping our hands at his chest.

"Anla na neesoo, anka ta linay et na lapay sahka. Suh Tunak me tunoo et kah Circe me sahka,"* he declared.

I laughed softly.

Then I said just as softly, "I don't understand you, baby."

He shook his head, his lips tipped up and he bent close. "Neesoo, kah Lahnahsahna."

"Neesoo?" I asked, and he didn't move back but his hand stroking my hair moved to my face where he gently touched each eyelid with a fingertip, my eyes blinking with each touch, then his fingertips glided down my cheekbone.

"Neesoo," he repeated softly.

"Rest?" I guessed.

"Quiet," he answered then he got closer and ordered firmly, "Loot *neesoo*."

"Okay, big guy, I'll neesoo," I muttered.

That got me a soft chuckle, something I'd never heard from him and something else about him that was appealing.

His fingertips trailed down my hairline from middle part all the way to my right ear. His eyes looked into mine before he tipped up his chin, his hands left me, he straightened from the bed and strode out of the tent.

"Neesoo," I whispered to the tent ceiling.

Then I closed my eyes and neesooed.

**Translation:* "Today you rest, tomorrow we see if you're healthy. The Horde does not ride if my Circe is not well."

It was late morning, and I was sitting on my bed laughing with my girls.

Gaal and Packa were lounging on my bed with me, and even Teetru, who appeared uncomfortable but was loosening up, had seated herself at the edge.

Jacanda and Beetus were running around the cham picking up things or pointing at them and telling me what they were called in Korwahk. I would repeat what they said then I'd tell them what it was called in English, and they'd repeat what I said. They'd all giggle like English was an insane language that made no sense and was silly beyond belief (like Korwahk wasn't).

I was feeling okay. I'd had a cool bath and the girls had brought more aloe vera stalks and we'd smoothed the moisture on my burns. I had a wicked, strange sunburn, crisscrosses on my feet, bands on my arms where the gold didn't cover me, pink at my belly, latticework on my chest and Lord knew what my face looked like since I was wearing my feathers all day. I probably looked like a dork, but the cool bath and aloe vera worked a treat. I couldn't say I felt great, but I didn't feel shit.

I was wearing much what the healer was wearing last night but mine wasn't gauze. Mine was a thin, soft silk the color of a green apple and it went down to my ankles and had slits up to my hips. I also had on a pair of pale-yellow silk undies. Ghost was oblivious to our game and was taking a baby tiger nap with her head in my lap.

And I was taking a rest from all the shit bouncing around in my head—about this world, about my world and about Lahn. Lord knew, I needed a break, and I was giving myself one.

"Poyah!" We heard and all of our eyes swung to the cham flaps to see Diandra enter.

Teetru shot off the bed like she was doing something wrong, and the rest of the girls also tensed.

But I called, "Poyah, Diandra!" and she didn't even look at the girls as she walked to the foot of the bed.

"How is my queen today?" she asked.

"Much better," I told her with a smile. "Sorry to call you so early—"

I stopped talking when she waved her hand in front of her face. "Don't mention it, Dahksahna Circe. It is an honor. Seerim is delighted I'm being of service to our new queen. He feels very important." Her eyes lit and she went on, "Which brings me to why I'm here. I have news!"

I grinned at her and patted the bed. She didn't hesitate but moved to lounge on it as she said something to the girls that set them scurrying.

I watched them go, my brows knitting but my focus went back to Diandra when she started speaking.

"You will never guess," she declared.

"Guess what?" I asked.

"Guess what the Dax asked my Seerim this morning," she answered, and I didn't reply, just looked at her, waiting. She pulled herself closer to me and leaned into a hand in the bed. "He asked Seerim if he knew our language."

Oh my.

I wasn't sure this was good.

"He did?" I whispered, and she nodded.

"Oh yes, my dear, he did. Seerim does know pieces but not much." She grinned big. "And he didn't know what the Dax asked him, so he came to our cham and asked me. It was of great import and the Dax expected swift answers."

"Wha..." I swallowed. "What did he ask?"

A huge smile lit her face. "He wanted to know what the words, 'baby,' 'honey,' 'big guy,' 'fierce warrior' and 'sweet' meant."

Oh.

My.

"What did you tell him?" I breathed.

She leaned back, tipping her head to the side. "Well, I told him what they mean, of course."

Oh God.

I wasn't sure Lahn would take to being called "baby" when he knew what it meant. Or "honey" for that matter. And I wasn't certain he'd like "sweet" either.

Damn.

"Um...Diandra—" I started.

She shook her head. "Do not worry, my queen. I explained that in your land, these are endearments, like kah fauna. Which, I assume, they are?"

I nodded.

Her head tipped further to the side. "'Big guy' is an endearment?"

"Uh...essentially," I muttered.

"Unusual," she muttered back.

"Did, uh...Seerim explain this to Lahn?" I asked, and she got that wicked, knowing look in her eyes.

"He did, indeed, my dear. He went right back to him and explained. Then he came back to me."

Seemed like Diandra had a busy morning.

When she said no more, I prompted, "And?"

Her eyes lit again. "Seerim tells me he has never seen the Dax laugh that hard *or* that long. Our king found all this very amusing."

Well!

I was *so* sure.

To hide my hurt, I looked to Ghost, slid my fingers through her fur and whispered, "Well, it's the way we talk where I'm from and it's not nice to make fun of the way people talk."

"Dahksahna Circe, linas please," Diandra requested softly, and I looked at her. "He has decided he likes the *meaning* of honey best, but he prefers how you speak when you *call* him baby. He is, of course, a 'big guy' and simply finds it amusing you would point this out. There were several warriors with him when Seerim explained all this and Seerim reports to me that they all found your words amusing but not in a bad way. It isn't making fun. It's good that your husband finds you amusing. Laughter is important to any relationship, but it's especially important in a marriage. No?"

I had to admit, she was right.

"What did...?" I hesitated. "What did he think of me calling him sweet?"

She grinned again. "I believe that he preferred you thought of him as a fierce warrior, but he took no offense to you calling him sweet, and it would be my guess he took no offense to this because you called him *your* Lahn before you did so."

I felt my eyes grow round. "He remembered that?"

"'*Out there, King Lahn is a fierce warrior, but in here,* my *Lahn*...kah *Lahn is sweet,*'" she recited. "Is this what you said?"

It was, and if memory served, it was word for word.

Holy moly.

"Yes," I whispered.

"Then," she said softly, reaching out and touching my knee, "I think my guess would be correct and he took *no* offense at all, my queen."

My stomach dipped before it warmed.

Oh man.

Here we go again.

"Now!" she exclaimed, and my body started. "I have more news."

I didn't know if I could take more news, but because I *was* a dork, I still asked, "What news?"

"Well, Seerim has found your Narinda."

I smiled and clapped my hands in front of me, so Ghost lifted her head and blinked at me with tiger cub irritation before she settled again.

"He did?" I asked.

"He did, indeed, my queen. She is the bride of Feetak."

I leaned into her. "Is she okay?"

Diandra smiled gently. "She is. Feetak is a strong warrior. A dependable one. Seerim respects him. And he tells me, Feetak is taken with his bride. This is why she has not been out and about, and he did not go to the games. He has been spending a great deal of time with her."

I hoped this was good news.

Diandra went on, proving it was.

"There are some warriors who do this. It is after the fact, of course, but it is what in our lands would be considered as wooing. He did not allow her to attend the selection, although he participated as is mandatory, and this is likely because, as you did, she would find it distressing. But Seerim says he was seen at the celebration with her last night. Though he took her back to their cham early before things got, erm...out of hand."

Yeah, out of hand.

She could say that again.

Diandra kept speaking.

"But she is well, and I know where their cham is so, when you are better and when Seerim says it is appropriate to approach, in other words, when Feetak would consent to it, I will take you to her or ask her to attend you."

Oh, thank God.

"That'd be cool, Diandra, thanks."

"Cool," she said on a smile. "You must tell me about your land one day, Dahksahna Circe. We share the same language and yet, we do not."

I'd bet that would be an interesting conversation.

I grinned at her while changing the subject. "And your other news?"

She pulled in breath then her face lit again, and she stated, "The Dax has spoken and we do not ride."

I blinked.

"What?"

"The Dax has spoken, and we do not ride," she repeated.

"I don't under—"

She leaned in. "We ride, always. The day after the selection, starting at daybreak, the camp is packed up and the instant it is packed up, be it early morning, afternoon or evening, we ride. But *you* are unwell. You had a turn last night, your king is concerned and he has decreed that, until he is content with your health, The Horde does not ride."

God, why was it that every time I convinced myself I did not like this guy he did something to make me like him?

"That was—" I started quietly.

"*Sweet* of him," Diandra finished for me on one of her wicked smiles.

"Right," I whispered, feeling my cheeks flame and not from sunburn.

She reached out a hand and touched my knee and she did this while laughing.

I, on the other hand, sighed.

She'd just leaned back when the cham flaps slapped open and my eyes went to it to see Lahn bending to enter.

And again, here we go.

I braced for him to be rude, bark orders and ignore me.

But he did not do this.

His gaze came right to me and then he did. Right in front of everyone, he carefully turned me (and Ghost, who made a purry mew and looked up at him) toward the side of the bed and then he leaned into me, fists on either side, body bent down at the waist, face super close.

Once in position, he spoke softly.

"Erm..." Diandra whispered, "your king asks how you are."

He didn't take his eyes from mine as Diandra translated and I couldn't take mine from his.

"I'm fine," I said softly, and Diandra translated, speaking one word.

Lahn spoke more and Diandra interpreted, "Did you do as you were told and rest?"

"Uh...yes," I replied.

"Meena," Diandra said.

"Good," Lahn rumbled then said more words.

When he was done, Diandra spoke. "When you take lunch, he wants you to take more medicine. Do you understand?"

I nodded.

"Good," he repeated on another rumble then spoke more.

He had finished talking and Diandra didn't translate for a few seconds then she said haltingly and with humor in her voice, "Your king wants to be between your legs tonight, Dahksahna Circe. He commands you get better in order that that can be so."

My eyes got wide, my cheeks again flamed, and I snapped, "Lahn!"

He grinned at me, totally unrepentant.

"I change my mind, you're not sweet in this cham," I declared irately.

Diandra translated and Lahn's hand moved swiftly. Cupping me at the back of my neck, he squeezed hard as he threw his head back and roared with laughter.

"I wasn't being amusing," I informed him, Diandra translated, and his waning laughter instantly waxed.

Brute!

I was glaring at him when his eyes came to me. He took one look and the smile remained fixed to his face.

Then he spoke.

Diandra interpreted, "It is clear my tigress feels well or at least well enough to bare her claws."

"Damn straight," I snapped.

Lahn grinned and Diandra asked, sounding perplexed, "Pardon, my queen?"

"He's absolutely right!" I snapped again, Diandra translated, and Lahn chuckled.

His face sobered and he whispered, "Neesoo, kah rahna fauna."

"Rest, my golden doe," Diandra whispered, and I pulled in a breath, but even though I tried to keep up the glare, I knew my face had gone soft.

My gaze slid away, and I whispered, "All right."

Lahn gently pulled me toward him, and I felt his lips at my ear where he murmured, "Rest, baby."

I closed my eyes and shivered then shivered again when I felt his wet tongue on the hot skin of my neck. He pulled back, looked deep in my eyes a moment, straightened and walked right out of the tent without another word or glance to anyone.

There was silence in the tent and then Teetru came forward and placed a plate of cut pears and grapes on the bed between Diandra and I just as Packa handed us cups of cool water. I smiled at her, took a long drink and set my cup on the ground before I grabbed a slice of pear and popped it into my mouth.

I looked at Diandra when she started talking.

"He always frightened me half to death, even as a young lad. So intense. So ferocious," Diandra remarked, still staring at the cham flaps. Her head turned to me. "But I'm beginning to like him." She grinned her wicked grin. "I'm thinking he *is* sweet."

I had to put a stop to this, pronto, mainly because of how it made my heart feel.

"He wasn't sweet when he made me sit in the burning sun and close to roasting firepits for nine hours yesterday, saying not one word to me and not even allowing me to feed myself," I reminded her mostly to remind myself.

Her face softened and so did her voice when she said, "I understand this would be upsetting to you, but it is your place to sit at his side. It is at all times but *especially* during a ceremony and a celebration. His people spend all day working in the sun, riding in the sun. He had no idea it would make you ill. It is true, there are other women from other lands who are wives to warriors, but there are few and King Lahn has certainly had no personal experience of any of them."

It sucked but this was true.

Diandra kept talking.

"And clearly, my dear, it cannot have escaped your notice last night...or just now...that you're falling ill and his responsibility for that troubled him deeply. Seerim and I were dragged from our bed, the healer, The Horde does not ride, and he visits you during the day when he normally attends his warriors."

It sucked but this was true too.

"Okay, I'll give him that," I allowed, and her lips tipped up. "But yesterday, he didn't speak to me for hours and—"

"Did you starve?" Diandra cut me off to ask.

"No," I answered shortly.

"Go without drink?"

I looked away and muttered, "No."

"My queen, please, look at me," she called, and I did. "You were correct in what you said to him. In here, he is *your* Lahn. But out there, he is the Dax, and the Dax is the mightiest of all warriors."

"But—" I started to protest, and she lifted a hand.

"There will be times, out there, when he shows you kindness, affection. But there will be times when he *will not*. I am sorry this distresses you, my dear, and I will tutor you now so, in future, when it happens, you will understand. A warrior does not ever show weakness, and whether you feel it is right or it is wrong, these soft feelings are considered a weakness. Therefore, most times outside this cham, he will be who he is, and if you are lucky, which it is clear you are, in this cham he will be who you need him to be. Your role as his queen, but also simply as his bride, is to understand that and find a way to live with it."

I made no reply because I had none. She was making sense which also sucked.

She went on, clearly thinking I hadn't yet gotten it.

"There have been warriors who have fallen victim to their wives' charms and have acted out there," she pointed to the cham flaps, "in ways a warrior not only does not respect but they deride." She leaned slightly toward me and whispered, "This, as I'm sure you can imagine, is not received well."

I bet it wasn't.

Diandra continued, "There are even warriors who stop acting on their own decisions and move to carry out the merest whim of their wife. This is even less well-received."

I could imagine.

She carried on, "But this does *not* happen often. It is extremely rare, and it is extremely rare because of how it is received and what befalls the warrior who succumbs to his bride's charms. But there is another reason and that is simply because these men are warriors. That doesn't happen often because they are who they are, and they're trained to be that way from the age of five. They don't know how to be any other way."

Fuck, that made sense too.

"Dahksahna Circe," Diandra continued. "I urge you to listen and understand this. It will make your adjustment to the Korwahk and to your new husband go much faster and it will make *you* far more content."

I bit my lip.

Then I nodded.

She smiled her approval.

I pulled in an unsteady breath and decided I was here, this was happening, I wasn't leaving, I needed to find a way to cope until that happened so I might as well know it all.

"Okay, Diandra, can I ask you to explain more?" I requested, and she nodded as she inclined her head.

"Certainly, it would be my honor to explain anything to you because you are my queen." Her eyes warmed. "And it would be my pleasure because you are my friend and I want you to be content."

Yep, it was official. I definitely liked Diandra.

"Thanks," I whispered then lamely threw out a hand. "And thanks for...

everything. You've been very kind and I don't know what I would have done if—"

She waved her hand and interrupted, "Let's not speak of it. Just know that, too, was my pleasure."

I smiled at her, reached out and took her hand to give it a squeeze.

She squeezed mine back.

I let her go, leaned back and she prompted, "You wanted me to explain something?"

I nodded. "It's the, um...last night, late...the celebration..." I trailed off. She lifted her chin encouragingly and I went on, "There were women there, um...dancing and, uh...*such* with the warriors and they were not—"

I stopped talking when Diandra's face changed. Her face was expressive but the look she was giving me I could not read.

"Xacto," she said the word like she'd prefer not to say it.

"Xacto?" I asked and she nodded.

"Xacto," she repeated.

"Uh—" I began.

"Warrior slaves," she stated, and I blinked.

"Warrior slaves?" I repeated and she nodded. "What—?" I began, but she sighed.

"Suh Tunak, or The Horde, as a collective own slaves. These are not owned by one warrior, and they have no duties to anyone but the warriors as a Horde. They are always young and attractive, and when they lose these traits, they are sold on to families who can utilize their services in different ways."

I didn't want to ask because I already pretty much knew.

But I asked.

"And what are their duties?"

She answered swiftly like she wanted to get it over with.

"They bathe the warriors, wash their hair and plait it or arrange it as the warrior sees fit. They paint them for battle or ceremonies. They massage the warriors after battle, campaigns or strenuous training. They also are available at all times to receive the attentions of the warriors should that warrior feel the need."

I stared at her.

She continued just as swiftly, "They also have duties to the young warriors. They erm...teach them things that will...erm...eventually, in future, benefit their wives greatly should the young warriors be good learners."

Oh my God.

Lahn was good in our bed because those women *taught* him how to be so.

"This is not a bad thing, is it my queen?" Diandra asked, then clarified, "The, erm...last bit, I mean."

I didn't answer because my heart started racing as my mind pulled up memories of Lahn dosing with water, but he didn't wash his hair, yet it was never dirty or greasy and it had been arranged in various styles.

And he had paint on yesterday, even his back which no way he could have done. And just now when he'd come in, he had no paint, and his hair was no longer loose and flowing. It was pulled back in a tail that started at the base of his neck and his hair was contained at intervals down his back with slim gold bands.

"Is Lahn—?" I started.

"Undoubtedly, my dear," she answered swiftly.

I sat up straight and Ghost lifted her head, but I didn't notice.

One of those *women* was washing my husband's *hair*?

Oh no, I did not *think* so.

"Dahksahna Circe, it would be best—"

My eyes cut to her. "Do you think Lahn is...is...has he...? Does he *fuck* them?"

She shook her head, scrunched her eyes closed then opened them and asked, "Fuck them?"

"Has he slept with them, had sex with them, had intercourse, *relations*," I snapped.

Her face got soft with understanding. "Oh, my queen, I see this disturbs you, but yes. Again, I'm sorry to say it is their way."

It was their way.

It was their way.

Last night, they were having their way right on the dance floor. And I knew some of them having their way with Xacto had to have wives at home in their chams.

I left him last night. Lahn was there at least an hour longer than me, likely more.

I left him last night!

Then he came to our tent and fucked *me*! Maybe after he had his fun with *them*!

"*Now?*" I shrieked.

Ghost mewed and jerked in surprise then read my mood and jumped off the bed.

"Now?" Diandra asked, her body tense.

"Is he fucking them now? I mean, since we were married?"

She shook her head, leaned forward and grabbed my hand.

"I do not know," she said quietly.

She didn't know. Which could be yes, or it could be no. Which could mean *yes*.

I yanked my hand from hers and looked away.

"My queen—" she started.

"If you say it is their way, I swear, Diandra, I swear...I'll *scream*," I snapped at the tent wall.

She was silent.

I deep breathed.

Then I made up my mind and looked at her.

"I must ask of you an important favor, and I will warn you that it will be one you won't want to grant. I am your queen, I get that. But I will tell you and mean it that you have every right to refuse what I ask and there will be no hard feelings," I declared.

"Erm...all right," she mumbled hesitantly.

"I want you here tonight to translate what I have to say when my husband gets home."

She instantly whispered, "Oh dear."

Oh dear was right!

"You can say no," I reminded her, and she held my eyes.

Then she leaned forward and grabbed my hand. "I advise you as your friend, Circe—"

I shook my head and squeezed her hand hard. "I get that, Diandra. I get it. Trust me, I do. Now, will you be here tonight when Lahn gets home?"

She studied me for long moments before she squeezed my hand and said softly, "Yes, Dahksahna Circe, as your friend, I will always be by your side when you need me."

Tears instantly filled my eyes and one spilled over before I looked away.

I let her go and dashed at it with the back of my hand before I whispered to the wall, "Thank you."

Diandra didn't respond.

I pulled in breath through my nose, looked at her, smiled a fake smile and suggested, "Why don't we have some lunch?"

12
WIFELY DUTIES

Night had fallen.

I was pacing the cham while Diandra sat at the table sipping from her third chalice of wine.

She was sucking back liquid courage.

I didn't need liquid courage. I was coasting high on adrenaline and emotion.

I did not allow myself to consider *why* the possibility that Lahn was having sex with other women and allowing them to bathe him and do his fucking hair upset me so much.

It just did.

A lot.

A lot, a lot.

And like when I saw something I wanted badly, I got irrational and emotional when I got upset. The difference was, when I got upset, I got *extremely* irrational and emotional and this, unfortunately frequently, mingled with a whole lot of stupid.

So I didn't question it in this world just like I never did in my own.

I just let that tidal wave sweep me wherever I got swept.

Which was what I was going to do the minute Lahn got home.

I was wearing my apple green nightgown and my long hair was pulled up in a messy knot wrapped with a piece of ribbon that I'd tied into it. I was too wound up to have it in my face and on my burned shoulders. It was driving me mad, so up it went.

"I wish you would sit, my queen, you're making me nervous," Diandra mumbled and then sucked back more wine.

I stopped, turned to her and started babbling. "I can't sit. I'm wound up. And, by the way, *I* wish *you'd* stop calling me your queen. I know I am to the people out there, but you're just my friend. No one but us knows what it means anyway, all my friends from home call me Circe mainly because that's my name and I'm not a queen there, but even if I was, not that that could ever happen, but still, I wouldn't let them. And you're my friend. So, I'd like you just to call me Circe."

She gave me a crooked smile that looked alarmingly tipsy, and I wondered with some concern if Diandra was a lightweight.

"I'd love that...*Circe*," then she giggled.

Oh shit.

The cham flaps slapped open. I turned to them and stopped breathing when Lahn bent low and entered.

Here we go.

His eyes cut through Diandra, across the bed and hit me standing at the far end of it. His face went soft, and he took a step toward me.

I lifted my hand swiftly and said, "Stop."

Diandra translated.

Lahn stopped and his brows drew together in a way that didn't loosen me up one bit. His gaze sliced to Diandra then back to me.

"We need to talk," I told him in a soft voice. "It's important. I asked Diandra to translate for us. Please, Lahn, will you talk with me?"

Diandra interpreted and Lahn stared at me with that scary look for a while then he jerked his chin up, crossed his arms on his chest and cleared his expression.

"I think that means yes, Circe," Diandra translated his look.

"I think I got that, honey," I said to her.

Lahn's brows snapped right back together again, and he looked over at Diandra.

"Lahn," I called, and his eyes came back to me. "Did you have sex with one of the Xacto last night?"

His face darkened ominously when I said the word "Xacto," and it darkened *more* ominously when Diandra translated what I said.

I held my breath.

He scowled at me.

I felt my heart start to hurt.

He continued to scowl at me.

My heart squeezed.

"Me," he finally grunted.

"No," Diandra translated a word I actually knew, and I felt my chest release.

"Okay, baby," I whispered to Lahn, watched his eyes flare briefly when I did but the scowl didn't shift. "Now," I went on carefully and quietly. "I know I'm living in your world. I get that. But I want to explain something about my world, something I want you to get, and I want you to get what it means to me. Will you listen?"

Diandra translated. When she finished, Lahn kept scowling but jerked his chin up.

"Shahsha," I whispered, got nothing but continued heat from his eyes and forged ahead. "In my world, men are faithful to their wives. They don't cheat on them. They don't have sex with other women or do *anything* with them, sexually or not. They don't allow other women to touch them, bathe them, um...etcetera."

Diandra translated and her translation became tentative as the raw, brutal energy Lahn normally exuded ratcheted up to the danger zone.

"I get that you do here, I mean, the warriors do and all that," I said swiftly, Diandra translating with me. "But in my world, we don't. We *so* don't, if a man does that to his wife, she has the right to leave him."

This was a mistake.

A *bad* one.

I knew this when his body tensed so fiercely, it seemed to grow and expand, and I heard the growl escape his throat.

No words, just a growl.

"Circe, my dear, I didn't know...you shouldn't...warrior wives do not ever—" Diandra started but Lahn spoke over her, and his words were clipped and seriously fucking pissed off.

When he was done talking, Diandra translated.

"You will not leave."

"I wasn't saying I was going to, just—"

Diandra spoke with me, and Lahn spoke over her and she translated but she didn't have to. He simply repeated his pissed-off words.

"You will not leave."

"I wasn't—"

He kept talking and Diandra interpreted.

"You will not call the wife of Seerim after me."

I blinked at this sudden change of subject as well as his words, which I did not get.

"What?"

Diandra translated, Lahn spoke and then she spoke again.

"You will not call Seerim's woman 'honey.' That is mine."

Oh man.

"It's an endearment," I explained. "In my world we say it to—"

"It is mine. You will not use it with anyone but me."

I studied him and decided this was not going very well.

Therefore, I decided to agree in order to try to soften him up for the hard part.

"Okay," I whispered.

"Okay," he bit off.

Then we started talking with Diandra translating.

"We need to talk about the Xacto," I told him.

"I will not discuss the Xacto with my wife," he told me.

"Um...this is important to me," I explained.

"This matters not. I will not discuss it."

Oh man.

Now *I* was getting pissed.

"But Lahn, I'm telling you this important to me!" I snapped.

"It is not your place," he replied.

"I'm your wife!" I shot back, my voice rising.

"And as my wife, it is not your place," he returned.

"That's crazy!" I cried.

"It is not," he retorted.

"Doesn't it matter to you that this is important to me?" I asked.

"No," he fired back, saying it in *my* language.

Oh yeah.

Now *I* was pissed.

"I beg to differ, big guy," I retorted. "And I will tell you right here, right now, right in this cham." I pointed to my feet then at him. "*You* will not let them touch you." I jerked my finger at him again. "*You* will not let them bathe you." Again with the finger. "*You* will not let them massage you, touch your gorgeous fucking hair, your fantastic fucking body or anything to do with *you* because *that*, baby," I swept him top to toe with an up and down sweep of my hand then jerked a thumb at myself and leaned in, "is *all mine*."

"Vayoo ansha," he ordered, uncrossing his arms and planting his hands on his hips and I retorted before Diandra could translate because I knew what that meant.

"I will *not* come there until you promise me you won't have anything to do with the Xacto. You want someone to bathe you." I jerked my thumb at myself again. "*Your wife* will do it. If you need someone to braid your hair," another thumb jerk, "*I* will do it. You need someone to massage the muscles in your body." This time I tossed my head, "You guessed it, big guy, *that* will be *me too*. And you need someone to fuck you, suck your cock and make you come," another jerk of my thumb, "that's *me* too and *only* me. Do you get me?"

Diandra quit talking and the instant she did, Lahn ordered, "Vayoo ansha."

I instantly retorted, "No, Lahn, I won't come there until I know you get me."

Diandra translated and Lahn repeated, "Vayoo ansha."

"Do you get me?" I shouted.

He spoke and Diandra said, "Lahnahsahna, sheathe your claws and come to your husband. Now."

"No!" I snapped.

He spoke then Diandra said, "Last time, Circe, you come here, or I come get you. Do you want that?"

I stared into his dark eyes. Then I realized I didn't want that. In fact, the look in his eyes, I *really* didn't want that.

Damn.

I stomped to him trying to look as pissed as I was, an endeavor which I was pretty sure succeeded.

I was four feet away when he leaned forward, reached out with his long arms and yanked me to him so I was plastered to his body and his arms were super tight around mine.

Um.

Uh-oh.

"Lahn," I whispered, pressing my hands against his chest.

He spoke and when he did, it was soft, and his eyebrows went up.

Diandra translated, "My wife will bathe me?"

Um.

Uh-oh!

Shit.

Now what had I done?

"Uh..." Shit! God, there was nothing for it. "Yes," I confirmed.

More from Lahn, more from Diandra.

"Plait my hair?"

Me and my big mouth.

"Yes."

"Paint me?"

I bit my lip because I liked the idea of doing *that*, then whispered, "Yes."

He grinned.

Then his face dipped close, and his eyes got hot before he spoke.

When Diandra translated, I realized I really had to learn the Korwahk language and fast. She was now a serious third wheel and if it wasn't embarrassing for her, it was for me.

"My wife will take my cock between her legs *and* in her mouth?"

"Y-yes," I stammered.

"Her mouth?" he reiterated.

Oh man, I felt a tingle between my legs, so they shifted.

He felt it, he knew what caused it and his eyes got hotter.

"Yes," I whispered.

Then he spoke and Diandra translated.

"Your king will grant this request. No more Xacto, Lahnahsahna, only my golden queen."

I stared at him.

Oh my God.

He gave in.

He gave in!

My warrior king gave in.

I felt my belly melt.

Then I whispered, "Shahsha, honey."

Lahn smiled.

I relaxed in his arms, held his eyes and licked my lips.

He watched me do that then he grunted, "Veeyoo," and Diandra didn't translate.

She got up instantly and headed to the cham flaps.

She stopped at them. I looked around Lahn to her, mouthed "thank you," and in return she winked before she mouthed, "well done," then slapped the flaps back and she was gone.

The minute she was, one of Lahn's arms went from around me, his hand curled around my jaw and moved my face to looking up at him all the while shuffling me back to the bed.

His head dipped to mine so his lips were so close, I could feel his breath.

"Kah Circe wahloo boh," he murmured, and I could tell by the heat in his eyes and the words I understood in that sentence that he meant I was starting now.

Oh man.

He turned us then sat on the bed, pressing me down to my knees before him.

Yep, I was starting now.

Right now.

His long legs were on either side of me, knees bent. He reached for my hands and guided them to the sides of his hides where both our fingers tugged the ties. Once we had two sets undone, he left my hands where they were, put his in the bed behind him and my head tipped way back to catch his eyes.

When I saw the look in them, my breath caught in my throat.

There was no need to translate that look. That look spoke volumes.

One could say my king liked his queen on her knees between his legs.

Mm.

"Kah Circe wahloo boh," he murmured, his voice thick.

I bit my lip. Then I reached out a tentative hand and rested it against his crotch.

He was, as ever, ready for me. My eyes dropped and I had visual proof.

Mm.

I felt a rush of heat between my legs and automatically my eyes went half-mast.

I had a feeling I was going to enjoy this so I decided I might as well do as my king commanded and start now.

I peeled his hides back and my present was instantly revealed.

"Oh yeah," I whispered, wrapped my fist around the base, moved in, and my eyes lifted to my husband to watch his face as I commenced with performing my wifely duties.

I was right, I enjoyed it.

But I knew for a fact my husband enjoyed it more.

THE TENT WAS FILLED with candlelight, and I was naked, on my side in bed with Lahn, the sheet up to our waists, his arms around me, our eyes were locked.

My hand slid to his chest.

"Chest," I whispered.

He tipped his face forward until his forehead was resting against mine.

"Fantastic," he whispered back.

I blinked then remembered I called his body fantastic when I was ranting and I was surprised, and impressed, that he heard the word and remembered it through the translation.

Jeez, he was good.

"Yes, baby, fantastic," I replied softly and slid my hand up his chest to his face. "Cheek," I told him when my hand rested against his. It moved and I touched his eye with my fingertips, both of them closed and I kept going, "Eye," then down, his eyes opened, and I whispered, "Lips," when my fingers touched there.

Those lips smiled then my hand sifted back into his hair that I'd let loose earlier.

"Hair," I said quietly.

He grinned. "Gorgeous."

There it was again.

I grinned back.

"Yeah, *definitely* gorgeous," I agreed, my fingers gliding down through the thick mass, and his hand moved from my waist, over my hip, down my thigh which he lifted and hooked over his hip.

His hand slid back up my thigh to my hip and up to my breast where he cupped it, gave it a gentle squeeze and lightly pressed his forehead against mine.

I got what he wanted. "Breast," I told him on a whisper.

"Fantastic," he whispered back, and my belly dipped.

His thumb slid gently over my nipple, and I pressed my lips together at the sensation that caused then breathed, "Nipple."

I watched his eyelids lower slightly, and damn, it was sexy.

"Gorgeous," he murmured, and my belly warmed.

His hand released my breast and glided down, his fingers curled in so when he stroked my belly, he did it using the backs of them.

"Belly," I said softly.

"Mm," he mumbled, and that rough sound glided through me like a soft touch.

His hand moved down between my legs, and he filled me with a finger.

I said no words because I couldn't. My lips had parted, and I'd pulled in a soft breath as my hips twitched.

"Sweet," he whispered, and my body melted into his.

"Shahsha, kah Lahn," I breathed.

His finger slid out and he rolled it once, hard against my clit. I gasped softly again then it slid back and filled me.

"My Circe is sweet," he told me, and my hand went from his back to wrap around the side of his neck.

"Lahn," I whispered, and his thumb went to my clit as his finger moved in and out. "Yes," I breathed.

"*Oh* yes, baby," he corrected, his thumb pressing deeper.

I vaguely realized my king *really* paid attention, but mostly I was concentrating on what his fingers were doing and the fact that my hips were jerking.

"Oh yes," I agreed, ducked my head down and shoved my face in his throat as my hips moved to ride his hand.

He added another finger, and I tipped my head back to run my tongue along his throat.

He kept at me, and I kept riding his fingers until he suddenly turned me so my back was to his front. He shifted my hips with his big hands, then he drove his cock inside. His arms moved around me, his finger returning to my clit, his other hand cupping my breast to tug at a nipple as he stroked deep.

My head reared back, and my body bucked.

"Oh yeah, baby, that's better," I breathed.

"Yes," he grunted. "Better, kah Circe."

"Fuck me, Lahn," I begged, and I guessed that was sort of universal because he added hard to the deep. "Yes."

I felt him shove his face in my neck and his tongue touched there as his thrusts drove even deeper and started to go faster.

I covered both of his hands with my own, my neck arched way back, pressing against his shoulder, my lips parted, and I moaned a long, silent moan as I climaxed a long, really fucking great climax.

A few minutes later, Lahn's forceful, rough groan wasn't even close to silent.

He stayed planted deep for a long time, his hands cupping me in two places, my hands covering his and my breath evened out as I listened to his do the same.

Then he gently slid out, but the minute I lost his cock, his long finger slid back in, and his mouth came to my ear.

"My Circe is sweet," he growled then his teeth nipped my ear.

I smiled into the candlelight.

His head settled to the pillows, and I pressed back into him as deep as I could go, my hands still over his where they claimed me.

And about two seconds later I fell asleep in the same position, claimed, in more ways than one, by my king.

13

WE DIDN'T DO ALL THAT BADLY

I wrapped the wide, absorbent cloth around Lahn's hips after having dried him. I secured it then, with my hands at his hips, I looked up into his eyes.

"You're done, baby," I whispered.

I'd used buckets of warm water and soap that the girls had provided to bathe Lahn while he stood in our tent. He was a mountain of a man so there was a lot of him—a lot of skin, a lot of muscle, a lot of *everything* and all of it was good, but it was even better wet, slick and soapy. The rugs on the ground were a sopping wet, soapy mess. But the bath was *seriously* fun.

His eyes dropped to my chest and one of his hands went to my waist as his other hand cupped my breast. I looked down to see my apple green nightgown was soaking wet, my nipples were hard, and nothing was left to the imagination.

"Not done," he growled.

My head tipped back just as his thumb slid over my nipple, my knees buckled, and it was good Lahn was as fast as he was big because his hands caught me at the waist before my legs could go out. He lifted me up, my legs wrapped around his hips, my arms around his shoulders and he took two long strides to the bed where he took us both down.

His hand slid down then up again, inside my nightgown as his lips trailed my neck.

Oh yeah, bath time was going to be fun.

~

IT WAS late afternoon and Diandra and I were headed to Narinda's. Seerim had given the all-clear for the visit and I was anxious to see her to check how she was doing.

But I had something on my mind.

"Um, Diandra?" I called.

She patted my hand in the crook of her arm and looked at me. "Yes, Circe?"

"Does, um...Seerim, uh...kiss you?"

Her brows drew together. "Kiss me?"

"Don't you have that word? Uh—"

"We have that word, of course we do, my dear. And yes, of course Seerim kisses me."

I looked away and felt my stomach clench.

Lahn had yet to kiss me. It was weird and this had lasted so long now *I* was afraid of kissing *him*.

"Ah..." Diandra murmured on a squeeze of my hand.

I looked back at her to see she was smiling. "What?"

"The Xacto," she started, I braced when I heard that word and she went on, "do many things for our warriors. They teach the young ones much. But they are not allowed to touch mouth to mouth."

"What?" I asked, and she turned to me.

"They aren't allowed to kiss the warriors."

I felt my brows lift. "Why not?"

She got close and her voice lowered. "Because their mouths have been many places, my dear."

Uh...gross.

I looked forward again and mumbled, "Other parts of them have too and by your account they don't avoid those."

She chuckled and explained, "Yes, this is true, and those places are private and special to those of us lucky enough to keep them so. But the mouth is close to the eyes and the eyes the Korwahk believe are portals to the spirit inside. They believe, if you open these portals to the wrong people, they can steal your spirit, cripple you, render you useless, lame. A warrior does not want *that*."

Portals to the spirit. Windows to the soul. I'd heard that before and I figured they meant the same thing in a way.

She kept talking. "They do not wish for such as the Xacto to be close to the warrior spirit. *That,* my dear Circe, is kept safe and given only to ones they trust...ones they love."

I bit my lip.

Diandra guessed. "The Dax has not kissed you."

"No," I mumbled.

"It could be, my dear, he does not know how."

This was such a bizarre notion, my step faltered, and my head snapped around to look at her. "*What?*"

Her head turned to me, and she stated, "It would not surprise me."

"That's...well, that's crazy," I told her.

"I see." She grinned her wicked grin. "He pleases you much in your cham."

He certainly did.

I felt my cheeks burn. She saw them and chuckled a wicked chuckle.

Then she stopped us, turned us to facing and I saw her eyes were not wicked and knowing but kind and understanding.

She wrapped her hand around my bicep and squeezed. "My beautiful Circe, your king is a ferocious warrior. He believes his spirit guides him into battle. It protects him. It keeps him strong. He would not allow anyone close to that. He would do anything to guard it and keep it safe just as he would do anything to guard his flesh and bone, his heart, his innards. He would no sooner allow a Xacto or whore or a girl he's taken during plunder to come anywhere near that."

Girl he'd taken during plunder?

Before I could ask, she started us walking again and advised, "And now, perhaps, he doesn't even think of it. If it is not part of the..." she paused and said with a smile in her voice, "*festivities,* I would suggest *you* introduce it to the..." her hand gave mine a squeeze, "*festivities.*"

"Maybe he doesn't want me near his spirit," I muttered.

She chuckled and squeezed my hand again.

"Oh, my dear, from what I've seen, I think you have no worries about that."

Hmm.

"Circe!" I heard.

My head came up and I saw Narinda walking out of a cham, her gaze turned our way.

"Narinda!" I cried, let Diandra go and ran to my friend.

When I got to her, I threw my arms around her. She threw hers around me, and we rocked each other back and forth as we embraced like identical twins cruelly separated by an evil stepmother and reunited after decades.

Then again, sharing the horrors of the parade, Hunt and wedding rite would do that to a girl.

Our torsos separated but we kept our arms around each other and smiled.

"I don't know, my queen, should I be touching you or bowed in a deep curtsy?" she teased.

"If you curtsy, I'll have your head chopped off," I teased back.

We grinned then we sobered. My gaze moved over her face, and I saw she looked healthy, fed, watered, her eyes were clear of the resignation I'd seen that night, and she looked like she might even be happy.

I pulled her back in my arms and whispered in her ear, "You're faring well?"

I felt her nod. "You?"

"Hanging in there."

Her arms tightened. "He treats me well, Circe, I think...I think..." she paused, and her lips came to my ear where she whispered, "I think he *likes* me."

I giggled and moved my torso back but kept my arms around her. "Rumor has it, he's kept you to your cham he likes you so much."

I watched pretty pink stain her cheeks. She started then let me go and looked over her shoulder to the tall, handsome warrior I saw with her that night. He was standing just outside the cham looking forbidding and his arms were crossed on his chest.

"Feetak, Queen Circe, erm...Circe, my husband, Feetak," she introduced, her hand moving back and forth between me and her husband in a shy way that was cute.

He bowed his head to me. "Kah rahna Dahksahna hahla," he rumbled with an added thump to his chest then his eyes turned to Narinda. I watched them warm, and he moved to his wife. He said some stuff to her softly and ended it with "Narinda sahna."

She looked up at him and nodded, but I knew by the semi-baffled look on her face (a look I was certain I'd adopted on more than one occasion the last few days) that she didn't catch half of what he said.

"Dohno," he said softly, moved to her, put his hand to her waist, bent his head and touched his mouth to hers.

Her cheeks got pinker, he jerked his chin to me and then Diandra and he strode away.

"He said, 'I will leave you to your friends, enjoy your time, beautiful Narinda,'" Diandra translated and Narinda's looked to her, eyes wide.

"Is that what 'sahna' means?" she asked, her voice breathy.

"It is indeed, my dear," Diandra replied on a smile.

Narinda's eyes took on a faraway look as she gazed in the direction where her warrior disappeared and she whispered, "Golly, he says that all the time."

I pressed my lips together and met Diandra's eyes which were dancing.

Welp, it didn't take a love doctor to see things were going well for Narinda and her savage brute.

Narinda seemed to shake herself out of it. She focused on Diandra, and her fingers went to her cheek. "Oh! I'm so sorry! We haven't met. I'm Narinda."

"Diandra," Diandra said, moving in to touch cheeks.

When they separated, Narinda asked, "Are you from Hawkvale?"

"I am Korwahk, but many years ago, yes, I was from the Vale."

Narinda smiled at Diandra then at me. "Well, isn't this wonderful? Now I have *three* people I can talk to and actually understand."

"Yep, it's pretty wonderful," I replied.

She jumped and cried, "Oh my goodness! What am I thinking? Come in, come in. I'll ask one of my...erm, people to get us some refreshments. Let's get out of this sun."

I smiled at Diandra as Narinda hustled us in her cham thinking the change was remarkable. That night that seemed years ago, Narinda might not have been cool, but she was collected. Now she was acting like a schoolgirl with her first crush.

My savior my first night in this world was in a good place and I was glad of it. It felt nice to have one worry off my mind.

We went into her cham, and I saw immediately that it wasn't like mine. It wasn't as big, for one. And there weren't as many trunks. Nor chests. Nor candlesticks. The furniture was nice but not heavily carved. The sheet over the hides of the bed (which was smaller) was gauze, a pretty gauze but not silk. And there weren't as many pillows, and only a few of these were covered with silk or brocade, the rest were covered in cotton.

Though, I had to say, her outfit was kickass, but it wasn't shot with silver or gold. The sarong was red, her belt was braided red, purple and blue and her halter top was purple. She had earrings on, some bangles but nowhere near my finery.

Okay, maybe it *was* good being queen.

We settled lounging on her bed, her girl brought us fruit juice and a platter with slices of cheese and grapes, and we chattered away. She told us she had picked up some Korwahk words while being transported and held prior to the Hunt but she wasn't even close to fluent and obviously hadn't lucked out and had an interpreter almost from the beginning like I did. And it was clear Feetak wasn't doing his talking with words. Nevertheless, it was also clear what he was saying was stuff Narinda liked.

After I ascertained she was settling, she took over the conversation, her attention coming to me. "I've been so worried about you. I tried to ask my girls and Feetak about you, but they don't know what I'm saying, or, when they answer, I don't know what *they're* saying. The king," she shook her head and shivered, "he was frightening. How are you handling everything?"

"It's taken a bit of time and I was lucky to have Diandra's help, but I'm adjusting."

She leaned into me and whispered, "It's all very strange, don't you think?"

I smiled at her. "You can say that again."

She returned my smile and leaned back. "But, I'm thinking, not a *bad* strange, just *strange*. Though, I'm also thinking it'll take a while to get used to it."

And I was thinking she was not wrong about that.

She turned to Diandra. "How long did it take you?"

"I, like you and our queen, was lucky to be claimed by a warrior who grew to care for me very deeply, very quickly. So, I'm happy to say, it did not take long at all."

Narinda's eyes came to me, and they were wide. "That large, fearsome man cares about you already?"

"Uh—" I started.

"Deeply," Diandra said firmly.

Narinda looked at her and then at me before she cried, "Isn't that lovely! Oh, Circe, maybe this won't be all that bad." I bit my lip, but she missed it when her head snapped to Diandra and she asked, "How long did it take you to learn their language?"

Thus commenced Narinda asking Diandra approximately one thousand seven hundred and twenty-three questions about all things Korwahk, Diandra answering these questions in great detail and then Diandra offering up juicy snippets of *my* life for the past week.

"Oh my," Narinda breathed. "How wonderful he was so worried for you when you were ill. It's almost, I can't believe I'm going to say this, but...*romantic.*"

Diandra beamed.

"The brute *did* leave me out in the sun for nine hours," I grumbled, the light shining from Diandra's face extinguished and she gave me a narrow-eyed look.

"Oh, I saw you," Narinda said. "I tried to catch your attention, but you didn't see me and I couldn't get Feetak to understand me when I said I wanted to go see you. Night had fallen and for some reason he didn't want me close to the dais."

Feetak was sounding better and better by the moment.

Narinda went on, "You looked kind of bored but *very* beautiful. All that gold. Your clothing was *amazing*. And your *jewelry*! Feetak has given me a chest full of it, but you were wearing more just during that celebration than I have in my entire chest."

Yep, there it was.

Proof it was good being queen.

"Our Dax showers great bounty on his golden queen," Diandra announced.

"I can see!" Narinda exclaimed, her eyes scanning my clothing and my jewelry which was again, I had to admit, a pretty spectacular show. She reached out and grabbed my hand. "But I'm sorry you were ill, Circe. I'm glad you're better now."

"Thanks, Narinda," I said softly.

"The golden queen," Narinda replied just as softly.

"That's what they say," I returned noncommittally.

She smiled a smile I remembered in a way I knew I would remember it until my dying day. It was small, it was weird, it was attached to not-so-good memories, but it still was a treasure.

"It was awful," she whispered her understatement. "But maybe we didn't do all that badly."

I recited words that I would also remember until my dying day, but I had forgotten until just then, "What has been has been, but what will be is what *we* make of it."

Her eyes got moist, and she squeezed my hand. I squeezed hers back at the same time I felt something settle in my heart.

What will be was what *I* made of it.

I needed to remember that.

There was a sudden commotion outside, all of our heads swung to the cham flaps, and when it penetrated the noises sounded urgent, we all jumped up as one and ran out of the tent.

People were running towards a cham a few down and there were shouts.

"What's going on?" I asked Diandra who I could see was listening to the shouts.

"A child in distress," she answered.

We three looked at each other then we all rushed to the cham. Once to the outside of the group surrounding it, people started noticing me and stepping back, clearing a path for their queen. I pulled my girls forward, and when we got to the cham, just outside, there was a child, maybe two or three, his face purple and he was clearly not breathing. His mother was shaking him, fear saturating her face.

"My God," I whispered at witnessing her distress then I noticed a large slab of dried meat on the ground. "Shit, that child is choking!" I cried, not thinking, and dashed forward.

It took some effort, but I pulled the boy out of his mother's arms. There were cries and shouts at my actions and she clawed at me to get him back, but I ignored her, turned his back to my front and did the Heimlich maneuver that I'd learned during the health and safety class I made all my father's movers take. It took four cautious (considering his age and size) heaves, but the meat finally flew out of his mouth and he instantly choked in air.

When he was sucking back his next mighty gulp, I turned him into his mother's arms and his arms feebly went around her neck. She collapsed on her ass, shoved her face in his little neck and burst into tears.

Shoo.

Well, thank God for that health and safety class. It was finally worth all the bitching the boys treated me to for making them take it.

I smiled down at mother and child, touching his hair then touching hers then I turned to see a sea of faces all watching me silently.

Oh man.

All eyes remained on me and not a sound was made.

Damn, *now* what did I do?

Then someone suddenly shouted, "*Kah rahna Dahksahna hahla!*"

"*Kah rahna Dahksahna hahla!*" another shout rent the air.

Then another. And another. Then a chant. Then they started the clapping.

Jeez.

It was just the Heimlich maneuver.

I looked at Diandra who was beaming ear to ear and Narinda who was looking at me funny but still smiling huge. I rolled my eyes at Diandra which made her break out into laughter.

I turned to the crowd and lifted my hands and pressed palms down to get them to stop chanting. It took a couple of palm presses, but I was their queen, my husband could kick anyone's ass, so they shut up pretty quickly.

I started to walk away, but my hand was grabbed, and I looked down to the mother who still had tight hold on her child, but she was kissing my hand.

"Shahsha, shahsha, shahsha kah rahna Dahksahna hahla. Shahsha," she whispered against my hand, and I did a knees-closed squat next to her, gently twisted my hand from her grasp and touched my fingers to her lips.

"It was nothing. Everybody knows how to do that where I come from," I said and heard Diandra close, translating. "And it was my pleasure," I added. Diandra interpreted then I smiled and finished on a whisper, "Nahrahka."

She nodded to me, eyes big and grateful.

I nodded back, got up, nodded to my, uh...*people*, then Diandra, Narinda and I went back to Narinda's cham.

14

THE BREAKING POINT

It was night and I'd talked Diandra into wandering the chams because it felt nice to be out in the cool air, the torches stuck into the earth every six or seven feet that lit the pathways between the chams cast a cozy glow, and I wanted to stretch my legs.

It had been a nice day. Another day with the Korwahk, another day waking up in this world, another hint that this may be my life, my old life might be lost to me forever, and unless I could do the impossible, figure out what had happened and reverse it, I was going to have to get used to it.

And in it I now had Narinda and Nahka. We'd spent some more time in Narinda's cham where she asked Diandra more questions, Diandra answered and then Diandra gave us both some Korwahk language lessons.

We suddenly heard a "poyah" from outside the cham and Nahka, the mother of the child who had been choking came in and offered us dinner.

We accepted because Diandra knew Nahka and informed us she was lovely. Because it was seriously doubtful Narinda was going to get swept from this world in her dreams and it would be good for her to get to know her neighbors. And because it was beginning to dawn on me that this might be my life and these my people, so I'd need to get to know them.

Even with the language barrier and Diandra having to translate, dinner with Nahka was what dinner always was amongst girls. Lots of food, lots of wine, lots of talk about the men in our lives (Nahka was a warrior wife too, her husband's name was Bohtan). Nahka spoke of her son (the child who was choking) and newborn daughter. Narinda and I spoke of our lands. And last, there was lots of laughter.

We left with promises to do it again soon, Narinda hugged me and Diandra after we returned her to her cham, and I talked Diandra into taking a walk. She agreed, so we were strolling through the torchlight in our normal way, bodies close, my hand wrapped around her elbow, her other hand covering mine.

"Uh...Diandra?" I called.

"Yes, my dear," she replied.

"Do all the Korwahk think they have a spirit or is it only the warriors?"

"All Korwahk believe they have a spirit," she answered.

"So...uh, they're spiritual?"

Her hand squeezed mine and she cut to the chase. "What are you truly asking, Circe?"

I smiled at a woman at a firepit outside a tent and replied, "Do they believe in God?"

"God?"

"Yes, God. A higher being, an omnipotent power, a divine creator, that kind of thing," I explained.

"Just one?" she asked, and I looked at her.

"Sorry?"

She looked at me too and her face was confused. "In your land, do you have just one god?"

I looked back at our path and shook my head. "Yes and no. Different people believe different things and some of them have more than one god they pray to, but me...I believe in only one."

"Unusual," she muttered.

I lifted my other hand, placed it over hers on mine and squeezed. "So? Do the Korwahk believe in a god or gods?"

"They do, my dear. They have many and for each person they choose which god will be their, erm...higher being. There is the Lion God, the Snake God, the Horse God, the Jackal God, the Tiger God and the True Mother. Most women pray to the True Mother. I would suspect," her hand gave mine a pat, "your king prays to the Tiger God."

I would suspect that too.

She kept talking.

"They do not have shrines. They do not have alters. They do not have churches. They have no holy men or women, and they don't carry talismans. They do not invest any spiritual significance in a person, place or object. The spirit is inside, prayers are silent, worship is individual and personal. Adults do not discuss it with adults. It is parents who pass down the teachings of the gods and inner spirits and they allow their children to adopt their own form of devotion."

Interesting. And kind of cool.

"So, if they're spiritual, um..." I trailed off.

"Yes?" Diandra prompted.

Shit.

Here we go.

"Well, you said something earlier I haven't been able to get out of my head. Something that doesn't, um...sit right if the Korwahk are spiritual. You mentioned something about Lahn taking a woman in plunder—"

I stopped talking when she halted us and turned to me but didn't let go of my hand.

I knew this meant something not good.

I looked in her eyes and she spoke.

"The Horde is revered," she said softly. "Even more than any god. This is because they protect the Korwahk nation *and* because they rain riches on it. And they do this through marauding."

Yep, this was not good.

"Marauding?" I whispered.

She nodded. "Korwahk is a warring nation, as is Maroo, Keenhak and other neighboring nations close and far. But Korwahk has riches that the others do not have. Veins of gold and silver. A vast wealth of diamonds in the earth. Mines of emeralds and rubies. These other nations covet these things and often wage war in order to take it for their own. The Horde rides against these armies that invade our land, murder the Korwahk people, rape our women. And The Horde never fails, Circe, *ever* in driving these armies back and bringing peace to the land. The Korwahk owe great debts to the blood of warriors."

"I can see that," I said softly.

She took in a breath then continued.

"There is no government, no law, but right and wrong is known by all and wrong is punished severely, either by the Dax amongst The Horde and those who travel with and serve it and by high counselors in settlements. Therefore, with no government, no treasury set up to do things like build roads and the like, the Dax does not tax his people and the Korwahk Horde rides into neighboring nations in order to acquire further riches for their own."

Okay, I was guessing this was the bad part.

"Go on," I urged tentatively, needing to know but at the same time not wanting to know.

She turned us and started us walking again.

"It is savage, this I will agree," she said softly. "But if The Horde rides and a village knows they are coming, if they are smart, they make offerings so The Horde will not plunder their village. The Horde will take the offering and move on. If the village is *not* smart and makes no offering or the offering is considered by the Dax as too little, they will ride against the village and take from it what they feel is their due."

I cleared my throat and walked but said not a word.

Diandra squeezed my hand and kept talking quietly.

"And they do plunder, my dear, and plunder as you would expect a brutal, warring tribe to plunder. I know you do not like it when I say this, but this is their way, it always has been." She was silent for a moment and then her voice got even quieter when she went on, "In getting to know you, I can imagine your mind is turning."

It must be said, she was not wrong about that.

"But I will share with you that your king's agreement to give up the Xacto surprised me greatly. This, too, is their way and has been since anyone can remember. This is a remarkable concession, my dear, and you should treasure it, hold it precious and tend it so the Dax never feels regret that he made it. But I will say, if you speak against the ways of his people who you must take to heart are now *your* people, I fear it would not have such a positive outcome."

I made no response mainly because I feared the same.

Diandra sighed then kept explaining.

"They bring these riches back, coin, slaves, all of it. Slaves are sold and they build tents, work in mines, serve households, provide a better life for the Korwahk. Coin and other booty is used and traded, given to wives who in turn provide custom to merchants who in turn order goods from farmers and artisans. These activities are the foundation of Korwahk life. The more The Horde showers down on their people, the better the Korwahks live, the more they revere The Horde. It is their cycle, their tradition, their *way*."

"Okay," I said, and my voice trembled. "But raping women and girls and killing people to steal their property?"

"It is their way of life," she said simply.

"Raping women and girls?" I asked quietly, shook my head and admitted, "Lahn doing that, Diandra, I have to say, it turns my stomach."

"Then stop him from doing it."

I stopped walking so Diandra did too and turned to me.

"Sorry?" I asked.

She smiled a small smile before saying, "You will not be able to talk to him and convince him to change the way of The Horde. Even *if* you were to be able to convince him, if he tried to rule his warriors and tell them they could not do as they see fit while warring and marauding, they would see this as a weakness. Although right and wrong is known, these are basics and mostly the Korwahk do as they wish. I do not know how it works and those across the Green and Marhac Seas see this as savage, and perhaps it is. But for the Korwahk, it works. The nation knows peace, wealth and safety. If an army invades, The Horde moves and puts a stop to it in short order. This is what it is. It is akin to Dortak and his bride. The other warriors know he is abusing her and many, I can assure you, find that contemptuous. But he is a warrior. He has endured training. He has leaked blood to rain riches on his nation. What he does in his cham and what he does to aid The Horde in procuring, they will make no judgment. It is not their business, and they will never move against him as long as he provides service to The Horde."

"Okay, so how do I stop Lahn—?"

She smiled and lifted a hand to my cheek, leaning her face close to mine.

"I, too, found great difficulty in understanding this way of life. This, especially this, did not sit well with me and it is the only thing that took me a great deal of time to come to terms with. I did not like The Horde doing it but especially I did not like knowing my husband did it, and he did, my dear Circe. He did, even after we were married."

I closed my eyes.

Diandra kept talking. "So I found a way to stop him from doing it."

I opened my eyes.

"How?" I whispered.

She dropped her hand. "Seerim always told me when there was a campaign. In most cases, wives stay with warriors. Wives are usually kept close. So, the night before *and the morning of* I made certain he had what he needed, *all* that he needed, *as many times* as he needed what he needed from me so he wouldn't feel the need to take it from someone else."

I got what she was saying.

"In other words, you fucked his brains out," I replied on a smile.

"Erm..." she muttered then grinned. "If I take your meaning then yes, my dear friend, I fucked his brains out."

I couldn't help it, the subject matter sucked but Diandra saying that made me giggle.

I stopped giggling and whispered, "Well done."

Her grin grew into a smile, and she replied, "Indeed. And my tactic worked. He did not speak of it, but he would come back from a campaign smelling of dirt, of sweat, of blood but never again of woman." She nodded smartly. "There are ways to get what *you* need out of your warrior. You just must be clever in finding them."

What will be was what I *make of it.*

"Right," I whispered.

She peered into my eyes a moment before she nodded smartly again and turned us back to walking.

I could tell from the familiar surroundings we were heading back to my cham, and I wondered, when we rode, how I would learn another layout or if The Eunuch always set up the Daxshee the same.

Then I wondered about Seerim and his age.

"Does Seerim ride with The Horde now?" I asked Diandra.

"Sometimes, during raids, if he so chooses, but he has charge of training young warriors and that takes most of his concentration. During the selection, he received ten new boys he needs to break as well as keeping charge of the twenty other boys he was working with. He is quite busy with this, and it is an important role. Only honored warriors as they get older are required to take on the training of the young. This is because their skills are considered desirable by the Dax, and he wants these warriors to pass down their expertise. It is a high compliment."

She spoke proudly and I squeezed her hand as my cham came in sight. "Well done, Seerim," I said softly.

"Indeed," she replied distractedly.

I looked to her and then I followed her gaze.

That was when I noticed what I hadn't noticed before. There were two warriors standing outside my cham. Feetak and the grinning one who Lahn spoke to the night of the games.

He was not grinning now. He was scowling, as was Feetak, and the instant they laid eyes on us, they turned to my cham, bent and entered.

"Is something going on?" I asked as Diandra, and I got closer.

"I do not know," she answered softly. "But I do know we soon shall see."

We made it to the cham, and I entered first. There was candlelight and the space was filled with warriors. Feetak and the grinning one and another one I'd seen in passing often speaking with Lahn. Seerim was also there. And Lahn.

My eyes stuck on Lahn who didn't look at all like he was in a good mood. I started to smile hesitantly and whispered, "Hey."

It was then he instigated the breaking point.

He took two swift, angry strides to me, his arm going down and across his body, and before I knew his intention, he swung it out and struck me with the back of his hand on my cheekbone.

He did this with all his substantial strength and therefore my vision burst in a firework of white lights, agonizing pain radiated out from my cheekbone, piercing through my eye and across my face and my brain bounced against the inside of my skull. I flew to the side and went down on the stack of hides.

I was blinking and concentrating on getting the excruciating pain to fade when I heard Diandra start, "Circe, are you—?"

I turned my head to see Lahn thrust her back with such force, she went flying into her husband. Seerim caught her, his fingers closing on her biceps as he held her steady but not tenderly. He, too, I noticed vaguely as the pain faded but did not, by a long shot, go away, looked seriously pissed.

Lahn was barking words and my eyes moved to him to see he was scowling down at me as he raged. My hand drifted up to my cheekbone and I stared dazedly back at him.

"He...he wants me to...to...translate," Diandra said haltingly then spoke a flurry of quick words in Korwahk.

I said nothing, just stared at my husband.

Lahn's enraged eyes didn't leave me when he snarled more words and Diandra started talking.

"He...the Dax...he says he did not know where you were. He says they've been looking for you. He says you are never to leave the cham without a guard." She paused and Lahn kept thundering then she went on, "He says you are queen, and you must understand this, and the possible dangers and you must never, never leave the cham without a guard." She stopped then she said, "Circe, I'm so sorry, I didn't—"

I took my hand from my face, lifted it toward her palm up, and she stopped talking.

Lahn had quit speaking, but his dark eyes were still filled with wrath, and they were burning into mine so fiercely I could actually *feel* the fire.

And I did not *fucking* care.

I pushed to my feet and turned my body to facing him.

Then I spoke, and when I did, so did Diandra.

"My father loved my mother. He loved her deeply. He said they were the perfect match. When I was ten and she was murdered..."

Diandra stopped talking and I heard her soft intake of breath but then she carried on because I didn't stop.

"He never got over it. Never got over her. Never. And he gave me all the love he would have normally given me *and* the love he would have given her. He thought I was precious, and he treated me that way. This was because I was his daughter, but it was also because I was the most important thing my mother gave to him, and I was all he had left of her."

I swallowed and watched my words start to penetrate Lahn's fury, but I didn't care about that either and kept right on talking.

"And I promised myself, *vowed*, that I would find a man like my father who would love me deeply and treasure me more than anything in the world."

I stopped talking when I saw Lahn's body lock.

Then I kept going.

"You raped me," I whispered and Diandra spoke softly. "And somehow, I found it in me to forgive you. You left me out in the burning sun even though I told you the harm it would do to me, and I forgave you. This is your world, this is your way, and I have struggled with it, but I have accepted it."

I pulled in breath and continued.

"But what you did just now, taking your anger out on me when I did something in all innocence, I *cannot* and *will not* forgive. You do not know your own strength, but it is formidable, so formidable it cows men, but I am no man. I am a woman, *your* woman, and you used *all of it* in violence against me, and that, kah Dax, is *unforgiveable*."

He held my eyes at the same time he held his body completely still.

I finished and I did it quietly.

"My father was an honorable man, and he would wish for me to be treasured. If he were here, he and all of his men would fall by your Horde's swords in order to protect me from the harm you've inflicted on me. They would do it, and before they did it, they...wouldn't...*blink*. And because of that, because I know that in the depth of my soul and because of everything he gave to me, all the love he showed me, in return, I loved him more than anything in this world. I respected him. I honored him over any man I ever met. But he is lost to me. He is gone and therefore could not be here to protect me. But you should know this, my king...if he knew you, he would *not* like you."

When I stopped speaking, I realized my chest was rising and falling rapidly, and I held his gaze as it burned into mine.

Then he barked out the words, "Tahkoo tan!"* and the instant he did, I felt the tent empty but I didn't tear my eyes from Lahn.

We stared at each other for long moments after we were alone, Lahn statue-still, me breathing heavily, before he said in a quiet voice, "Vayoo ansha."

I shook my head and whispered, "*Never*. For good and always, you have lost me. Na me lapay kah Lahn. Not anymore."**

I watched him flinch, but I didn't care about that either.

When he recovered, his voice was soft when he said, "Vayoo ansha, kah rahna fauna."

I shook my head again and moved. Skirting him, I went to the trunks and dropped to my knees to open one to get a nightgown, thinking I had no escape. I had nowhere to go. I didn't even have another fucking *room* where I could hide and let lose the tears that were burning in my throat.

I felt him come at me before he got to me. His arms closed around me from behind, trapping mine tight to my front and he pulled me to my feet. He held me close and bent at the waist so his face was in my neck. There he spoke more soft words and I pushed hard against his arms caging mine, but, as usual, there was no give.

That burning in my throat grew so hot it rivaled the pain I still felt in my cheekbone, and I felt the additional sting of tears in my sinuses.

"Let me go," I whispered on another attempt to jerk my arms free.

He spoke more soft words and I jerked again. Then he let me go, I started to step away, but before I could I was up in the air, cradled in his arms, but they were like steel bands, locking me close. I tried to arch my back and buck, but this was to no avail.

He turned and took two long strides to the bed, sat then fell to his side, my back to the bed, my hips in his lap, thighs over his, and I couldn't swallow the sob that tore from my throat, filling the tent with the sound of sorrow.

"Kah Lahnahsahna Circe," he whispered, his hand cupping my head, forcing it into his chest as his other arm locked me in place.

"Let me go," I sobbed into his chest, my hands flat against it on either side of my face, pushing, but he didn't move. I gave up and whispered, "Let me go."

He didn't let me go. He kept my face in his chest and his arm tight around me as I cried, I sobbed, I bawled, I let it all hang out.

Everything.

Everything I was feeling. Everything that haunted my headspace for days. Being in this world and not knowing why. Being hunted and raped. Being confused and hurt. Watching a man die while his chain was hooked to me. Losing my world, my father, my job, my friends, my culture and everything I knew. Finding friends and building friendships at the same time not knowing if they would be torn away. And struggling against starting to fall in love with a man I didn't understand, whose ways frightened and repulsed me, but I was drawn to him by something I couldn't deny because it was just...that...*strong.*

And then, with one swing of his mighty arm, falling right out of love and landing with a crash so brutal, it shattered me.

In other words, I cried a lot of fucking tears.

So many, it exhausted me. So much emotion, I couldn't get it all out. It was impossible. The effort felt like it would kill me, and my body had to shut down just to survive.

Therefore, I fell asleep in Lahn's cradling arms even as the tears continued to fall.

**Translation:* "Leave us!"
***Translation:* "You are not my Lahn."

~

I WOKE in the night still in Lahn's arms and I didn't hesitate in pulling away, rolling and getting up from the bed.

Candlelight still spluttered, as it always did—he never extinguished them in the night—and it led my way to the trunks. I opened one, selected a nightgown, pulled it out, took off my clothes and jewelry, dropping them unheeded to the rugs at my feet, and I slid the nightgown on.

I moved to the bed of hides by the flaps and laid down, my head to the cushions, my back to Lahn in the bed.

I barely got settled before I was going up, his arms around me, cradling me to his chest again and I was back in bed. He jerked the silk out from under us, settled it over us and pulled me under his body, his heavy legs tangling with mine, his arm nearly fully around me, his weight pinning me to the bed.

As ever, no escape.

So I escaped the only way I had.

I twisted my neck to turn my face away.

But I was with Lahn, and Lahn being Lahn, he didn't even give me that.

His big hand curved around my jaw, and he turned me so I was facing him. His fingers glided into the hair at the side of my head, his thumb against my cheek, forcing my face into his throat and keeping it there.

I felt the burn in my throat and pulled in a deep breath that broke in the middle, loudly, communicating my struggle against tears.

Lahn's fingers tensed into my scalp but otherwise his hand didn't move.

It took a lot out of me, everything I had left, but I succeeded in holding them back.

When my breath evened, communicating I won my battle, Lahn's neck bent, and I felt his lips on my hair as his fingers again tensed gently into my scalp.

There he whispered, "Na lapay kah rahna Dahksahna. Na lapay kah Lahnahsahna. Na lapay kah Circe. Fahzah, Circe. *Fahzah.* Farzah kay markan nahna rah ruhnee zo kay. *Farzah.* Kuvoo sah, Circe, loot farzah danhay."***

One couldn't say I had the Korwahk language down pat, not even close, but I knew enough to know what he was saying.

And from the way he said it, I knew he really meant it.

And there it was.

I had no choice. I had no escape.

I had nothing.

So I closed my eyes, forced my body to relax and tried to find sleep.

This took a while before I succeeded, and his hand never left my head until I was out and when I went out, I went *out.*

Thus,I didn't feel nor even sense Lahn's hand drifting down to curl around my neck nor did I feel the pad of his thumb tenderly press up on my jaw to expose my face to him.

And lastly, I didn't feel his lips brush mine before his arm curved around me, he pulled me deeper under him and then he fell asleep.

****Translation:* "You are my golden queen. You are my tigress. You are my Circe. Always, Circe. *Always.* Never will I allow your gold to be taken from me. *Never.* Understand this, Circe, and never forget."

15
THE GIFTS

The noises of the Daxshee being disassembled and packed up were all around me, but I didn't see it, nor did I hear it.

I was completely in my head.

Being in that world was no good place to be and being in my head wasn't much better.

Still, it was better so that was where I was going to be.

It was early afternoon the next day after Lahn struck me and I knew from the noises invading the cham that woke me up (alone in our bed, might I add) that the packing up had already begun.

The minute I moved in bed, my girls swung into action, feeding me, bathing me, dressing me like the queen I was and then quickly went to work to pack our belongings for the ride.

Now, I was sitting outside on a big, soft hide with some cushions under a piece of gauze that had been set up on a slant to protect me from the sun. I had a plate of untouched food in front of me, a jug of water, a cup, and Ghost was rolling around, playing with some toy one of my girls had made for her (in other words, tearing the thing to pieces).

The activity was intense, the hustle and bustle all around, and I watched with distraction six young men who were likely around fourteen or fifteen, clearly Horde warriors in training considering they were all tall, fit and muscular, pulling down Lahn and my cham.

They were good at it. They were strong, fast and clearly had some practice.

I felt it before I saw him round the tent. That raw, brutal energy.

Lahn was coming.

I braced and then saw him move toward me wearing nothing but his hides, his boots, his hair still in the braid I'd plaited in it the day before.

He moved well, I noticed. He'd been trained since he was a little boy to know what his body could do and command every inch of it and that was exactly how he looked when he moved.

All that power was at his complete command.

And now I knew in a way I never wished to know just how much power he wielded.

His focus was on me the second I was in his line of sight and in that same instant I caught his flinch.

He'd marked me. I knew it. I didn't have a mirror and I didn't need to see his reaction to be made aware of it. The skin on my cheekbone was tender to the point that even the lightest touch caused significant pain and it was swollen so badly the skin felt stretched to the breaking point.

But even if I couldn't feel it, I saw it in the eyes of my girls the minute they saw me that morning, and then, all day, the eyes of those moving around me. Or more to the point, those eyes in faces not smiling at me, heads not nodding but avoiding my gaze, and after seeing my husband's mark, looking swiftly away.

I noticed even with the flinch his gait didn't stutter as he made his way to me. I tipped my head way back to watch him as he didn't hesitate to bend, his hand finding mine, engulfing it, and without a word to me, he pulled me gently to my feet.

He started moving us, his hand in mine, and he still said nothing to me, but he barked, "Teetru, Ghost," and in two short words gave the order to his busy slave to take time out from her important tasks to look after my pet.

He strode around our now-fallen tent and into the disappearing pathway that was fast becoming a clearing, and I hurried to keep up.

Not, this time, protesting his pace.

Not, this time, speaking a word.

But I knew his head turned because I felt his eyes on me then his hand squeezed mine and his gait slowed so I didn't have to half run to keep up.

I didn't even look at him. I slowed my step and kept my gaze to my sandals.

We entered an area where there were no chams or belongings to pack away, but the activity seemed more extreme. I looked up to see we were at the outskirts of the disappearing Daxshee. There were lines of wagons being loaded and there was also a line of horses standing in wait.

I immediately saw Lahn's. Firstly, because it was at least one hand higher than all the rest, a visibly powerful beast, huge, regal, absolutely perfect for him. Secondly, I saw Lahn's steed because beside it was a blinding white horse the beauty of which I'd never beheld in my life, and I'd spent some time around horses.

My father had scraped and saved to give me horseback riding lessons from the time I was eleven to the time I was fourteen. He did this because he loved me, and he did this because he had a daughter who lost her mother and he wanted her to have what she most wanted in the world. I wanted my mom back, but since that was utterly impossible, horseback riding lessons were going to have to do.

When I realized how much it was costing Pop, and how little he could afford it, I asked him to quit paying for them. But I bought time on the back of a horse every weekend for the next two years and I bought it by mucking out six horse stalls for free in order to get it.

And lastly, I knew Lahn's horse because Diandra and Seerim were standing in front of it.

I searched her face and body for hints that Seerim had taken his hand to her too in what appeared to be his anger last night, but she had none. However, the minute her eyes could see my face clearly, her expression grew soft, her shoulders drooped slightly, and even over the distance, I saw her eyes get moist.

Yep, definitely, absolutely and truly, I liked Diandra, and if I ever made it out of this godforsaken world, I would miss her.

Lahn walked us right up to Diandra and Seerim, then stopped. Dropping my hand, his arm curled around my shoulders, and he turned me so my front was held against his side. On display to his people and with no choice, I slid my arms around his waist and looked at Diandra whose eyes were on me as Lahn spoke.

Then Diandra did. "He has asked me here to translate for him."

"Ordered you, you mean," I replied, and she pressed her lips together.

Then she whispered, "Yes, Dahksahna Circe."

She called me my title as she was now not just my friend but in the presence of her king.

I nodded.

She nodded to me then looked to Lahn.

He turned me toward the white horse and reached out a long arm to catch the horse's bridle, doing this without letting me go. He pulled the horse's gleaming white nose—a nose that was so white it seemed an aura of the coolest ice blue shimmered from it—close to us and he spoke.

"This is my gift to my tigress," Diandra said, and my gaze flew to Lahn who was still talking. "When The Horde rides, their queen rides."

I stared at him without a word. Then slowly my eyes moved to the beautiful beast in front of me.

Lahn spoke as did Diandra. "She has no name, Circe."

I nodded, my attention still on the horse and I lifted a hand cautiously to her nose. She allowed the touch, so I stroked her.

"Hey, girl," I said softly.

She jerked her head up slightly, the movement controlled by Lahn's hand still on her bridle, but my hand flew away. She came back and butted my hand with her nose, so I smiled at her and stroked again.

"You're gorgeous," I whispered, moving in close. Lahn's arm fell away from me, he let go of her bridle and she butted the side of my head gently. "Seeing you, there is no name to capture your beauty so why don't we try to capture your coat," I told her. "How do you feel about Zephyr?"

She lifted her head again, shook it briefly then I got three down and ups.

Assent.

I grinned at her, caught her nose with a hand on either side and brought it down so we were eye to eye.

"Zephyr it is then," I said.

She snorted what I hoped was her approval (alas, I could not understand this beast in this world), and my grin turned to a smile.

"Lahnahsahna," Lahn called, and I closed my eyes, gave Zephyr a last stroke then let her go and turned to my husband, dropping my head back to catch his gaze.

He didn't hesitate to pull me gently into his arms. I placed my hands lightly on the warm skin of his chest then he spoke as did Diandra.

"She pleases you?"

"Meena," I replied in his language.

"Good," he replied quietly in mine, and I felt my heart wrench.

His eyes moved over my face and caught on my cheekbone. He studied it for long moments before they moved back to mine, and he spoke softly.

Diandra translated, "I do not like it when my tigress weeps."

Then you shouldn't have made her weep, I thought but made no verbal reply.

He waited for it, but I didn't give it to him. He was a man who could have anything he wanted, and if not, he was a man who was strong enough to take it.

Except one thing.

Me.

He sighed. Then he lifted a hand to my jaw and his thumb swept the skin under my bruise in a whisper-soft touch that still caused a hint of pain that made my brows draw together in protest. He caught the movement, and his jaw went hard.

He spoke again and Diandra translated. "I do not like it that my queen bears my mark."

Then you shouldn't have marked her, I thought but remained silent.

He waited.

I gave him nothing but my gaze.

Then he spoke again, this time in a mutter as if to himself, but Diandra still translated, "She keeps even her claws sheathed from me."

Damn straight, I thought but made not a sound.

His eyes focused intently on mine then came more. "I've no doubt I'll very soon earn your claws again, my tigress."

Don't hold your breath, I silently advised.

He waited and so did I.

He spoke again and Diandra said, "Very well, my Circe, I'll allow you time to retreat and lick your wounds."

Well, thanks so much, asshole, I thought sarcastically.

He watched my face, drew in breath and let it out slowly. Then he pulled me closer, his arms going tighter, he bent and whispered something in my ear I did not understand and Diandra didn't hear.

Suddenly his body tensed, his head came up and he looked over his shoulder. He let one arm drop and turned to my side.

That was when I saw Nahka, carrying her baby daughter strapped to her chest, her hand holding on to her little boy's. He also had a hand in Narinda's who was walking with Nahka, the boy in between them. They seemed to be rushing but not having an easy time of it with the boy slowing them.

In front of them at least five paces was a warrior wearing a grave expression, carrying a long, squat box made of gleaming wood. His attention was on me, and he seemed to be heading our way.

What on earth?

My gaze went back to Narinda who was smiling at me, and I knew the minute she caught my mark because her lips parted and her step stuttered. Her eyes flashed to Lahn and her face filled with fear.

But Nahka kept dragging her little boy and Narinda had no choice but to keep on coming.

The man stopped in front of Lahn with something obviously on his mind. He did not wait to say it and Diandra immediately started translating.

"Dax Lahn, I'll have a word with your wife," he stated.

"You'll have a word with me first," Lahn replied, his meaning clear.

"Then you have not heard," the man declared.

"Heard what?" Lahn asked.

"Yesterday, in front of my wife and many witnesses, our true golden queen saved the life of my son."

Lahn's arm around the middle of my back tensed.

Then Diandra translated his, "What?"

"He was not breathing. She executed some maneuver she said she learned in her land and expelled a piece of meat he was choking on. If she had not done that, my son would not have lived to serve his Horde," the man explained, and I felt Lahn's regard on me.

"Is this true?" he asked, and I looked up at him.

"It was nothing," I said softly, and Diandra translated then kept doing it when words flew from the warrior's mouth.

"I do not agree, my queen, that it was nothing, for my son lives today instead of being prepared for his pyre," the man stated, and I looked from Lahn to him.

"Uh—" I mumbled.

Diandra didn't translate my mumble but did translate his words.

"I serve my king, I serve my Horde, and before yesterday, as was my duty, I served my new queen. Now, my debt to you will never be paid. My family stands strong. My wife does not peek from under the veil of mourning. We have our time with him before he leaves us to take the paint. Gods willing, he will live to gather his own bounty and spill his seed in his wife to guarantee the future of The Horde, as I have done, and my father did before me. This is not nothing. This is everything, my queen, and when you owe everything, it is a debt that cannot be repaid."

"Um..." I whispered, "okay."

"But, even so, with Dax Lahn's consent, I offer you a gift," he stated then opened up the box.

I blinked as the sun flashed on the gleaming silver and jewels.

Then I stared with my mouth hanging open.

It was a dagger made of perfect, shining silver, the hilt covered completely in jewels. These were not roughhewn but perfectly crafted so their brilliance reflected everywhere. There were emeralds and sapphires, in abundance, but there were also diamonds and not a small amount of those either. It was not small, it was not large, but just the number and size of the jewels made it obviously valuable, and the craftsmanship, even from someone like me who knew nothing about it, could not be denied. In my world, the thing would be worth tens of thousands of dollars. Maybe hundreds of thousands.

Holy crap!

I looked at him and started, "I can't—" but he (and thus Diandra) talked over me.

"The silver and jewels were pulled from deep within Korwahk, but the artisan who created this is from your land. It is Valearian and it signifies our queen, once of the Vale, now Korwahk, forever bound together to create beauty."

That was so beautiful (albeit untrue) that tears sprang to my eyes, and I whispered, "It was just the Heimlich maneuver. Seriously. A lot of people from my, uh...land know how to do it."

"It is not just anything, my true golden queen," he retorted.

Lahn spoke softly on a squeeze of my back and Diandra translated, "Quiet your protests, my doe, and take the dagger. You do Bohtan a dishonor by hesitating."

Quickly, my hands came up. Bohtan placed the box in them, and I blinked the tears away as I looked up at him.

"I...I don't know what to say," I whispered, Diandra translated my words and his reply.

"Say nothing, my queen, except that you will grace our cham in future, make my wife laugh and do it casually as you did even just hours after you saved our son's life."

"I, uh...okay," I replied, his serious face melted, and he smiled at me.

I smiled back.

Then he looked at Lahn and jerked up his chin with a, "Kah Dax," turned and strode away.

I watched him reach Nahka, who was stopped some feet away, and swing his son up into his muscular arms, attach him to his hip, throw his other arm around Nahka and guide her away.

She looked back and waved as did her son.

I waved in return.

Narinda remained rooted to the spot, staring at me, and I was about to mouth something to her before I heard Lahn bark and my body started. I started paying attention to my immediate surroundings and saw The Eunuch was close and clearly had been there awhile. He had something to say too, and he was biding his time to speak.

But his eyes dashed to me twice in the brief time mine rested on him and something about that struck me as wrong.

Before I could put a finger on it, he spoke and Diandra translated. "The Daxshee is nearly dismantled, King Lahn, we ride in an hour."

"Dohno," Lahn muttered on a jerk of his chin.

The Eunuch inclined his head and his eyes darted to me yet again before he turned and moved quickly away. I lost sight of him when Lahn curved me into his front again, both arms around me and I looked up to him as he spoke and Diandra interpreted.

"We ride soon under a sun that still holds heat. Will you be all right on Zephyr or do you need cover?"

"Zephyr," I replied instantly, ignoring the fact that he was being solicitous and therefore sweet.

Lahn went on after a squeeze of his arms, "My tigress, the pink in your skin has turned to honey, but the sun will beat for four to five hours yet before losing its strength. I do not wish you to have another turn."

"I'll be fine," I assured him, and I would. Late afternoon sunshine was a lot different than sitting in it all day. I now had an enforced base tan, and anyway, I had to do something about these whacked-out tan lines. I hadn't seen myself, but I had to look like a freak.

"This is a promise?" he pushed, and I locked eyes with him.

"It is a promise, my king, I'll be *fine*," I stated, and his jaw clenched.

Then he muttered, "Nahna Dax."

Your king. Not just Lahn.

He didn't like that, I could tell.

Whatever.

I held his eyes as I waited. He held my eyes as something worked behind his.

Then he gave me a squeeze and muttered, "Okay, Circe. Veeyoo..." then a bunch more stuff that Diandra translated as "I will see you as we ride."

I nodded. He gave me another squeeze with another sigh, he looked over my shoulder and jerked his chin up, and I looked too, to see a warrior nod and move our way.

My guard.

Then he let me go.

I moved away quickly, closing the box and shoving it under my arm, and Diandra was instantly at my side.

Before she could say a word, I spoke.

"Are you okay?" I asked, and she blinked.

"Pardon, my dear?"

"Did your husband take a hand to you last night?" I clarified.

"No!" she exclaimed. "Of course not."

"He was angry," I reminded her.

"He was, Circe, but he just yelled at me. I yelled back because you were right, neither of us knew we were doing anything wrong. It was all innocent. It took a while for me to calm him down, get him to hear me, but I did, and he realized it was an innocent mistake and all was well."

"So he doesn't hit you?" I asked.

She eyed me.

Then she answered quietly, "Not anymore, my dear." Then quickly, "And not for some time."

"Right," I muttered.

"My goodness!" We heard and both our heads swung to Narinda who was standing in front of us, and we would have bowled her over if we didn't stop. She lifted a shaking hand toward my cheekbone then she dropped it, grasped my hand and tugged me close. "Oh Circe," she whispered. "What on earth happened?"

"I displeased my husband last night," I told her shortly.

Narinda reared back in shock, her face paling instantly and Diandra sucked in breath.

I turned to her, and she had her mouth open to speak.

I knew what was coming so I lost it.

"Don't," I whispered on a hiss, shaking my head at the same time tears sprang to my eyes. "Don't. Do not tell me more of how this place and these people work, what they do, what are their ways. No more explanations of who they are and why they behave the way they do."

She blinked with obvious hurt. I let Narinda go, turned fully to Diandra and grabbed her hand, squeezing hard.

"I adore you, my friend, you already own a piece of my heart. But you and I know there is no excuse for what he did last night. There is no Korwahk explanation that enlightens me to the ways of him and his people that would justify him unleashing his fury on me the way he did. You cannot look at my face, see his mark and know the woman I am and think I could ever do, no matter the wrong he perceives, anything to make him strike me the way he struck me and that would be in any way okay. You know it, Diandra," I squeezed and shook her hand sharply. "*You know it.*"

"Circe," she whispered, squeezing my hand back. "Please listen to me. There are things you don't know. Things you have yet to learn. Things Lahn knows, and Seerim told me last night he was wild with worry—"

I shook my head hard, let her go and took a step back. "No. No, I won't listen to you now. Maybe later when I don't feel the ache of the back of his hand smashing into my face. But not now."

Then as quickly as I could, before she could say another word and without a glance at either of them, I hurried back toward where my cham used to be.

My guard followed.

~

I STARED at the stars overhead and there were a lot of them. They blanketed the dark sky in a twinkle of lights that was breathtaking. I'd never seen anything like it. Not in my life.

I moved my legs and my entire body protested.

We'd ridden from afternoon into the night. It had been years since I'd been on a horse and my body wasn't used to it. I forgot how much it took out of you physically, riding. Now I remembered.

We didn't make camp. Once we stopped, I dismounted from Zephyr, a strapping young boy was instantly there to take her away and then Teetru was there, grabbing my hand. My girls gave me water to wash my hands and face, served me a simple meal of dried meat, cheese, flatbread and dried fruit with a cup of water and a chalice of wine. This was cleared away and I was led in the clothes I wore that day to a stack of hides that I took to be my bed. They were out in the open, as everyone else appeared to be bedding down, though somewhat removed from the others.

I wasn't keen on camping, though I was an experienced camper. I was the only child of a man who was *a man* and he liked fishing, hiking and shit like that. So he took me with him. But I'd never slept under the stars and was uncertain I wanted to. I wasn't in Rome, but I was in Korwahk, and therefore had to do what the Korwahks did.

Bed under the stars it was.

I slipped off my sandals and slid under the top hide. They were set on a slab of cream stone but there were a lot of them (giving me an understanding of why Lahn had that huge pile in his cham) so although it wasn't the softest bed I'd ever lain in, it wasn't hard stone either and my aching body was glad to recline.

The girls had rolled some hides at the top to act as pillows and I lay on my back and stared at the stars.

I had seen Lahn that day, several times. He rode mostly at the front of the procession of hundreds of horses that was followed by at least double that amount of wagons, but he would often drop back to ride next to warriors and speak with them. I caught his eyes on me twice, but he never got near me.

I rode with the women who rode behind the men. I did this but I did it while avoiding Diandra on her roan mount because I felt badly for my outburst. Not that my words were wrong, just that I should have weighed them before hurling them at a woman who had been nothing but kind to me.

I lost sight of Lahn the minute we stopped and hadn't seen him since.

The stars were drifting from sight because my eyelids were drifting closed when I heard Lahn's boots approach. I turned to my side away from his side of the hides and heard one after another his boots hit stone. Then the top hide moved. Not a second later, I was hauled across the hides and my body was forced to curve into the large, hard, warm one at my back.

He spoke quietly into the back of my hair as his hand drifted up to cup my breast and I stilled. He kept speaking and I waited for him to do something. It would be just like him to try to have sex with me with hundreds of people camping just feet away.

But his thumb did not wander across my nipple, his hand just cupped me warmly as he continued to speak words, most of which I didn't understand.

He stopped talking and his head moved. I felt his beard against the skin of my neck as he used his chin to pull my hair away and then I felt his tongue taste me from the back of my ear down the length of my neck and further down the length of my shoulder.

Throughout its journey, I steeled myself against the shiver and fortunately succeeded in beating it back.

At the point of my shoulder, he rubbed the long hairs at his bearded chin back and forth, which felt sweet and nice and made my nose sting with tears that this time I held back with sheer willpower.

He did this for a long time as if he was staring into the darkness deep in contemplation at the same time delivering to me a preoccupied caress that was still, nevertheless, a caress.

Then his arm around me pulled me deeper into him and he settled back into the hides. He tilted his big body slightly into mine and I listened until his breath evened out.

Only then did I allow my eyes to close and my body to fall asleep.

16
TAKE HEED

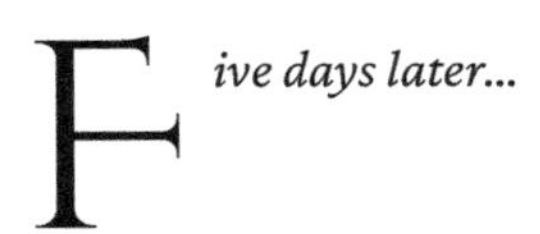

ive days later…

I WAS RIDING WAY BACK amongst the wagons, the ones that carried the chams and belongings and the slaves who were also belongings, of course, a fact I found loathsome and yet another thing I could do nothing about for it was my people's *way*.

This was my new tactic.

Not that I really needed one.

I had not talked to Lahn since the day he gave me Zephyr. He clearly had Dax business to attend to and he was gone from our hides in the morning before I woke, and three of the four nights after our first one under the stars, I was so exhausted from the ride, I was asleep and didn't even feel him slide in beside me. I only knew he was there when I woke in the deep of the night, felt his arm around me, his warm body curved into mine and then I drifted back to sleep. The one night I was awake, it was still late, and he attempted no conversation, didn't speak soft words or rub his beard gently against me, just curled me into him, and he was asleep within seconds, and shortly after, so was I.

But it was now days later, and it was a now when I'd avoided Diandra, and also Narinda, who was riding with the wives who were in wagons, and it had been so long since I'd spoken to either of them, it was too long.

I'd screwed up. I'd been overemotional (with cause) then got stuck in my head for days and it was getting past the point of rude, not apologizing to and spending time with my friends. I was their queen. It might be they couldn't approach me and certainly Narinda couldn't as she didn't have a mount. But I could do what I wished (sort of) and I hadn't approached them.

So now I was avoiding them both, and Lahn, by riding in the back like a sissy.

My pop would be pissed. He hated sissies, he wasn't that fond of rude, and he'd always told me procrastination was the work of the devil, *especially* when you practice it before righting a wrong.

Damn.

On this thought, I noticed there seemed a commotion amongst the slaves, so I looked to the wagons at my side then the direction they were looking which was forward. That was when I saw the warrior galloping toward us. He was well out of warrior space—they all rode up front with their Dax. He was also the warrior I saw in the cham the night Lahn hit me.

Shit.

He galloped right by me, but when I twisted in my saddle to see where he was going, I saw him circle back quickly then come up on my left side. Before I knew what he was doing I was plucked right out of my saddle (yep, right out of my saddle, *while* both our horses were moving) and planted in front of him. He yanked Zephyr's reins out of my hands. She whinnied with irritation and then he touched his heels to his mount, made a clicking sound with his tongue and we took off on a gallop, Zephyr running alongside us.

Hmm.

It appeared the queen didn't ride with the slaves.

So noted.

We kept going and he slowed when we were coming abreast of Diandra's horse.

Shit!

With both horses still moving, he plopped me right back *on* Zephyr's back. Before I flew off in a horse mishap that might include a broken neck, I quickly grabbed the lip of the saddle (they had no pommels on their saddles) swung my leg around and both feet found my stirrups. He tossed the reins to me, touched his heels to his mount and took off toward the warriors.

Fantastic.

These guys.

He could have just grabbed my reins and moved Zephyr and I forward, but *no*. He had to manhandle me.

I watched him go then stupidly looked beyond the warriors to the leader of the pack.

As suspected, the leader of the pack was turned in his saddle. He was far away but I could see him, and I knew Lahn's eyes were on me because he couldn't miss me. Zephyr's coat shone in the sun like a beacon, not to mention I was the only blonde in the bunch.

Fantastic again.

I watched him turn to face forward and I sucked in breath.

With nothing for it, and because my pop taught me well, I got my head out of my ass and turned to Diandra whose attention was on me.

Then I said, "Uh...hey."

She burst out laughing.

I stared at her and when her laughter waned, her eyes caught mine. "Our king grows impatient with his queen, I see," she remarked.

Uh...what?

"Um..." I mumbled.

She faced forward and announced, "It took years before Seerim saw the errors of his ways, putting his hands on me in anger. He didn't do it often, but when he felt the need, he didn't hesitate to do it. It was only after he hit me so hard, he bloodied my nose that he stopped. Something about him shedding my blood struck something in him and he never did it again. Not once. In fact, when he'd get angry, all I had to do was flinch, thinking he might hit me and his anger would vanish," she lifted a hand and snapped, "just like that. It appears, my dear, our king is learning this lesson much more swiftly than my Seerim."

"I'm not trying to teach him a lesson," I said softly and in all truth.

"Well, maybe not, but you're doing it all the same," she replied.

I pulled in another breath. "Diandra—" I started on the exhale, wanting to apologize but more wishing to give her an apology, and her kind eyes came to me.

"Don't speak of it," she whispered. "I remember, my beautiful Circe, it was long ago, but I remember the tumult of my mind when I was brought here, claimed and forced into a life I did not understand. I have had twenty-two years with these people, I have built a life with my husband, I have come to love him deeply, we have created and nurtured a family, and I have become Korwahk. But I have had much time to adjust. I was like you many years ago and I remember it because it is something you do not forget. You have done far better than me and I am very proud of you. But our emotions get the better of us on occasion, and if you cannot allow them to do so with people who care about you, you are in trouble."

I felt my eyes fill with tears, "Diandra—"

"Though," she cut me off, a twinkle in hers, "*I* didn't have a gifted interpreter to guide my way like you do. So along with being proud of you, I am also quite proud of me because, as far as I can tell, I'm doing an excellent job."

Then she grinned huge, and at that, it was me who burst into laughter.

When my laughter slid to a giggle I saw her smiling, looking ahead and she noted, "We make camp tonight, I'm sure of it."

"Sorry?" I asked.

"You have a very appealing laugh, my dear. It is like a song that rings into the very air, traveling far, I would suspect, considering while you did it, your husband turned on his mount and watched. I am getting old, but my eyesight is just fine and by his scowl I would guess he has not heard your laughter for some time and misses it, wants it for his own and therefore, being of The Horde, when he wants something, he will do something about it. So, we make camp tonight. I'm sure of it."

It took a lot out of me, but my gaze didn't move to Lahn as I repeated, "Sorry?"

She looked at me. "Have you been receiving his attentions since our unpleasant...erm, incident?"

"Um...no," I muttered.

"I would guess he misses that too," she stated.

I felt my stomach drop.

"Diandra, I think...well, actually, I *don't* think that I've ever laughed with Lahn, and he can get attention whenever he wants from a variety of Xacto who follow at the back of this convoy."

"You don't have to have had something to want it or need it, but when you have something you liked...very much...and it is taken away, and you want it back, it can become a hunger. Your husband is hungry, Circe. Warriors don't stay hungry long before they find ways to assuage it. So he will need his cham because *you* will need *your* cham for what he intends to do. Thus, we make camp tonight," she repeated. "I'm sure of it."

I sucked in breath and looked ahead.

This was not great news.

"Now, my dear, before you face what you will face tonight, you must go in prepared," she stated, and I knew what was coming.

"Diandra, I'm not sure I'm ready—"

"Ready or not, Circe, you have no choice. You are queen and must know this as queen, but you are married to the king, and you must understand what drives him and you must understand all of this for your marriage, for your husband, for your people and for you."

I sighed before I muttered, "All right, my friend, let's get this over with."

"Circe, I'm trying to keep you alive."

I blinked and my head snapped toward her.

Then I breathed, "*What?*"

She was looking at me and saw she had my devoted attention therefore she nodded before facing forward again.

"I have explained much about Korwahk and its people. They are savage, primitive even in some ways. They have no government, but they have riches, they have land and they have a king. That king has no court but that does not mean there are no courtly intrigues and politics."

I looked forward too and said, "Diandra, sweetheart, I'm not following."

"That man, Geoffrey, do you remember him?"

I looked at her again and when she turned her eyes to me, I nodded.

She faced forward and I did as well as she went on.

"He is from Middleland. Middleland is ruled by King Baldur. He came into his kingdom as a very young man and ruled before I left the Vale, but also Seerim tells me of him as he is known far because he is a greedy man, wicked and even cruel. He cares little for his people and a great deal for gold. And *land*. And any kinds of riches he can get his hands on. The kinds of riches Korwahk has in abundance."

Oh shit.

As was her way, Diandra continued.

"I have seen this Geoffrey, not often, but I have seen him more than once. Now, there are many men who come from far away to watch the Wife Hunt. They are despicable. They watch it for sordid reasons, and they have no honor. The Dax cares not about them. His focus is The Horde, and they bring coin that they use with his merchants, so he allows it."

I'd noticed those men. And any man who watches a Wife Hunt like a spectator sport definitely had no honor.

Diandra carried on.

"Then there are other men who come who do so to study The Horde, its practices and the Korwahk people. This is usually for academic reasons, but those reasons *could* be nefarious. These men, the Dax considers carefully before he lets them observe, but he does not share openly with them. He is cautious about what they learn and anything they learn, he controls. It would not do for training and tactics to be revealed. The Horde is successful because no one knows the entirety of what makes a warrior and how they wage war. Indeed, you likely missed it but there were no outsiders at the warrior selection or ensuing celebration and there never are. It is forbidden. Another reason Geoffrey's visit to you was not taken kindly. And had you not been a new queen not of the Korwahk before your claiming having recently been claimed in a rite that distressed you, who, it is highly likely, would be alarmed by any violence close to your person, it is also highly likely your honor guard would have dealt with him differently and *swiftly*. We have not seen him since, and I would not need to try very hard to guess why."

Oh man.

I had a feeling Geoffrey was toast.

What an idiot.

"Then," she went on, "there are men who come as ambassadors from other lands. These, the Dax deals with too."

Wow.

There was a lot more to this Dax business than I realized.

Diandra wasn't done.

"I have little doubt that the news the Dax has installed his Dahksahna at his side is news that has traveled far and wide. It has been but two weeks, but horses will have lathered, and boats will have sailed with missives and messengers. The news will travel this earth within months and plots will be hatched within moments of it being reported. And this news will be the news that our new queen is the golden queen of legend. That makes you a valuable commodity, my dear."

I felt ice slide through my veins as I looked at her again. "A commodity?"

"What would the Korwahk people, and The Horde, trade should their golden queen be kidnapped and held for ransom?" she asked back.

I blinked.

"Oh my God," I whispered.

"Held and tortured, parts of her traded for wild riches in hopes of gaining her returned alive if not intact?"

I looked forward again and swallowed.

"Riches would not be traded, Circe, you should know that. The Horde would ride, and blood would be spilled. A great deal of it. Warriors would fall, widows would be made, children would lose fathers."

"Okay." I was still whispering. "I'm getting it."

"No you aren't, not the half of it," Diandra replied.

I closed my eyes and opened them when she kept talking.

"That Geoffrey thought you were from Middleland and having problems adjusting, seething against your claiming, hating your king. He told you he was your friend, but he wanted to earn your trust, even though he is not trustworthy, in order to turn you against your people, whisper in his ear their secrets, provide him the information he needs to give Baldur to take these lands, and their riches, and do it by wiping out The Horde."

"Okay," I repeated, my voice trembling. "I'm getting it."

"No, I'm sorry, Circe, you aren't," she said softly. "He is one of many. Men from anywhere and everywhere will send agents to do the same. But even amongst the riders in this procession, there are those who plot against the Dax, and they too will see you as an instrument to his downfall. They will watch you, my dear, and they will seize on any intimation you give that you might conspire against our king. And to do this, there are eyes and spies everywhere, watching your every move. Including now."

This immediately made me think about The Eunuch, but my thoughts were turned when Diandra kept speaking.

"Our Dax is our Dax because he is strong, because no one can defeat him in battle, but he is also exceptionally bright. He would never remain the Dax if he did not continue to keep the peace, to keep his nation wealthy, to deal with these outside influences with cunning. If he did not, and there have been those who have not, the challenges would be so thick he would face another clash of swords even before the last warrior fell, until he was so exhausted, his head would be gone before he could lift his weapon."

Yikes!

Diandra went on, "Dax Lahn does not fear your turning traitor. He fears your abduction. You did not know it and I did not know it until my husband and I nearly shouted our cham down, but Seerim informed the Dax we were going to the marketplace and the Dax commanded a guard to follow. Teetru sent word we were intending to walk through the camp, and again, a guard followed. Our decision to go visit your friend Narinda was not overheard by Teetru, none of your girls were around, so when we left, they did not see us and did not know where we were going. When Teetru discovered us gone, she sent word to the Dax."

She took in a long breath and kept going.

"Later, too much later, he heard from Feetak that you were with Narinda, but when Feetak went to his cham, we were with Nahka and he had no idea where we were. By the time this was discovered, you and I were wandering the Daxshee, and through very bad luck, we somehow evaded the warriors who had been sent out to find us. This is an extremely unfortunate set of circumstances that, as the minutes ticked by, especially since he saw Geoffrey make contact and knows the ways of King Baldur, which usually are insidious, but no one would put it past him to be violent, made your king very anxious. So, by the time we arrived at your cham, *his* emotions got the better of *him*."

I felt my mouth get tight and I said through stiff lips, "That's still no excuse."

"Yes, my dear, in your land with the father you described you were fortunate enough to have, I can see you believing that, but again, I remind you with some hesitation as I know you dislike it, that you are married to a *Korwahk Horde warrior*."

I turned to look at her, and when she turned to me, I locked my eyes with her.

"That's still no excuse," I repeated quietly.

She held my gaze then heaved a sigh before nodding.

She looked forward again and so did I.

"You're only agreeing in order to agree to disagree, aren't you?" I remarked.

"It seems wise at this juncture," she replied, and I smiled.

Then I couldn't help it, my friend was funny, and after she shared some not so fun information (to say the least), I needed to release some emotion and I decided I'd do it a better way this time. So I burst out laughing again.

Diandra laughed with me.

When I sobered, before I could stop them, my eyes went to Lahn to see he was again turned on his mount toward me.

Oh man.

He called to someone, and I looked away.

Diandra missed this, I could tell, when she urged gently, "Take heed, my beautiful friend, to what I say."

I nodded, turned to her to see she was sober too, very sober and very serious.

And then I said, "I do not agree with the way these people, now *my* people, live their lives, but I promise you, Diandra, I vow that I would do nothing that would bring harm to them." I smiled at her before I whispered, "They *are* my people, you know."

She returned my smile and whispered back, "Use caution, be watchful and stay safe, my queen."

I nodded then I heard galloping hooves and looked forward in time to see the warrior from earlier returning.

"What now?" I muttered as he passed me, circled, came back, and again, this time with a small cry (coming from *me*), he plucked me off Zephyr and he grabbed her reins. She gave a *really* irritated whinny, but he pierced Diandra with a look and barked, "Vayoo!"

Then off we were again at a gallop, but we were heading straight to the front of the line.

Straight to Lahn.

Oh shit.

The warrior slowed us to a walk, got close to Lahn and then *he* plucked me off the warrior's horse and planted me in front of him. Before I settled, his arm got tight around me, my ass slid into his groin, and he looked to the side and said something.

I looked where he was looking and saw Diandra next to us, the warrior gone, Zephyr riderless going with him.

Yep.

Oh shit it was.

"He wishes for me to translate for you both, Dahksahna Circe," Diandra told me.

Great. Just great.

Oh well, again, I had no choice.

"Okay, Diandra," I said softly and aimed my eyes forward.

Lahn spoke and thus commenced our conversation with Diandra interpreting.

"You ride with me until we make camp," Lahn ordered.

There it was. We were making camp.

Damn.

"Okeydokey," I replied flippantly (Diandra didn't translate that, and it got me a squeeze from Lahn's arm when I said it, probably because I said it flippantly).

Lahn spoke. "While we ride, I wish to learn about your mother."

All flippant disappeared, my back went straight, and my gaze went to Diandra. She tipped her head to the side in an "I'm sorry" gesture and I turned to face forward again.

Lahn's arm gave me another squeeze and he growled, "Circe."

I gave in because I didn't have any other choice.

"Okay, what do you want to know?" I asked.

"She was killed," he stated but I shook my head.

"No, she wasn't killed. You can be killed in an accident. She wasn't in an accident. She was murdered."

"By whom?"

"A robber, a thief. She walked in on him while he was in the middle of stealing. He turned his weapon on her and murdered her."

"Was this during war?" he asked.

"No war. No one else died that day. He was a petty thief. It was just an average day. Bad luck, Mom being in the wrong place at the way wrong time, and then she was gone."

Lahn was silent for long moments.

Then, "You had feelings for her?"

"She was my mother," I replied.

"You had feelings for her?" he repeated.

Yeah.

Shit yeah. I had feelings for her.

I sucked in breath and said softly, "I loved her more than anything on this earth, except my pop. She was a good mom. No, a *great* one. She died a pointless death at the hands of a stupid, reckless man, and I've lived with that knowledge my whole life...or the length of it I led when I didn't have her."

Again, he was silent for a while.

Then, "And who took your father's life?"

I closed my eyes.

"A dream," I whispered.

"What?"

I pulled in breath and opened my eyes.

"He died in his sleep," I lied a lie that cut me to the quick. "I don't know how."

"He commanded men?"

I smiled a sad smile. "Yeah, he commanded men."

"Was he a king?"

My smile got sadder. "Yes, of a very small kingdom."

"So you were princess."

I pressed my lips together to bite back the tears.

Then I nodded my head and whispered, "Yes, I was definitely a princess."

"And now you are queen."

"Yes, now I am queen."

"Your father would want that for you, is this not true?" he asked, and I blinked.

Boy, he orchestrated that well, clever bastard.

"Kah Dax—" I started but stopped when his arm squeezed the breath out of me.

I felt his lips at my ear where he growled, "Lahn."

"Lahn," I wheezed, and his arm loosened but I said no more.

This got me a, "I asked you a question, Circe."

"No," I answered. "No, he would not care if I was queen. He'd be happy I married a peasant, just as long as it made *me* happy. He'd even be happy that I was a slave, just as long as I spent my days doing something that made me content."

"No king would want that," Lahn stated.

"They would if they loved their daughters."

"You are wrong," he informed me.

"I most definitely am not," I informed him.

"You are, my tigress. A man would want his daughter showered with riches. He would want an army to be at her service to keep her safe from harm. He would want her to have the adulation of a nation of people. He would want her to be the consort of a leader of men. And if he could not find that for her, he'd want her to be in the bed of a free man, a strong man, a brave man, one who provides for her and one who has the respect of his brothers. I am a man, we may have daughters, and this is what I would wish for them."

I blinked at the landscape.

Oh my God, God, *God.*

How could I...?

Oh my *God, God, God.*

How could I forget about birth control?

Oh my God!

"Circe?" he called on another arm squeeze.

"What?" I whispered.

"Did you hear what I said?"

"Yeah." I was still whispering.

"You have no response?"

"No, uh...you're right. Showered with riches, army at her service, adulation, consort to a leader. That all sounds good. Pop would dig all that."

"Dig?" Diandra asked.

I turned distracted eyes to her.

"Like. He'd like that," I explained.

Diandra nodded and translated.

I looked forward.

"She jokes," Lahn muttered (but Diandra still interpreted).

"No," I said softly and shook my head once. "No, I'm not joking. But the truth is, Pop wouldn't like that. What he would like is that a man would wish to give his daughter that and that man would want the same for *his* daughters."

Diandra hadn't finished translating when Lahn's hand came up making his arm slant at an angle across my chest so his fingers could curve around my neck, and he could pull me so my full back was tight against his chest.

"We will make warriors," he told me quietly, his voice deeper than normal.

Oh God.

"Right," I whispered.

"But we will make daughters too so I can find them kings who wish to hand them kingdoms."

Oh fucking God.

"Right," I repeated on another whisper.

"You have rare beauty the like I have never seen, but you will be more beautiful heavy with my seed," he stated softly.

At his words, my breasts swelled, and my head got light both at the same time. The combination was an unusual sensation and one that I did not like.

Oh man, if he didn't shut up, I was going to pass out.

"I really need to learn the Korwahk language so Diandra doesn't have to translate conversations like this," I grumbled, Lahn chuckled then his lips went to my ear.

There, he murmured in my language, "Yes, my Circe, you do."

I blinked.

Jeez, was he some kind of language savant or what? He was picking up

English *way* faster than I was picking up Korwahk, and he only had me and Diandra to listen to.

"You're freaking me out," I whispered.

"Sorry, my dear, I didn't catch that," Diandra said, and I didn't even have to look at her to know she was fighting back laughter. And losing.

"He's freaking me out, um...shocking me, surprising me but in a not so good way. He's learning our language very fast and it's not natural."

"It isn't surprising that he would pick things up quickly. He meets often with ambassadors, dignitaries and foreigners from many lands. It is important for him to hear and understand them therefore it is known widely our Dax speaks seven languages fluently, my dear," Diandra told me.

I whipped around so fast Lahn had to jerk his head back and I stared up at him.

"You speak seven languages?" I breathed, Diandra translated, and he nodded so I leaned in and kept breathing, "*Seven*?"

His eyes roamed my face and one side of his lips twitched before he replied in English, "Yes, Circe, seven."

"Then why don't you know English?" I shouted. "I mean, Valearian or whatever!"

He waited for the translation and then Diandra translated his response. "Because it is spoken in Hawkvale and Lunwyn, which are peaceful nations that do not cross the Green Sea to make war or find trouble. And it is spoken in Middleland, which is ruled by a tyrant who I would not honor by learning his language."

Shit, that made sense.

Still, it was annoying.

"Well, unlucky for you that your wife speaks the one language probably in this world that you don't speak."

"No," he replied. "There are many lands too far away to wage war on Korwahk whose languages I do not know. None of them speak Valearian, which brings me to the question of what small kingdom *you* are from."

Uh-oh.

I turned forward, mostly to buy time.

"Circe," he called then Diandra translated the rest. "Look at me."

I bit my lip and turned back to him.

His eyebrows went up with his question. "What kingdom are you from?"

"Um..." Shit. Well, here goes. "Seattle."

His brows descended but only to knit over narrowed eyes. "Seattle?"

"Yes, it's a *very* small kingdom," I told him.

"Like Bellebryn?" he asked.

Hell, I didn't even know what Bellebryn was.

Well, I had a fifty-fifty chance of getting it right.

"Yes."

He nodded.

Shoo.

"Where is it?" he went on.

Shit.

"Uh...over the Green Sea?" I made another guess.

"Are you *asking* me where it is, my tigress, or *telling* me?" he queried.

God, why was he so cunning and clever and kingly and never missed a trick?

The jerk.

"Telling you," I answered. "But, uh...I can't really say *exactly* where it is because I'm not very good at geography. I never was."

At least that was true.

His eyes narrowed again. "Tigress Circe, you were on a ship that was overcome and looted by pirates, and when they docked, you were taken by Korwahk scouts as they were moving you to shore. How could you travel from a faraway land and not know where you'd traveled to get where you landed?"

Uh...*what*?

"What?" I whispered.

"Do you not remember how you came into the possession of a Korwahk scout?"

No, actually, I didn't. And actually, I never thought about it.

Shit.

"Circe," Lahn warned.

I focused on him and thought fast.

"Well, uh, when we were, you know...*traveling* and uh...*sailing*, um... most of the time I was seasick and the rest of the time I was reading a book, so I didn't pay a lot of attention and the, uh...pirates weren't very chatty."

He stared down at me. Then he looked over my head.

"I have never heard of this Seattle," he muttered.

"It's tiny," I told him, and his eyes came back to me. I lifted a thumb and forefinger with about a half an inch of space, squinted through it to look in his eyes and emphasized, "Teeny tiny." I dropped my hand. "It isn't even like a kingdom, as such, more like a...*city*."

He stared at me a moment before he again looked over my head and murmured, "Bellebryn."

Whatever.

I needed to move us on.

"My mother looked like me," I told him in an effort to change the subject. His focus came back to me so I kept going. "It's weird, um...strange. My pop was dark, uh...like you. He even had olive skin. But she was fair, very fair. Usually dark is a dominant trait, but I didn't get anything from Pop. I got my mom's hair, her eyes, her skin—"

He cut me off to ask, "Her eyes?"

I nodded and suddenly he dipped his face closer to mine and his hand came to my jaw.

I braced at this quick movements and it was a good thing I did when he spoke.

"If you're given the opportunity to look deep enough, you can see a person's spirit in their eyes, but usually they are guarded, kept safe. Not you, my tigress. The night of your claiming, even in the moonlight, I could see your spirit shining from your eyes. You hold your spirit close to the surface for all to behold and it is the most beautiful thing I have ever seen."

Oh.

My.

God.

Unfortunately, he kept talking.

"So if she gave you your eyes, my golden doe, I can see your father mourning your mother long after her death. If you share your spirit with someone, their hold on you will never fade away."

"Stop talking," I whispered and felt the tears shimmering, ready to fall.

Lahn saw them and his hand glided up to my cheek, his thumb sliding below my eye, releasing the tear suspended there and capturing it against his skin.

"My tigress weeps," he murmured.

My eyes slid away.

He again spoke. "You've had enough, my Circe. Face forward and ride with your husband in silence. We make camp soon."

Great, something else to look forward to.

I nodded and turned around.

Lahn said something to Diandra, and I looked her way to see her smiling at me, eyes alight, as they would be considering she was my

Korwahk- crazy romantic friend, and I just stopped myself from rolling mine.

Her horse faded back into the warriors.

I looked forward and tried to focus on the landscape and my next trauma and anything else that entered my brain that was *not* the words my husband just said to me.

But this was difficult when his arm slanted across my chest again, fingers curling around my neck in order to hold me close, his thumb sliding up and down my throat in an idle caress I tried not to think was sweet (but it was).

So, the fact was, it wasn't difficult.

It was impossible.

17
THE CHALLENGE

I was turned and lifted then moving, cradled in Lahn's arms.

I opened my eyes to see the Daxshee was up around us, torchlight glowing everywhere.

We'd stopped by a small, rushing creek where there was an abundance of spiked grass and bowing, wispy willow trees, their green so green against the backdrop of the stark cream stone, dirt and sand landscape that it was stunning.

It became clear to me in short order that the Dahksahna didn't assist her slaves in setting up the cham.

This became clear when hides and cushions were produced, a small jug of wine, another of water and a platter of food. Further, Ghost, who had (my poor baby) been caged for nearly six days, was let loose so I could feed and watch over her while my girls worked, and the young men erected our tent.

And this was clear because Teetru made it clear with lots of shakes of her head and hands up pressing the air to tell me I was to take a load off while they worked their asses off.

This did not sit well with me, but again I had no choice. And, truth be told, I was exhausted from the ride. And I was exhausted from my chats with Diandra and Lahn. And after I had three glasses of wine while I ate, watched with no small amount of fascination what could only be described as a practiced dance of the Daxshee rising (they didn't mess around, they clearly did this often, it was swift and also weirdly graceful) and played with Ghost, it wasn't a surprise that, when Ghost grew drowsy, I grew drowsy with her.

Thus, I tucked her to my front, settled in on the hides and cushions and fell asleep.

Now I was half-awake, in Lahn's arms and heading to our cham, which was glowing with the candlelight dancing within.

I turned my head, whispered, "Ghost," and got a squeeze of Lahn's arms as my eyes found my pet who was being scooped up by Gaal and carried away.

Well, I guessed that meant Ghost was sleeping elsewhere that night. Not unusual. Lahn had allowed me my cub, but he had yet to allow her in our bed.

He bent low, me in his arms, entered the tent, and I sleepily took it in.

It looked exactly the same and everything was set up. It had to have been only a couple of hours and it was all done.

Jeez, these people knew what they were doing.

Lahn set me on my feet by the bed, moved away and Jacanda and Beetus were there immediately. I tried to blink away the exhaustion that fogged my mind and the dull ache of fatigue that made my body heavy and helped them disrobe me. Packa came forward with a warm, wet cloth and glided it over my limbs which felt like heaven. Except for quick wash ups, I had no bath for five days and had been wearing the same clothes since we left. When they packed up our belongings, they stayed packed while we rode and only the bare necessities were produced to eat, drink and sleep.

Jacanda dropped a Korwahkian-style nightgown over my head, this one a lilac so pale it was nearly cream. She tied the drawstring over my breasts then looked up at me and gave me a tired smile.

I lifted a hand to cup her cheek and smiled back at her.

"Shahsha, kah Jacanda, boh na trahyay, kah fauna," *Thank you, my Jacanda, now you sleep, my doe,* I whispered and was too tired to see the warm surprise flash in her eyes.

I just turned, pulled back the silk, collapsed into bed, tugged the silk up and closed my eyes.

I was out within seconds.

I was back in what felt like no more than a minute.

And I was back because the silk was pulled off me and there were big hands at my hips turning me to my back. My eyes opened as those hands spread my legs and my fatigue disappeared when my eyes focused on Lahn settling between them, his hands pulling the silk of my nightgown up to my hips.

"What are you doing?" I asked.

It came out breathy, but he didn't answer. His weight hit me, but he was taking most of it in a forearm in the bed. One of his hands came up, and quickly, his fingers yanked the drawstring above my breasts and the tie came undone.

I wrapped fingers around his wrist and snapped a repeated, "What are you doing?"

His eyes came to mine and his were burning.

Oh shit.

I already pretty much knew what he was doing but now I *seriously* knew what he was doing.

His head started to descend.

I blinked because it was doing it in a way that it looked like he intended to kiss me.

I turned my head swiftly to the side at the last minute. I also put my hands on his shoulders and pushed at the same time I bucked, but the massive weight of his hard body didn't move.

"No," I stated firmly when his lips touched my neck. "This isn't happening. I'm tired, kah Dax, and I need sleep."

His head came up sharply and his hand rounded my jaw, turning my head and forcing me to look at him.

"Kah Lahn," he growled.

Oh no.

No, he didn't. He didn't get to do this, and he didn't get to tell me what he was to me.

No...he...did...*not.*

"Kah *Dax,*" I hissed.

His face got close to mine so his eyes were all I could see, and when his mouth moved, I could almost feel it against my lips.

"Kah *Lahn,*" he growled again.

I glared into his eyes and whispered furiously, "*Never.*"

"Oh no, Circe, not never. Boh," he returned quietly, his head slanted, and I swear to God he intended to kiss me.

Before his lips could touch mine, my hands pressed down on his shoulders and I heaved myself upward, sliding up the pillows.

This was a mistake. My nightgown was loosened, and it slid down, exposing my breasts and my heave had taken that area right into the target zone of his mouth.

And being Lahn, he didn't miss the opportunity. His hand left my jaw, curved under my breast and lifted it as his other arm pushed under me, locked around me, and then his mouth closed over my nipple where he instantly sucked hard.

Automatically, my back arched.

Oh man, that felt good.

Fire shot through me, and before I knew what I was doing, the fingers on both hands curled around his head.

Damn.

No, no, he didn't get to do this.

My fingers fisted in his loosened hair and pulled back.

"No," I whispered.

He stopped sucking but only so his tongue could swirl, and it was debatable, but I was thinking that felt better. Then I was wondering what on earth I was thinking.

"No!" I cried.

He started sucking again and I felt a curl of excitement in my belly and wetness surge between my legs.

Crap!

As he continued to draw my nipple in (and alternately swirl), I squirmed under him and his hand left my breast, trailed down my ribs, my belly and then in and I felt his finger fill me.

Oh God, I liked that.

Shit, but I liked that.

His mouth released my nipple, his arm around me yanked me down under him but his finger stayed planted and his thumb tweaked my clit.

My hips jerked.

"My Circe," he said, his voice low and thick. "Wet."

I was thinking it was not good he could pick up languages so easily. I was thinking it sucked.

I held on to my fight and snapped, "You don't get this, kah Dax."

"I do," he returned.

My eyes narrowed, and with everything I had, I bent my legs, planted my feet in the bed, surged my hips up and pushed at his shoulders, succeeding in bucking him off, taking him to his back. Then I was straddling him, bent over, looking down in his annoyingly beautiful face that was surrounded by his unbelievably fantastic fucking hair.

"You *don't*!" I yelled.

His torso knifed up and his arm still around me locked tight.

Uh-oh.

Clearly, I hadn't thought my strategy through.

He looked up into my eyes and I saw his were burning, but there was a light in them. It was bright, and if I read it right, it was permeated with both humor and triumph.

"She bares her claws," he muttered, and I knew he liked it.

Yep, humor and triumph.

"*Argh!*" I cried on another heave to get away, but there was no getting away.

Nope. None.

And my battle was about to get a lot more difficult. I knew this when his hand still between my legs moved to wrap around his cock and his arm around me moved me so he could slide the tip of it in the wetness between my legs.

I bit my lip. That felt nice and I knew it felt a whole lot nicer when his shaft was embedded deep inside.

And I wanted it.

"Kah Lahn." His words were an order for me to repeat it, his voice was growing even deeper, getting rough.

He wanted inside.

Oh God, I liked that too.

"No," I denied, and the tip of his cock slid over my clit.

My hips jerked again.

Lahn smiled.

God!

He was so annoying!

"Kah Lahn, Circe," he ordered again, and when I made no response, his hard cock slid over my clit again. "Kah Lahn," he repeated, his voice now rough.

"No," I whispered.

"Kah Lahn," he growled.

"No!"

He pushed me slightly down and started rubbing the tip of his cock hard against my clit in a way that felt so good, my bones dissolved, and my hands moved to either side of his neck to hold on so I didn't melt into a puddle.

My lips parted, my head went slightly back, and my eyes went half-mast.

His arm didn't need to hold me to him, not anymore. I was holding on, moving my hips to rub myself against his shaft so his hand slid up into my hair, tilting my head to face him and my eyes focused dazedly on his.

"Lahnahsahna, *kah Lahn,*" he ordered, his voice now hoarse.

Oh well, fuck it.

They were just words.

Right?

"Kah Lahn," I whispered, his hand instantly shifted his cock so the tip was inside me then moved away, his arm curved around my hips, and he drove me down, filling me.

My head flew back, and I ground down with my hips to take him deeper.

"Yes," I breathed, my fingers digging into the muscles of his neck.

His arm around my hips tensed, drawing me up then pushing me down, and I started moving, slow, my head tipping forward again so I could look in his eyes.

Triumph, desire, satisfaction—God, it was hot.

His hand moved from my head, down my shoulder, my arm, to wrap around my wrist. He shoved our hands between us, pressing my finger to my clit and rolling. My hips jerked and I whimpered, but I took his hint, took over, gliding up and down, slow, sweet, as my finger rolled. Both his hands slid up my body to rest, palms at my jaws, fingers in my hair cupping the sides of my head.

Then he tipped it toward his, slanting his own, and again, I thought he was going to kiss me.

I had his cock inside me, and I liked it. No, I fucking *loved* it.

I'd give myself that, and in doing so, I'd give it up to him.

But he couldn't have all of me.

I moved my head at the last second, sliding my lips down his jaw to his neck. I buried my face there, shoved my hand under his arm and wrapped my arm around his back.

And I drove down on him faster, grinding harder, taking him deep as I circled my clit with my finger and whimpered into his skin.

His hands glided down, arms curving around me, fingers drifting as mine dug into the muscles of his back, and I went faster.

"Kah bahsah lapay rah. Zah xaxsah lapay hahnee rah. *Sahna,*"* Lahn whispered in my ear.

The rumble of the words gliding along my skin, over my breasts, down between my legs, it happened. My back arched, my hair flew out and I came.

I was nowhere near done when Lahn flipped me, yanked my knees high and pounded hard and deep. His hand cupped around my jaw, thumb one side, fingers against my cheek and he held my face steady as his bent into mine.

I was staring into his heated gaze, my eyelids lowered, my orgasm taking its sweet, sweet time to drift away, my thighs pressed deep into his sides, my hands low, fingers curled into the clenching muscles of his ass as he drove hard and deep while our breath mingled.

"Fuck me, baby," I breathed, and he pounded harder.

"Yes, kah Lahnahsahna," he whispered.

"God," I whispered back, my nails digging into his skin, my thighs pressing tighter, "I love the feel of you."

He closed his eyes, his fingers tensing on my face and his head snapped back, the muscles in his neck straining, veins popping out as he planted himself deep and tight and grunted his climax so loud the sound filled the tent.

It had to be said, I liked that too.

When he was done, his head dropped, his hand at my jaw tilting mine to the side, and I felt his heavy breaths against my neck. My arms moved to circle him, and his head came up. He tilted my face back toward him, his eyes caught mine, his breath still labored, and he moved again to kiss me.

I jerked against his hold, and it instantly got tight, but his mouth stopped moving toward mine.

Our eyes clashed and I knew he knew I was withholding from him, and my breath caught because I also knew a Korwahk warrior would not like that, not at all.

Then he growled, "You're *my* gold, nahna xaxsah is *my* hahnee rah. Kay jahnan nahna lisa, na *uvan tee luh kay*. Ana kay jahnan nahna pahnsahna, Circe. Kay nayeesan tee. *Fahzah.*"**

Okay, it couldn't be said that I understood everything Lahn said, but I understood enough that I knew I'd managed to lay down a challenge. He was a warrior who had been trained since he was a little boy to face any challenge and best it, and he'd just vowed to me that he would win.

Shit, I had a feeling I was screwed.

But being me, I didn't give up.

"You got lucky tonight, big guy," I whispered. "But so did I. Now, I'm *really* tired so will you get off me so I can *trahyay*?"

He scowled down at me a second, his hand still holding my face. Then his eyes moved. Drifting, they caught on the bruise still marking my cheekbone. I watched the glower fade slowly as his expression went soft. His hand tipped my chin down and held me still while his lips slid across my bruise.

I closed my eyes.

Shit, I really freaking *hated* it when he was sweet.

I felt his forehead on mine and my eyes opened.

"Yes, my Circe, you sleep," he said softly then he moved his head, let my jaw go and rubbed his nose along the side where his thumb had held me. He gently pulled out and slid his body down and partially to my side, tucking me underneath him, tangling his legs in mine.

I sighed and was so exhausted and sated I couldn't help but let his warmth relax me.

My eyes drifted closed.

They drifted right back open when his arm tightened in an affectionate squeeze and he whispered in my ear, "Anka, ta linay tera leenyahso na lapay, claws against steel."***

He sounded tired, satisfied and like he was looking forward to tomorrow.

Like, a lot.

Seriously, Lahn learning English so fast sucked.

And even more seriously, I knew I was screwed.

**Translation:* My wife is gold. Her cunt is liquid gold. *Beautiful*."

***Translation:* "You're *my* gold, your cunt is *my* liquid gold. I will have your mouth, you *will give it to me*. Then I will have your spirit, Circe. I will own it. *Always*."

****Translation:* "Tomorrow, we see how skilled you are, claws against steel."

18

THE HORDE

My eyelids floated open when I heard the cham flaps slap back and I took in the bright sunlight on the walls of the cham.

It had to be late morning.

I arched my back slightly in a light stretch and tipped my chin down on the pillows to see which one of my girls had come in.

I blinked when I saw a pair of muscular legs in hides coming my way.

My eyes flew up and Lahn was looking down at me with a seriously hot, seriously satisfied look on his face.

He aimed his ass to the bed as I rolled to my back and that was when it hit me that my nightgown was bunched at my waist, exposing me top and bottom. He hadn't pulled the silk over us last night, instead, warding off the chill with his body.

My hand flew to my nightgown but didn't make it even close. It was captured in a firm grip, pushed back and pressed to the bed. My focus shot to him as I tried with my other hand which was captured too. Both were pulled up over my head and held in one of his while his eyes followed his other hand that drifted palm flat from my chest, between my breasts, down my midriff, over the silk then he cupped me between my legs.

Shit.

His eyes came back to mine, and I skewered him with a glare.

"You love the feel of me," he whispered, and my glare slipped as I blinked.

"Wh-what?" I whispered back.

His finger slid inside and that felt so flipping great, coupled with that look on his face, my lips parted, and a swirl of pleasure uncurled in my belly.

He bent slightly more toward me and repeated, "My tigress loves the feel of me."

His finger moved.

Shit.

"Lahn," I breathed as it hit me. I'd said that to him last night, and this morning he'd seen to finding out what it meant. "You've been talking to Seerim."

He smiled, and damn, it was sexy.

Yep, he'd been talking to Seerim.

First on my morning's agenda, find Diandra and kill her.

His finger moved, sliding out and in. "Sah me lapay the part of me you love gahn tee jahkal,"* he murmured.

Okay, no.

First up, Lahn was going to play with me, give me an orgasm and *then* I was going to find Diandra and kill her, the crazy Korwahkian matchmaker.

And I was right about the morning's agenda, with one hand holding my wrists over my head, his other hand worked between my legs until my back arched, my hips ground down on his fingers and I cried out when he made me come really freaking hard.

It was still washing through me when he let my wrists go and tugged me gently into his lap, wrapped his arms around me, buried his face in my neck and cradled me.

"My Circe's claws are not so sharp," he whispered there.

My body tensed.

Seriously, he was *annoying*.

I lifted my hands to his chest and shoved hard enough that he moved back an inch as I snapped, "Go away, Lahn, I need a bath."

His head came up and his silently laughing eyes caught mine. "Yes, kah Dahksahna, me too."

Oh shit.

He went on, "Kah bahsah bathes zah Lahn, kay bathe kah bahsah."

He said, "My wife bathes her Lahn, I bathe my wife".

Oh *shit*!

"Lahn—" I started, he grinned then turned his head and barked, "Teetru!"

The cham flaps instantly opened and I pressed my chest to his, my arms going around him to hide my nudity (not that I needed to, my girls had seen me plenty of times, but it was habit) as my head twisted around to see all five of my girls traipsing in with buckets of steaming water, cloths and rough, creamy disks of soap. They set them down in a new area I hadn't noticed last night that was stone and grass and no rugs.

The mess we made with Lahn's bath was not to be repeated, I saw. We now had a shower area.

Crap.

They shuffled out without looking at us.

"Lahn—" I started, but I was up because he was up and carrying me. "Lahn!"

"Quiet," he ordered.

"Lahn!" I snapped.

He dropped my feet, they hit stone and my nightgown immediately slid down to my ankles. Before I could decide to go for the nightgown or just make a run for it, his hides were at his. He stepped out of them and bent to grab the handle of a bucket. I prepared for flight, but he caught me at the waist, yanked me into him, my body slammed against his and not a second later he poured a whole bucketful of warm water on our heads.

The bucket clattered to the ground as Lahn's arm tightened around me and the fingers of his other hand slid up the back of my neck and into my wet hair as I spluttered.

Once I'd blinked the water away, I saw his face close and felt his hot, slick body sliding against mine.

It went without saying that felt nice.

"Kah bahsah bathes zah Lahn, I bathe my Lahnahsahna," he said softly.

Then he bent us both to the side as he reached for the soap.

Oh well, whatever.

I needed a bath, and he undoubtedly did too.

"Whatever," I muttered, pulled the soap out of his hand and pressed it against the gorgeous brown skin on his massive, fantastic chest and it didn't take long (approximately a second) before I really got into what I was doing.

About a second after that, both his arms locked around me and he burst out laughing.

He knew I was into what I was doing.

Yep, he was definitely *annoying*.

When he'd stopped laughing, I tilted my head back and gave him a scrunchy face in an effort to show him exactly how annoying I thought he was.

His dark eyes took in my scrunchy face, his lips gave me a smile and his arms gave me a squeeze.

Again, whatever.

I focused on the task at hand. Then he focused on his task.

Needless to say, this added nuance to bath time with Lahn made it even more fun.

Yep, I was definitely screwed.

**Translation:* "This is not the part of me you love but it must do."

"Oh Circe, my lovely, I'm so sorry. Golly, I can't imagine my Feetak ever taking a hand to me," Narinda breathed.

Her Feetak.

Yep, ole Feetak was in there and I meant that in more ways than one.

That didn't take long.

"I'm okay," I promised her, reached out and squeezed her hand. She gave me her small, weird smile and squeezed mine back.

Then I looked out into the Daxshee.

Narinda and I were lounging on hides and cushions outside Lahn and my cham while I kept my eye on Ghost, who was wandering around, being cute, attacking things and generally annoying passersby, to which I'd call out, "Kay tingay," which meant, "I'm sorry," and I'd get smiles as they moved away.

Our cham had been set up a bit away from the others, close to the creek on a slight rise, so we could see most of the Daxshee spread out below (this gave evidence that The Eunuch did not set up the Daxshee the same every time).

It was late afternoon. Narinda had come around earlier, we'd had lunch, and now we were sipping fruit juice, chatting and watching the activity of the Daxshee. There was a long, wide gauze fall set up that provided shade that we could laze under. This was welcome but unnecessary. Nearly my whole body was a golden honey color from riding for days in the sun. But it was nice to have a break from it.

I'd just told Narinda the story of the bruise that she informed me looked a lot better.

But it wasn't gone.

And I couldn't allow myself to forget it, no matter how sweet and sexy my husband was being.

He might be the tiger and a warrior who thrived on challenge, but I was a tigress raised by the kind, loving king of a small, loving kingdom, and I knew what I deserved and it was *not* what Lahn handed me a week ago.

So he had a fight on his hands, one I was determined to win.

"Oh look! There's Diandra! Poyah, Diandra!" Narinda exclaimed, waving frantically.

I followed her gaze.

Then mine narrowed.

Diandra grinned shamelessly at my narrow-eyed look, came right up and gave Narinda a "poyah" as she dropped into a lounge on the hides, grabbed a big cushion and shoved it under her side and then helped herself to fruit juice.

Her dancing eyes came to me. "How are you, my queen?"

Now she was just *trying* to be irritating, calling me her queen.

"I'm not talking to you," I informed her, and she burst out laughing.

"What's this?" Narinda asked.

"Oh, nothing," Diandra answered as I glared at her. "Unless you're talking about our Dax's groan of gratification that half the Daxshee heard ringing from his cham last night. Seerim and I aren't that close, but it still woke us both up."

Narinda's wide eyes flew to me, and a wobbly smile hit her lips.

I kept up the glare but ratcheted it up as high as I could take it.

Diandra ignored me, and just like Diandra, kept right on yapping.

"Angry words were heard from our queen, but I have inside information that she told our king she loved the feel of him so I suspect things eventually went well for her last night too."

Narinda let out a giggle you could tell she tried to suppress...and failed.

I turned my face away.

Narinda's voice came to me. "Have you forgiven him, Circe?"

"No," I bit off.

"Her head hasn't but other parts of her have," Diandra chimed in, and my attention sliced to her.

"Are you *trying* to irritate me?" I snapped.

"Yes," she replied. "You're very endearing when you're angry." She looked at Narinda. "Our king calls it his tigress baring her claws. My husband tells me he speaks openly and often about it, so far as *bragging* about it. He, too, clearly likes it...even more than me."

"Will you *shut up*?" I clipped, and she threw her head back and laughed.

She focused on me, still chuckling. "The Daxshee is abuzz, as usual, and as usual of late, it's all about their Dax and golden Dahksahna. The Dax emerges bathed from his cham and doesn't visit the Xacto. His laughter is heard ringing from his cham, amongst other things. He delays the ride until he's content with her health. He rides at the front of his warriors with his wife tucked close. He gives her a horse—"

I cut her off with, "You have a horse."

Her chuckles died, her eyes got serious, and I knew Korwahk wisdom was coming even before she replied quietly, "I do, my dear. My Seerim gave me a horse two years after I was claimed."

She looked at Narinda.

"You see, the warriors, they war which means they fall. The Horde is everything. They do form friendships, in battle they will act to protect their brothers-in-arms, but they hold themselves distant. Too many opportunities to lose people who are in your heart. It beats down the spirit, weakens it. But a warrior's horse, now that's a different story," she explained. "Warrior and horse ride into battle connected. The horse of a warrior is part of him. They actually consider their steeds an extension of their own limbs. I've heard Seerim tell me battle stories of warriors receiving wounds they would not get if they didn't move to protect their horse from steel."

"Golly," Narinda whispered.

"Indeed," Diandra stated. "This is why, my dears, a newly claimed wife is set to straddling her husband's steed. It is akin to straddling *him*. But it also is a ceremonial offering from warrior to horse on the night a warrior lets in the new most important being in his life, as, while straddling his horse, his new bride will leak his seed which, I think you both have come to understand, is vital to any warrior. Therefore, they feel it is an extremely worthy offering to a creature they feel keeps them safe, makes them strong and is an extension of themselves."

Yeah, any man, in this world or my own, thinks that kind of offering is "extremely worthy."

Jeez.

I scrunched my nose at Narinda, and she scrunched hers back.

Diandra ignored our looks and kept speaking.

"So, obviously, horses as a whole are revered greatly by The Horde. It would be a guess, but a good one, that a vast amount of warriors pray to the

Horse God. And, therefore, owning a mount is considered a privilege. One must *deserve* their own mount. Young warriors do not get their own mount until they are chosen to perform their first kill which means they'll have trained for more than a decade before they acquire a steed. That said, it is no surprise that a husband does not bestow such an honor on his wife until he feels she deserves it. For instance, after she has successfully given him their first son or she has spent much time being a good warrior's wife, providing for his needs. Therefore, the Dax, bestowing a mount of such beauty to his new bride is cause for much gossip. Gossip," her eyes came to me, "which was mostly speculation until, of course, his cry was heard last night, and his mirth heard this morning."

Her face grew wicked as it returned to Narinda.

"It would seem, sweet Narinda, our Dax's new wife is providing quite well for his needs."

I stared at her, too shocked at the knowledge that Lahn had given me a horse far earlier than most wives earned one to be irritated at her teasing.

"He is a contradiction," Narinda muttered, and my gaze slid to her to see her staring unseeing into the Daxshee. "From what Circe told me about his mark, I do not wish to like him, and every time I see him, he frightens me. Yet much of what you say shows there is a great deal of soft under that hard."

"I'm not certain, sweet Narinda, it is the soft our queen likes..." She paused and finished with emphasis, "But *the hard*."

"Diandra!" I snapped but she chuckled as another giggle escaped Narinda.

Just then, the object of our conversation strode around a cham. He wasn't close but he wasn't far, and still his raw energy invaded all around.

I drew in breath as he stopped to talk to two warriors who waylaid him. Then I allowed my eyes to move over my husband.

Okay, well, I wouldn't admit it out loud, but I did have to admit to myself that I definitely liked the hard.

"Oh, what's this?" Diandra muttered.

I tore my attention from Lahn and glanced to my right to see a young boy, slight, perhaps eleven, twelve years old and definitely not of the warrior sort. This was probably why he wasn't off training somewhere but instead at my cham carrying what looked a great deal like a guitar. And it sounded like one when my eyes hit him, he swallowed, looked up to a woman who was standing beside him and he started strumming and then, falteringly, singing.

The woman moved forward and laid a flower carefully on the hides well away from me or my girls before she scuttled back, her gaze shooting in Lahn's direction and back to me as her boy sang.

He looked nervous and kept screwing up the chords and he wasn't the greatest singer in the world, it must be said, but he didn't do half bad and it was definitely sweet.

But his mother gazed down on him like the sun's rays sprouted out his mouth with his voice and I could tell she thought he could do no wrong and that was probably why she took him to her queen to bestow what she thought was a precious gift.

I smiled encouragingly at him as he lost his way. He found it and kept going and I nodded my head continuously to keep him going.

I saw movement out of the corner of my eye. I looked that way and tensed. I knew Diandra and Narinda saw it too because I felt them tense.

Dortak was striding through the chams, a dirty-looking, rough-woven bandage around his middle, the carves on his chest and face had not been stitched but were glistening with goo and were clearly not going to heal very well. But they were healing.

His bride, clean but bruised up her arms, around her neck and with a cut lip, stumbled behind him.

She was wearing her claiming necklace. He was wearing a claiming chain around his waist. It was attached to her necklace, but he had it in his fist and was yanking on it as he dragged her behind him.

Jeez, seriously, this guy was the king of dicks.

He stopped at a warrior that was about five feet from Lahn and he started talking to him. As he did, he yanked her to her knees beside him and his hand fisted in her hair to hold her there. Not that he had to, she wasn't going anywhere. Not without his permission.

My eyes moved over her, and my heart hurt as they did, clenching more and more the more I took in.

Whatever girl she once was, now was gone. Everything was gone. Her expression was blank, her eyes distant. She was so deep in her head that she probably didn't even know where she was.

I looked swiftly at Lahn to see he and the two warriors he was talking to were eyeing the couple with tight faces.

But they did not say a word. Lahn simply turned his back on Dortak and resumed his conversation.

Without thinking, I turned to the boy singing, pushed to my knees and reached out toward his instrument, wiggling my fingers at it and smiling at him. His strumming faltered as did his singing. He looked up at his mother. She jutted her chin to me. He stopped making music and handed his guitar-like thing to me.

One of my two lost loves was guitar crazy. He had four of them, two acoustic, two electric, and he taught me how to play. Then he got shitty when I took to it and quickly got better than him (one of the reasons, I kid you not, why I was convinced he broke up with me, but when I threw it in his face, he swore it wasn't, but I knew it was).

When he left me, I bought my own guitar and always, every week, twice, three times, sometimes every day, I found time to play.

And I couldn't give anything to Dortak's wife, me being queen or not, except what that boy gave to me.

So I sat back on my calves as I tested the strings and the frets, found my way and then started to sing Israel Kamakawiwo'ole's "Over the Rainbow/Wonderful World" but with a guitar and not a ukulele.

You couldn't say my singing voice was a lot better than the boy's, but it didn't have to be. Even if you couldn't understand the words, the song couldn't be anything but beautiful. I kept my eyes glued to her as she stared at the ground, and I hoped somewhere in her head the words to two sweet, hopeful songs meshed together in one beautiful one penetrated and colored that dark world she was living in with all the vibrant shades of a rainbow.

Then, slowly, her head lifted, her eyes found mine, and I did what I thought any good queen would do. And that was all she *could* do to provide what she could for her people—even if it wasn't much and it was just one of those people.

And I knew right when the song got in there. Her eyes drifted closed, her face grew soft, and I hoped to all that was holy that in that moment she was over the rainbow in a wonderful world.

When I stopped playing, her eyes opened, and I smiled at her.

But Dortak yanked her chain which wrenched her neck and the soft look disappeared instantly from her face as a flash of pain replaced it.

The moment he did this, I heard a deep, male voice call out tersely and that voice was really pissed off.

And it was not Lahn's voice.

I looked to my left and saw it was Bohtan. I also saw I had drawn a crowd.

I further saw Lahn's dark eyes riveted to me in a way he'd never looked at me before, but one that made my belly dip and my heart feel light.

"You disrespect your queen," Diandra whispered, and I started then looked at her to see her eyes on the action in front of us and I realized she was translating.

I followed her gaze and saw that Bohtan was striding swiftly toward Dortak and words were being exchanged.

Diandra interpreted.

"I care nothing of women singing." That was Dortak.

"You care nothing of women." That was Bohtan with a jerk of his head to Dortak's wife.

"Caution, Bohtan," some other warrior said.

"Yes, caution, Bohtan. My wife is not your concern," Dortak warned.

"You're right. Your wife wouldn't be my concern. But I'm not talking about your wife. I'm talking about your dog. You've made your wife your pet. Do you like to thrust your cock into animals, Dortak?" Bohtan returned.

I pressed my lips together because those were fighting words in my world so I was guessing amongst The Horde they were *serious* fighting words.

Bohtan went on, "Do not answer that, I know you do. This could not be missed considering you rarely miss an opportunity to show us what a warrior you are by thrusting your cock into in any hole your animal provides."

"My bride is none of your concern!" Dortak shouted, yanking on her chain again.

"But she isn't your bride!" Bohtan shot back. Having made it to Dortak, he leaned in dangerously. "She's nothing but an animal you've brought to heel. You sully The Horde with your actions, thrusting into her face at the games, challenging our Dax while armed, disrespecting our queen *in front of our king*."

Diandra gasped at Dortak's reply and I knew not only by her gasp but the fact the air went still that something very, very bad had happened.

A glance showed she'd gone pale, and I whispered urgently, "What?"

She didn't tear her eyes off what was happening when she whispered back. "Dortak said, 'I care not for our queen or a king whose new wife *rides* so soon after the claiming. The yellow one has had his cock two weeks and she's leading him around by it. Our *king* is the one who has come to heel.'" Her eyes slid to Lahn, and she finished, "That is a challenge."

Oh shit.

My eyes moved to Lahn too. He was surveying the scene with his arms crossed on his chest and an expression on his face that stated clearly he found it mildly interesting. But only mildly.

"You challenge the Dax?" Diandra interpreted what a warrior standing with Lahn called to Dortak.

"What *Dax*?" Dortak spit the words then he spit into the ground in Lahn's direction. "I see no Dax."

Finally, Lahn spoke, and he did this mildly too.

"I advise you stop taking your fists and your cock to your bride, Dortak, so you can heal. I want you fit before I bring you to your knees and take your head."

"I claim the Dax," Dortak shot back, "the first thing I do is thrust my cock into the yellow one, spilling my seed until it leaks out of every orifice in her body."

I sucked in breath, but Lahn grinned and I stared at his reaction in shock.

Then Diandra gasped again but quickly translated Lahn's words.

"You take my head, the Gods would weep because the world is falling from the sky. You get near my tigress, she'll sink her claws in you and you'll be looking at your innards spilling out before your last breath escapes your body." Diandra looked at me. "This is a grave insult to any warrior, my dear, to infer a woman could best him."

It would be a grave insult to anyone. Still, it was a pretty awesome comeback.

Diandra started translating again as Dortak spat, "The yellow one owns your cock!"

To this, Lahn returned, "You speak truth and I'm glad of it. She knows what to do with it and she likes what she knows how to do. While I was driving it inside her last night, my queen gasped that she loved my cock right before I planted my seed in her womb. Seed that might make a warrior. Seed that's already more warrior than you."

"Holy crap," I whispered.

That was a good comeback too, perhaps a little on the personal side, but a good one.

"I don't even know what that means, and I'll say you can say that again," Narinda whispered.

Diandra translated Dortak shouting, "I take your head tomorrow!"

To which Lahn replied, "No. I want you fit before we toss your headless carcass on the pyre. You've got two weeks, Dortak. Then our steel clashes."

Dortak glared at Lahn a second before he swung his angry gaze to Bohtan who was still close.

Diandra interpreted.

"Before I claim the Dax, *you*," and he jerked a finger at Bohtan, "watch yourself and keep your mind off my bride."

"*You*," Bohtan returned, "treat her like a bride and I will. You keep treating her like a dog, I'll be forced to put her down like one to put her out of her misery."

I pulled in breath at Bohtan's words (words I hoped he didn't mean) as Dortak's face got so red I thought his head would explode then Lahn entered the conversation.

"Bohtan, enough. Your point is made."

The king spoke so Bohtan took a step back, but his eyes didn't unlock from Dortak.

Then Diandra translated Bohtan saying, "After the Dax cuts your tail from your lifeless head and it falls from his saddle, I will be the first to seize it and present it to your *bride* as my wedding gift."

Then he turned and walked away, his eyes coming to me briefly before he bowed his head for a second and then he stormed out of sight.

"What's a tail?" Narinda asked softly while I tried to catch my breath but instead caught my husband's eyes.

"It is their hair." I heard Diandra answer. "After a challenge, the victor ties the head of the vanquished to his saddle and rides through the Daxshee. When he's done celebrating, however long that takes, he releases the head from his saddle by slicing it off at their tail. After that, the head is at the mercy of whoever grabs it. They can do whatever they wish with it and the warrior's body is burned headless on his pyre. It is important to anyone to have their pyre so their ashes can drift to the heavens, body joining spirit. The Korwahk, Maroo, any person from the Southlands has this same belief and any body not fired is thought to roam this realm as an unseen, unheard, powerless phantom. Not burning the head is a final indignity for a warrior's defeat, for they will wander eternity headless, a reminder of their humiliation."

I was listening but I was also, weirdly, communicating with my husband. As Diandra talked, his eyes stayed on mine then he jerked his chin up slightly, once. I knew he meant to ask if I was all right, so I nodded. Once I did, he turned away.

And that was when I remembered I had the boy's instrument.

My body jerked and then I turned to him and smiled, offering it up to him and saying, "Shahsha."

Boy and mother were both clearly shaken by the events that took place and he swiftly took it back as I asked Diandra to tell him to come see me again with his instrument so we could play and sing together. The mother's face beamed, but the boy looked like he wanted to do this about as much as he wanted to be forced to run naked through the Daxshee with his hair on fire. Therefore, I decided when he came, I would play and he could take off and have fun with his friends.

They wandered away as Narinda asked, "Do these...erm, confrontations amongst warriors happen often?"

"No, sweet Narinda. It happens, they are men, so it is bound to. But it isn't frequent. Though Dortak is not a favorite of anyone, and I have seen warriors get impatient with him or he says things that force them to have words. Bohtan is a good man, a good father. Seerim says he is a good warrior. He and Nahka didn't leave their cham for nearly two weeks after her claiming, he was that taken with her. The Horde rode after the selection, leaving them behind. He is a good husband and cares for his wife." Diandra smiled gently at Narinda, a smile that spoke volumes about the warrior who had claimed her. "There are some men, no matter what blood flows in their veins or what teachings were drilled in their heads, who are just good men."

Narinda smiled back and there was nothing small or weird about it.

Gaal came forward and set a plate of candied fruits on our hides. I smiled at her, and she smiled back then scuttled away.

I watched her go thinking that Teetru was a little distant because she was older, she seemed to take her duties very seriously and I'd learned yesterday that part of her duties were keeping an eye on me. But Jacanda, Beetus and Packa were younger, friendlier and more talkative. As the days passed, even Packa was coming out of her timidity and becoming more outgoing. Our conversation was halting, but even with Teetru, I felt like we were all forming a bond.

But Gaal remained distant and watchful, and after what Diandra said to me yesterday, I hated to do it, but I wondered about it.

Shit, I was going to have to keep an eye on my girls, especially Gaal.

Then I heard it, a rumble like distant thunder. It was familiar and yet seemed strange.

It hit me what it was the minute the horizon filled with horses. It was the sounds of the hooves of a vast number of horses beating the earth. I'd heard it for the last six days, but this was different and it was different because the horses coming our way didn't number in the hundreds.

I stared as more and more came visible.

Holy fuck! There had to be thousands of them!

I tensed, my first thought was to run to Lahn when Diandra said calmly, "Oh look, The Horde arrives."

My head snapped her way, and I asked, "The Horde?"

She was reaching for some candied fruit. She popped a piece in her mouth and looked at me while she chewed.

She swallowed then she said, "The Horde."

"But," I blinked, "I thought we were *with* The Horde."

"We are, my dear, some of them. Warriors who attended the Hunt, others whose sons were up for selection, trainers who'll need to take charge of new warriors, others who enjoy or their wife enjoys the celebrations. But the rest are out patrolling or on campaign."

I looked to the horses moving our way and the wagons, vast numbers of them, could now be seen coming up the rear.

"The rest?" I whispered.

"Circe, my beautiful friend, a few hundred warriors cannot keep an entire nation safe. The Horde numbers at a little over seventy-five thousand, the last I heard. It could be more."

My mouth dropped open and I stared at her.

My husband commanded an army of seventy-five thousand men?

Oh my God!

"That isn't even all of them," Diandra tipped her head to the approaching procession. "Not even half. Just the warriors who ride with the Dax. While he was presiding over ceremonies, they were taking care of business. They always join the Dax when he's done with official matters. Further, there will be other large squads off on patrol throughout Korwahk or others executing campaigns the Dax has ordered. Why do you think he attends his warriors all day and into the night? Being a Dax, there's a lot to do."

I looked to Lahn who now had five warriors huddled with him and he had his hands planted on his hips, his eyes on the horizon, watching his warriors draw near. The men were talking to him, and I saw that he was watching and listening when he nodded once to something one of them was saying. Then he crossed his arms on his chest, moved his gaze from the vista and turned his attention to the man who was speaking to him.

I had no idea. None. In fact, a savage, primitive horde of just a few hundred seemed enough for a savage, primitive horde. In fact, too many. I had absolutely no idea he commanded such a legion.

"Circe?" Narinda called.

I shook my head, tore my gaze from my husband and aimed it at my friend.

"Are you all right?" she asked.

"Yes, yes," I said distractedly then looked to the horses getting ever closer. "I'm fine."

"I see it is now penetrating," Diandra said softly, and my dazed eyes swung to her to see hers, not dazed but understanding on me. "I kept telling you, my dear, you are a queen. I see you now understand you are a *queen*. A queen of a vast number of men, their wives, their children and the nation of people who they protect..." She paused. "All of whom serve you."

"Yes, Diandra," I whispered. "It's penetrating."

She leaned into me.

"You have saved a child's life, and your people witnessed it. You have sung a beautiful song to a woman whose spirit has been tramped to death inside of her, giving her mind a brief moment of harmony, and your people witnessed it. You make your husband's laughter, something *never* heard before by those other than his brothers, as well as the sounds of his pleasure ring out from your cham, and your people hear it. I tell you there are whispers, and these whispers are soaring, Circe, with a speed that would astonish you. You don't know it, but your actions have already built strong bonds of loyalty in the hearts of people you've never even met, and you've been our Dahksahna *for two weeks*. Your king builds loyalty through providing riches, safety and cunning. You, my beautiful Circe, are building yours, and therefore his, through matters of the heart. This makes you strong and it makes you weak. There will be those who will seek to target those weaknesses. Use caution, be watchful and *stay safe*."

I swallowed and nodded, my gaze flitting to Narinda who was looking on, her eyes wide and her face slightly pale.

Then I turned to the advancing procession and watched part of my husband's ginormous army arrive.

"LINAS, RAH," he whispered before his lips moved over both of my eyes.

I was in trouble.

My king had just made love to me...yes, *made love to me*, slow, sweet, gentle, tender. It was—no other words to describe it—*beautiful.* And I liked it, *a lot.* So much, I didn't think I'd ever forget it, not a touch, not a taste, not a stroke, not a second, not any of it.

And now he was lying on top of me, his weight on a forearm in the bed beside me, his other hand curled around my neck, thumb gently stroking my jaw, and he was whispering to me.

Man, he was good.

"Yeah, I guess you could say that, but really, my eyes are more a very light brown," I muttered to try to break the mood.

His chin tipped down, his eyes locked on mine and at the look in his, my belly melted.

Okay, message received, Lahn didn't want the mood broken.

"Eyes, *rah,*" he whispered then his hand slid up my cheek, fingers sifting through my hair at the side of my head and down before he bunched a length of it against my neck. "Lipa, rah," he muttered, his thumb back to stroking my jaw.

"In my world, we don't call it gold. We call it blonde," I whispered, his eyes caught mine, that warm, sweet, contented look was still in the depths of his and my heart skipped.

Then his head dipped, I braced, and his lips skimmed the skin on my cheek. "Leeka, rah," he rumbled in my ear.

I wasn't going to argue with that. That was true, with all the sun I was getting, my skin *was* gold.

His head came back up as his thumb swept over my lips, his fingers moving so his hand could cup my jaw, "Lapay nahna lisa rahna, kah Lahnahsahna?"

I knew what he was asking. *Is your mouth golden, my tigress?*

My heart skipped another beat.

Shit.

"Lahn," I whispered then closed my lips as his head dipped again and he brushed his against mine.

Okay, he might not have kissed a woman before, but he did *that* really freaking well.

"Mm, kah rahna fauna?" he urged quietly, his mouth moving against my lips.

Oh yeah, he was good.

I just stared in his eyes which were all I could see and did my best to keep my mouth shut.

What I wanted to do was kiss him.

And I wanted it *bad*.

He stared back.

"Lapay tee?" he whispered, *Is it?*

I shook my head and watched up close as his eyes smiled at the same time I felt his lips do the same.

Then, his gaze never leaving mine, his tongue traced my lips.

I shivered and my limbs, all four of which were wrapped around him, tensed.

Oh shit, *yeah*, he wasn't good. He was *good*.

"Yes it is, Circe," he whispered against my lips. His tongue slid along them again and then he murmured, "Rahna honey."

Okay, I'd had some nice compliments in my life. One, I had to admit, was Lahn telling me I had rare beauty the like he'd never seen. Another was, of course, him telling me the spirit that shone from my eyes was the most beautiful thing he'd ever seen.

But his telling me my mouth was golden honey just notched itself right smack in the middle of that list.

"Sahnahsoo kay neenkah," he whispered.

I knew that too. *Let me inside.*

My belly dipped, my heart surged and the area between my legs tingled.

Shit!

I shook my head again and got another touch of his tongue.

Oh God.

"Sahnahsoo nahna Dax neenkah, kah Dahksahna," he murmured.

Let your King inside, my Queen.

Oh God!

I had to stop this, like, *now*.

One of my hands slid up his back, under his arm, up his chest, his neck and I cupped the side of his jaw, sliding my thumb between our lips.

"No, Lahn, kah lisa lapay kahna," I whispered, *No, Lahn, my mouth is mine.*

His eyes smiled again, a knowing smile, therefore a *scary* smile.

"No, baby, your mouth is *mine*," he whispered back then his thumb swept across my cheek, my lips, taking my thumb with it, and when he had access, he bent his head and touched his mouth to mine again.

I held my breath, but he only lifted his head and whispered, "Okay, my Circe, anah na vatay. Anka, ta junay tooka."**

I didn't catch any of that, but I felt extreme relief mixed with almost devastating disappointment when he slid off my side but tucked me close under him, tangled his legs with mine and muttered, "Trahyoo."

I wanted to trahyoo. I *needed* to trahyoo.

But all I could do was feel the specter of his lips against mine and the phantom of his tongue.

So it took me a while.

Then, tangled with my warrior king, I trahyooed.

***Translation:* "Okay, my Circe, tonight you win. Tomorrow, we play again."

19
THE JUDGMENT

Six days later...

"Poyah, kah rahna Dahksahna!" I heard, turned my head and saw Keenim, the boy who sang to me days ago, in an open space. He was with a bunch of other boys kicking around what looked like a ball. It was bigger than a football but shaped like one without the pointed ends.

"Poyah, Keenim!" I called back, waved.

He waved and his friends all stared at me in shock, their eyes then turning slowly to their friend in more shock that the queen would know his name and wave. Clearly, he had not told them he'd been to my cham twice since his initial visit (where I played his guitar and he played with Ghost), or they didn't believe him.

This made me smile, until I made my way back into the sea of chams.

My smile faded and my thoughts wandered.

I was walking, thinking and most importantly, being seen. With the return of The Horde, there were thousands more warriors, their wives, their children, their slaves and other hangers on. The din of the Daxshee had escalated as had its sprawl.

The good news about this was that Lahn's returned army kept my husband busy.

And the bad news about this was that his returned army kept my husband busy.

Therefore, for the last six mornings, he woke me with his hands then wasted no time getting me hot before he fucked me fast, hard and brilliant. He always forced my orgasm before he let his go. It was sweaty, it was energetic, it was heated, it was freaking great, but it never lasted long.

Then he'd demand my mouth. I'd refuse. He'd grin his knowing, scary grin that told me, clearly, he was biding his time. Then he'd drag me out of bed so I could give him a quick bath and braid or arrange his hair how he instructed. He'd pull me to him with one arm, wrap his other hand around my jaw to position my face so I couldn't escape, touch my mouth with his and then he'd be gone.

As in *gone.*

I didn't see him all day, and even though I tried to stay awake at night (though, I was not admitting this fact to myself), I was never awake when he slid in bed beside me.

The good news about *this* was it made it easier to resist his sweetness, his hotness and all other things Lahn.

The bad news about this was I missed him. It sucked to admit but there it was.

I missed my scary, savage brute, king of a marauding horde in another universe husband.

How whacked was that?

The other bad news about this was that it gave me plenty of time on my own.

Diandra had a husband, a daughter and a cham to see to, and I wasn't her only friend. So although I spent time with her every day, as the days went by, I opened my eyes and saw cham, it seemed I was settling into this world and doing it on a permanent basis. This meant I actually had to find some way to *settle* into this world and I couldn't have Diandra by my side every second.

The same with Narinda who had a very attentive savage on her hands, and he didn't have a legion to command. So she was tied up a lot of time (hopefully not literally, or, maybe, if he was sweet about it, then hopefully literally).

Nahka, the same with cham, husband and two kids.

And my girls seemed to be always busy pounding rugs, rinsing out baths, cleaning my sarongs, polishing candlesticks, baking flatbread in a clay oven, roasting meat on a spit over the fire and the like.

I tried to help (more than once), but Teetru had a fit when she saw me laughing with Jacanda and Beetus while pulling my tops and sarongs off a drying line, and she lost her mind (in her quiet, solicitous Teetru way) when she caught me rinsing breakfast dishes at the creek with Packa so I stopped doing it.

I was a queen. I needed to do queen things. And queen things clearly didn't include doing the dishes.

The thing was, I knew no other queens of primitive savage hordes to tell me what queen things I should be doing, and although Diandra was a great advisor, she'd never been a queen. My husband wasn't around to advise me, I wasn't sure he'd be good at it and his advice might be scary.

So I decided the best queen thing I could do was to get out amongst my people, smile, nod, talk (as best I could), get to know them and let them see me.

Therefore, every day I took walks through the Daxshee followed by whoever was guarding me that day.

Today it was Bain, or the grinning warrior, who was friendly. Unlike Zahnin, the other warrior who kept watch over me (and the one who had plucked me off my horse twice that day we were riding).

Bain walked with me and talked with me all the while scanning the people and chams.

Zahnin walked two feet behind me and never looked at me. However, he *did* look like he was in a perpetual bad mood.

The first time he was with me, I tried to engage him in conversation.

This was so unsuccessful, I didn't try again.

And talking with Bain was fun. He had no clue when it came to English so I was forced to try out my Korwahk on him. This made him laugh (a lot, my Korwahk was really bad), but after he quit laughing, he was a patient teacher. He would correct me, and as we walked, he would point things out and tell me what they were called (for instance, firepit, *pahkah,* torch, *pahkan* and just fire, *pahk*). He also intervened when I chatted with my people, often miming what they were saying which made *me* laugh.

But today, I was in my head and Bain sensed it. So, although he walked close and often spoke softly to me, he was letting me have my thoughts.

Bain doing this made me think that perhaps somewhere his new bride was grinning too.

I was in my head mainly because the day seemed weird. I couldn't put my finger on why, but it was weird. I woke up feeling it in the air and it hadn't gone away.

But also, I was thinking about what Lahn said about how I came into the possession of a Korwahk scout. He clearly knew, thus must have asked how that came about. This was not surprising—curiosity about your new mate—and that didn't bother me.

What disturbed me was that there was a story to tell. I thought I'd woken in a pen filled with women.

How could I be on a pirate ship?

That didn't make any sense in a situation that made no sense. I was here, I'd been here nearly three weeks and it seemed I wasn't going home.

But how did I get here?

And who was the Circe (or whoever) who was on a pirate ship?

I needed answers but I didn't know how to go about finding them and I wasn't sure I wanted them. The knowledge might be more frightening than the reality.

That said, Diandra had said something I hadn't paid attention to at the time because I felt crap, was shaking uncontrollably and Lahn was extremely pissed, so I had other things on my mind.

But when I had sunstroke, she told me the medicine was natural, not "witchcraft."

If you could hear animals in this world (and Ghost spoke to me, she was a baby, she didn't have a lot of words and all of them were Korwahk so I didn't know what she was saying half the time, but I still understood her mews and purrs and growls like human language). If horses could be so white they shone ice blue. If innocent women could go to bed in Seattle and be transported to an alternate universe.

Then there could be magic.

And perhaps someone here practiced it.

And perhaps that someone knew what the fuck was going on with me.

And, if I knew what that was, then maybe I could figure out what I should do.

"Dahksahna Circe," Bain muttered, and I belatedly noticed that he'd tensed at my side.

I came to myself, looked up at him then looked where his eyes were aimed.

The Eunuch was headed our way and his attention was on me.

"Tee lapay lee Xacme," Bain said under his breath to me, *It is the Eunuch.*

I looked back up at Bain, and before he rearranged his features, I saw distaste in them.

Oh man.

"Kah Dahksahna," The Eunuch murmured, bowing his head as he stopped before me.

Hmm.

He called me "kah Dahksahna." Most everyone called me "rahna Dahksahna" or "rahna Dahksahna hahla" or "Dahksahna Circe" if they knew me pretty well.

No one simply called me their queen.

How weird.

"Poyah," I greeted, and his head came up, his face masked.

Oh man.

"I am The Eunuch," he stated, and I blinked.

"You know Eng...I mean, Valearian?" I asked.

"I speak the language of the Vale," he answered, lifting his chin a bit.

He spoke English. *Very* weird. Why didn't Lahn use this guy as an interpreter?

"Well, um...cool, uh, that's great. I mean. Lovely to, uh...finally meet you," I stammered. "Uh, what's your name?"

He stared at me.

Then he repeated, "I am The Eunuch."

"Uh...okay. I've um...heard that but..." Yikes! "I was asking your name."

"My name?" he asked back.

"Yes, the one you were given at birth," I told him.

His face, already masked, closed down.

"That name was taken with my manhood, kah Dahksahna," he informed me coldly.

Okay, there were a lot of uncomfortable conversations a person had to have in their life. When they broke up with someone, for one. When they fucked up and had to admit they were wrong, for another.

But talking to a dude who had his balls cut off about his balls being cut off beat them all.

I held his eyes a moment before I said softly, "Right, but you *are* still that man no matter that atrocity happened to you so...I'd like to know your name."

At this point Bain said something that sounded like he was asking, "What does your queen require of you?" but I wasn't sure.

"Kah trooyha," *My name,* The Eunuch answered (there it was, I was right about Bain's question).

"Uvoo tee luh zah," *Give it to her,* Bain ordered firmly and impatiently.

The Eunuch looked hard at Bain for a brief second then turned to me. "Karrim, my queen," he answered on another slight head bow.

"Shahsha," I said softly.

He stared at me a second and then said, "I will beg your pardon. I have had many things to do. The Hunt, the selection, the ride. I have been too busy to present myself to my queen. I am giving you my apologies."

"There's no need, I understand." I threw an arm out to indicate the busy Daxshee at the same time I gave him a smile. "Your responsibilities are vast. Anyone can see that."

Another obsequious head bow and a muttered, "Shahsha." His eyes slid to Bain and back to me so fast it was almost like I was seeing things, before he went on, "I am asking you if you are managing well with tahna Dax."

I tipped my head to the side. "Sorry?"

His gaze pointedly went to my cheekbone, now, I would suspect, without any discoloration, and then back to me. "You and tahna Dax, I have the hope that all is well in your cham."

A tingle slid up my spine before I said, "Everything is fine." Then, because I wanted Bain in on this conversation, I said in Korwahk, hoping I got it right, "Jak lapay yahka." *All is well.*

"Jak lapay yahka? Zut tela?" Bain asked, and I looked up at him.

"Kay loot kah Dax," I answered his question of, *All is well? With what?* then I looked at The Eunuch. "Kah Lahn lapay uh...busy gahn we are, um, coping well, uh, ta lapay yahka. Fahnahsan." *Me and my King...My Lahn is uh...busy but we are, um, coping well, uh, we are well. Happy.*

The obsequious bow from The Eunuch again then, "Dohno, kah Dahksahna, very dohno." He was obviously avoiding Bain's eyes, and perhaps the unhappy vibe Bain was emanating, and it was clear he wanted to seriously avoid it, and I knew this when he said with another mini-head bow, "I will leave you to your...wanderings. Goyah, kah Dahksahna." A bow without any eye contact to Bain and a muttered, "Goyah, Tunakan."*

After he delivered that, he hurried away.

It could be said I didn't like how that went and when Bain touched my arm to move us forward again, I knew by his continued unhappy vibe he didn't either.

Then he spoke in Korwahk and used easy words so I could understand. "I do not like that man."

Uh-oh.

He went on to warn, "Be cautious, Dahksahna Circe."

I pretty much got that.

"Okay," I whispered.

At that point, an almighty scream pierced the air, so hideous it sent ice shards tearing through my veins.

Instantly, one of Bain's arms lifted high, his hand going behind his neck where he smoothly and swiftly unsheathed his sword while the other arm went around my waist and he pulled me to him, inching back even as people all around were running to a cham three tents down.

Bain barked a question at someone who was running the other direction, got an answer and the man spoke so fast, the only words I could make out where "Dortak" and "zak bahsah," *his wife.*

Oh shit.

Another scream split the air.

Oh shit!

Bain's body went solid at the answer and then he tried to pull me back, but I planted my feet and twisted my neck to look up at him.

In Korwahk, I did my best to shout, "We need to go to her!"

"Me, kah rahna Dahksahna," he denied.

"Bain! *We need to go to her!*" He kept pulling me back, so I screeched, "Nahna Dahksahna tahnoo tee!" *Your Queen commands it!*

He stared me in the eyes for a heartbeat, clearly read something then muttered, "Tooyay kay."

Diandra had told me what "tooyo" meant and it didn't have a literal translation, but the description made it sound like it meant "fuck." This meant Bain just muttered, "Fuck me," which would have been funny any other time but obviously not then.

He let me go but took my hand, kept his sword unsheathed and we jogged to the tent. He shouted orders at the people surrounding it. They turned, saw me, parted, we got to the front of the cham, and I beheld a nightmare.

Dortak had his wife on her knees in front of him, his hand fisted in her hair. He was bent to her, the blade of a knife at her throat, and he had blood dripping from a huge, gaping gash at his shoulder. His face was red and twisted with rage.

She had clearly been recently beaten about the face and we weren't talking a little slapping around, which would be bad enough, but *fists.* Her cheeks were awash in a river of tears, and I knew he was about to slit her throat.

Thus, without a single thought, I whirled, gripped the hilt of one of the knives in Bain's belt, pulled it out of its sheath, whirled back and advanced like a shot until I had the knifepoint at Dortak's jugular.

"Stop," I commanded in Korwahk.

He glared hatred up at me and then the blade sliced her flesh, blood immediately dripping from the shallow slash, but she screamed her terror in a way it crawled along my skin.

I pressed the point of my blade in his neck. "*Stop!*"

"Kah rahna Dahksahna," Bain said softly. He was close.

"Your queen commands it!" I shouted in Korwahk at Dortak, ignoring Bain, my eyes glued to the dark, cruel ones of a monster.

He slid his blade in deeper and another scream rent the air. She twisted in his arms (not the smartest thing to do, I thought vaguely, considering his blade had opened her skin) and tears dropped off her chin.

"*Your queen commands it!*" I shrieked, pushing my knifepoint in deeper and a bead of blood surrounded the point.

He stilled and glared at me, and I held his eyes. We were in a staredown. I was breathing heavily, my chest expanding deep and falling so hard I could feel every breath.

"Your queen commands it, Dortak, drop your blade," Bain said in Korwahk from behind me and Dortak's eyes slid to him.

"Your queen commands it, *drop...your...blade.*" Another voice came from a little further away. One that was familiar, but I was concentrating on not shoving my knife in his throat and/or passing out so I didn't have the capacity to place it.

Dortak's gaze came back to me, and I held it.

"*Drop your blade!*" Bain thundered.

Dortak's eyes moved over my shoulder and up again then slid across me to take in something else. His lip curled in a sneer, and he dropped his blade but shoved his wife so she fell face first in the dirt in front of their cham.

I started to move to her, but I didn't even get a step. Bain's hand curled around mine and he took off, dragging me with him. When he pulled me through the crowd of people, I caught a glimpse of several warriors including Zahnin who was the voice I couldn't put my finger on (mostly because he'd never said much to me, most of what he said was monosyllabic and all of that was grunted).

I was surprised he took my back.

I was also running through the Daxshee to keep up with Bain's quick, determined, urgent strides, and I was shaking like a leaf.

When we got to my cham, he shoved me inside, snatched his blade out of my hand, sheathed it then bent, put a finger in my face and growled in Korwahk, "Do not leave."

His face was scary but there was also something else there.

Concern.

Oh shit.

I'd fucked up.

As he stalked out, he barked something at Teetru who was standing just inside the flaps. Her eyes went wide but she nodded. He prowled out, she called to the girls, and they all came dashing in. They all listened to Teetru talk. Then they all nodded and stood at the flaps.

I looked at my girls lined across the flaps.

I guess I wasn't going anywhere.

And I had a feeling I hadn't fucked up.

I'd *fucked up*.

**Translation:* "Farewell [until later], Tunakan." [*Tunakan:* Warrior of Suh Tunak or the Korwahk Horde]

~

"*What possessed you?*" Diandra cried.

I was right. I hadn't fucked up.

I'd *fucked up*.

"I don't...I...I d-don't...I don't even know where to begin!" she yelled.

It was at least two hours later, but it felt like two years. My girls were no longer at the flaps. No, they'd disappeared. In their place were two large, scary-looking warriors standing inside the cham at the flaps.

I was definitely not going anywhere.

Diandra had arrived fifteen minutes ago already in the know about what went on mainly because it was spreading through the Daxshee like wildfire.

She was pacing.

I was sitting cross-legged on the bed silently panicking.

"Did I *not* tell you what happens in a warrior's cham is nobody's business?" she shouted.

"They were outside the cham, Diandra," I said softly.

She stopped mid-pace and whirled on me.

"This is not amusing, my dear, *nothing* about this is amusing," she hissed, even though I wasn't trying to be amusing, just informative. But I didn't share that when she took two quick steps to me, bent and snapped, "You held a weapon to a warrior."

"Yes, but—"

"You are a *woman*, and you held a *weapon* to a Korwahk Horde *warrior*!" she bit out.

"Diandra—"

"It matters not that you are queen, you are a *woman*, and he is a *warrior*!" she clipped.

I lifted a hand.

"Sweetheart," I whispered, "please."

"He was not trying to force himself on you. He was not looting your cham. He was not mishandling your slaves without your permission and refusing to stop at your request. He was with *his wife*!" she shouted.

"But he was—" I tried again, dropping my hand.

"What he *was* or what he *wasn't* is *not* your concern!" she yelled.

"He was going to kill her!" I exclaimed.

"And if he did, he would face the Dax for that, not *you*. Not you, Circe. *The Dax*."

"Two members of The Horde took my back," I told her quietly.

She straightened and snapped, "What?"

"Bain and Zahnin both backed me up. They supported me," I explained.

"Yes, I heard that too. And you can only hope that the Dax, who never but *never* in all the years I've known him as Dax has been tolerant, today feels tolerant, for he could order their heads for standing against their brother."

I sucked in breath, felt my throat close and my eyes widen all at the exact same time.

She saw my look and nodded once.

Then she said softly with strained calm and more than a little fear, "Yes, he could do that, Circe." She paused before finishing, "And, he could order yours."

"Oh my God," I whispered.

"That's a good idea, my friend, pray to your God. I fear you will need Him right now," she whispered back, and I saw fear had saturated her eyes and her hands were shaking.

Yep, I'd seriously fucked up.

The tent flaps slapped opened. My eyes snapped in that direction to see the warriors tense then step aside as Lahn bent and entered.

I stopped breathing.

Bain, Zahnin and Seerim followed him, but I only had eyes for Lahn.

I took him in, trying to read him, but his face was blank as he took four steps toward me, stopped and crossed his arms on his chest. He was watching me the whole time but giving nothing away.

When he stopped moving, he kept watching me.

I didn't know if I should bow before him, ask him if I could explain, plead for my life (and Bain's and Zahnin's) or burst into the terrified tears that threatened to singe my throat.

So I just sat there staring up at him.

This lasted awhile.

Then he turned his head and jerked a chin at Diandra, which I didn't know what that meant until he immediately turned back to me and started talking.

Diandra, catching his drift, translated.

"My tigress, it seems, unsheathes more than her claws."

Oh fuck.

I didn't think that was a good start.

I felt it prudent to stay silent.

Lahn spoke.

"You drew a warrior's blood, my queen."

I pressed my lips together and stayed quiet.

"You were the second woman today to draw his blood. He caught steel from his wife before you."

The wound in his shoulder. She'd fought back.

There was something tragically beautiful about that.

I didn't share this with Lahn. I kept my mouth shut.

He stared at me.

I withstood it and kept my peace.

Then he said softly with Diandra interpreting, "I see it, even from here, shining in your eyes."

I sucked in a breath that I dearly needed and ventured softly, "Linay tela?" *See what?*

"Your spirit, my warrior queen," he replied just as softly using my language.

Okay, was that good?

He kept talking softy but reverted to Korwahk with Diandra translating.

"I have passed judgment, my tigress, and it will not be a decision you will like. But I am your king, and it is my ruling, so it will be done."

"Wh-what is your decision?" I whispered when he didn't go on.

"My warriors stood by their queen. They are not to be punished. They have been assigned as your personal guard and were doing what I commanded. They have vowed to take a blade should they need to do so in order to save your life. The situation you placed them in was grave, Dortak's intention was to end his wife's life and your intervention meant, once he'd used his blade on her, he would have turned that steel on you. In order to keep you safe, they acted on their vows to me. They did what they were expected to do, therefore they will not feel my censure."

Well, that was good.

"O-okay." I whispered.

"You, my Circe, should not have put them in the position to have to choose between their queen and their brother. It was not them but you who made a bad decision."

Oh shit.

He stared at me again.

My mouth went dry.

As his gaze stayed locked on mine, I watched as something I didn't get flashed in his eyes before he murmured, "Kah teenkah rahna tunakanahsa."

Diandra whispered, "My little golden warrior."

Okay, I didn't know.

Was that good?

Lahn fell silent. I swallowed.

Then he spoke with Diandra translating. "I ask, in future, my tigress, that if you intend to *be* a warrior, you *think* like a warrior, and that would mean, before you bare your claws or unsheathe your steel, you... actually...*think*."

Okay, he said "in future," which would intimate I had one.

"Lahn," I whispered.

He spoke over me (as did Diandra). "I must have her life, Circe."

I blinked swiftly before I asked, "What?"

"She took steel to her husband. This is forbidden. I must have her life."

My lungs contracted as I repeated, softer this time, "What?"

"This is my judgment," he declared.

He couldn't be serious.

"You know how he treats her," I whispered.

"I do."

"She had no other choice," I explained.

Lahn nodded.

"She didn't," he agreed. "And now, neither do I."

"But you're king," I said quietly.

He took a step toward me, and I used my hands to scoot back on the bed. His eyes dropped to my body, he stopped then his eyes came to mine.

"I am king," he said quietly. "And in one week, I face the challenge of Dortak's blade. But today, I face the responsibility of releasing his wife from the prison he has made of their cham. Dortak will fall. She had to wait one week for release. She decided not to wait that week. She is Korwahk. She knew exactly what she was doing when she took steel to him. She knew, if he didn't end her life, I would. She was asking for this judgment, Circe. She is asking for this release. She knows, I know and you, my tigress, know that her treatment at his hands has broken her spirit. It is dead inside her. It is gone to another realm. She wishes to rejoin it. And you will sit on your throne beside me as I cast this judgment and the sentence is carried out. You will be there as my queen, as is your duty to me and your people. But you will also be there for her. It is your eyes she wishes to see before she moves to the next realm. It is your spirit so close to the surface that will guide her."

I had my focus glued to him and I was panting as he finished in a gentle voice.

"This is my judgment, my golden doe. Prepare yourself for your throne."

With that, he instantly turned and strode out of the tent, all the warriors following him.

I stared at the cham flaps for long moments after they were gone and even after my girls came bustling in.

Then my gaze slid slowly to Diandra.

"Did he just say I was attending that woman's execution?" I whispered, but she was close to the bed, reaching out to me, her manner hurried.

"He did, my dear, and we must not delay. For the sake of that poor girl, we need to end her suffering quickly. Therefore, we need to get you prepared."

She grabbed my hand, tugged me to my knees and automatically I crawled out of bed.

And then, without a word, stuck in a haze of horror, I allowed my girls and Diandra to prepare me to take my throne and witness an execution.

20
THE EXECUTION

Korwahk Queens had execution apparel.

I learned this when my clothes were taken off and new ones put on. A large, square piece of black silk, folded and tied around my breasts, the end dangling down and coming to a point at my navel from which two gold disks were stitched and hung down, one to each point, two more hitting me, cold and heavy, from the tie at my back. A black sarong shot with gold. A black belt made of woven leather with gold chains braided through. A gold choker made of links that covered my neck from base to chin. My gold bands were pushed up to my biceps, long, wide gold loops fixed to my earlobes. Black leather sandals were tied to my feet.

My makeup of the day was gently but swiftly washed off and black kohl went around my eyes, charcoal gray eye shadow, the dusting of gold powder along my cheekbones and temples and deep berry lip tint was painted on my lips.

My hair was left as it was, hanging long in twists and curls, but the pins and clips adorning it for the day were removed and Teetru slid her fingers through, shaking it and ratting it out a bit so it even felt big.

The golden band of feathers was laced through my hair and tied around my head.

The minute Diandra walked us through the tent flaps, I saw the warriors. Not one, two or four...but ten. As Diandra guided me toward the sea of chams, they fell in, four in front, one on either side, four in the rear.

The Daxshee was eerily silent, and as we walked, we saw not a single soul. Night had fallen and torchlight lit the vast space. I could see the open space on the rise nearly to the opposite end of the Daxshee was blazing with fire, and even from a distance, I saw people gathering there and this was because there were a lot of them.

I knew that was where we were going.

The air was wrong, as it had been when I woke up to it that morning and all day. But now it was worse. It pressed in. It felt thick.

I couldn't breathe.

"The Dax was tolerant, my dear," Diandra whispered to me as we walked. She had, as usual, curved my hand around the inside of her elbow, pulled me close and held her other hand over mine. "It is a blessing," she went on. "He does not punish you or his warriors. He took his time to explain his judgment to you. He did this gently, beautiful Circe. I am astounded. It is a blessing."

I kept my eyes straight ahead as I whispered back, "I adore you, my sweet friend, but right now, I need to prepare myself for what's going to happen so can I ask that you please be quiet?"

She removed my hand from her arm but slid hers along my waist and pulled me even closer as she murmured, "Of course, my love."

I slid my arm around her waist, and we walked through the silent, vacant Daxshee. It was a long walk but not long enough for me to prepare myself to witness the execution of a woman whose only crime was to be beautiful enough to capture the attention of a Korwahk scout.

Finally, in front of us, through the warrior guards I saw a wall of people, shoulder to shoulder. They saw us and parted slowly so we could pass. When we did, I held on to Diandra tighter, looked straight ahead and avoided all eyes.

They thought I'd done wrong, many of them probably thought I should be punished, but that wasn't why I avoided their eyes. I didn't think I had it in me to face this and I needed to hold together what I had so I didn't lose it. Not now. Not this early. Whatever brought me here, I was their queen.

I needed to act like one.

We walked into a clearing lit relatively brightly with torches all around and firepits burning on the rise and my eyes immediately went to what was in it.

Dortak, standing, feet planted wide, arms crossed on his chest, bandage around his shoulder, back to us but his neck was twisted so he could watch us arrive.

I barely took him in before my eyes dropped to the stone to see his bride at his feet. She was on her knees, bent fully forward, forehead to her hands that were resting on the stone.

From what I could see, she was wearing a stark-white gauze sarong.

My attention shifted to the rise where I could see Lahn standing on a platform with our thrones side by side, firepits next to it, torches surrounding it.

He was painted.

I felt something at my side, looked there and saw Seerim was next to Diandra. He had his hand on her but suddenly looked to the rise. I followed his gaze to see Lahn shake his head once. I looked back to Seerim who was nodding. He dropped his hand to take his wife's, and even in the torchlit night I saw the firm squeeze before he moved away and disappeared.

I was to have my friend.

Thank God.

My friend was to have a front row seat at an execution.

She walked tall and her step didn't falter, nor did she leave my side.

As promised.

Damn, but I owed her huge.

I looked back to the rise and noticed that Bain and Zahnin were both standing behind my throne. As we approached, Lahn sat on his. He was in king mode. I knew this the minute his blank, painted eyes left me and he sat on his throne.

I did not dally. The guard peeled off and I walked right to my throne and sat down, Diandra standing at my side.

The drums started pounding, the small ones, but the noise thumped like a giant mallet into the night.

My hands went to the armrests of my chair, my fingers curling around, and I squeezed.

Suddenly the drums stopped and the instant they did, Lahn shouted and Diandra bent to my ear to interpret.

"We are here because the new bride of Dortak took steel to her husband!"

No one said a word. The torchlight danced, the firepits crackled. My fingers tensed into my throne.

Lahn spoke.

"Now, she must receive my judgment!"

I swallowed and my gaze dropped to the woman who was still bowed low to her king.

Then a whisper went through the air. I looked up and saw a warrior push through the crowd. He strode into the small clearing that was nowhere near the vast space of the ceremonial clearing of the other encampment and stopped.

It was Bohtan.

He shouted and Diandra translated, "I wish to speak, my king!"

"You will be heard!" Lahn shouted back.

Bohtan didn't delay.

"Our golden warrior queen has championed Dortak's bride. She has a bond with the wife of Dortak and she has a bond with my wife Nahka. My wife Nahka has felt this bond constrict, linking her through our true golden queen to Dortak's bride, and should it be your command to spare her life, she wishes to assist our queen in resurrecting the new bride of Dortak's spirit."

My lungs seized and my body went solid right along with them.

Another whisper went through the air as Lahn remained silent.

The girl five feet from the base of our thrones didn't twitch but Dortak's face twisted with disgust.

Another warrior pushed into the clearing. My eyes went to him, and I saw it was Feetak.

"I wish to speak, my king!" he shouted.

"You will be heard!" Lahn returned.

Feetak also didn't delay.

"My new bride, Narinda, also shares a bond with our queen. She tells me she too wishes to assist our queen in resurrecting the wife of Dortak's spirit."

I felt Diandra's hand curl tight into my shoulder indicating she was gravely surprised at these proceedings.

I was too, especially considering Narinda didn't have near enough command of the Korwahk language to inform Feetak of this, but somehow she'd either managed it or he'd assumed it, and for her, or simply because he was a good man, he stepped forward.

I held tight to my throne as I stared and tried to control my rapid breaths.

Another warrior pushed forward. "I wish to speak, my king!"

And another, "I wish to speak, my king!"

I shiver slid over my skin.

Oh my God!

Diandra's fingers squeezed so hard, they caused pain.

And then came another, "I wish to speak, my king!"

And another, "I wish to speak, my king!"

Three more came in simultaneously from three different sides. "I wish to speak, my king!"

Dortak's arms dropped. He took a step back and his head swung around to take in his brothers, his face now distorted with rage.

His bride didn't twitch.

More warriors came forward and shouted the same words.

"Enough!" Lahn boomed.

I looked to him and saw he had his hand up.

He did not look at me.

I turned back to the clearing to see it now nearly filled with warriors, Dortak and his bowing bride in white.

The air pressed in as I and the silent crowd held our breath.

Finally, Lahn spoke.

"Bride of Dortak, give your king your eyes."

She didn't hesitate to push up to sitting on her calves and her gaze lifted to Lahn. She was wearing a wide strip of gauze around her breasts and a thin one was wrapped around the cut on her throat. Her face had been cleaned but her left eye was nearly swollen shut, purple and bruising.

I swallowed again.

"The warriors of Suh Tunak speak for you," Lahn told her.

She lifted her chin.

"Their wives speak for you," Lahn went on.

She lifted her chin again.

"Is it your wish for my queen and her women to resurrect your spirit?" Lahn asked, and I held on to my throne as Diandra's fingers clenched into my shoulder.

He was giving her an out!

She shook her head.

No!

I tensed to shoot out of my chair but Diandra's hand held me down.

"You understand that judgment has been passed?" Lahn asked.

She lifted her chin.

"And you accept that judgment," Lahn stated.

She lifted her chin again.

No!

I felt my lips tremble as my body shuddered with the effort to stay seated and unmoving.

I wanted to reach out to Lahn. I wanted him to tell her that it was his decision that she must allow me and the wives of Suh Tunak to resurrect her spirit. I sent this thought into the night and hoped it found his mind.

It didn't.

I knew it when he said quietly, "Very well, my sister."

My head snapped to the side, and I saw his head turned away and he was lifting his chin at something. My focus flew there, and I saw The Eunuch come forward with a long thin blade.

Lahn turned back to the woman, and I did too, seeing her sitting on her calves, apparently calm. I looked at Dortak to see him smiling.

God, God, *God* but I fucking *hated* that man.

My fingers tightened so deeply into the horns I feared they'd break through as The Eunuch positioned behind her, bent forward, cupped her what appeared to be strangely tenderly under her jaw and held the blade to her throat.

Then he lifted his eyes to his king.

"Do you have words, sister?" Lahn asked softly.

The woman in white stared at him.

Then, slowly, her gaze slid to me.

A small, tragic smile drifted across her mouth, and she said one word.

"Rainbow."

And, so fast it was almost as if I didn't see it, her hands shot up. She grasped the knife, tearing it away from The Eunuch who shouted in surprise. She took it by the hilt, pointed it to her belly, shoved it in and drew it up.

Blood spewed from the wound, loud gasps, cries and exclamations could be heard all around, but I shot to standing, my arms straight down, my head tilted back, and I shrieked to the heavens.

"*No!*"

At the exact same time I cried, lightning rent the sky, a crack of thunder filled the air, the heavens opened, and rain poured down.

"End her misery!" Lahn shouted.

Somehow, I knew he was now standing but I didn't look. My head tipped down to see she had fallen forward.

The Eunuch didn't delay. He dropped to his knees, his hands went to Dortak's bride, he pulled her back across his thighs and he tore the blade from her belly. Her pained eyes captured mine and I held them as he swiftly drew the blade across her throat. Blood surged out, wetting the stone, and I watched, my eyes locked to hers for the terrible, brief seconds it took the life to drain away.

The rain came down in sheets, already washing her blood in a dark river across the light stone.

"No," I whispered as the tears filled my eyes, the rain beat against my skin, my hair, my clothing, all of it soaked within seconds.

Dortak roared in triumph.

My attention went to him, and he pounded a fist in his chest then punched it in the air, turned and pushed his way roughly through the crowd.

I saw movement out of the corner of my eye. Two men and four women. The men were carrying something and one of the women had a huge wad of white material in her hands. They made it to the fallen woman and the women arranged the material flat on the wet stone as the men lifted her with care and then set her at one end. They moved away as the women gently rolled her lifeless body, wrapping her tight in her wet, white gauze shroud, the blood still seeping from her wounds staining it red.

Once she was wrapped, the men came forward, lifted her onto a stretcher and swiftly all of them moved out of the clearing.

"Kah Lahnahsahna," Lahn called.

Fogged like I was in a dream, my head slowly turned to him, and I saw his paint dissolving down his body as the rain beat into him.

His arm was extended to me.

I stared at him.

"Go to your king," Diandra whispered in my ear, her hands at my waist, pushing. "Now, my love."

I moved to my king.

He took my hand, pulled me near, bent our arms and held my hand tucked close to his chest, me to his side, and we stepped off the platform, walked down the rise, through the gathered throng that was standing, silent and unmoving (except to let us through) in the driving rain.

I kept my head up, my eyes straight, but that didn't mean I didn't cry the whole way home.

My girls were in the cham when we arrived, and they sprang into action.

My clothes and jewels were taken away, but before Packa could put a cloth to me to dry my wet skin, Lahn murmured, "Tahkoo tan," and they hurried out of the cham.

Lahn, also still wet, his black paint seeping, but now hideless, came to me and gently he pulled me into bed, not only under the silk sheet but also under the first layer of hides.

Then he pulled me into his arms, face to face, his hand cupping the back of my head pressing my face to his throat.

I listened to the rain beating on the top of the cham and wondered how the material didn't get saturated and the wet didn't seep through.

As I wondered this, Lahn held me close.

Then I whispered, "Your Hunt did that to her."

"Rayloo, kah rahna fauna," Lahn said softly, giving me a squeeze.

He understood my words even though I spoke my language, I knew it.

"Your Hunt drove her to that." I was still whispering.

"Rayloo, Circe."

"She was beautiful." I kept whispering.

Lahn didn't respond.

"He killed her beauty and slaughtered her soul."

Lahn said nothing for a moment then he asked quietly, "Soul?"

"My people's word for pahnsahna, her spirit," I said just as quietly.

That got me another squeeze.

Then his hand slid from the back of my head and around to cup my jaw where a thumb under my chin pressed up gently so my head tipped back. He was looking down at me, his eyes, I could see, soft in the candlelight.

"The heavens wept," he said in Korwahk.

I knew the air felt wrong all day because of the impending storm but I still replied in English, "That happens when innocents are punished."

"Innocents?" he whispered.

"Ones who did no wrong," I answered in Korwahk.

His head tilted so his forehead could rest on mine.

I closed my eyes.

I opened them and whispered in Korwahk, "You were right, she wished that."

"I know, my tigress," he whispered back in English.

I kept whispering when I said in Korwahk, "Thank you for not punishing me."

His chin jerked back slightly, and his forehead came away from mine before he replied, "I would not punish you for being what you are."

I blinked and asked softly, "What?"

"Kah Circe, you are kah Lahnahsahna, you are my warrior queen. It is who you are. It is not what anyone made you. It shines from your eyes. It is what I see in the boys I select to serve Suh Tunak. It is why I chose you. It is why we suit. It is why together we begin the Golden Dynasty of legend."

His thumb started stroking my jaw as he went on.

"I cannot say I do not wish you would have thought before you acted today. If Dortak took her life, it would have ended her torment sooner and saved her from what she endured tonight. But I recognize it is who you are."

I stared up at him, heart in my throat. He was speaking in Korwahk, but he was doing it slowly and I understood most of what he said, and what he said, I had to admit, moved me.

I watched his mouth twitch before he finished, "Though I will caution you at least to attempt to rein it in in future. I do not like my queen in black."

My clothes were kickass here, it was true. But I was with him, and I hoped I never had to wear that black outfit again in my life.

"Okay," I whispered, and his lips curved as his thumb swept mine.

"Okay," he repeated.

I had more to say so I called, "Lahn?"

"Mm?" he murmured with another stroke of my jaw.

Okay, shit, it must be said there were some times when I really liked my husband.

Now was one of them.

"Thanks also for not punishing your men," I said, and his grin turned to a smile.

"My Circe," he started. "On your claiming, you stole my blade. No one, no other man, no other warrior, has ever taken my weapon. Not once. I know when your little warrior shines through, you will stop at nothing. I could not punish Bain for his weapon being seized when you had a mind to seize it, for you did the same to me. He could not control you so he and Zahnin sought to control the situation. This is not grounds for punishment."

Again, he was talking in Korwahk, so I didn't catch it all, but I got the gist of it.

And the gist made me stare.

When he received no response, Lahn spoke quietly. "I like my paint on you, my golden doe, because I like how I put it on you. But I like it more that your warrior spirit deserves the paint."

I kept staring.

Then I asked (in Korwahk), "No one has ever taken your weapon?"

He nodded.

"Wow," I whispered, and he smiled again.

"I do not know what that means, my tigress, but the way you say it and the look on your face, I do not have to ask."

I felt my expression grow soft. Then I tilted my head until my forehead rested on his chin. To that, he tilted his until his lips rested on my forehead.

There, he murmured, "The heavens wept at my wife's command."

I blinked at his throat and tilted my head back to ask what he meant, but before I could say a word, from outside the cham I heard a man shout, "Kah Dax!"

Lahn's head turned and then, to my shock (and horror, I must add), he shouted, "Enter!" in Korwahk and lifted up to sitting in the bed, *taking me with him*. The hides fell as he pulled my back to his front so I was facing the cham flaps, his arm across my breasts somewhat covering my nudity from the three warriors who bent and entered our cham.

He didn't have to shield me. They only had eyes for their king.

Rapid fire Korwahk was thrown but I got this from it:

"You are needed, my king," one of the warriors.

"I attend my bride," Lahn (which I thought was nice).

"It is important, my king," another warrior.

"I leave my wife in our bed, it had better be," Lahn.

"You have my vow it is," the second warrior who spoke, spoke again.

Lahn hesitated before he sighed. Then he turned me in his arms, his hand came up to curl around the underside of my jaw and he dipped his face to mine.

"Rest and try to sleep, my tigress. I will return," he said in English.

I nodded.

He held my face steady and touched his lips to mine before he set me in bed, threw the hides over me, exited off the side, went to the trunks, pulled out then yanked on another pair of hides and left the cham still tying them at his hips.

The warriors followed.

The rain fell.

And I lay in bed in the tent, listening to the drops slap against the cham and I tried to do as my husband ordered: rest and sleep.

But all that filled my head was the beautiful, tragic bride of a monster saying a word she did not know but a word I knew in my soul she understood.

"Rainbow."

And I hoped she was over it, her spirit now inhabiting a wonderful world.

I WOKE when Lahn's arms shifted me into his body.

Sleepily, I lifted my face to his and my eyes fluttered open.

"Is all well?" I whispered.

"Yes, my golden doe. Now sleep."

I nodded but kept my face tipped to his as his moved closer to mine.

And when his lips pressed against mine, groggy and not thinking, mine parted.

And the instant they did, his tongue swept inside.

It felt great and he tasted even better.

My body snuggled closer to his as I drowsily offered my mouth to my husband, he accepted, his arms growing tight around me, and he drank deep.

When he ended the kiss, I felt his lips move against mine as I heard the rough, whispered words, "Golden honey."

I mumbled, "Mm," dipped my chin and tucked my face in Lahn's throat.

Then I fell asleep in his strong, tight arms.

21
THE GOLDEN GODDESS

"Wake, my queen." I heard Lahn's voice.

My eyes fluttered open, but before I was fully awake, he plucked me out of bed, planted my ass in his lap, knees bent, one arm circling my calves and waist, the other hand sifting in my hair from the neck up.

I focused drowsily on his handsome face and whispered, "Hey."

I watched his eyes smile as he whispered back, "Hey."

I was pretty sure my eyes smiled too mainly because I knew my mouth did it. Then his gaze dropped to my mouth, his eyes grew heated, and his head bent.

I was registering the heat in his eyes when he murmured against my lips, "Your king wants your golden honey."

A vague memory of the night before filtered into my brain, and I didn't hesitate before I parted them in invitation and immediately felt Lahn's tongue sweep inside.

Nope. It wasn't a dream I had last night.

My husband could *kiss*.

My arms slid around his shoulders as he dropped back then twisted. My back hit bed and Lahn's body hit mine, all the while we kissed, our tongues dancing. He shifted and I knew what that shift meant. My legs parted, his hips fell between, and his hand went to the ties on one side of his hides.

Seconds later, his tongue plundering my mouth, his cock slowly invaded me.

I moaned into his mouth.

Oh, this was good.

He started moving, slowly, his sweet strokes unhurried, his mouth never leaving mine.

No, *this* was good.

His lips finally moved to trail down my cheek to my ear as I lifted my knees and pressed my thighs to his sides to take him deeper and held on tight with my arms.

"My golden queen commands the heavens," he whispered in my ear.

I turned my head to ask what he was talking about, but he turned his head too, his mouth came back to mine and my question evaporated as all thought moved to his mouth, his weight, his heat, his cock...*him*.

His eyes were open as his tongue slid back into my mouth and I felt my belly plummet, my limbs tense, my lungs burn as I saw it.

I saw *it*.

Golden, shimmering, bright and brutal and deep...God, so deep in his eyes.

But I saw it.

My hand slid up into his hair to keep his head to mine so I wouldn't lose it as he kissed me, made love to me and showed me his spirit.

I'd never seen anything like it and it...was...*beautiful*.

With nothing but kisses, light touches and slow, sweet, deep strokes, Lahn built the fire until I had to let his spirit go so I could close my eyes with my climax, my moan drowned in his mouth.

Mere seconds later, not yet fully recovered from my own orgasm, my mouth received the gift of his groan.

Once he recovered, his lips swept my cheeks, my eyes then his face disappeared in my neck.

I held him tight and stared at the roof of the cham, not able to stop myself from feeling moved that he showed me his spirit. Something so precious to him. Something he kept safe. Something he did not share. And further not able to stop myself from being dazzled by the display.

Shit.

I pulled in a breath, turned my head, and mouth at his ear, I whispered, "You're a natural at this kissing business."

His head came up and his eyes came to mine, the shimmer gone but his gaze was warm.

"Natural?"

My hand slid to cup his jaw.

"Have you ever kissed a woman, my king?" I asked my question softly in Korwahk.

His gaze held mine in a way it felt like he was trying to read me before he grunted his clearly guarded negative admission of, "Me."

I was his first.

He'd given that to no one else. He'd given it only to me.

Shit. I liked that.

I smiled at him.

"Well, you're good at it," I said softly in English. "A natural." He stared at me, so I lifted my head two inches, my lips a breath from his where I whispered, "Kay anhay tee." I paused then finished with emphasis, "*Chah.*"

I liked it...*a lot.*

I watched again as his eyes smiled.

Then they grew intense, and he whispered back, "Kah rahna tunakanahsa pahnsahnalla."

I blinked.

This was new. He called me, *my golden warrior goddess.*

"What?" I asked then in Korwahk, "Tela?"

Instead of answering, he pulled out, rolled and sat up, taking me with him so I was straddling him. His hand cupping my head tipped mine down and his arm around my waist squeezed tight.

Then he said in Korwahk (most of which I caught, some of which I guessed), "I am sorry, my tigress, but you have a difficult choice this morning. Either you attend the pyre, or you do not. It is your choice, but I urge you to watch the ashes of Dortak's bride drift to the heavens."

All thoughts of what Lahn called me flew from my head.

Last night, I attended an execution-slash-suicide.

This morning, a funeral.

Fantastic.

It must be said, sometimes this queen business sucked.

My gaze slid to his ear, and I whispered in Korwahk, "I will go."

"Lahnahsahna," he called, and I looked back at him. "This is not the easy choice," he told me then gave me a squeeze. "But it is the right one."

It was way cool he understood and even cooler that he seemed proud of me.

I didn't tell him that. Instead, I sighed and nodded.

Then I asked in Korwahk, "What was her name?"

Instantly, he answered, "I do not know."

I blinked again before I stared and asked, "You don't know?"

He shook his head, "I do not."

Was he crazy?

I pulled back an inch and felt my eyes narrow. "You ordered the death of a woman whose name you don't know?"

His arm tightening brought me back and his brows knit as he studied me.

"She is the wife of a warrior. Of course I do not know her name."

Of course he didn't know her name?

He *was* crazy.

Then it occurred to me that never, not once in all the times she interpreted for us, had he called Diandra by her name. If he referred to her at all, he called Diandra "wife of Seerim" or "Seerim's woman."

"You know," I informed him, "women are wives of warriors, but they are also a lot of other things. They are mothers. They are friends. They are healers. They are—"

"Circe," he cut me off with a mini-squeeze, speaking patiently. "They are also the most beautiful women in the land. For that reason, they do not exist to Suh Tunak as anything other than a warrior's wife. They cannot. It is forbidden."

I now stared in confusion *and* curiosity. "It's forbidden?"

Lahn nodded.

"I must tell you that with your beauty, which far exceeds any woman I have ever seen, there are times when I regret you are my Dahksahna. This means people know who you are. You are on display. You sit at my side and men's eyes can study you and they do. I see it. I see they take great pleasure in their study, and it often lasts a long time." Another squeeze. "This I do *not* like but this is my burden as Dax."

Uh-oh.

My belly was getting melty.

Lahn kept speaking.

"It is a high crime for a warrior's wife to share a bed with a warrior not her husband. If this were to happen, both would be punished severely. In olden times, it happened frequently. Warriors are men and wives are beautiful. To maintain necessary distance, to warriors, all wives are known only as the wife or bride of a warrior. Contact is minimal and personal relationships between warriors and other wives are very rare and only occur when permission is granted by the husband and usually is always supervised *by* the husband. Another burden I must carry as you form attachments to your personal guard and wander the Daxshee amongst your people."

He knew about that?

"You know about that?"

"Bain and Zahnin report your activities to me daily, my queen."

Oh. Well.

That wasn't entirely surprising.

Intrusive, but not surprising.

The good news was, this wasn't about possession or stripping women of their identities, but about stopping infidelity.

And, for once, there really wasn't any bad news except the "punished severely" part, which I did not want to know so I was not going to ask.

I looked into his eyes and saw he had braced for my response so when I said, "Okay," his chin jerked back half an inch before he smiled and gave me another squeeze.

Then he repeated, "Okay."

Why did I think it was so sweet when he said that word?

I needed to move on.

I started to push away, muttering, "I guess I should bathe..." when I trailed off and fully took him in.

Last night, he had rivers of paint on his body. Right now, he didn't but I did—the paint he transferred to me when he held me after the judgment.

Last night, his hair had been plaited (something I had done yesterday morning). Right now, his hair was flowing free.

And lastly, last night, *he'd been painted.*

My body froze.

He'd been painted!

And it wasn't *me* who painted him.

"Lahn," I called and his hand in my hair slid down to rest between my shoulder blades as he grinned.

Then he murmured in a deeper than normal voice, "My tigress, you sit astride me leaking my seed in my lap, you do not have to call my name."

Okay, that was kind of hot, but I wasn't in the mood for him being hot.

I put both my hands to his shoulders and asked, "Who painted you last night?"

He stared at me, and I watched the shutters cover his eyes.

Not a good sign.

"And," I went on, "who bathed you this morning?"

His arms curled tighter around me, and he said a soft, "Circe—"

Oh no, I did not *think* so.

"Did you visit the Xacto?" I inquired in a dangerous voice and his arms got tighter.

"Kah Lahnahsahna—" he murmured.

That meant yes.

Oh no, I did not *think* so.

"You promised!" I exclaimed, reverting to English, pushing hard against his shoulders and he went back but he took me with him, twisted, and then I was on my back, him on top of me again. "Get off me!" I yelled, still pushing. "You promised!"

"Quiet, Circe," he ordered softly.

"I will not be quiet!" I shouted.

His arm moved from around me so his hand could cup my face, his thumb coming to my lips and pressing lightly.

"Quiet, my queen," he said in English then reverted to Korwahk, most of which, luckily, I understood. "You were in no state to paint me last night, and by tradition, in a ceremony where I would be passing my judgment, I needed to be painted. I had no choice, and although I promised, you must understand I broke it with a thought to your state of mind. This morning, I swam in the creek to rid myself of my paint and in order not to further break my vow to you."

Oh. Well then.

That was understandable.

It was even nice.

Shit.

"Well," I whispered against his thumb. "Okay then."

He looked into my eyes for a heartbeat then he threw his head back and laughed. Before I knew it, his thumb left my lips, his still laughing mouth replaced it, his tongue slid into my mouth, and he kissed me hard and deep.

Totally a natural.

I kissed him back and he rolled so I was on top, both his hands moving to hold back my hair.

When he broke our kiss, I saw from close up that his eyes still held mirth.

I would know why when he stated with not a small amount of arrogance, "My tigress is stubborn, and her claws are sharp, but I knew I would win her mouth."

He was gloating.

He was also not wrong.

So, I rolled my eyes and muttered, "Whatever."

This made him chuckle which made me roll my eyes again.

He stopped chuckling and called, "Circe," and when my eyes went back to him, his hands dropped my hair and his arms wrapped around me. "I will not be attending the pyre with you. I have much to do. You will be escorted by an honor guard. I command that you not leave their sight and," his arms tightened, "if Dortak should have the insolence to attend the pyre of the bride he drove to take her own life, you will show no response. I will deal with him in less than a week and then you and Suh Tunak will only have bad memories."

Again, he was speaking in Korwahk, so I didn't understand all of what he said, but I followed. Even so, I was stuck on the concept that Dortak would be there, which was such bad taste, it *defined* bad taste, and that my king wanted me not to grab the nearest blade and send it flying at him.

"Circe," Lahn called again. I focused on him, and he asked in English, "Okay?"

I stared down at him. I heaved a sigh.

Then I forced out my, "Okay."

He grinned before he lifted his head, and in my ear, he whispered, "Kah teenkah tunakanahsa," telling me he knew it was difficult for me to agree to his command, but he was pleased I did.

Then he kissed the skin of my neck, rolled me to my back, grinned down at me a second while I tried to recover from how hot he looked smiling at me with his hair flowing down his shoulders, chest and back then he bent forward, touched his mouth to my forehead and exited the bed.

I rolled to my side and watched him tie the ties on his hides as he barked, "Teetru!" And without looking back, he slapped the flaps aside and he was gone.

I rolled again to my back, pulled the silk over my naked body and hoped they didn't wear black to funerals in Korwahk.

I listened to my girls calling "poyah" to me as they rushed into the tent dragging the bath, and I heard the tinkling silverware, which meant breakfast was soon to be served, as the rest of this morning washed over me. Lahn's mouth on mine. My husband sharing his most precious possession with me. Him telling me I was beautiful, and he didn't like other men watching me. His thinking of me when he needed to be painted and still thinking of me when he washed it off, doing so without breaking his promise. And just how much I liked his hair down and how much more I liked to hear him laugh.

Shit, shit, *shit*.

I was in trouble.

It was not until much later when I would remember that I forgot to ask him about why he kept saying I commanded the heavens and why he called me a new name.

His goddess.

~

I WORE ice blue to the funeral and none of my signature gold.

An ice-blue sarong shot with silver, an ice-blue, wide suede belt (that was so plush to the touch it was shocking, and I fell in love with it instantly), another fold of silk to cover my breasts, also ice blue with heavy, silver ovals dangling at the ends.

My jewelry was minimal, just silver chandelier earrings and the seed pearl bangles I bought at the marketplace.

My makeup was pearlescent, and for the first time, Teetru arranged my hair in twists and curls pulled back at the top and sides into a fall at the back that was created by pins she slid in so they were invisible.

I heard the horses before I walked out of my cham but was surprised how many there were.

Four horses held warriors I had not seen before. Diandra was on her roan, Seerim beside her on a black mount. Feetak held Narinda in front of him on his chestnut. A dapple gray held Bain with his new bride, Oahsee, sitting behind him, her arms about his waist. Zahnin, alone but on his feet, his hand holding the bridle on a buckskin horse. Bohtan with Nahka on a palomino. And Zephyr was there for me.

The women all held flowers, and as I approached Zephyr, Jacanda handed me a beautiful, vibrant orange bloom that looked like a tiger lily except with twice as many petals.

I noticed right away that no one was in their finest finery, even if it was never as fine as mine.

Attending the pyre clearly was not a cause for celebration, an opportunity to show off or a fashion parade.

It was what it was, a sad occasion, the marking of the end of a life—this one more tragic than most and every death held tragedy so that was saying something.

Zahnin moved forward to spot me while I mounted then instantly walked to his steed, swung up and off we went, two warriors in front followed by Feetak and Narinda next to Bohtan and Nahka. Me with Diandra's roan falling in on my side. Seerim behind us next to Bain and Oahsee, Zahnin then the last two warriors.

"The pyre is far away, my dear," Diandra said to me then she lifted her chin to the air. "The wind," she finished as an explanation.

She was right. It *was* windy.

Luckily, the rain had wet the dust and sand so it wasn't swept up to bite us. Not that the wind was fierce, but it was no cool breeze either. It was good the pyre was set far. We didn't need a spark to fly and the Daxshee to burn to the ground. We'd had enough heartbreak for a while.

"Are you all right?" I asked her.

She turned her head and gave me a small smile.

"This is what I was going to ask you." I returned her small smile and reached out a hand. She grabbed it and gave it a squeeze. Then we dropped hands and she answered, "I am sad," she turned forward and said with feeling, "*It* was sad."

She could say that again.

"You?" she prompted.

"Lahn took care of me last night," I replied and felt her regard on me, so I knew her head turned my way. I sighed, thinking of my crazy romantic Korwahkian friend and how she would take this news. Then I admitted honestly, "It's true. He was lovely."

I felt her regard leave me as she muttered, again with feeling, "I am pleased."

I was too.

Damn.

We rode through the chams at a sedate walk for a while in silence.

Finally, Diandra spoke, and I was surprised to hear her voice held a vein of hurt. "Why did you not tell me you held magic?"

I blinked and looked at her. "What?"

She didn't answer my question.

Instead, she said, "I do understand, my friend, why you would hide it. I must admit, I have long since given up many of the beliefs I held growing up in the Vale, but the ones I have given up do not include my disdain for magic. So, you growing up in that part of the world, I can see you wishing to withhold this information perhaps thinking it is the same here. But you should know," she looked at me, "that the Korwahk do not hold such disdain for those who have magic. They are few and they are revered."

I kept staring at her.

Then I repeated, "What?"

Again, she ignored my question and stated, "But I do wish you would have trusted me enough to tell me. It was a grave surprise to see you command the heavens."

There it was again.

"Diandra, I didn't command the heavens," I told her, and she looked at me.

"As I explained, you do not have to hide this. In fact, I wish I had known earlier." She faced forward again. "You are my friend, and even if you shared your secret with me, it would not change how I feel about you. It is obvious, considering your personality, that you hold noble magic."

"Diandra, sweetheart, I *don't* hold magic, noble or any other kind," I asserted, and her eyes came my way again.

"Circe, I was *there*," she replied. "I saw you shout your lament to the heavens and the instant you did, they wailed."

"*I* didn't do that. That storm was brewing all day," I pointed out.

"This is true, but you called it down," she returned.

I shook my head and whispered, "That's insane."

"It is? I do not see why you think this, considering I and thousands of Korwahks witnessed the same."

I shook my head again and started, "I—" but she cut me off.

"This, too, has been whispered through the night. Many a cham stayed lit as husbands and wives put heads together, neighbors met with neighbors." She looked forward. "Your storm coupled with the unprecedented acts of the warriors on behalf of Dortak's bride..." She nodded her head once and finished, "If there were any nonbelievers, there are none now."

I blinked then again asked, "What?"

She turned to me. "The golden queen of legend, her fierce king, the Golden Dynasty, there are many stories, and as the years pass, these stories, as they have a tendency to do, grow and build until they become mythical, fantastical."

"And what is the fantastical story of the Golden Dynasty?" I inquired, although I was uncertain I wanted to know.

Of course, Diandra told me.

"The one I always thought was a flight of fancy was the one that stated the mighty king and his golden queen were god and goddess. He had strength that was unparalleled, cunning beyond compare and his queen had magic. He was impossible to kill and she commanded the moon and stars, the sun, the rivers and seas, the heavens and the earth."

I stared at her.

She kept talking. "The story tells that they never grow old, they live in youth until their first son succeeds the Dax. Then they fly on winged horse into the heavens."

"That's absurd," I said softly.

She peered at me closely.

"Circe, last night, I could *feel* your despair. I could *feel* your frustration at your powerlessness. It shone off you like an aura. And when you stood and shouted your lament, your one word felt like it pierced my skin. And it was your word that did that, my dear, not the thunder and lightning, which I will remind you, does not come at once while the heavens open at the same time they pour down their tears. They start distant and one follows the other, they offer warning. They do not come one on top of the other *with* the wet. I have lived many years on this earth, and I have not once seen that until you called it upon us last night."

Okay, I had to admit, I lived many years on the earth, *my* earth, but still, I'd never known that to happen, and I lived in Seattle where it rained a lot.

Oh man.

Still, it couldn't be true. It had to be a fluke.

"Diandra, my sweet friend, I'm telling you, I don't hold magic," I whispered, and she studied me closely.

Then she said quietly in return, "Perhaps you do and you did not know you did until last night and it flooded out from you when your emotions were careening out of control. But it matters not, now your people believe you do. They believe you hold great power. They believe your king cannot die. They believe you will never age. And they believe, deep into the depths of their spirits, that the Golden Dynasty is upon us."

I faced forward thinking, *holy shit, now what do I do with* this?

"There is more to this than last night, my dear," she continued. "You fit the description of the Golden Goddess exactly. Golden hair, golden eyes and now, with your time in the sun, golden skin. You sing like the seraphs and your heart is as golden as your eyes. But you are the queen of the warrior nation because you *are* a warrior, fierce of spirit, a match to your formidable king from the very beginning, the night of your claiming. The warriors themselves respect you like no other woman. You have earned great loyalty in a short period of time as evidenced last night when so many came forward to intervene, an occurrence so extraordinary, I still have trouble believing it. The same holds true for the mighty Dax. Seerim has told me for years he has never seen a warrior like your King Lahn. Even when he was younger, he had no compare. He has never been unhorsed. He has never been disarmed. He rode out for his first kill at the age of fourteen, for his trainers had nothing left to teach him, he so excelled in his studies."

Oh man...*really*?

Fourteen?

Holy crap.

She kept talking. "I have seen him face challenges and his strength and speed is astonishing. It is superhuman and now, it would seem this is because he is not a human, but, like you, a god."

"Diandra, I'm not—" I started but she held up a hand and I stopped.

"We will talk more later. Not now, my love, for we approach the pyre."

Considering our bizarre and scary conversation, I hadn't noticed it, but now I did.

We had left the chams and climbed a small rise that we were now descending. Others on foot and on mount moved in the direction of the tall, wooden pyre on which a body wrapped in white gauze rested. There were many still approaching, like us, but it seemed there were thousands already gathered and waiting, silent and respectful.

As our procession approached, the thick crowd parted at the orders of the front of the guard and, since I was queen, we road straight to the pyre.

See?

Sometimes it was *not* good being queen.

We stopped close to the pyre, and I saw that the wood leading up to the top was mingled heavily with flowers, hundreds of them of all colors, shapes and sizes, even the body had flowers resting on it from those who had been able to toss their blooms that high.

Zahnin's horse trotted forward, and he dismounted to spot me as I swung off my horse.

My women and I approached the pyre, each of us lost ourselves in a moment of reflection before, in our time, we laid our flowers in the wood.

We stepped away and stood, waiting, as silent as the rest of the crowd as the trail of horses and people joined us and gave their blossoms in offering if they had them.

As I stood close to the pyre, I felt eyes, many of them. This was not unusual, but after Diandra and my talk, my senses were heightened to the point this attention felt physical.

I shook this off and noted our numbers were no longer swelling, however I didn't look around very much. I did this not because I didn't want to encounter people who thought I was a goddess (crazy!), but because I didn't want to see Dortak amongst them. I made a promise to Lahn, and I needed to keep it. To do that, I needed to adopt the ignorance is bliss strategy.

I also noted that no time was wasted, for the gray-haired female healer who had attended me when I had sunstroke was standing to the side bearing an unlit torch, which another woman was lighting.

Interesting, women lit the pyre.

Then I sucked in breath when her torch was lit, and her gaze came to me before her body started my way.

Oh shit.

No.

Was this a queenly duty?

She kept coming.

Oh God, it looked like this was a queenly duty.

Great, fucking great.

She stopped in front of me and spoke. "My golden queen, I watched as you held her gaze when her spirit moved to the next realm. It is my honor to offer you the torch which will send her ashes to the heavens so her body can join her spirit."

With that, she offered me the torch.

Crap.

Well, there was nothing for it, so I took the torch and looked at the pyre.

I looked back at the healer and asked, "Do you know her name?"

She examined my face a second before her eyes warmed and her lips tipped up in a small smile.

"Her name was Mahyah, my true, golden queen."

I nodded, took in a deep breath and walked to the pyre.

I looked up at the body so high up I couldn't see much except they'd changed the gauze. There was no blood to be seen and her face had also been shrouded.

And I thought about a young Korwahk woman who possibly walked through the parade and looked over the warriors in their avenue while wondering which one would be hers, maybe excited about her life as a warrior's wife. And in three short weeks she'd been debased, defiled, beaten and abused.

I turned around and called to Diandra.

Quickly, she moved to me.

When she arrived, I whispered, "Can you translate?"

She nodded.

"You can say no if you're uncom—" I started, but she shook her head and touched my arm.

"I will speak your words, my queen."

I smiled at her.

Then I wasted no time so I wouldn't lose my nerve, turned to the crowd and spoke loudly in Korwahk, doing the best I could do and hoping I didn't fuck it up.

"I am only recently Korwahk, and I am new to your tongue. I have not yet learned it enough to honor young Mahyah on her pyre before we send her ashes to the heavens. So my friend Diandra will be translating for you the words to a song I sang to Mahyah some days ago in hopes of reaching her spirit and giving her a few moments of peace. Before her death, she told me the land that I sang of was the land where she wanted to go. Now, I will sing the song to you so you can know where Mahyah is, and she is somewhere happy."

I looked to Diandra who nodded to me.

When she did, I sang without accompaniment. I didn't do great, I didn't suck. I certainly didn't sound like seraphs, though I didn't know what they sounded like. The good news was, once I closed my eyes and gave my mind over to the song, I remembered all the words. And I was so into it, I didn't even hear Diandra translating the words while I sang.

When I was done, I opened my eyes and saw a sea of faces. There were some women crying, their eyes wet, their hands to their mouths, but every eye was on me.

"I don't know what lemon drops are, Circe, and they don't have chimney tops, but I did my best," Diandra whispered to me, and I turned my head to her and smiled.

I grabbed her hand, squeezed and whispered, "I'm sure it was perfect."

She smiled and squeezed my hand back.

I turned to the pyre and looked up at the gauze shrouded body.

"I hope, beautiful Mahyah, you're over the rainbow," I whispered.

I threw the torch into the flower-strewn wood and instantly was pulled back by Zahnin as Seerim pulled Diandra back to stand at the front of the crowd some feet away from the quickly catching inferno, the flames coaxed to great heat swiftly by the wind.

The tears stung my nose as the flames licked Mahyah's body.

But I froze as my attention caught on something, lifted to the sky and my breath stuck in my throat as I heard gasps all around, felt the astonished shuffling of bodies and Diandra's hand came to mine and held tight.

This was because, as the flames danced high, arching through the sky over the pyre, there was a brilliant, perfect rainbow.

I stared at the rainbow with my mouth hanging open.

Oh.

Shit.

22
THE FAVOR

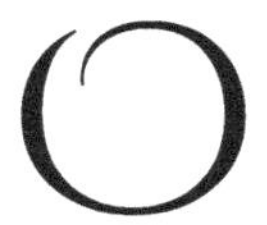kay, it couldn't be denied. Evidence was suggesting I held magic.

Shit.

Our ride home was silent, everyone in their own thoughts.

It was also wired.

This was because, for no reason at all since the rain had stopped in the night and the wind and sun were quickly drying the wet, there was no way a perfect arc of a rainbow should grace the sky.

Unless I commanded it.

Shit!

Maybe I *did* have magic, as completely insane as that seemed. Maybe I *did* command the heavens accidentally last night. Maybe I filled the sky with a rainbow so Mahyah's ashes could drift over it to meet her soul.

And maybe this magic had brought me to this world in the first place.

Maybe it was *me* who was responsible for bringing me here.

Which would mean it was *me* who had the capacity to send myself back (somehow).

In my world, thoughts like this would lead me straight to my car where I would drive to the nearest psych ward and voluntarily check in.

But in *this* world, apparently anything went.

And the point was, I was *in this world*, which meant I was not insane, but instead, screwed.

As we rode back into the Daxshee, horses carrying my friends peeled off on a variety of trails winding through the chams, quietly called farewells the only things piercing our silence. When Seerim had lifted his chin at his wife before his horse took him down another path and it was only Diandra and I, I decided it was time to have a chat with my friend.

I didn't get this chance.

Zahnin barked an order, the four warriors gave him chin lifts, peeled away and Zahnin's horse trotted up to me.

I looked up at him to see him glaring down at me. His gaze swung to Diandra then back to me and I watched his jaw turn rock hard.

I was thinking this wasn't good.

Maybe he didn't like rainbows. Or witches. Even those who held noble magic who didn't know they were witches.

I braced before I asked, "Is all well, Zahnin?"

His glare turned to a scowl. A muscle jumped in his cheek.

Then he grunted, "Me."

I felt my body get tight as I looked beyond him to the winding paths that led through the chams, wondering, if all wasn't well, why he dismissed our guard.

"Um—" I started.

He interrupted me by forcing out between his teeth, "I request a favor from my golden queen."

You could tell he didn't wish to request this favor, like, he *really* didn't wish to request this favor. Or, maybe, *any* favor.

My gaze slid to Diandra who was looking at Zahnin. She felt my eyes on her, looked at me and shrugged. I turned back to Zahnin.

"What favor do you wish to request?" I inquired.

He scowled down at me and a muscle again jumped in his cheek.

Then he grunted, "My new bride."

These were not words I expected or understood why he was saying them, so I gazed at him silently, and when he said no more, I prompted, "Your new bride..."

His buckskin horse, catching his warrior's vibe, danced with agitation under him and Zahnin tightened his hold on the reins so the horse stilled.

Suddenly, so quickly it took all my concentration not to miss any of it, he explained, "My new bride is like you. She has great beauty. In the parade, I knew it was only her for me. I fought four brothers to claim her. She is also not of Korwahk, like you. She does not speak our tongue. She does not speak..." he hesitated, and his eyes narrowed, "*at all.*"

Oh man.

That wasn't good news.

I bit my lip.

Zahnin went on tersely, "Unlike you, she does not settle into my cham and her new life. The favor I ask of my true queen is that you speak to her and help her settle into her new life as my wife as you have done with my king."

I was sensing (rightly) this was why Zahnin was in such a bad mood.

I was also sensing (rightly) that the proud warrior before me didn't often request favors.

As in...*never*.

Therefore, I stated, "Take us to her."

He stared at me, and without looking at Diandra, he said, "The wife of Seerim—"

I cut in, "She will accompany me. She is the reason I have settled in my life with Suh Tunak. She will be of great assistance with your bride."

He scowled awhile longer, his jaw still hard, that muscle jumped, then he jerked his chin, jerked his reins and Diandra and I pulled our horses around and followed him back through the chams.

As we did this, her eyes came to me, and they were twinkling.

I pressed my lips together and tried not to laugh.

Zahnin stopped in front of a cham that was bigger than most (not as big as Lahn and mine) and a girl ran forward as he dismounted. He tossed his reins to her without a word and rounded his horse to spot me as I swung off Zephyr. When my feet were on the ground, he did the same with an already dismounting Diandra. Once the girl had the reins of all three horses, Zahnin stalked to the cham flaps and slapped them aside, entering.

Diandra and I followed.

When we got inside and my eyes adjusted to being out of the sun, I noticed instantly that Zahnin's tent was not like Feetak and Narinda's nor Bohtan and Nahka's (which was slightly grander than Narinda's). It was nearly like Lahn and mine. Bigger bed (not quite as big). Silk on the bed and pillows. More trunks (not as many as Lahn and I had). Nice furniture. Many candlesticks and tall candleholders. Also, there was the smell of incense, the scent of musk and bergamot. It smelled lovely and I instantly decided I needed to talk to Teetru about incense.

I decided this as I watched a girl scoot with some alarm off the bed. So much alarm, she toppled over the head of the bed and landed on her ass.

She shot up and quickly backed away, her eyes glued in fear to Zahnin, her body shaking.

I studied her.

Yep, this was why Zahnin was in such a bad mood.

Three weeks and she was still like this?

Not good.

I looked at Zahnin and he was watching his bride and he was not happy. So not happy, he looked extremely pissed off and that look on a huge, savage Korwahk warrior was fearsome.

Okay, it was clear Zahnin needed a few lessons in romance, but I needed to focus on the girl first.

I turned back to her to see she hadn't torn her frightened eyes from her husband. I also recognized her as one of the women in the pen who I thought was like me. She had been visibly terrified back then and she was no less terrified now.

She was, however, as Zahnin had described her, quite beautiful. Light-brown hair, green eyes, a pixie-pretty face and very petite. Her ass and breasts were not much to write home about, but her skin was peaches and cream all over and there was something delicate about her, something graceful even as she stood still. Something that many men, not Zahnin (I would have thought before that moment), would be drawn to in a protective way.

But clearly, I was wrong about Zahnin.

Nevertheless, this would not help Zahnin. He was not as tall as Lahn, but he was still tall and extremely muscled. Lahn dwarfed me and I was just above average height. This girl was small and Zahnin must seem like a giant to her.

I stepped forward and her focus shot to me before going back to Zahnin.

"Hello," I said quietly in English and her gaze moved quickly back to me, "I am Circe, Queen of Korwahk."

She stared at me.

I took another cautious step forward and went on softly, "We're here to help. You're safe."

I watched her swallow then lick her lips, but she did not speak.

Another step forward and I said, "Can you tell me your name?"

She blinked at me, bit her lower lip and then quickly she said something in a language I recognized with one of the words being, "Valearian."

She was speaking French.

Shit.

I took French in high school for two years, but that was high school. It had been ages. I recognized it, but there was no way in hell I could speak it.

"She is Fleuridian, my dear," Diandra whispered to me. "A language I do not know."

Great, they didn't call France France and Diandra didn't speak Fleuridian (or whatever).

Shit again!

"Uh..." I began, pulling up my high school French. "*Bonjour,*" I tried. "*Je m'appelle* Circe."

Her eyes grew big, then they grew wet, then her hands came up clasped in front of her and she shot rapid-fire French at me all the while her gaze slid back and forth between me and Zahnin.

I didn't catch a lick of it.

Shit, shit, shit!

I smiled at her and lifted my hand.

She stopped speaking and I turned my head slightly to Diandra. "Is there anyone in the Daxshee who speaks her language?"

"Yes, Circe, several, and I know of someone who will be happy to help. She, like me, has been here many years," Diandra answered and turned to Zahnin and said in Korwahk. "Have one of your slaves find Claudine, wife of Veenuk."

Zahnin scowled at her but jerked his chin then slapped out of the cham.

As he did, I watched the girl relax.

Not good.

I took another step to her and asked softly, "*Comment tu t'appelles?*" and she looked back at me, her eyes soft, her manner relieved.

"Sabine," she whispered.

"Okay, Sabine, *ma*, erm...Fleuridian *no c'est bon*, uh...but we're getting help."

She blinked at me then she nodded in a way that I knew she understood what I said in her language but not in my own.

Boy, I hoped Claudine lived close.

Zahnin slapped back into the tent and grunted something to Diandra, and Sabine grew instantly tense.

I approached Zahnin.

His attention came to me.

He still looked pissed, that look was still scary, but I sucked it up, stopped close to him and whispered in Korwahk, "Your wife's name is Sabine, did you know that?"

His head jerked so slightly I could convince myself I didn't see it, same with a flash that flared in his eyes.

But I didn't miss the angry look slightly fading from his face as his head turned toward his bride and he murmured, "Sabine," in his deep, rough voice, making a pretty name even prettier.

He didn't know his wife's name, but he was clearly glad to know it.

I pulled in a calming breath.

I could work with this.

I turned to Sabine who had wary eyes on her husband. I waited until they flitted to me, and I smiled. My smile didn't alleviate the fear shadowing her entire frame and I knew this was because Zahnin was in attendance.

It occurred to me that in all likelihood Zahnin was doing the same thing to his wife that Lahn had done to me.

That was, he'd raped her during the Hunt, she either had no idea what was happening to her (my guess, she too was "sheltered") or knew about it and hated it. She took that hit then kept taking it as he kept using her body for the last three weeks as any warrior would feel his due from his wife.

I studied her.

She was clean and clearly fed. There were no signs of visible abuse, no cuts, bruises or swelling. Her sarong, bandeau, belt and jewelry were very nice. She was wearing quite a bit of silver. Her hair was artfully arranged, and her makeup was expertly applied, which meant she had a girl or girls who were taking good care of her. The entire package saying that her husband was doing what he knew how to do to provide for his wife.

He was just not providing for her the way a woman needed to be provided for.

And he didn't understand it, but he'd been forcing her to live a nightmare for three weeks.

Okay, maybe I couldn't work with this.

Not, of course, without reinforcements.

I turned back to Zahnin and whispered, "I need my king. Can you send a messenger to him, and if he's not too busy to attend me now, can you ask that he does? It is not urgent, but I would look favorably on him granting my request."

Zahnin examined me, clearly uncertain about how he felt about Lahn being called into our current situation.

Then he grunted and slapped out of the tent.

I took that as a yes.

I also took that as a sign that Zahnin wanted his wife to settle in her new life with him.

I turned back to the woman to see Diandra had gotten close and was talking softly to her.

And I sucked in breath and waited for Claudine and, hopefully, Lahn.

STANDING with my husband outside of Zahnin's tent, I watched his eyebrows knit ominously and his eyes narrow dangerously before he whispered angrily in Korwahk, "My tigress wants me to do *what*?"

I moved in close (or closer, I was already pretty close), put a hand light on his chest (a chest that he had his arms crossed over), got up on my tiptoes and bent my head way back to reply on a whisper as best I could in Korwahk and I essentially repeated (with more detail), "You need to talk to Zahnin. He requested this favor of me, but *he* needs to do his part. He must stop taking her against her will. He needs to back off, start wooing her, take meals with her, bring her presents, flowers, candy, jewelry. He needs to try to talk to her, teach her the Korwahk language. He needs to take her for rides and show her her new country. He needs to speak gently to her, look on her gently, touch her gently. And when he tries anything with her, he needs to do it like *you* did it with me and seek to give her pleasure before he takes his own. And I can't tell him any of that, Lahn, *you* need to tell him all of that."

Lahn stared down his nose at me.

Then he asked, "My queen called me away from my warriors to ask me to tell another one of my warriors not to fuck his new wife." (There it was, I knew *tooyo* meant *fuck*.) "But instead to bring her candy and take her for horseback rides? Do I have this right, Circe?"

I didn't think this was going very well.

"Um...yes?" I asked back, now not so certain about my strategy.

Lahn kept staring at me. He stopped doing that to look over my head. Then he sighed. And finally, without looking at me again, he turned on his boot and walked away.

I was taking that as a no.

Great.

I walked back in Zahnin's cham to see Diandra and Claudine (who was older than Diandra, but she still held great beauty, maybe it was something in the water or just that the Korwahk scouts had good eyes) sitting on either side of Sabine on the bed, Claudine murmuring to her. This happened under Zahnin's glower from where he stood a few feet inside the tent flaps, legs planted, arms crossed, focus riveted to his wife and the two women.

If he kept glaring at her like that, she'd never calm down and let him in.

I got close to him, touched his arm, jerked my head to the tent flaps, and without looking to see if he followed, I walked back outside.

He followed.

When he did, I got close, looked into his dark eyes and saw that he was scary, but he was still handsome. He had a scar that slashed through his eyebrow, which only served to make a hot guy hotter. If he didn't constantly wear an expression that made him look like he wanted to rip someone's head off, he'd be super-hot.

I sucked in breath, hoped that he truly wished tranquility in his cham, and then, in Korwahk, I told him exactly what I told Lahn. I faltered in the middle when his glower looked like it was flashing to rage (this was around about the time when I told him he needed to stop taking his wife against her will), but I sallied forth.

I finished with, "Zahnin, my protector, I know you do not wish to hear any of this. But if you want peace in your cham, if you want to hear cries of pleasure and sounds of mirth, hers and," I leaned in, "*your own*, instead of the sound of tears and the feel of fear, then you must take heed to what I say."

His pissed-off stare didn't waver, so I kept on.

"I will do my best, with Diandra and Claudine, to teach her your language and the ways of your people, to help her to understand her new life and to be able to communicate with you and you her. But that is all we can do. You must do the rest."

He continued to stare down at me angrily.

Shit. There was nothing for it.

I kept right on going.

"Your king did not break through with me until his touch stopped taking and started giving, and until, in our cham, he treated me with kindness. He is the mightiest of Suh Tunak. He recognized the battle he had on his hands, he analyzed it, created his strategy and then he went about winning that battle using any means necessary. And, Zahnin," I edged closer, and for the sake of this man who pledged to guard me even if it meant giving his life, who backed me against Dortak and who clearly wanted his wife to settle in her new life with him in his cham, I admitted to him at the same time I admitted to myself, "*my* Lahn won that battle. I now lay awake at night waiting for him to return. When he does not, I fall asleep looking forward to the morning when he will wake me with his hands. He is my king. He is my warrior. He is my husband. And I am proud to say above all...he is *mine*."

Zahnin said not one word and kept staring at me.

I returned his stare, all out of ideas.

Finally, he grunted and jerked up his chin.

I took *that* as a yes.

I smiled up at him hopefully. He watched me smile, shook his head, the scowl left his face and I saw his lips twitch.

Yep, definitely hot. If Sabine had it in her, there were hints that, soon, she would think she didn't do so badly.

Then, hopefully, Zahnin would share with her his greatest gift, and she'd feel touched and loved.

Like I felt that morning.

Good news for Sabine and Zahnin, confusing and worrying news for me.

Shit.

"My wife creates rainbows," Lahn muttered to the roof of our cham.

It was late. We'd just gone at it hot and heavy, so hot and heavy I came *three times*, (yep, *three*). I was sated, drowsy and in a really good mood mostly because my husband had come home before I fell asleep, but it must be noted it was also because he'd given me three orgasms. My mood was too good to let all that was weighing heavily on my mind weigh on it. So I'd set it aside.

I was curled up against him, my legs tangled in his, my arm resting on his abs, my cheek to his shoulder. Lahn was on his back, his arm was under me, curled around, his fingertips trailing random patterns on the skin of my hip.

"Lahn," I whispered to his chest.

"She is also mad," he kept muttering.

I pushed up onto a forearm and looked down at him.

"Mad?" I asked.

His eyes came to me, and he used one word to explain.

"Zahnin."

I pressed my lips together.

Lahn kept talking. "Do not ask me to do something like that again, Circe. I understand your heart guides you in many matters. But I am warrior, *he* is warrior, and this is a line we never cross. Am I understood?"

I kept my lips pressed together and nodded.

His gaze dropped to my mouth then his arm tightened around me, pulling me up on his body. His other hand lifted to shift my hair from one side of my face and hold it behind my neck.

When he spoke, it was in a murmur, "I do not like my queen's lips pressed tight."

I relaxed my lips, and he gave a slight nod of satisfaction before his eyes locked on mine, and when he spoke again, his voice was soft and even, fuck me, tender.

I liked it.

"It means much to me that you let your heart guide you. It guided you back to me after I marked you and forced you to guard it from me."

Oh God.

He was being sweet again.

He kept talking.

"But this, I fear, will cause you harm, my doe. And I want you to use caution as you open that heart. Zahnin is my closest lieutenant and I know much of him. He did not come to training direct from his parents' care. His father was a warrior who died before he was born. A sickness took his mother not long after. His family took him in, but they didn't show him a great deal of kindness in the short time they had him. This would lead me to believe he does not understand how to provide this to his wife. Much time has passed since the Hunt, so you must not hold high hopes for him winning her, for if you do, and he does not succeed, I know you will be crushed. This can happen and does. There are warriors who do not break through with their wives. If this does not happen, they can then cast them aside and attend another Hunt. It is their reward, as a warrior of Suh Tunak, to be provided a beauty to warm their bed, to do this willingly, to provide for their desires and to give them sons. And it is their right to keep seeking until that is found."

My head tilted and I whispered, "Cast aside?"

He nodded. "Those cast aside are taken care of, given chams, even a slave. But they do not live the life of bounty that a warrior's wife lives. Although the basics are provided, many of them must learn a trade to live a decent life. Sometimes, they will find a free man who will wish to take them as bride, and do, but this is rare. A warrior's wife who is cast aside bears the reputation that she is unfit or unable to provide for a man's needs, and although beautiful, will be avoided."

Well, that sucked.

"Would...um, Sabine, Zahnin's wife, if, um...this happens, since she's not from Korwahk, will she be returned to her homeland?" I asked.

His eyes flashed and he stated firmly, "Absolutely not."

Hmm.

"Why?"

"She is claimed, she is Korwahk," Lahn stated just as firmly.

Hmm.

Time to change the subject because this one might irritate me, and I wasn't in the mood to be irritated.

"Did, uh...you, um...grow up under your parents' care before training?"

It was the first personal question I'd ever asked him.

And he didn't hesitate in answering.

"I did, my tigress. My father was Dax, and my mother was Korwahk, a great beauty. There was tenderness in his cham even though my mother could only give him one son, a difficult delivery rendering it impossible to provide him more. He was happy with the warrior she bestowed on him, and he was happy with her." His hand in my hair fisted when his voice dropped as he shared, "And I watched my father die during a challenge. I was warrior then and attended. As Dahksahna and as was her duty, my mother attended as well. His end marked her, as it did me, and she cared deeply for him. She would have lived a pleasant life as a deposed Dahksahna, the Korwahk people and myself providing for her, but she chose not to live on without him. She took her own life the day after his body burned on the pyre."

Oh my God.

That was awful.

I felt myself melt into him as my hand lifted to cup his jaw and I whispered, "Lahn."

His eyes held mine. "I regret she did not live to see her son best the Dax who bested her king. He was a man it was difficult to respect and not simply because he took my father's head. It was a triumph in more ways than avenging my father to take his."

"Honey," I breathed, and his hand moved to the side of my neck, his thumb beginning to stroke my jaw as I watched his eyes grow warm.

"Would that you were in my bed those years ago, Circe," he whispered, staring deep into my eyes. "Sharing with me like you are now, your golden spirit to balm my own." I held my breath as the silk of his words glided through me, then he grinned. "And also here to celebrate my triumph when I took my vengeance."

God, he was *such* a man.

I couldn't help it, I grinned back at him.

"I take it that would have been..." I paused, searching for the word in Korwahk and hoping I found it, "*Energetic.*"

His thumb stopped stroking and his fingers sifted up into my hair, putting pressure on so my lips touched his.

There, he whispered in English, "Oh yes."

I found the right word or *a* right word.

I smiled against his mouth.

His eyes heated and he growled against mine.

Then his head slanted. His fingers pressed further, he ground my lips against his, they opened, and his tongue instantly invaded. I made a noise in my throat, and he rolled me to my back.

And he demonstrated how energetic he would have felt after he seized the Dax.

It was years later, but clearly the glory hadn't faded, and I knew this mainly because, even after an already hot and heavy session, it... was...*phenomenal.*

So much so, my loud moans, whimpers and cries were noted by passersby, those inhabiting close chams and spies paying attention, as were his groans, grunts and his final shout of climax.

And after he was through with me, *thoroughly* through with me, I fell into an exhausted sleep not thinking about holding magic. Not thinking of calling to the heavens to make them weep, to sending a rainbow arcing through the sky. Not thinking that I might have the magic in me to send myself home. And not thinking about Zahnin and his wife, hoping all would soon be well in their cham.

No, I didn't think any of that.

Instead, in the seconds before my husband's warm, hard, big body settled next to and partly over mine, his arm wrapped around, our legs tangled, I didn't think about anything.

23
THE CONTEST

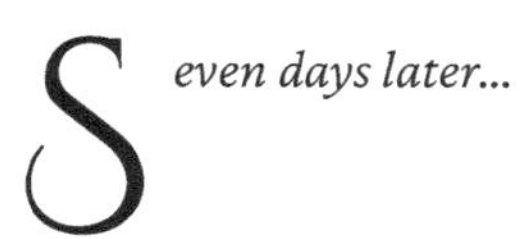

even days later...

I DIPPED my fingers into the pot of black paint and saw they were trembling.

I had to get a hold of myself.

But soon, very soon—in fact, I was all dressed and ready to go in my golden finery—and as soon as I painted my husband, we would be out of our cham and on our way to Lahn facing Dortak in the challenge.

I knew one thing: Lahn would beat him.

I knew something else, as much as I hated Dortak and as little as it said about me, I cared nothing about the fact his life would soon end.

But I still didn't look forward to watching my husband cut his head off.

I knew one last thing, Dortak would not hesitate to cheat and I didn't want Lahn to get hurt when he did.

I *so* didn't want that that I knew I didn't want it not because I simply didn't want another man, an abuser and a cheater, to harm a man who would fight with honor.

And I knew I didn't want it not because Lahn had kept me fed and sheltered and showered in jewels and kickass clothes.

I didn't want it because I cared about my husband and this feeling ran deep.

And because of this I was terrified out of my mind.

THE LAST SEVEN days had been good.

Very good.

Too good.

I had kept up my wanderings with Bain and Zahnin, but now Zahnin was chatting. We didn't have deep conversations where he bared his soul, but he talked. He didn't ask for advice or share how things were going in his cham, but he did more than grunt unintelligibly at observations I made. He corrected my Korwahk and he often waded in to try to explain when I was speaking with my people on the (rarer and rarer occasion) I was messing it up.

Daily, however, I went to his cham to attend Sabine.

At my request, Diandra and Claudine had sought and found the other girl not of Korwahk who was hunted with us. She was Fleuridian too, her name was Anastasie, and although her warrior had been gentler with her, without the assistance I had or Sabine was getting, she was still lost in a culture she didn't understand and more than a little alarmed by it (she had not, for instance, been sheltered from the selection *or* the celebration after).

With Narinda, Diandra and Claudine gave all of us lessons in Korwahk, and often Nahka would come by, sometimes bringing her friends, and lessons would descend into girlie time with Diandra and Claudine translating.

With this, it didn't take long for laughter to ring from Sabine's tent.

And this laughter was ringing once when the flaps slapped back and Zahnin entered.

Sabine did not scurry away, but her eyes did snap to him. She held her body tense but not tight nor terrified, just guarded.

I counted this as progress.

He took in the scene, his eyes went to his bride, and he asked, "All is well, wife?"

Claudine interpreted, and after a moment's hesitation, she nodded.

Zahnin tipped his chin up to her, walked forward and executed a smooth move right in front of all her new girlfriends.

He ran the backs of his fingers gently across her cheek even as she visibly failed to fight back a slight wince.

He wisely ignored this and whispered, "This pleases me."

Then, without another word or glance at anyone, he turned and walked out.

Nice.

Very nice.

Sabine stared at the tent flaps in open-mouthed shock.

Diandra, Claudine, Nahka and even Narinda and I shared knowing and amused glances.

In our time with her, Sabine did not share how things were going and we didn't ask. But Zahnin's move made me hold hope that even if he wasn't raised with kindness, he was the kind of man who was born with it.

I had heard and processed Lahn's warnings, but still, I couldn't help it.

I was hopeful.

It became clear to me the night of the day of the rainbow that Lahn had settled his horde and therefore he came home much earlier.

This meant more lovemaking. It also meant more chats. Some of them heartfelt (for instance, when I told him stories of my father, his men, horseback riding lessons and the like). Some of them informative (Lahn explaining things about Korwahk, how he spent his days, how I spent mine, me telling him how I learned how to play guitar (though, mention of another man in my life was not looked on favorably so I made a mental note not to do that again)). Some of the chats were amusing and I realized my husband had a dry wit.

I also realized that he found me hilarious in a resigned way that, even if resigned, he felt it was appealing. He thought I was quite mad, I knew, with half the shit I did and said, the way my heart guided me, the easy way my temper flared, but he found it attractive, and he didn't hide it.

I liked that.

He even once came home in time to take dinner with me in the cham, and as he did, I realized I'd never seen him eat. I also realized he ate a lot. He was a big guy, and he had a big appetite. With the way he ate, how he kept that six pack was anyone's guess. But I liked that he enjoyed his food, and he did not hide it.

He was also gentle with me in many ways and took time and patiently began to assist Diandra in her teachings about the Korwahk and The Horde. He was king, he could do as he pleased and expect to do it without being questioned and his people had lived their way of life for eons. But I liked that he took the time to explain things to me.

Truth be told, I was beginning to like everything about Lahn.

And, stupid me, I did absolutely nothing to stop it.

~

I often spent time with Diandra, Nahka and Narinda, but I did not broach the subject of my magic and my possible goddess status with any of them, and they didn't with me either.

I didn't know why they didn't.

But I didn't because I was stupid.

And I didn't because I wanted Zahnin to win his wife, and Sabine, who was very sweet, to settle and find contentment and even happiness after what she'd endured. I wanted her to have what Mahyah never found. I wanted that a lot. And I wanted to do what I couldn't do for Mahyah, and that was to help her have it.

And I also didn't because I liked wandering the Daxshee, talking to my people, gabbing with Bain, exchanging comments with Zahnin, learning Korwahk, getting to recognize faces and beginning to share in the lives of my people. Knowing who was sick. Who was pregnant. Whose son was to go before my husband in the next selection and the like.

And I also didn't because I liked my nights with Lahn, our chats, our lovemaking.

And I liked our mornings, his baths, sometimes my baths with him, the soft talks we'd have as he sat cross-legged in front of me while I sat on the pile of hides and braided or bunched his hair and...um, our lovemaking (that was good enough to repeat).

Diandra was right and so was I.

After Lahn hit me, he listened to what I said to him, and inadvertently I had taught him a lesson, at the same time he realized he had a battle on his hands and set about winning it. He had changed, sharing with me his time, his wit, his sweetness and his patience as well as his body, and in so doing, he succeeded.

And he was enjoying his spoils, for he knew from one look at me in the parade that I was what he'd been waiting for for years (he told me this during one of *his* heartfelt chats). And he now had it, and he was not only content, he was openly happy.

I liked that he was, but further that it was me that was giving it to him.

Therefore, I wasn't broaching the topic of magic because I was actually *enjoying* being with the Korwahk, with my husband, with my friends.

This didn't mean I wouldn't kill for a burrito or a cell phone where I could call Diandra or Narinda rather than traipsing all the way to their chams with one of my guards in hopes they were home when I wanted company.

But as the days went on, these longings faded, my memories of home faded, and Korwahk became my reality.

When I allowed myself to think of it, I told myself I would, and soon, find out what was happening and then make a decision about what I would do next.

But, for now, I would give myself this.

Because I liked it.

See?

Stupid.

I totally should have sorted that all out before Lahn faced Dortak in the contest for the Dax and maybe got himself injured. Something I would have to watch or, God forbid, the gods of this world wept because the earth was falling from the sky and Dortak took my husband's beautiful head, then he turned to me.

See?

Totally.

Stupid.

I SET the pot on the table and turned to Lahn.

Not looking in his eyes, I started at the indentation of his collarbone and drew a heavy line down his chest, starting to paint the design I hadn't realized until then I had memorized.

"Uh..." I mumbled in order to take my mind off the day's events and take Lahn's off the fact that I hadn't quite controlled the trembling of my hand. "You only wear black. What do the other colors warriors bear signify?"

I didn't look at him when I asked my question, but I knew he'd tilted his head down to look at me as he answered.

"White is an unseasoned warrior, new to the kill. Red indicates those who go on campaign. Blue, those who go to war or patrol Korwahk. All colors, those who are seasoned, who have gone on raids and handled themselves well in war and therefore have proven themselves. They can choose to raid or war or both. Green, a color you may not have seen, are warriors who now spend their time training. Those wearing only black are my lieutenants, warriors who have my ear, who lead troops on assignment or who belong to The Horde that travels with the Daxshee. In other words, they have also proven themselves in battle. They are our finest warriors and therefore hold a high rank."

"Mm-hmm," I mumbled, listening but not listening then, twisting, I grabbed the pot, gouged out more paint and turned back to him, lifting my hand to start on the arcs.

I didn't touch his skin.

This was because his fingers wrapped around wrist.

"Give me your golden eyes, Circe," he said softly in English.

I bit my lip then lifted my eyes to his. I knew I was not hiding anything when his went soft and his hand tightened around my wrist.

"He will not best me," he whispered, again in English.

"Right," I whispered back, but that one word trembled.

His brows rose slightly. "You do not have faith in your king?"

I shook my head once.

"No, I do." I was still whispering, my voice continuing to tremble, when I said, "He cheats."

"I know this," Lahn replied, and when I made no response, his other hand came up and curled around the back of my neck, holding me warmly there. "Because I know this, do you not think I have planned for it?"

Um...actually, no. That thought hadn't occurred to me.

"Uh," I started then admitted, "No. I didn't. I've been too busy freaking out."

Whereas, when amongst the Korwahk, I almost always spoke Korwahk, when Lahn was in our tent, he demanded we converse in English. He caught on quickly, proving maybe he actually *was* a god or at least he was super clever.

Further, this aided in softening my heart because I liked that he wanted to learn my language and share that with me.

So now he asked, "Freaking out? You use this expression in many different ways."

"Well, this time, I mean worried, upset and a lot of both," I explained, and his eyes roamed my face.

Then his hand at my neck pulled me in and up as he bent so his lips could touch mine.

He moved away an inch before he whispered, "He will not best me, Circe."

I pressed my lips together.

His eyes flared.

I quickly released them and whispered back, "Okay, Lahn."

His hand gave me a squeeze and he repeated, "He will not best me." He went on with another squeeze, but this time, his hand held tight. "This is my vow to you. I face this contest to defend my title as the Dax, but I also face this challenge knowing that, if he were to take my head, I would die and spend my time in the other realm knowing he would handle you and he would do it worse than he did his bride. I would not allow that to happen, and I am not about to fall and *let* it happen. I am your husband. I will keep you safe and I will do it by keeping my feet on this earth, breathing the air and being there to *make* you safe. Do you understand this?"

Okay. Okay.

Shit.

Okay.

There it was. I *really* liked my husband.

And after his declaration, the only thing I could do was whisper, "Yes."

"Okay?" he asked on another squeeze of my neck.

"Yes, Lahn, I'm okay."

"Okay," he returned then let my neck go and moved slightly back, ordering, "Make it heavy, my queen. In less than two hours, I want there to be enough on me to cover your naked body in my black."

That got an all over skin tingle.

"Uh...okay," I breathed, that word not trembling at all, and he grinned.

"Okay," he replied, and he let my wrist go.

I dipped my head and commenced painting my husband's fantastic chest, arms, back and face in killer, kickass streaks of black.

Lahn and I walked together through the Daxshee to the clearing with the platform where Mahyah had (essentially) taken her own life.

Lahn did not touch me, but he walked at my side through the parting sea of people who had come to watch. He wore his belt with knives and his sword strapped to his back, the only weapons he was allowed during a challenge. Though, I was told by Lahn, this was done on an honor system. Like the fights at the games, there was no referee. During a challenge, anything goes, and no one checked to make certain that someone was not intending to fight fair.

When we made it to the clearing, I saw Dortak was already there, painted in black and red, his wounds exposed and healing but not healed. He was grinning, and God, I would be happy when that grin was frozen on his face in death.

I tore my eyes from his as I walked with Lahn to the platform. When we both lifted a leg to step up, the drums started. Hearing them, it took superhuman effort not to start trembling again.

This was not because I didn't believe in Lahn. It was just because I hated those fucking drums. It was an automatic reaction and one I managed (quite proudly, might I add) to beat back.

Lahn guided me to my throne, a throne that, again, Bain and Zahnin stood behind.

I was looking at them so I didn't see what Lahn did to make them both jerk their chins up at him, but I didn't like that. That said Lahn was planning for an eventuality that was different than the one he'd vowed he'd make for me. It was nice and all that, he was covering his bases and doing it to ascertain that I would be safe. For I knew from those chin lifts that Bain and Zahnin had both vowed they would stand against Dortak should he best Lahn and turn to me.

But still.

I beat back the fear that too sent surging through my system, sedately turned and sat on my throne.

Diandra didn't attend me because she no longer had to. My Korwahk was still not fluent, but I'd been exposed to it long enough that I more than knew my way around.

I was going to miss her.

I looked up at Lahn to see him standing at the edge of the platform, his painted back to me, hands on his hips, focus on Dortak.

The drumming stopped.

Thank God.

Lahn didn't move and the crowd stayed silent.

Then Dortak shouted, "When I take your head, your body will not be thrown on the pyre." He lifted a hand to point at a pyre already set up some distance away on top of the rise we went over to get to Mahyah's. "I will toss it in the river. Then I will mount your head outside my cham and keep it there so every time your yellow one enters and leaves my cham, she will see it as the flesh rots to skull."

I clenched my teeth together and forced my hands to stay loose in my lap.

Lahn didn't move or speak.

Dortak didn't like that and, being Dortak, pushed it even further.

"Before that, I will strip your yellow one naked and ride with her through the Daxshee while I force her to hold your head. Then I will rip off her yellow crown of feathers, shove them up her cunt and take her through her ass. In the months to come, while I use her until she is no longer of use to me, the sounds coming from her in *my* cham will be much different from those she cried in yours."

Yep.

One could say it was official.

I wasn't going to lose a lot of sleep when Lahn took his head.

At this, Lahn moved and what he moved to do made me suck in breath and hold it.

He removed his belt, turned to me and handed me his knives. My eyes darting up to him, my hands automatically lifted to accept them. He then unbuckled the strap on his chest and slipped off his sword. After he had done this, he laid it across my throne so it was resting on the arms.

Still bent so his face was level to mine, his painted eyes came to me, and I saw it...*I saw it*...his golden, bright, brutal spirit was shining close to the surface and let's just say it...was...*pissed.*

Uh-oh.

Dortak was *in trouble.*

The breath flooded my lungs, the tension evaporated from my body, and I grinned at him.

"Give him hell, tiger," I whispered.

He held my eyes a second before he blinked and his spirit was hidden, his fury gone.

Then, swear to *God*, he *winked at me.*

No joke! Winked!

I stifled a giggle.

My husband turned and moved off the platform.

Dortak guffawed as he lifted his arm and unsheathed his blade.

Then his eyes narrowed, and he spat at the advancing Lahn, "*Fool.*"

"I take your head with your own steel," Lahn told him casually.

"Ha!" Dortak cried. "I've never been disarmed."

"Then today will be your first and your last," Lahn returned, still moving to him, closer and closer, his arms relaxed and dangling at his sides, his stride steady, and Dortak finally got smart(ish) and realized that, even unarmed, a threat was closing in.

That was when he took his stance, and without hesitation and with a mighty roar, he charged Lahn.

Dortak didn't wait to be just what Dortak was.

An asshole, a jerk, the king of all dicks, and lastly, a fucking, dirty, little *cheat.*

For during his charge, his left hand came up and swung out, leaving a trail of yellow dust. He whirled himself to avoid it getting in his face, advancing through it with his back and my guess was that whatever it was would blind his opponent.

A hush of shock settled instantly over the already quiet crowd.

I held my breath again, but as Lahn promised, I needn't have worried.

He was prepared.

I knew this when he instantly dropped. Tucking in his body, he landed on a shoulder, rolling legs over head. He then twisted and rolled again sideways several times, landing on his back well clear of the dust. Without delay, he did one of those awesome knee lifts where he kicked out and, using the power of his legs and strength of his abs, he regained his feet without using his hands.

Oh yeah, my husband was a badass.

It was then I held my breath yet again but not from fear.

From awe.

I had heard a lot about what a fierce warrior my king was, how strong, how swift, how smart. I knew his strength personally.

But I had no idea.

No freaking clue.

Dortak charged again in full-on attack.

And then again.

And again.

And repeat.

Each time he did, Lahn's body moved or swayed gracefully, every swing or thrust Dortak threw, Lahn avoided it, and not just by a whisper but by a mile. It was like Lahn was in his mind and knew exactly what move Dortak would make.

He did ducking twirls, the plait I'd braided in his hair flying as Dortak's blade whistled through the air six inches above him.

He jerked his torso back and Dortak's steel whizzed by him.

Dortak would thrust and Lahn would turn full circle and Dortak would catch nothing but air.

After this went on a long time, suddenly, Lahn closed in on him, avoided his sword, took his arm, and with apparent ease, he flipped warrior and sword, Dortak landing on his back on stone. Without hesitation, Lahn kicked him in the mouth and blood spewed as his head jerked fully around.

Lahn took a step back, declaring, "First blood."

This must have meant something, for the crowd, watching in silence until that moment, went berserk as a cheer rent the air.

And they continued to cheer as Dortak jumped to his feet, and infuriated, yet again attacked, his swings and thrusts no longer calculated in any way, but clearly, even to someone like me who knew nothing of this kind of stuff, no longer strategic, but angry.

Lahn, too, changed his tactic. He no longer swayed, turned and ducked. With every swing or thrust he avoided, he finished his movement by landing blow after blow on Dortak. A powerful jab to the ribs that made Dortak grunt. A strike to the jaw that made more blood spew from his mouth. A heel to the back of his knee that made Dortak fall hard to that knee. And so on.

Again, this went on a long time. So long, Lahn had opened an oozing cut on Dortak's cheekbone, blood was pouring from his mouth from lost teeth and two cuts on his lips, there were fierce, angry red welts all over Dortak's torso and back where Lahn's fists had connected, and Lahn reopened the wound Mahyah had delivered to his shoulder.

Blood was leaking and Dortak's anger had turned to wrath. His grunts of pain and effort filled the air. His sweat mingled with his blood and his movements became jerky and uncoordinated with the beating he was taking, the effort he was expending and the emotion he should have kept in check.

Then, so fast it was hard to believe I'd seen it, Lahn's hand snaked out. He stole Dortak's knife at his belt and planted it in his shoulder. Without hesitation, as Dortak shouted with surprise, pain and frustration, Lahn's hand darted in again, stole Dortak's other blade and planted it in the old, now-bleeding-again wound Mahyah had given him.

Dortak retreated five steps all the while bellowing in rage.

The crowd, however, went wild with sheer glee.

Someone close to the front shouted, "*Puntay zan, kah Dax!*" *End him, my king!*

And this shout struck up a chant, *Puntay zan! Puntay zan! Puntay zan!*

But Lahn wasn't done playing, and when Dortak yanked the blades out of his flesh one by one, tossed them aside and rushed Lahn with his sword raised high, Lahn ducked to avoid his steel but lifted an arm. Grabbing Dortak's sword hand and keeping it held high, Lahn punched him in the stomach on Dortak's advance, then delivered a blow to the kidneys at the back. He whirled, lifted a leg and planted a boot in Dortak's back at the same time he yanked down on Dortak's arm so viciously, I could hear the bone break even though I was at least twenty feet away.

The crowd roared at the sound, as did Dortak, but his cry was of pain. He fell flat on his face and dropped his sword, no longer able to carry the heavy weapon in hand on an arm attached to a fractured shoulder.

Lahn stepped several feet away as Dortak struggled to his healthy(ish) hand then got his knees under him.

"Again, my brother, I'd like to hear it. What did you intend to do with my tigress?" Lahn called.

Dortak, on one hand and both knees, turned his head to look over his shoulder and up at Lahn. His face was red, sweating, bloody and twisted, not just with hate but with not a small amount of pain.

Lahn kept talking.

"My golden goddess opened the heavens and commanded their tears when your bride left this earth. She drew a rainbow in the sky to guide her ashes to the next realm. When *you* fall, the heavens won't weep and she won't waste her magic on a rainbow. When your lifeblood hits stone, that is the closest you'll get to the heavens. My golden bride will need to waste no energy in guiding your spirit to eternal agony. Your spirit will know exactly where it's meant to go."

With visible effort, Dortak pushed himself to his feet, grunted with pain when he bent to retrieve his sword in his left, non-dominant hand, and he lifted it clumsily toward Lahn.

Lahn stared at him for a short moment before he turned only his head to me.

"Are you bored yet?" he inquired.

I kind of wasn't.

It was gruesome, but it was also, I had to admit, kind of cool.

But I had the feeling my husband was done, so I called out, "Meena, kah Dax. Na weykun kay nahna quaxi. Ta jahnay boonahn keeta jahko. Kay zookay juno." *Yes, my king. You promised me your paint. We have better things to do. I want to play.*

At my words the crowd, again, went wild.

Lahn grinned.

I grinned back.

And with a mighty roar that probably took all the energy he had left, Dortak charged.

Lahn's head turned back then I stopped thinking this was in any way cool and stared in a horror I hoped I hid as my king ended the contest.

With ease, he dodged the charge and disarmed Dortak as he did so. Dortak ran past Lahn, but Lahn didn't delay. After Dortak came to an awkward stop and whirled lumberingly to face his challenger, Lahn had already swung Dortak's steel wide and instantly executed a low, powerful, smooth sweep, cutting Dortak off at the knees.

Literally.

With a bellow of agony that hurt to hear even coming from a monster, the legless Dortak again fell to his face.

The crowd, clearly delighted beyond reason with grisly dismemberment, became crazed—their cries, chants and cheers clogging the air.

But Lahn wasn't done.

He bent and used Dortak's hair to drag the still living but definitely fallen warrior within five feet of my throne, leaving his legs behind.

There, Lahn lifted Dortak's legless body clean in the air, hefting it up with an almighty heave.

I forced my eyes to stay open as I stared into the hated, bloody, now pale and agonized face of a man who it could be said was getting his just desserts—in a *serious* way—before Lahn let his hair go.

As his body started its plummet to the ground, fast as lightning, Lahn quickly two-handed Dortak's sword and swung it in a downward arc, slicing him clean through the neck, Dortak's body dropping straight to the ground, his head flying off in a sickening gush of blood.

I couldn't help it. It was so freaking gross, I winced.

Luckily, I didn't think anyone noticed, not even Lahn. He was staring down at the headless, legless, very, very, *very* dead body of Dortak and the crowd was going insane.

As was, I was getting, their way, the Korwahk did not delay with completing the festivities. Men ran forward, one grabbed both severed legs, two grabbed an arm each on Dortak's body and they dragged and carried the carcass pieces out of the clearing, moving toward the pyre. Another man rushed forward with Lahkan, Lahn's horse, and Lahn himself had moved to the head, which he snatched up by the tail.

While striding back to his mount, he tossed Dortak's bloody sword on the platform. It clattered across the wood and his eyes went beyond me to Bain and/or Zahnin.

"Unahyoo see," he grunted. *Melt that.* His gaze came to me, and he reverted to English. "You've had enough and will not ride with me. Drink and be cheerful with your people. I will return and we will celebrate."

I nodded.

He jerked his chin up, attached Dortak's head by his tail to a stirrup on Lahkan (something that I saw the start of then averted my eyes because, seriously, *gross*).

Then, without delay, Lahn swung up into the saddle, jerked his reins, Lahkan veered around, and Lahn sent his heels into his steed.

Immediately, Lahkan burst forward in a full gallop.

The crowd had moved in, and the clearing was not a clearing anymore, but they'd been around these contests enough. They swiftly got out of Lahn's way, but they did it shouting, clapping, punching their fists in the air, pounding them against their chests and generally being boisterous and exceedingly rowdy. A stream of men, women and even children raced after Lahn on Lahkan, likely in hopes to be close when Lahn severed Dortak's tail so they could claim his head.

Lahn disappeared from sight, casks were produced, jugs came out and leather covered cups were passed around.

It was time to party.

Bain and Zahnin moved to flank my chair at the sides rather than the back.

A woman came forward and handed me a leather-covered, resin-lined cup, which a sniff told me held zakah.

If I had a choice, I would have preferred wine. Korwahk wine was excellent.

But zakah was offered so zakah it was.

I looked up at Bain, lifted my cup when he dropped his eyes to me and then turned my head to Zahnin who was already looking down at me.

"Suh Dax!" I cried. *The Dax!*

And then I belted back a slug.

Before I righted my head, I heard both warriors chuckle.

Yes, even Zahnin.

~

Oh yeah.

Yeah, yeah, *yeah*.

"Harder, baby," I begged, so close, *this* close, and damn, it was going to be huge.

I had paint on me. I even had another man's blood on me, and I also had on my hands a savage warrior who bested a challenge for his throne and took the life of a man not fit to walk this earth.

And he was in the mood to celebrate.

I was on my hands and knees in front of him. Lahn was thrusting inside, deep and hard.

He'd already gone down on me, not letting me come. Let me ride him while he rolled my clit with his finger, not letting me come. Let me take him in my mouth while touching myself, again not letting me come. And now he was fucking me hard.

I was primed. So primed, I'd never been this primed.

When it came, it was going to shatter me.

Lahn was leaned over me, one arm wrapped around me, fingers tugging not very gently but ever so effectively on my nipple, his other hand was wrapped around my jaw, holding my head back much like the first time he fucked me in a way I liked...but better.

So much fucking better.

His hands released me, and one went into my back, shoving me down.

"Atoo luh nahna Dax, kah Dahksahna, uvoo zan nahna xaxsah," he grunted through his thrusts. *Bow to your king, my queen, give him your cunt.*

I did as ordered, arching my chest into the bed, pressing my cheek to the mattress. My arms straight in front of me, I reared my ass back to meet his drives.

His big hands spanned my ribs, and he yanked me back hard even with my violent jerks.

"See lapay tee, kah rahna Dahksahna," he growled, "uvoo kay nahna rahna xaxsah." *That's it, my golden queen, give me your golden cunt.*

"Yes, my king," I breathed, coming closer. "Kah rahna xaxsah lapay nahna." *My golden cunt is yours.*

"Kahna," he growled. *Mine.*

"Nahna," I gasped. *Yours.*

"Jak kahna," he grunted, pounding deep. *All mine.*

And I lost it, my head shooting back, my hair flying, my hands clenching the hides and my hips slamming back into his. It overwhelmed me, making me cry out in ecstasy, no joke, *ecstasy*, as I went into a mini-orgasm trance as the sheer force of it swept through me.

But I still didn't miss my king's powerful shout of release as he buried his cock deep, yanking me to him one last time, his hands tightening fierce on my ribs.

I was nowhere near recovery when he jerked my body up roughly, like he had what I liked to consider our (real) first time, so I was virtually suspended, impaled on his cock. His hands moved from my ribs to cover my breasts and his breathing in my ear was still labored when he spoke, his voice thick and hoarse.

"Kahna," he grunted, squeezing my breasts.

"Nahna," I agreed, turning my head and pressing my forehead in his neck.

One of his arms circled to hold me around my midriff as his hand cupped our connected sexes.

"Kahna," he grunted again, tweaking my clit.

My hips jerked and I whimpered before whispering, "Nahna."

His hand slid up my body, up my throat and he forced his thumb between my lips. I accepted it readily and instantly sucked it deeper. This time his hips jerked, and I heard his growl emanating low from his throat.

"Kahna," he grunted yet again.

My tongue swirled his thumb, he slid it out and it glided along my lower lip as I whispered, "Nahna."

"Uvoo nahna lisa luh kay." *Give your mouth to me.*

I tipped my head back and he took my mouth until I moaned down his throat.

He broke his mouth from mine, but I opened my eyes and his captured them as his hand went to my belly and he reverted to English.

"Tonight, I planted my seed in your womb, my Circe. Tonight, we made a warrior. Tonight, your gold and my paint mixed, and we created the greatest warrior this world will ever see."

Okay, um...that scared the freaking shit out of me. I was steadfastly ignoring the fact that I was having unprotected sex, repeatedly, with a very virile man whose "seed" was probably as virile as he was. I was handling it in an "I'll deal with it if it happens" kind of way (the "if" in that sentence as the days went by truthfully being more like a "when").

In other words, I was ignoring it and stupidly hoping that what would be was meant to be.

But, honestly, even if threatened with death, I couldn't kill the mood.

"That's impossible, my Lahn," I whispered, lifting a hand to curl it around his neck. "The greatest warrior this world will ever see already walks this earth and right now he's inside me."

I watched his eyes blaze, exposing the golden spirit within before he growled and took my mouth again, plundering it until I was whimpering. Then he broke free.

When he did, my hand not at his neck slid between my legs, going deep until I was cupping him.

"Kahna," I whispered and watched his golden spirit glow brighter.

"Nahna," he whispered back.

Yes, *mine*.

My fingers at his neck squeezed and I repeated, "Kahna."

Without hesitation, he agreed, "Nahna."

I stared into his heated, gleaming eyes and said softly, "*Kah* Dax. *Kah* tunakan. *Kah* Lahn." *My* king, *my* warrior, *my* Lahn.

His lips came to mine, and he whispered, "Meena, my Circe, jak nahna." *Yes, my Circe, all yours.*

My lips curved into a smile seconds before his tongue slid between them, the tip of mine met his for a sweet touch before he broke that connection, pulled me off of his cock, turned me and planted me on my back in the bed. He pulled my legs apart, came down on top of me then yanked them around him as I circled his broad shoulders with my arms. His hand roamed my body, all the skin he could touch that wasn't being touched by his body as his other arm rested in the bed taking on the bulk of his weight.

All the time he did this, his beautiful, dark, painted-black eyes stayed locked to mine.

Eventually, my limbs gave him a squeeze and I whispered, "I like our paint, honey, but I don't like Dortak on me. Can we take a bath?"

He dipped his head and touched his mouth to mine as his hand came up and curled at the side of my neck.

Then he spoke softly, and I knew he meant what he had to say because he didn't bother with English. He used Korwahk.

"I understand this is not of your world, my Circe, but he shares our bed tonight."

Oh no, I didn't like the sound of that, like, *at all*.

Lahn kept talking.

"His body has been burned on the pyre. His head has become a toy or trophy. The Korwahk celebrated his death with cheers and chants, drink and dancing. And he knew humiliation, beaten, disarmed and immobilized, before his defeat, cut down by his own steel. But I am not done with him. His blood shares our bed as I take you with my mouth, with my cock, with my fingers, your mouth sucks me deep and I make you beg and gasp and cry out. And he shares it as you sleep underneath me, my seed leaking from between your legs. Tomorrow, I will bathe him away from you. Tonight, if there is any part of his spirit left in this realm, he will know the beauty we share in our cham, and since he threatened to defile my queen, this is my way to shove it up *his* ass."

All right, I could get where he was coming from. I knew my man was pissed after what Dortak said. But now that the passion was spent and the cuddling had begun, I wasn't all fired up to sleep with some guy's blood on me.

I started to tell Lahn this. "Lahn—"

He shook his head and his thumb moved to my lips. "No, Circe. This will be. Your king commands it."

When he slid his thumb from my lips, I whispered, "But, baby, it's *gross*."

He blinked. "Gross?"

I nodded. "Gross. Icky. Yuck. Blech. Nasty. *Gross*."

He grinned.

Then he reminded me, "You didn't think it was...*gross*...when you gave me nahna xaxsah while carrying his blood and my paint."

"But—"

"Or when you begged for my cock harder."

"But, La—"

"Or when you pushed your hips into my cock so violent—"

My arm moved from around his shoulders and my fingers covered his mouth. "Okay, okay, I get it. You're right. And this means something to you, so all right." I moved my hand from his mouth, sighed and gave in. "I'll sleep with icky blood on me."

I caught his grin before his face disappeared in my neck where he murmured. "Shahsha, kah rahna Dahksahna."

"Nahrahka," I muttered, sliding my hand down his neck to the back and then down between his shoulder blades, thinking, *Jeez, the things I do for my king*.

"Kah teenkah tunakanahsa was very brave today," he said in my ear and lifted his head, his thumb moving to sweep my cheekbone. "I know that took effort, Circe, to watch that. I was very proud of you."

I felt my pique fade away as his sweetness invaded.

"Thanks, honey," I whispered.

His gaze moved over my face, and he whispered back, "I could not dream a better you."

Oh my God.

Oh...my...*God.*

Did he just say that?

I stared into his warm eyes.

He just said that.

And that was *so* sweet, *so* unexpected, but *so* welcome, my breath arrested and all I could do was continue staring at him.

He wasn't done. "A better wife, a better queen. Not even in a dream could I create better than you."

"Stop it," I whispered because I couldn't take anymore, and I couldn't take anymore because the happiness blooming inside me threatened to overwhelm me.

He lips tipped up slightly, but his eyes warmed even more. "Okay, kah Lahnahsahna, I will stop it."

I sucked in breath through my nose to control the tingling there, and then I lifted my head and shoved my face in his neck, holding on tight with all my limbs.

Lahn spoke in my ear. "My queen, do not get drowsy. I am not done fucking you."

Okay, maybe I shouldn't have taught him the f-word. Sure, when I explained it to him, he laughed loud, then he picked me up, threw me on the bed and acted out its meaning.

But his saying it was *hot*, too hot.

My head dropped back on the bed, and I stared up at him in disbelief.

"You're not?"

"No. Not close."

I felt my eyebrows shoot up. "Not close?"

"No."

"Wow," I whispered. "Maybe you *are* a god."

He burst out laughing and he did this a long time, his massive body shaking with it, moving mine as it did in a way that I didn't like.

I *loved.*

Then, still chuckling, he dropped his forehead to mine and whispered, "Kay *lapay* el Pahnsahnak, kah Pahnsahnalla." *I* am *a god, my goddess*. "And I will prove it to you."

Then his mouth took mine and he proved it to me.

Boy, did he ever prove it to me.

I thought my man kicked ass on a field of battle, and he did. I was in awe.

But I was more in awe at what he could do in our cham.

Much, *much* more.

24
THE DECISION

month later...

"Circe, oh, *Circe,* I couldn't," Diandra breathed as she stared at the heavy gold bracelet inlaid profusely with garnet and amethyst that she'd been examining with obvious yearning, but being so weighty with gold and gems, likely could not afford—a bracelet that I'd just cuffed on her wrist.

"You can, my friend, and you will," I whispered, and her head tipped back from her study of her new bracelet. I saw wet shimmering from her eyes, and I finished, "As you promised me, you stood by my side and I know, my sweet friend, I *know,*" I shook her wrist once for added emphasis, "that there were times it wasn't easy. But I want you to know there will be times when being at my side will provide you with the bounty you deserve because you are kind, you are patient, and you are generous. I want you to have this gift, from Lahn and me, as a token of our gratitude for all you have given us."

I watched one tear slide down her cheek as her hand not captured by mine lifted to cup my cheek.

"You made every minute, even the difficult ones, a pleasure, my true, golden queen," she whispered back.

I felt the tears fill my own eyes and I smiled at her.

Then, to lighten the mood before I burst into unqueenly tears, I joked, "Even now, you're being generous. I know I can be a pain in the ass."

She stared at me a second, probably not knowing what a "pain in the ass" was but definitely understanding it. After that second was done, she burst out laughing, pulled her wrist from my grip and yanked me into her arms for a tight hug.

I gave it back as good as I got.

When we pulled away, I grabbed her hand for one last squeeze, smiling into her shining eyes. Eventually I let her go and smiled at Teetru.

"Give the man some coin, sweetheart," I said in Korwahk.

Teetru jerked like she'd been pulled from a trance even though her eyes were on Diandra and me. She nodded and jumped toward the merchant, opening the drawstring leather pouch she carried that was filled with Lahn's coin.

I grabbed Diandra's elbow and turned her away from the stall, looking back and smiling at my entourage.

The night before, a large traveling band of merchants had approached and through the night set up on the outskirts of the Daxshee. This morning, the people of the Daxshee fell on it like it was the day after Christmas sales.

So, of course, I gathered my girl posse of Diandra, Narinda, Sheena, Nahka, Oahsee, Claudine, Sabine, Anastasie, and Nahka's two BFFs who had been adopted by the troop, Char and Vuntus, and away we went...shopping.

Being queen, and followed by Bain, who carried weapons, was huge and muscular and barked orders, I or my girls got to go to the front of any stall that caught our fancy.

It was awesome. I was having a great time, the vibe in the air was excited and I was happy.

I was happy because I was with my friends. I was happy because I was shopping, something I loved to do. And I was happy because my friends were happy, giggling, talking and buying.

But mostly I was happy because Lahn would be home tomorrow.

Needless to say, I'd made my decision.

Magic or not. I had the power in me or not. Savage nation or not.

I was staying.

This was because, here, I was queen.

This was because, here, I had awesome clothes.

This was because, here, I held beautiful magic.

This was because, here, I had great friends whose friendships had been tested beyond anything I could ever imagine, and they held strong and true.

And this was because, here, I was in love.

Perhaps not with the man of my dreams, but with a man that was more man than any I'd ever encountered. He was savage, no doubt about it. But, to me, he was unbelievably sweet.

And he thought I was a woman beyond his dreams.

And that worked for me.

I PRETTY MUCH KNEW I had been denying the pull of the crazy Korwahk world for a while.

And I had been denying, too, the strange connection that held strong as steel between Lahn and me throughout the weeks we'd been together, the dramas and the heartbreaks.

But after he defeated Dortak and celebrated with me, I knew.

I knew I was in love.

What would happen the next day would only prove it irrefutably.

HE HAD WOKEN me with a gentle, "Wake, my Circe," whispered in my ear.

When my eyes fluttered open and my head turned to take him in, I saw something on his face I'd seen once before—when he was looking at me after I sang to Mahyah.

God, that look was beautiful.

"What?" I whispered back.

"You will see," he replied quietly then bent. I heard water splashing and he came back to me with a wet cloth. "We will bathe properly later. But you must see now and Dortak does not share this with us."

He then set about tenderly washing the blood from my skin and I saw that he'd already done it to himself.

I came up on my elbows and started, "Lahn—"

His gaze went from my chest to mine. "Quiet, my golden doe."

His strange tone and that gorgeous look on his face, which hadn't faded, made me quiet.

He didn't wash off all the paint, but he made certain to wash off all the blood. Then he dropped the cloth in a bucket by the bed, scooped me up and put me on my feet. He walked to grab my robe from where it was hanging on the back of a chair. He was already in hides.

He held it out for me. I slipped my arms through and tied it around my waist.

Then he took my hand and guided me to and through the cham flaps.

I saw it was just dawn. The Daxshee was still, most were asleep.

With his hand in mine, he took me around the cham to the back where the creek flowed past.

But I saw it before I got there, and I couldn't believe what I was seeing.

All along the banks of the creek was a riot of flowers like the one I'd put on Mahyah's pyre. They had been there before but not nearly as many and most of those had been cut by the Korwahk to give to Mahyah. Now, those cut blooms had been replaced—*overnight*—and their number had more than tripled.

And they weren't just the vibrant orange of the bloom I gave Mahyah but also there were white, yellow and scarlet, as far as the eye could see, trailing along the edges of the creek. The willows dotted along the sides drooped their bowed branches, the ends dipping into the gentle flow of water.

It was astoundingly beautiful.

Lahn stopped me on the rise behind our cham just up from the creek and pulled my back to his front, one hand on my belly, the other arm slanted across my chest, hand curled around my neck the same as he had held me to him on his horse when we were riding.

I vaguely noticed that there were people about, not many, here and there on our side of the creek and on the opposite one, all of them silent, all of them staring at the spectacle.

Lahn bent so his mouth was at my ear, and he spoke quietly as he pressed my belly lightly.

"I see we did not make a warrior last night. My golden goddess, I would hope, would not create a riot of flowers if my seed produced a warrior." His voice dropped, his hand pressed deeper and his arm tensed. "We made a daughter."

A shiver slid across my skin at his words, another one following when it dawned on me he was not disappointed at the thought of a girl...not at all.

He touched his mouth to the skin of my neck then his head lifted and he rested his jaw at the top of my hair and held me as I stared at what he thought I created.

Then something unbelievably cool happened.

Without me thinking them, memories sifted through my head.

Lahn relenting when I wanted Ghost.

Lahn lifting me to his back to carry me to the games.

Lahn grinning down at me the first time I drank the zakah.

Lahn holding me while I was trembling with sunstroke.

Lahn preparing medicine for me and holding it to my lips to drink.

Lahn checking on me during the day after I was sick.

Lahn giving me Zephyr.

Lahn holding me on his horse, asking about my mother, my father, telling me I was beautiful, explaining to me how my claiming—something that had been hideous for me—had been, to him, a gift he held precious.

Lahn's eyes holding mine, asking nonverbally if I was all right after Dortak extended his challenge.

Lahn taking care of me after Mahyah's death.

Lahn offering me the greatest gift I'd ever received, more than once, his spirit.

Lahn telling me he was pleased my heart guided me back to him.

And Lahn telling me last night he couldn't have dreamed a better me.

And as each memory shimmered in my brain, I watched in stunned silence as a new blossom sprouted out of nothing and bloomed in a flash of color somewhere along the bank.

Except for the memories of Lahn giving me his spirit and the last of him telling me I was better than a dream, both of which caused dozens of flowers to explode and grace the banks with astonishing vibrancy.

Holy *shit*.

I totally had magic.

And it wasn't noble.

It was awesome and it was freaking *beautiful*.

The eyes of those sharing this turned to me in wonder and Lahn's arms gave me a squeeze as he murmured over my head, "My wife thinks happy thoughts."

Yes. He was right, I did.

I...*so...freaking...did*.

And I did because I was in love with a savage, warrior king and I knew straight to my soul that he loved me.

My arms crossed over his hand at my belly and I stared at the beauty I created.

That made me happy too.

And I smiled when a bloom burst to life at that thought.

Lahn chuckled.

He was happy too.

Another bloom burst open.

Freaking cool!

"Loolah." I heard the tired mew.

I twisted my head to look around Lahn and my bodies to see Gaal emerging from the tent she shared with all the girls, Ghost padding toward us, still blinking sleep from her beautiful blue eyes, and I noticed with the weeks passing my cub was becoming less of a cub and growing into a tigress.

"Poyah, kah teenkah lahnahsahna," I called to her.

She made it to us, bumped her head against Lahn's and my legs then her booty collapsed and she sat leaning against them.

Lahn's arms gave me another squeeze and I knew another bloom had opened but I was looking down at Ghost and didn't see it.

One of my hands twisted so I could wrap my fingers around his at my belly.

Then I whispered, "I love you, my Lahn," and heard the swift hiss of his intake of breath.

He buried his face in my neck and whispered back, "Loot kay hansah-nalay na, my Circe." *And I love you, my Circe.*

At his words, the banks of the creek burst forth in a riot of blooms. So many, no bank could be seen as one blossom crowded the next.

And that was when I knew.

I loved my father. I loved my friends. I had a good life at home in Seattle and I was happy there.

But nowhere near as happy as I was here.

And I was never going back.

LIFE CARRIED on as normal for the next two weeks. I wandered amongst my people with Bain and Zahnin. I spent time with my girls. My Korwahk improved to the point I no longer needed lessons. My mornings were spent with my husband in bed then at his bath. My evenings with him at our table then back in our bed.

And I was not content.

I was gloriously happy.

Dark moments drifted through as I considered exploring my magic, maybe finding out if I could go home and explain things to Pop, say good-bye to him, his boys and my friends and come back. Maybe even plan trips back and forth.

But there would be time for that, I decided. And I would know when that time came. I would then speak to Lahn and Diandra and plan for it.

But my worry was, if I went home to Seattle, I couldn't get back to Lahn.

And in the now, I was happy just to exist in a crazy dream that had become a beautiful reality.

AFTER TWO WEEKS, when Lahn and I were taking our evening meal together, he told me that the Daxshee would pack up the day after the next and ride.

And we did, for eight days, until, on a bleak cliff with not very much scrub but a lot of stone, dirt and sand, we set up again. It was a weird spot and not very attractive, especially compared to our spot by the creek. But what did I know? I was no Dax.

The morning after the Daxshee rose, Lahn told me he would be leaving the next day to lead a raid and he wouldn't return for five days.

And he wouldn't be taking me.

I didn't want him to go because I didn't want him to be away from me, but there was more.

This alarmed me.

Diandra had told me that the warriors kept their wives close while they were out plundering. And if Lahn was out plundering, I needed to be close.

And when I told Lahn firmly I wanted to go with him, we had our first knockdown, drag-out fight.

He flatly refused and I flatly refused to allow him to refuse. I shouted and he thundered. This lasted a long time and got heated. He was angry, actually furious, not only that I was questioning his decision as Dax that I not go but that I wanted to go at all considering he thought such a journey would be dangerous for me as we would be entering a neighboring country. Even in his fury, though, not once did he let it get out of control enough for him even to raise a hand with the intent to strike me.

This was good.

What was bad was me finally sharing with him what was on my mind.

"If you're off marauding, then I can't take care of you before you do!" I snapped, and he blinked in surprise at my words which clearly bewildered him.

"What?" he clipped back.

I planted my hands on my hips and swept his body with my eyes. "Don't forget, honey, *that's* mine, *all* mine. You said it yourself. And I'm not sharing it with *anyone*. I know how you get when you're celebrating, *boy* do I know, and you sure as *hell* are not going to be off collecting booty and plundering villages without *me* being the one you celebrate with, before *and* after."

I couldn't believe I was saying this shit but there it was.

I was.

He stared at me, and I didn't know if he was staring at me in shock, he didn't know what to say or he was controlling his anger so he didn't say anything he would regret.

Too far gone, I stupidly kept going.

"In other words, Lahn, I'm not a big fan of raiding and looting. I know it's your way. I don't like it, but I won't speak against it. But you are *not* going to add raping to your looting. No *fucking* way. You take no other woman but me."

I knew light dawned when his face turned to granite and he was silent again for several heartbeats before he asked softly, "Am I standing in my cham with my wife telling me what I can and cannot do?"

His tone was dangerous, as dangerous as the stony look on his face, and lucky for me, I was smart enough to read it so I let my silence be my answer.

Lahn went on, "A husband and wife, Circe, they do not speak of this." He paused then finished, "*Ever.*"

"We are not just any husband and wife," I shot back.

"That is agreed. I give you your head in many ways. I will not with this. This is not your concern, and we will never speak of it again, my queen. Not ever. Am I understood?"

Oh no.

Hell no.

My voice quieted too when I replied, "You come back smelling of anything other than dirt, sweat and blood, I get that first *fucking* clue you've taken a woman who is not me, we're done, Lahn, no joke. I will leave you."

His eyes flashed and his body tensed but I didn't stop talking.

"You find me and bring me back, I'll leave you again. I'll keep going until I can stay gone. And in the meantime, you will never, *ever,* get me sweet again. I tell you in my world it's important that a husband remains faithful to his wife, you must understand that it is *important.* It is *crucial* I know that I can trust you don't use your body with anyone but me. When I say it's mine, I mean that outside of you sharing your spirit with me, it is the most precious gift you've ever given to me. I treasure it. I *worship* it. And it will tear me apart inside to think you've tarnished it by forcing it on another woman."

I was breathing heavily when I was done speaking and Lahn held my gaze but kept his silence as his body continued to exude raw, pissed-off, brutal energy.

Then it hit me that if he did go out raping with his pillaging (which was bad enough), I was not lying. It would kill what we had, and I loved what we had. He didn't know it, but I'd given up everything to keep what we had. And staring at my husband just then, I knew he was not going to give in. This was who he was and what he did, and it would be the end of us.

And that was why tears filled my eyes and I felt my lips quiver as those tears spilled down my cheeks.

But I held his angry gaze until it melted with the wet.

Then I looked to the side and whispered, "You will tear me apart. You do this, you do it *knowing* you will destroy me." I pulled in a breath and dashed the tears away with the back of my hand. When my vision cleared, I straightened by shoulders and looked back at him. "But you are Dax, and you are warrior, so obviously, you are free to do as you will."

That was when he growled, "You will not leave me."

I didn't respond.

"You will *never* leave me."

I kept my silence, held his eyes and we went into staredown.

He broke it by stating, "You will never leave me, Circe, in any way you could leave me."

I didn't know what that meant exactly, but I didn't ask, nor did I get the chance because he kept talking.

"To make that so, I will not ever take another woman but you."

I sucked in a hopeful breath as I felt my eyes grow round at his capitulation. But he wasn't done and when he spoke his voice was way lower than normal and it rumbled through the tent.

"You have this one warning, I will not repeat it and I will point out that

I have not once asked you to alter any of who you are. *Not once*. You are not of my people, and you behave in ways that are strange to *me*. Yet you seem not to understand that this is true. But never have I asked you to change *who* you are."

I winced because this was true. He expected me to accept his way of life, but he never asked me to change who I was.

He continued, "This is the last concession I will make for you. I am who I am. I am Korwahk. I am warrior. I am Dax and you must accept me as what I am. I may have forced my body on yours, but I did not force your love. You *gave* it to me knowing who I am. As we live our lives, you cannot decide to disagree with parts of that and then decide to take your love away, Circe. I'll not live like that. Therefore, you need to reflect on this, come to your peace with it and never, my golden queen, *never* request another such concession from me."

My lips parted to respond but he didn't give me the chance. He prowled to the cham flaps, slapped them back and he was gone.

He didn't return until very late, but I was awake when he did. I stayed still in our bed until he joined me in it, and I knew how angry he still was when he didn't curl into me or pull me to him but settled on his back not touching me.

So I whispered hesitantly into the cham, "Thank you for..." I paused then, "It was important to me, thank you."

Lahn didn't respond.

I forged ahead. "I will, um...process things and come to peace with my life with you and the Korwahk."

Nothing from Lahn.

I kept going. "I'll, uh...never ask for another concession again, I promise."

To that I got a growled, "Promise never to leave me."

I closed my eyes tight, rolled, scooted to him and got up on an elbow but rested my other hand on his chest.

When my eyes locked with his, I whispered, "I promise never to leave you, baby."

And I said it like I meant it because I did. And in that moment, he didn't know that I actually gave up a world for him. But the weight of my words still communicated that.

He glared up at me, then his arms shot around me, pulling me down, his lips captured mine and he rolled me to my back.

The next morning, he left.

And tomorrow he would be home.

I know it sounded crazy, but I couldn't wait.

I missed my king.

"Oh, Circe!" Nahka called through the throng surrounding the fabric stall. She was holding up a bolt of pure gold silk that shimmered in the sun. "You must have this! It was *made* for our golden queen!"

She was beaming at me brighter than the gold silk she held in her hand.

I smiled back at her and twisted my head to Teetru who stood just slightly behind me. "Could you go buy some of that for a sarong for me?" She nodded then I went on, "And, choose something you like for you and pieces for Jacanda, Packa, Gaal and Beetus. My girls need something pretty. For sarongs and tops too."

She blinked at me in shock and stayed unmoving.

I grinned at her, took her hand, gave it a squeeze and urged with a jerk of my head toward the stall, "Go."

Her body jolted physically before she nodded then hurried forward.

I felt a hand curl around my elbow and looked to my other side. It was Sabine.

"Can I speak with you?" she asked in Korwahk.

She'd taken to the language and was getting pretty good at it. She wasn't as good at it as me, of course. I was, I was pleased to say, nearly fluent. But she hadn't had as much practice, though she was better at it than Anastasie, who was struggling. Claudine was still giving them daily lessons.

She had also not shared what was happening with her and Zahnin and not one of my posse pried.

That said, I was in her cham twice when he came in. The first time was some weeks ago and she'd instantly gone tense but not with fear, still simply guarded. The second time was two days ago, and she'd bitten her lip before she'd offered him a tentative smile. Neither time did he repeat soft words or a gentle touch like he had weeks ago, but both times his eyes went warm and his mouth went soft when he saw her.

My hope was, he was breaking through.

At that moment, when she pulled us slightly back and out of the crowd, Bain moving with us, I would find out he definitely was.

She looked shyly at Bain, and I knew she didn't want him to overhear.

I gave him a look and asked, "Can Sabine and I have a moment of privacy?"

His eyes went from me to Sabine to me again. Then his mouth twitched, and he stepped out of hearing distance.

Sabine didn't delay. She launched right in.

"Can I be forthright?"

I nodded.

She studied me then said, "I mean, *really* forthright."

I struggled against a giggle and nodded again.

"I, er...need your advice," she stated.

"About what, sweetheart?" I asked.

"About," her eyes slid away, she bit her lip and then they came back to me, "er...Zahnin, my, um...husband."

I turned to face her, folding my hand on hers still at my elbow and whispered, "I'll do my best. Tell me what you need."

She was looking up at me again and I saw pink tinge her cheeks.

Then she spoke quickly in somewhat broken Korwahk, "He doesn't, er... he has been...for some time, he has been...*changed*. At first, he was, it was...*not good*. I was, you know, I've told you, I had no idea what was happening. But I got to the point where, I don't know, I decided...er, since it kept happening, I knew it wasn't going to stop. So, uh, anytime he touched me, I just..." Her face flamed deeper pink and she whispered, "Got to my knees, pulled up my nightgown and put my face in the bed, like he always took me so he would just...*get it over with*."

Oh God.

How hideous.

I let her hand at my elbow go, grabbed her other one, held it to my chest and whispered, "I'm so sorry, my sweet girl."

She nodded and bit her lip.

"Thank you," she whispered back, then she drew breath into her nose and kept whispering, "He was my first."

Oh *God*.

She was a virgin.

I squeezed her hand. "Oh Sabine, I'm *so* sorry."

"I...didn't like it," she shared what I knew was an extreme understatement.

"You wouldn't," I told her. "Of course not. I understand that."

She nodded again and then moved an inch closer. "But he has not done that to me. Not *for weeks*."

It was my turn to nod, but I kept quiet.

Sabine kept talking.

"And he has been, like I said, changed. Er...*greatly* changed. His tone has gentled, and for some time, except to stroke my face or shift my hair off my shoulder, he didn't touch me at all. Not even in bed."

I nodded again when she stopped talking to urge her on, so she took a deep breath and continued.

"Then he, er...started to chat with me. I didn't know much of what he was saying but he would come to our tent at night and talk to me...quietly. Then, one night, when he left...um, he started always to leave to give me time to prepare for bed," she explained then went on, "He, er...kissed my forehead before he left, which felt..." She squeezed her eyes shut then opened them and breathed, "*Nice.*"

She stopped again.

I squeezed her hand and prompted, "Go on."

"Well, that started...it started, er...then he started to change again but not to go back to how he was before. He just kind of, um...*kissed* me. Not my mouth or anything. My eyes, my forehead or when he would sweep the hair off my shoulder, he would bend low, you know..." She paused and her eyelashes fluttered a little in a very cute way before she whispered, "He's very tall."

"I know he's very tall, Sabine," I whispered back when she didn't go on.

"Well, he would bend low to kiss...er, my neck. And then...then, one night he pulled me into his arms when he got in bed with me, and I was terrified he was going to...you know."

I nodded again and held her hand tight. "I know."

She leaned further into me. "But he *didn't*. He just held me. And I... I...*slept with him like that*." Her eyes grew round. "Like a *baby*."

I smiled. "This is good."

"I...is it?" she asked hesitantly.

"Yes," I answered without any hesitation at all. "Has he continued to—?"

She nodded. "Yes, every night he holds me. But...um...the other night... er..." Her eyes slid away, and she went quiet.

"Sabine, you can tell me," I whispered, and her gaze came back to me, her face now aflame.

"He *touched* me," she whispered reverently. Her eyes warming, she leaned in and went on quickly, "He was holding me then he turned my back to him, and his hands moved on me and they did this awhile, soothingly. I relaxed because it felt rather...*nice* and then he started using them in ways... such ways..." The look in her gaze drifted faraway and a small smile played at her lips as she breathed, "Such *ways*."

Well, good for Zahnin.

Well done, warrior!

I squeezed her hand, and when her focus came back to me, I stated, "It was good."

Her eyes got huge. "No, Circe, it was *beautiful*."

All right!

Zahnin was definitely *the man*!

"Then this is definitely good," I informed her, and her face fell. I felt my brows draw together and I asked carefully, "It isn't good?"

She shook her head, looked to the side and said softly. "He hurt me."

Oh man.

"Yes, he did," I confirmed softly back, and her attention again came to me.

"But I want it again," she breathed her admission and I blinked but she carried on, "He just hasn't...*done* it again and I don't know how to...er...*ask* him to."

I stifled a giggle, released my hold on her but lifted both hands to cup her jaw and I dipped my face to hers.

"Okay, then, my sweet girl, I will give you my advice. If you want this, if you know in your heart you want this change, then my guess is, your husband has shown you a hint of the beauty he wishes to give you. Now that he has done that, he is waiting for you to give him a sign that you liked it and wish for him to give more."

I actually felt her face heat under my hands but kept talking.

"So, the next time he kisses your forehead, tilt your head back so he will instead kiss your lips."

I watched close up as her eyes got wide again and carried on.

"Or, if you have the courage, touch him as he holds you when you're in bed. All you'll have to do is glide your hand across his chest or find his and move it to your body. He will take your hint, and then your part will be done and he will lead the way."

She stared up at me and whispered, "I...Circe, I don't know if I can do that."

I smiled at her. "You can, Sabine, if you want what he can give you, and I promise you," my hands tightened on her jaw, "you have my word that, since he knows how to give you the gift he's already given you, he knows other ways, *better* ways to give it to you again. And if you liked what he's already shared, I promise you will like even more the bounties he has yet to offer."

"Really?" she breathed, clearly astonished but liking that idea.

"Oh yeah," I whispered.

She studied me and whispered back, "Claudine says that you enjoy, er...*this*, um...greatly and, er...*often* with our Dax."

"Oh yeah," I repeated, dropping my hands but capturing both of hers. Then I told her, "You know what happened to you is the way of the Korwahk and I do not condone it. This does not happen in my land either. I endured the same as you and I didn't like it any more than you did. I did not endure it for as long, but I endured it. What I do know is that your husband is a proud warrior, and he wanted your happiness enough to put his pride aside and ask for my assistance in helping you settle in your new life, with him, in your cham. This was not an easy thing for him to do, but he did it." I squeezed her hands. "For you."

She pulled in her lips, and I finished.

"He did what he did because he knows no other way. This is not an excuse. It is simply the truth. He does what he does now, and what he has been doing these past weeks since he brought Diandra and me to you, because he cares for you and wants your happiness. I would try to focus on that instead of the path you took to get here, and my hope is, my friend, that he will continue to show you tenderness and work for your happiness. And I care for you enough to wish that for you in your life with him and tell you this as the truth I believe it is and not lie to you in the hopes that you will simply find a way to tolerate a cruel life that was forced on you."

Her eyes filled with tears, her teeth bit her lip and she nodded before she said softly, "I believe you, Circe."

I nodded back and gave her another squeeze of her hands.

Then I shared one last thing, for her and for Zahnin.

"Zahnin told me when he saw you in the parade, he knew you were the only one for him."

I watched her face go soft as this surprising compliment penetrated, and I continued sharing.

"Lahn told me that, when he claimed me, even in the moonlight, he saw my spirit shining in my eyes and it was the most beautiful thing he'd ever seen. To me, he was raping me. To him, he was receiving a gift he'd treasure always. This is a contradiction that it is difficult to come to terms with. And although it does not heal the pain we felt, a memory seared into our brains, the terror we experienced, I cannot say it does not provide just enough balm to allow me to live with it."

She licked her lips, nodded and squeezed my hands.

I concluded, "Find a way to forgive him, sweet Sabine, and he will reward you. I promise."

"I hope so," she whispered.

"I do too," I agreed.

She grinned at me. It was tentative but it was still hopeful.

I grinned back.

Then I turned us toward the stalls lined in front of us, wrapped my arm around her waist and she mine, and that way we walked back to our posse.

I searched for Teetru and found her holding folded bolts of material, my gold shimmering grandly against five other fabrics in different colors that were pretty but nowhere near as luxurious. She was standing at the side of a stall that had a table that held nothing but a sparkling array of bangles. I let Sabine go and moved to her to see her finger extended, timidly touching a silver bangle that sparkled with inset blue stones.

I reached beyond her, picked up the bangle and she jumped, her head snapping to me.

"I am sorry, my golden—" she started to say, but I looked at the merchant.

"I will take this for my Teetru." I looked down at the bangles and quickly selected four more that would complement my girls. "And these." I held them up to the merchant. He told me the price and I turned to Teetru, slid the pouch from her frozen hand, dug in and pulled out coins.

I realized I had no idea what value they carried and thus ensued a back and forth with Nahka coming forward to make sure I didn't get gouged as I paid for my gifts. Once the payment had been made, Nahka faded back, and I took Teetru's forearm and slid the bangle on her wrist.

"Beautiful," I said, my eyes moving to hers to see her head tipped down to the bangle.

It tipped back to me, and I saw something I couldn't read shining in her eyes.

"You cannot—" she started.

"Funny," I cut her off on a smile. "I just did."

Before she could say another word, I slid my arm around her waist and pulled her away from the table. I let her go, dropped the other bangles in the pouch and handed it back to her.

"When we get back home, you can give those to the girls. The green one is for Jacanda, the yellow one, Gaal, the pink one, Beetus and the red one, Packa. Yes?"

"Yes, my golden queen," she whispered.

I smiled, lifted a hand and squeezed her upper arm then I looked to my girl posse who were all huddled together admiring a bolt of fabric the color of violet shot with copper that Narinda was holding out.

"Let's get lunch!" I called, and when the queen spoke, everyone listened.

So we got lunch.

But, even if I was queen, we'd been shopping for hours, and I knew my girls had to be hungry.

25
THE ATTACK

Late that afternoon, when Bain escorted me back to my cham, I knew it was the changing of the guard because I saw Zahnin standing outside.

I smiled at him. He tipped his chin up at me, but for some weird reason he watched closely, his head turning to do it, as Teetru scurried beyond him and into the tent.

He turned back and called loudly to Bain, "Do not go far."

I froze at these words, but my neck moved so I could look back at Bain who was studying Zahnin intently. He gave a jerk of his chin to Zahnin then moved away. I watched him fade into the chams and turned back to Zahnin. Then I moved to him.

"Is something amiss?" I asked.

"I do not know," he replied. "But I am warrior. I am trained since five to trust my instincts and my instincts tell me something is not right."

Oh shit.

"What?" I asked.

"Again, my golden queen, I do not know. Let us just hope that my instincts are wrong."

"Are they ever wrong?"

He held my gaze.

Then he grunted, "Me."

Great.

"You are safe," he announced, and I focused on him. "Nothing will harm you. Ever."

The good news was, he sounded firm about that. Very firm.

I decided to leave it at the good news without exploring the bad partly because he sounded firm but mostly because he didn't look in the mood to continue that particular conversation. And when Zahnin wasn't in the mood to talk, queen or not, we didn't talk.

I decided to change the subject to something he *would* wish to talk about.

I got closer to him and said quietly, "All right, my protector, this goes against all the girl club rules, but for her sake and yours, I'm going to share."

He stared down his nose at me and crossed his arms on his chest. From my experience with Zahnin, I knew this meant I had his attention even though he likely had no clue what I was talking about at this present time.

"I had a chat with Sabine today," I informed him, saw his eyes flash but that was all he gave me before I continued. "Or, she had one with me."

I stopped talking and waited for his response.

He just stared at me.

Seriously, Sabine said he chatted with her, but I couldn't believe it. I knew he had words, just not many of them.

I laid it out for him. "You're in, Zahnin."

That got a reaction.

He blinked in puzzlement.

"I'm...*in*?" he asked

I grinned.

"In. In. *In*," I answered. "Whatever you're doing and whatever you did a couple of nights ago," I watched his body jerk slightly in surprise that I had this knowledge but again that was all he gave me, so I kept right on talking. "She likes it. Like, *a lot*."

He stared at me but said not a word.

I sighed. "What I'm saying is, you were her first. That didn't go so well for, um...*her*, so she has no idea what she's doing, but she wants..." I leaned in, "*more*. She just doesn't know how to ask."

There it was.

His eyes warmed and his mouth curled up slightly at the sides.

He got me and what he got was hot. *Way* hot. If I didn't have the super hottest guy around, I would think it was *ultra*-hot.

Boy, Sabine was going to get lucky.

"So, I advised she make a move and you're going to have to watch for it," I went on sharing. "It might be timid, shy, maybe awkward and will definitely take some courage for her to do. But she's going to make a play, you're going to need to receive it and take it from there...*gently*."

"Right," he grunted.

"I can't stress enough that she's still a little scared of you *and* her feelings. She's not experienced. You're going to have to teach her."

The lip curl got bigger, and he said low, "I can be a teacher."

I bet he could. And he looked like he was looking forward to it.

Still, I cautioned, "A *patient* teacher."

His lip curl spread into a smile.

"I can be a *patient* teacher," he assured me.

Oh yeah. He was looking forward to that too.

Sabine was definitely going to get lucky.

I grinned up at him.

Then I whispered, "Have fun, my protector."

I moved to walk around him, but he caught my bicep in his hand, so I tipped my head back to look at him.

He dropped my arm as I noticed the smile had faded but intensity was deep in his eyes.

"Shahsha, kah rahna Dahksahna hahla," he murmured.

"Lapay fahnahsan, kah jahnjee," *Be happy, my protector,* I murmured back.

He jerked up his chin.

I moved around him and into my cham. As I moved in, Teetru was scurrying out. I smiled at her, but she tipped her head slightly to the side in a weird way, not returning my smile, looking hurried and nervous, and she left the tent with all due haste.

I stared at the flaps as they swung back in place behind her.

Okay, now *my* instincts, instincts I didn't know until then I had, were saying something wasn't right.

I felt my body tense as I gazed around the tent. The gold fabric I bought that day was laying folded on one of the trunks. My eyes moved and scanned as they did but nothing seemed different.

Until I saw the table.

And when I did, I stared at it.

Then, woodenly, I walked to it.

On it was the gleaming wooden box Bohtan had given me, opened, the dagger brilliant even in the muted light of the cham. At its side, a fold of blue fabric and on top of that, the blue bangle I gave Teetru. The money pouch was not there nor were any of the other bolts of fabric or bangles I'd bought the other girls. Teetru, I noticed, had carried the fabric out. The pouch she did not have, but I reckoned she'd locked it away in its trunk.

I stared at the table and what was on it as a tingle slithered up my spine.

Then, without thinking, my hand snaked out.

I grabbed the dagger and screeched, "*Zahnin!*"

But it was too late.

From all around, I heard the sounds of ripping fabric and I looked to the side of the cham to see a dagger had been planted in it and was tearing through.

I whirled and took them in.

There were daggers all around!

Shit!

I was surrounded!

My arm shot out and I grabbed a heavy candleholder in my left hand as I heard steel clash with steel at the front of the cham. The candle toppled off my holder as huge men with skin the color of Teetru's pushed through the slashes in the cham.

"*No!*" I shrieked as they came at me.

Suddenly, out of nowhere, something came over me, and whatever it was was coming from inside me.

In a weird way I saw but did not see. In a weird way my body was not at my command. It just moved of its own accord.

I bashed out with the candleholder with all my strength and caught the first man who got to me upside his head. His eyes rolled back into his head, and he careened to the side as arms closed around me from behind, picking me up.

I kicked out with my feet with all my might as I turned the dagger in my hand and tried to strike at his head behind mine with the candleholder and missed. But my tactic worked, he was having trouble defending himself at the same time containing me.

Then I kicked out with my feet again as I plunged the dagger back and connected its blade with the flesh at his side.

He howled, his arms loosened, and I was dropped to my feet. My fist still wrapped around the hilt, I yanked out the dagger, whirled, and even as I felt more hands start to close on my waist, quickly, before his hand could make it to the knife on his belt, I sunk my blade into his chest, aiming at his heart then pulling it out.

My aim was true.

Blood spurted and he dropped like a stone.

But another one had me.

For a second.

I heard a ferocious growl I'd never heard before in my life and I was suddenly free.

This was because my sweet, little tigress cub came out of nowhere and jumped him. Surprised by the attack, he stumbled to the side and her not-quite-so-baby-anymore tiger teeth went right for his jugular.

I had no time to watch. I was again captured from behind and this one came smart. The blade was nearing my throat before I tossed my dagger up, caught its handle and again thrust back, finding flesh. At the same time, I jerked my head back and it collided with his chin. He went back and I again moved the dagger in my hand, whirled and slashed out, opening skin at his chest.

I felt the presence of more bodies in the cham, heard the clash of steel and the sound of men's grunts, and my guess was Zahnin and/or Bain had entered the tent. I didn't look as I slashed another slice through my attacker's chest. On my third go, he caught my wrist and twisted it. Pain shot up my arm so strong, it took me to my knees. His other arm came back to my throat with the knife, but I moved quickly. Dropping the candleholder, I grasped his wrist, jerked it with all my might and leaned forward using the only weapon I had at my command.

My teeth.

I bit hard. So hard, blood spurted into my mouth and he yelped. Then he let me go. I turned swiftly on my knees and plunged my blade into his belly, my other hand going to cover the one on the hilt. I jerked it up, slicing him open, blood spurting out and flowing down.

He stumbled back then fell to his knees.

I gained my feet, lifted one and kicked him as hard as I could across his face. As he fell to the side, I was shoved out of the way, and then I watched Bain heave his sword in an arc, separating head from body, blood spraying out as his body dropped to the rugs and his head flew away, fell and rolled behind the bed.

Bain's arm hooked me at the waist, and he pulled my back tight to his front as he shouted, "Lock down the Daxshee! Every warrior on alert! Search parties sent out to see if there are more Maroo!"

My eyes lifted to the tent flaps, and I saw a warrior I didn't know nod then exit immediately.

My eyes moved round the tent, searching for new threats and automatically counting the bodies on the ground, bodies (or, disgustingly, body *parts*) that seemed to fill all the available space. One, two, three, four, five...I got up to what might amount (if put back together) to ten, taking in the blood that was splattered throughout Lahn and my cham before I froze.

Zahnin was at the back of the tent, his body heaving with the deep breaths mine was sucking in and I felt Bain's pulling in against me. Zahnin held his bloody sword in one hand, pointed down, an equally bloody knife held in the other. Ghost was sitting at his feet, jaws bloody, tongue lolling, blinking like she was bored and ready for a nap.

And I also saw a jagged slash of opened flesh scored down Zahnin's chest and through his abs.

"No," I whispered as I watched the blood drip down his hides. "*No!*" I shrieked, and Bain's hold tightened around me.

"It is fine. He is fine, my golden queen. It is a flesh wound," Bain whispered.

These *fucking* savage brute warrior guys.

A flesh wound!

His blood was *dripping* down his *hides.*

With a heave I tore from Bain's hold and ran across the cham on a direct route to my protector. That was to say, I ran over the bed. Ghost jumped to all fours and crept back, clearly reading her Loolah's mood and wanting nothing to do with it.

When I got to him, I put a gentle hand on him and tilted my head way back to look at him.

"We need to get you down. We need to cleanse this. We need—"

He cut in to grunt, "Queen Circe, I am fine."

I stepped back and screeched, "You are *not* fine!" Then I turned to the tent flaps and screamed, "*Jacanda! Get in here!*"

"My golden—" Zahnin started, but I whipped my head back to him, raised the point of my own bloody dagger toward his face and his mouth snapped shut as his eyes went to my weapon.

"Quiet, Zahnin, you will allow me to see to your wound. Your queen commands it!" I ordered.

His gaze moved from my blade to my face, his lips twitched and then his attention slid to Bain.

"Our king told us of this," he remarked drily.

"Indeed, our queen gets something in her head…" Bain trailed off, sounding amused—yes, *amused*—as he agreed with his brother from behind me.

I turned to glare with narrowed eyes at Bain then I swung my glare back to Zahnin and I snapped, "No more banter. *You*!" I jabbed my dagger at Zahnin. "Lie down." I swung the blade to the bed. "I'm seeing to your wound."

"As you wish, warrior queen," he muttered, also sounding amused…deeply.

My narrowed gaze got squinty and Jacanda scurried in, face pale, eyes wide, fear visible on every inch of her frame.

I turned to her. "Boil water. I need soap, clean cloths and cleaner bandages. I'll need a needle and thread, uh…" I stopped because I didn't know the Korwahk word for "sterilized" then said, "Cleaned." When she looked confused, I explained, "Boil those too…*for a long time*." She nodded, though now she looked less afraid and more perplexed. I ignored it and kept going. "Bring the healer to me. And send someone to get some zakah. *A lot* of zakah."

"I could use some zakah," Zahnin muttered, and I whirled to him.

"You're not going to *drink* it. I'm going to use it to clean your wound."

He stared at me with unconcealed surprise.

"Don't question me," I ordered. "They do it in my land. It's a good thing to do."

"It's a waste of good zakah," Bain commented under his breath from across the tent, but I caught it and I turned to him.

"Don't you have a Daxshee to lock down or possible enemies to round up or *something*?" I prompted.

He pressed his lips together I knew to suppress a twitch and I squinted at him.

"Yes, my true golden queen," he muttered, his amused gaze slid through Zahnin then he left the tent and I noticed Jacanda was still standing there.

"Go, sweetheart, *now*," I urged.

She nodded and shot off.

I turned to Zahnin and noted, "You're not lying down."

"Right," he muttered.

I moved to the bed and pulled the bloody sheet off and also any hides that had blood on them. Then I shoved off any pillows that had been bloodied.

What I didn't do was look at any of the cut-up bodies or body pieces littering my tent or think of the fact that I, myself, had taken at least one, possibly one and a half lives (I might have delivered a killing wound, but it was Bain who definitely executed the kill, so I was counting that as a half). Nor did I allow myself to think about the obvious news that my Teetru had betrayed me to her people.

She betrayed me, yet got out my dagger, exposing it openly both to warn me and to give me a fighting chance by providing me with the only weapon she, or I, had at our disposal.

And lastly, I did not think about why she would do either of these things, betray me first then warn me second.

"May I have my queen's leave to find a warrior and ask him to gather other warriors to collect these bodies?" Zahnin asked solicitously from behind me, far more solicitous than he ever spoke to me (mainly because he never spoke to me solicitously). I heard the humor in his tone. Something about it made the adrenaline surging through my system and subsequent temper flare evaporate.

I straightened from the bed and turned to him.

"I'll do that," I said softly. "Can you please, for me, lie down?"

He read the change in my tone and his face softened, the amusement faded, and warmth hit his expression.

"I am fine, my golden queen, this is my vow."

"You bleed for me," I whispered. "Please, *please*, I know you don't need it, but *I* need to take care of you. *Please*."

He studied me. Then he nodded and lay down.

I ran to the flaps of the tent, stuck my head out and saw two warrior guards on either side.

"We need clean up in here, if you don't mind," I said to the one on my left.

He nodded but didn't move. Instead, he bellowed my order to a warrior standing post some ten feet away. That warrior nodded, turned and bellowed my order to someone else.

I didn't hang around to watch the rest. I saw Packa running toward me with the big bath cloths Lahn and I used and I moved back into the tent.

Needless to say, everyone was a little surprised, and get this—*sickened*—by the medicine I explained was practiced freely in my land.

They did not sew flesh together, Bain informed me with curled lip, eyes filled with disgust.

Yes, this from a man who cut up a bunch of the enemy in what amounted to my freaking house. And, after, stood amongst the carnage bantering with his comrade.

Furthermore, they didn't have a word for germs because they didn't know what germs were. So my explanation of why I would waste good zakah cleansing Zahnin's wound fell on deaf ears.

Luckily, I was queen so they had no choice but to give into my commands, and they did.

Though, Bain and Zahnin did it obviously humoring me.

However, when I commanded a clearly squeamish Gaal (Jacanda told me she was a very gifted seamstress when I demanded she find the best one in the Daxshee) to sew together the edges of Zahnin's wound, the healer, standing and observing, saw the wisdom of this.

"Very clever," she muttered as Gaal, swallowing with nerves and aversion but still game, started to use the needle I'd further sterilized in a candle flame and thread that Jacanda had boiled in a pot over the fire, and I'd soaked in zakah to sew Zahnin's wound together.

Gaal looked like she was about to heave a couple of times (and I was right there with her, talk about *gross*), but she stuck with it mainly because I stayed close for moral support. Her eyes kept lifting to me, I nodded to encourage her, and eventually she lost her distaste for it and did, from my extremely limited experience, what looked like a very good job.

For Zahnin's part, he didn't even wince but lay on my bed with pillows I'd shoved under his head, one arm bent, hand behind his head, chatting amiably through the whole thing to Bain who was standing at the head of the bed, arms crossed on his chest and one ankle crossed over the other in a casual warrior pose, which didn't fit with what had become a minor medical procedure in a primitive examination room.

Once closed, I cleansed the wound again with zakah when Gaal moved away. The healer gooped him up with some salve she promised aided healing (after I made her wash her hands with soap and rinse them in zakah) and then he sat up so she could press a long bandage down his front then roll a clean gauze tight around and around his torso, tying it expertly at the end.

The bodies, by the way, had been removed by young trainee warriors, and Packa and Beetus, faces pale, had grabbed the sheet and pillows and pulled up the rugs to take them out as Jacanda went to work wiping down furniture and trunks.

Boy, I needed to go back to the market and buy my girls more gifts. They already went beyond the call of duty and got nothing for it except food, cham and minimal clothing. Wiping up blood went so beyond the call of duty, it wasn't funny.

Ghost, by the way, was lying on her side at the foot of the bed, napping in a dead-to-the-world fashion, and I knew this because, even with all the people and activity around, she didn't even twitch.

When I put pressure on Zahnin's shoulder to press him back, he went without complaint, but he looked at me when he was fully reclining.

"Can I have some zakah now?"

I studied him. He was not pale. He had never been faint. And his eyes held no pain. None at all. In fact, he looked totally normal.

Boy, they trained these boys to within an inch of their life.

Literally.

I sucked in a calming breath and answered, "Yes, my protector, you can have—"

I stopped speaking when the cham flaps slapped, and I was turning toward them when I heard a soft, feminine intake of breath.

Sabine was standing inside my cham, Diandra and Claudine entering the flaps at her back.

Sabine was also staring at her husband and his bandage, her eyes wide, her face pale, her mouth soft. I watched those eyes drift up his chest to his face then I stared as they got bright with unshed tears.

They slid to me.

"Circe?" she whispered.

"He's fine, sweetheart. We've fixed him up," I assured her.

She held my gaze for several moments before she nodded. Her gaze went back to Zahnin who I noticed had not moved and he was watching her silently. Then it swiftly came back to me.

It hit me that she didn't know what to do.

I was sitting on my knees in the middle of the bed next to her husband and I extended my arm to her.

"It's okay. You can come to him. He's fine and you won't hurt him," I called softly.

Her body jerked slightly, and she bit her lip.

I held my breath.

Then slowly, foot in front of foot, she walked to the bed. When she made it to the end, she put a knee to it and crawled on all fours to me.

Zahnin watched without a word.

I scuttled back and she stopped when she took my place, sitting ass to calves, knees an inch from his hip.

My feet hit stone at the side of the bed when I heard her whisper, "You are all right, husband?"

"Meena," Zahnin replied instantly.

A pause, then from Sabine, "Are you in pain?"

"Me," Zahnin answered again instantly.

I heard her soft intake of breath and let out my own when her hand tentatively lifted. She settled it lightly on the bandage at his stomach as she whispered, "Dohno."

At her word and touch, with his gaze warm on his wife, his face soft, Zahnin lifted his hand, and her body didn't move or even tense as she allowed her husband to cup her cheek.

And she did something that proved I was right about how sweet Sabine was.

She slowly and carefully dropped gracefully to her side and curled up next to him, her head on his shoulder, her hand light on his bandage. As she moved, Zahnin's fingers slid through her hair, so when she was settled, they cupped the back of her head.

My eyes went to his to see his were on me.

And they were communicating.

I nodded, getting the message loud and clear.

His fingers started sifting through his wife's hair.

"Everybody out," I ordered softly, and I didn't need to ask twice.

Jacanda quit wiping, grabbed her bucket and scurried. The healer and Bain moved to the tent flaps that Claudine had exited and Diandra was currently moving through. Gaal was already gone.

I wanted to look back but didn't. It wasn't right. But I really, really wanted to.

I didn't need to.

I heard Zahnin mutter, "Thank you for coming to me, my beautiful one."

Before I dropped the flaps behind me, I heard Sabine's soft sigh.

And as the flaps settled, I heard Sabine ask with cute, quiet surprise, "Oh my, Zahnin, is that a *tiger*?"

This was followed by a quiet manly chuckle.

Hmm.

It seemed I never shared about Ghost with Sabine, and it occurred to me I'd never hosted her at my cham.

I walked toward Diandra and Claudine thinking I was going to have to do that. I'd had lunch or dinner at all my posse's chams. I was falling down. It was *way* my turn.

These thoughts were wiped from my brain when Diandra's eyes came to me and drifted the length of me.

Then they filled with tears.

"Oh, my Circe," she breathed.

I stopped moving, looked down and saw I had blood all over me.

I hadn't even noticed.

I looked up to assure her I was fine when suddenly the air changed and I heard the thunder of hooves.

My head turned to the left just in time to see Lahn on Lahkan clear the cham closest to us. I had no time to experience shock at his early return, or delight.

I didn't because he was coming at a full gallop, and he wasn't slowing.

I registered vaguely he was followed by a number of other horses, but I didn't pay much attention because suddenly his body was swinging off his horse *while Lahkan kept galloping*!

"Lahn!" I cried, frozen stiff in panic when his feet solidly hit ground and Lahkan zoomed by me so close, I felt the breeze of motion and a whisper of touch from his tail, but I couldn't concentrate on that either.

Lahn was on me.

Or his hands were. Traveling over my limbs, my shoulders, my breasts, my belly, my waist, drifting over the dried blood, he jerked me so my back was to him and did the same.

It finally hit me what he was doing, and I tried to turn back, saying, "Lahn, I'm okay."

I didn't turn around. He *jerked* me back around and my body swayed with the force of it and only remained standing because his hands clamped on either side of my jaw.

He stared into my eyes, and I held my breath because his spirit was there, right there, right at the surface, burning golden, bright and brutal more than it had even after Dortak called out his threats.

He was not pissed. He was not angry.

His spirit was filled with wrath.

Oh shit.

"I'm okay, honey," I whispered, my hands lifting to curl my fingers around his wrists and his fingers pressed in so hard they caused pain. "Honestly, I'm—"

I didn't finish because he released me but threw back his head and roared with rage. No words, just a primal shout he thundered to the heavens that came straight from his gut and was filled with a fury unsurpassed.

I took a step back in shock and surprise at this uninhibited, savage display as he dropped his chin and roared again, thumping his fist on his chest and turning his massive body toward the phalanx of warriors on their horses who had crowded thigh to thigh in the limited space.

He thumped his fist on his chest again and thundered, "We ride on Maroo!"

Oh shit!

The warriors on horses, those standing around, others standing sentry and all of those guarding our cham roared in response, punching fists in the air or thumping their own chests.

"The blood of our enemy stains the gold of *my* queen!" Lahn kept bellowing, thumping his chest on the word "my" then swinging a powerful arm around to point at me. "They closed on her in *my* cham," another thump, "shattering the safety *I* provide her," another thump, "and spilling the blood of our brother!" He beat at his chest with both fists. "In return, we will create *rivers* of Maroo blood. The stone of our earth will *weep* with it, and we will know *vengeance*!" Another thump and another returning roar from his warriors, now, their numbers were growing as more were joining or closing in.

I felt Diandra and Claudine move in on my sides, Diandra's hand finding mine as Lahn turned, but he didn't look at me.

He looked beyond me and ordered, "Bathe their blood from her golden skin. Remove our possessions and burn this cham, *now*. Order a new one made. I want it up and sheltering my golden bride in a week." He paused, leaned forward, I turned my head and saw Gaal and Beetus staring at him, frozen, and he boomed, "*Move!*"

They moved and they did it fast.

Lahn again didn't look at me when he turned back to his warriors and kept thundering, "My seed has been planted in her womb and she carries my child. They attacked *my tigress* and *your golden warrior queen*. They attacked all that is the beauty of Suh Tunak *and* my unborn. They will know a vengeance that their *grandchildren* will understand, and knowing it through the ages to come, they will *still quake in their beds*!"

Okay, he wasn't calming down, like...at all.

"Lahn," I whispered, for some reason my voice not able to get any louder, but Diandra squeezed my hand.

"No, Circe, not now. Not at all," she murmured in my ear. "Even a normal warrior's wife is off limits, and the enemy knows it. The Daxshee is never penetrated, *ever*. In times far past this happened, and in that past Suh Tunak has ridden just like our Dax now describes, and the brutality of their vengeance has not been forgotten...until now."

I looked up at her and she finished quickly.

"To invade a cham is akin to them taking you by force. It is symbolic. It is the safety he offers you as your husband and it was violated. He will taste vengeance and the Maroo will bleed for it."

Oh God.

My eyes snapped to Lahn when I heard him ask, "She is taken?"

I saw he was glowering at a warrior who jerked up a chin.

Lahn ordered, "Bring me the traitor."

Oh no. No.

No.

My body got tight.

He wanted Teetru.

"Still, my friend, still. Be strong. He will know vengeance," Diandra murmured, her arm going around me and Claudine, at my other side, did the same.

I was glad for it, for I was suddenly shaking and not just a little.

"Send messengers, my brother," Lahn barked at another warrior. "They ride out tonight. Suh Tunak amasses."

That warrior nodded, turned and stalked through his brethren, quickly disappearing.

Lahn suddenly turned and again looked beyond me. I looked over my shoulder and saw Zahnin outside the tent, his arm around his wife who looked tiny next to him and was visibly shaking at his side. He had her turned, front to his side, and held close with his arm around her shoulders, but his attention was focused on his king.

She'd seen, heard and understood and she was pressing her lips together probably in the effort not to whimper.

That was my girl.

Her eyes darted to me, and I smiled at her. I knew it trembled. Hers trembled too when she returned it.

Yep, that was my girl.

We weren't Korwahk, but we sure as hell were learning to be.

Fast.

Lahn spoke and I turned back to him.

"Your blood will be avenged."

From behind me, Zahnin replied, "Yes, my king."

He jerked his head my way. "It will also be rewarded."

"Yes, my king," Zahnin repeated, and Lahn's gaze cut to Bain who was standing several feet from him.

"The stains on your steel will be rewarded," Lahn stated.

Bain jerked up his chin.

Horses sidled, a pathway cleared, and I sucked in breath.

Diandra and Claudine held on tight.

Thinking quickly, knowing in my heart what would happen, I twisted and caught Zahnin's gaze.

"Hide her eyes," I called.

He grunted unintelligibly but his big hand lifted, covering Sabine's eyes as he turned her to his front, burying her face in his bandaged chest.

He bent to her and said gently, "Cover your ears, close your eyes. I will tell you when it is done."

I turned back when I heard a pained cry and then winced when I saw that Teetru had been tossed to the stone ground.

She'd also been mishandled, gravely. She wore no clothes, bruises had already formed around her arms, her wrists, her hips, her knees, her throat, and there was a dried, white substance liberally splattered everywhere on her body including her face, and I knew what that was.

My knees gave out, but Diandra and Claudine closed in, holding me up until I forced my legs to stand strong again under me.

Teetru's body was on its side but down, only her head lifted up and her eyes came to me then they traveled through the blood on my body.

They were full of pain, but to my shock it was not just the pain she felt in her body. Mingled with it was a different kind of pain.

I heard her whisper, "You should not have been kind to me."

My body jolted and tears filled my eyes.

"Prepare her," Lahn barked.

Her gaze stayed locked to mine as Bain strode forward, and using her hair causing her to cry out, but she still didn't break her connection to me, he pulled her to her knees.

The wet streamed down my cheeks and pain burned my throat.

With a hiss of steel, Lahn unsheathed his sword.

"I wish you hadn't been kind to me."

Those were her last words before Bain stepped free and Lahn severed her head from her body with a vicious swing of his sword.

I turned into Diandra's arms and shoved my face in her neck, so I missed the flash of lightning that rent the sky, trailing down the cliff five hundred yards behind me.

"Throw it off the cliff. Return the head to the Maroo king with one of their warriors you captured. Unman him before you free him. Her head and his balls, my gift to their king before we lock steel," Lahn ordered.

I stifled a painful sob by swallowing and that hurt even more.

"Bathe my fucking *bride*!" Lahn bellowed.

I felt Diandra nod and then she and Claudine gently guided me toward my girls' cham, and I heard Zahnin's soft, "Attend your queen," as I went.

But I heard no more and felt no more, and this was because I slunk into my head to sort it out.

I was Korwahk, Queen of Korwahk and we were at war.

I was Korwahk, I repeated to myself, Queen of Korwahk and we were at war.

I had to find some way to get my shit together.

Somehow.

"You must eat, my golden queen."

I turned and looked down at Jacanda.

I was in her tent. Whatever belongings she and the girls had were gone, whereabouts unknown (to me). Our bed with a clean silk sheet had been moved in, our scrubbed trunks and our cleaned furniture. The tent was smaller, the stuff crammed in the space.

I was bathed, my hair washed and the skin behind my ears and at my wrists had been anointed with perfumed oil. I was wearing my robe of blue.

Incense Teetru had sourced weeks ago at my request burned, smelling of berries.

Packa set this to burning because she knew I liked it and probably thought it would soothe me. But I would find the stash and get rid of it later when they weren't around. It reminded me of Teetru, whose actions could have killed me, or harmed me, they did harm Zahnin, but at the same time she did what she could to save me. A paradox I would never understand because she was no longer breathing for me to ask.

"You sleep with Diandra's girls tonight?" I asked, and Jacanda nodded.

"Yes, my true queen. But we will be here before the dawn in case you need us."

"Sleep in, my doe, today has been busy. You and my girls need your rest. I will get on," I assured her.

"We will be here," she replied firmly.

"I will—"

She cut me off, "The king will expect it."

I stopped talking and nodded, because this was true. Lahn would expect it.

Then I lifted two hands and put them on her cheeks, dipping my face to hers.

"I'm so sorry about Teetru," I whispered.

I watched with surprise as her eyes went hard.

"She is a traitor," she hissed, pulled away, turned her head to the side and then made a spitting sound with her mouth though no spit came out before she turned back to me. "I was born slave. I was lucky to have good masters, like Beetus. Packa and Gaal were not. This makes Packa timid and Gaal guarded. But we have talked many nights of you, our golden queen, who laughs with us and speaks kindly, touches kindly, whose warrior provides us with plentiful food, better than we've ever had. You are our true golden queen, and she was of Maroo, but she knew the gold of your touch, just like us all. Slaves are normally commanded, not asked and not included. We do not exist, even though we serve. We exist for you. It feels *good* to exist. She nearly took you away from us. This is unforgivable and this will not be forgiven, not by warrior, not by warrior bride, not by free man or woman, not by slave, not by anyone Korwahk, and most especially not by what you call us. Your Girls. She was honored to be among us and now her headless body rots at the bottom of a cliff, a body that will never join her spirit in the next realm. We will not miss her, not one of us. Your Dax was too good to her. He should have turned her over to the warriors to do what they are forbidden to do even to the Xacto instead of taking her head."

Okay, mental note, do not get on Jacanda's bad side.

This was what I thought.

What I said was a whispered, "All right, sweetheart."

She nodded and moved to the cham flaps but stopped and turned back.

"I burned her bolt of fabric with your cham as well as her other belongings, and Beetus threw her bangle over the cliff. She no longer exists."

I nodded.

I got the message. I was not to speak of her again.

She nodded back.

"Goodnight, Jacanda," I whispered.

"Eat something," she tipped her head to the table where she'd put food. "Then sleep well, my golden queen," she whispered back then exited the cham.

I sucked in breath, lifted my hands to my cheeks and pressed in.

I felt the tears and shakes come again and I struggled to keep them in check.

I won this fight as the tent flaps slapped back, my gaze flew there, and I watched my husband bend low and enter, accompanied by Ghost.

I stared at him as he took a step in and stopped. Ghost didn't stop. She ambled to me, so I bent in a knees-to-chest squat, and she kept coming until I had her head in my hands. When I had a hold on her, I started to scratch behind her ears.

"The animal sprung to your aid," Lahn declared, and I kept scratching as I tipped my head back to look at him. "From now on, she sleeps with us."

I nodded and studied his face.

He still looked pissed.

I bit my lip.

This made him look more pissed.

I stopped biting my lip.

His eyes dropped to Ghost, and he looked even more pissed.

What on earth?

He looked back at me and ordered tersely, "Rise, wife, and come to me."

I didn't want to, mainly because he looked pissed, but I did. I gave Ghost's head a rub, straightened and walked to him.

I stopped a few inches away.

"Put your hands on me," he commanded, and I felt it prudent in the face of his continued anger to keep quiet and do what he said.

Therefore, I lifted my hands and rested them on his chest.

The minute they touched, his hands came up, and as they did earlier, they clamped on either side of my jaw, but this time he pulled me roughly in and up so I was on my toes as he bent toward me.

"No one," he ground out, his eyes an inch from my own. "*No one* touches my queen."

"Okay, baby," I whispered.

"No one threatens her with steel." He kept grinding out his words between his teeth.

My hands drifted up to his neck.

"All right," I said softly.

"No one betrays her," he kept going. "*No one* and especially not one she's shown generosity and kindness, who has felt her golden touch."

I nodded as best I could with his hands on me. "Yes, honey."

He scowled into my face.

Then he asked, "You have no words for the collaborator?"

"I..." I started, shook my head, again as best I could with his hands on me, then went on, "Honey, I promised you before you left that I wouldn't again question who you are and what you do, and I'm keeping that promise." His burning eyes didn't leave mine and I continued, "It's hard, of course, because, you know me, I have something to say about every—"

I didn't finish. His hands left my jaw, his arms locked around me, one hand at the back of my head, he tilted it to the side, slanted his the other way and his mouth crushed down on mine.

I held on to his neck as his mouth and tongue took their fill and then he tore his lips from mine. He shoved my face in his chest. I turned it so my cheek was pressed there, and I pushed my hands under his arms and wrapped them around him.

"You came home early," I noted (a little breathlessly) in order to take our conversation to the mundane.

"Zahnin says you felled a Maroo," Lahn returned, not, obviously, in the mood for mundane.

"Tee..." I hesitated then went on cautiously, "She knew the attack was imminent and left the dagger that Bohtan gave me out for me. I had a moment to prepare."

"That *kut* did not save your life, Circe. Zahnin, Bain, Ghost and *you* did," he growled on a squeeze of his arms. "I'll listen to no talk of her giving you a moment to prepare."

Kut.

He'd called her a bitch. That was big. Even Korwahk warriors didn't say that very often.

At least not in front of their wives.

"Uh...okay," I whispered.

Another mental note, don't mention Teetru around Lahn either.

He was silent. This lasted awhile.

Then he said quietly, "I give thanks to my god you are warrior."

I nodded.

I gave it to mine too, on several occasions the last few hours. I had no idea I had it in me but I sure as hell was glad I did.

Lahn went on, "And I give more thanks you hold magic. As you were battling, your lightning filled the sky. Warriors and everyone in the Daxshee knew the lightning storm was not natural but something to do with their queen. This gave warning and meant the traitor did not escape and other Maroo warriors lying in wait for the return of their brethren were also captured."

Whoa.

Wow.

I didn't know that. Any of it.

"Yes, magic is good," I agreed. The light pressure he was exerting on my head relaxed. I tilted it back to look at him and changed the subject. "Why are you home early?"

"Early this morning, we had a messenger from Keenhak. Keenhak spies close to the Maroo king heard of the plot and came to me. This decision was smart. They build alliances while Maroo seeks to end the Golden Dynasty. Keenhak will be rewarded for this act." I nodded and he finished. "We rode hard to return to the Daxshee, but we were too late."

"I'm okay," I said quietly.

"All day, I rode blind, the only thing I saw, visions of my golden queen covered in blood."

Oh God.

That had to suck.

"I'm okay," I repeated.

"And I ride into the Daxshee only to see you covered in blood."

My arms gave him a squeeze. "Honey, I'm *okay*."

"I can see that and feel it, my doe, but I do not care. Vengeance—"

I pulled an arm from around him and lifted my hand to touch my fingers to his mouth.

"I know, Lahn. Rivers of blood. I *know*. It freaks me out and scares me, and I don't want you or anyone to be hurt, but I know. This is what you must do. So you will do it. But now can I ask a favor, and can you be quiet for just long enough so that I can give you a welcome home kiss to add to your, 'thank God my golden queen is all right' kiss? Then you can rant all you want about vengeance."

He stared down at me.

Then he said against my fingers, "Remove your fingers, Circe, you can hardly kiss me with your hand over my mouth."

I smiled up at him as my body relaxed in his arms and I moved my hand. I went up on tiptoe, he bent his neck, and I gave my husband a welcome home kiss that was, I was guessing, pretty damned good. I guessed this because he lifted me up in the middle of it, my legs wrapped around his hips, and he strode to the bed. I went down, him on top of me.

Ghost growled with irritation and jumped off her perch.

Eventually, Lahn's mouth left mine and he buried his face in my neck as my limbs tightened around him.

There he was.

So big. So strong. My husband. There with me. In our bed.

On these thoughts, it hit me, and I couldn't hold it back. My breath hitched.

His head came up and his eyes found mine. When they did, his warmed.

"Baby," he whispered, and my breath hitched again.

"I killed one and a half men today," I whispered back, a tear sliding out of the side of my eye.

His head twitched and he asked, "A half?"

"Bain cut his head off, but I'd already sliced through his innards, a wound he survived right then, but he wouldn't survive it for long."

I watched Lahn's jaw get hard and I didn't know if it was to bite back laughter or a roar of fury.

Then he informed me quietly (and scarily), "I am glad you did, for if you had not, they would have killed you. The plot was to capture you, take you outside the Daxshee but murder you close and leave your body for us to find. Instead, they encountered a warrior queen, her extraordinary pet and guards with good instincts. As things did not go as they had planned, they would have needed to execute their plan as best they could and instead would have killed you in our cham."

I knew this to be true. The first man had grabbed me and done it unarmed, probably underestimating me. The last had not done the same and came at me with a knife.

That scared the shit out of me, but I sucked it up as best I could and nodded.

Another tear slid out of my left eye followed by one from my right and I felt my nostrils quiver.

"She betrayed me," I whispered, and Lahn's face went soft, his hand lifted to cup the side of my head, his thumb moving through the wetness at my temple. "Why would she do that?"

"I do not know," Lahn answered in his own whisper.

I sucked in a breath that broke twice on the way in. "And since she did, why would she put out my dagger…warn me?"

"I do not know that either, my golden doe."

I didn't either.

I thought of Teetru's face looking at mine after I gave her the bangle.

"She was my girl," I said so softly it was barely audible, my breath hitched, and my vision melted as my body started shaking with sobs.

"My Circe," Lahn murmured, rolling off me but pulling me tight and cradling me close as I cried into his chest.

Lahn didn't get the chance to rant about vengeance. It could be said that I had a tough day, so I pretty much passed out right in the middle of bawling. I didn't know what he did.

But later, I woke to feel his weight and heat, the sheet up to our waists and Ghost asleep at the foot of the bed.

For that moment, I was safe, my husband was home, and all was well.

So I drifted back to my dreams.

26
KORWAHN

S*ix weeks later…*

It was official.

I was most definitely pregnant.

I spit into the chamber pot then sucked in breath hoping more would not come up my throat and out my mouth.

Seriously, I hated puking. And doing it in a chamber pot made a not very fun activity a lot less fun.

When the nausea subsided and it seemed I had the all-clear, I moved to the basin, poured some water from a jug on a cloth, wiped my mouth, rinsed the cloth, wiped my face and rinsed it again. Then I rinsed my mouth with water and grabbed the thin, split branch that Jacanda had given me to brush my teeth and tongue. I used that, rinsed again, grabbed the cloth and folded it as I wandered out of the bathroom type, um…room.

Lahn was in bed, on his side, silk sheet up to his waist, elbow in the pillow, eyes on me.

My really not-so-little-anymore tigress was lounging on a big, fluffy, hide-covered pad in the corner, her pink tongue licking a bone.

My stomach roiled as the nausea returned and my eyes moved back to Lahn.

Even nauseous, it wasn't lost on me my husband was hot.

It was just that with morning sickness, I was in no mood to do anything about it.

I went to the bed, pulled back the sheet, lifted a leg and collapsed on my back, head to the pillows. I pulled the sheet up and slapped the folded, cool cloth over my eyes.

I felt Lahn's heat against my side then I felt his large hand on my belly.

"Perhaps I was wrong," he murmured. "If you carry a golden daughter in your womb, she would not be so rough on you." I felt him get closer and knew I was right when his soft voice came at my ear and his hand pressed gently at my belly before he whispered, "I believe we made a warrior, my doe."

"I don't care what it is, just as long as you're happy with it because it's the only one you're gonna get, big guy," I muttered back and heard him chuckle in my ear but felt his mouth leave that area after it brushed skin.

Nice move and I loved to hear Lahn's amusement.

But I was not being amusing.

I lifted one side of my cloth so I could slide my eyes to him to see he was still grinning, and I informed him, "I'm not kidding. I don't like puking as in, *really* don't like it."

I watched his eyebrows go up in a face that was still smiling. "Puking?"

"Hurling, calling Buick, heaving, throwing up, vomiting, *puking*."

He chuckled again.

I found nothing funny.

I dropped the cloth and announced, "After this, birth control all the way."

Through another chuckle I heard Lahn ask, "Birth what?"

"Birth *control*. After little Lahn or little Lahnahsahna makes his or her entry into this world, you're sheathing your sword, big guy."

An amused but confused, "Sheathing my sword?"

I lifted the cloth again, glared at him then moved my glare down to the area being discussed and just to make certain he got it, I gave a little nod in that direction.

He got it. I knew it when he roared with laughter.

Again, I found nothing funny.

I dropped the cloth and tried not to let his big body shaking the bed make me hurl.

Finally, he quieted his humor but remarked, "I've heard of this practiced in the Northlands. We do not practice the same in the Southlands, my queen."

"Well, you're going to be a trendsetter," I returned on a mutter.

"Trendsetter?"

"Setting the fashion, being the first."

His hand still at my belly slid up, curled around my breast and his voice was partly amused, partly serious when he informed me. "I'll not have anything between me and my golden queen."

I opened my mouth to say something smart, but he kept talking as his hand slid back to my belly.

"And we will have many children, many warriors to serve Suh Tunak, many golden princesses so their father can behold your beauty on more than your face."

That was sweet and all, *really* sweet, but...

I did not *think* so.

"That's sweet, Lahn, but I'm being very serious."

"Then I will be serious as well and tell you I will not use these...*things*."

"Then you'll pull out before the festivities culminate. It isn't foolproof, but it'll be something," I muttered.

Suddenly, the cloth was gone, and Lahn's face was in mine, his big body looming over me, and I noticed immediately he no longer thought anything was funny either.

"I will not spend my seed on your skin."

Uh-oh.

I stared in his face and knew I'd said something very, very wrong.

"Lahn—"

"A warrior's seed is his essence. It is the future of Suh Tunak. It is not wasted unless used to deliver the worst insult he can give or released on the body of a Xacto. Traitors, enemy warriors weak enough to get captured alive, spies foolish enough to be detected, *they* receive wasted seed. And a warrior does not plant his seed in Xacto, and you, my golden queen, are *not* Xacto."

Okay, it was safe to say this conversation had taken a drastic turn down a road I did *not* want to go.

I had to detour us, pronto.

"Okay," I whispered.

He glared at me.

Then he clipped, "Okay."

"I, uh...didn't know," I said quietly.

"Now you do."

I sure did.

I lifted a hand to cup his bearded jaw and whispered, "I'm sorry, baby. I won't speak of it again. I just really don't like being sick."

"I don't like it either. It means I cannot take your xaxsah in the mornings. I *like* to take your xaxsah in the mornings. What I do *not* like is having to wait until the evening."

Hmm.

Clearly my apology hadn't put him in a better mood.

I sought to better his mood and suggested softly, "How about you try to take my xaxsah with your lisa and we'll see how it goes."

"I do not wish courting you being sick with my mouth between your legs, Circe."

Okay, well, that didn't work.

I rolled into him, fighting the nausea as I ran my hand down his chest and then wound an arm around his back, whispering, "Lahn—"

Suddenly, he pulled in breath through his nose, and he did this so sharply, I shut up.

When he expelled it, his eyes locked with mine and he whispered, "We ride on Maroo in two days."

I closed my eyes and tipped my head forward.

I knew this and I didn't want to talk about it. Not then, not ever. I'd be living it soon enough.

A second later, I felt his lips on my forehead, so my eyes opened to see the beautiful column of his throat.

Against my skin, he said, "We could be on campaign a month, or we could be on campaign a year. And you will be here, and I will not."

All right, he wasn't pissed about the birth control discussion, he was worried.

That was good.

What was bad was, for my husband, I needed to talk about this and I didn't want to.

"I'll be okay," I said gently.

"I know you will be okay." His hand again pressed into my belly and I felt his mouth move from my forehead so I tipped my head back to catch his eyes. "But every day, he or she grows in you and this I will not see. You will grow heavy, and I will not be here to watch your beauty bloom to be even more beautiful. And he or she could come, and I will not be here to cut the connection and be the first being they gaze upon so they will know their father."

"They'll know you, honey, even if you're not here. They'll know."

He stared down at me in mild affront, his brows drawn. "I must be at the birth. It must be me who pulls him from your womb. The first being a child must see, Circe, is their father. The first touch they must feel is the touch of their father. Their connection to their mother is established for months. Their father must have those to establish *his*."

Wow, that was beautiful.

But as beautiful as it was, I was hoping for someone like a midwife who would "pull him from my womb." Even the midwife serving a savage, primitive horde. My guess was my husband hadn't handled or even attended very many births (as in, *none*) and she'd likely have experience I might need.

You know, just in case.

I decided it was wise not to share this.

Instead, I sighed before I gave him a squeeze.

Then I said, "Well, you better kick some Maroo ass, baby, then get *yours* home to me..." I paused then whispered, "*Safe*."

His eyes roamed my face for long moments before his lips twitched up.

"This is the plan," he muttered.

I grinned at him.

He grinned back.

It faded and he whispered, "I must go."

I nodded and waited.

I didn't wait long before it came, his hand at my jaw, his thumb sweeping my cheekbone and his eyes wandering my face with such intensity it was like he was trying to burn the vision of it in his brain.

This happened every morning right before he left me since the day after the attack. This, I guessed (but did not ask), was an indication of a psychological wound he'd endured while riding hard to get to me after learning of a plot to murder me that included a traitor in his very own cham. Then arriving home to have his first vision of me being a me covered in blood. It was clear this had marked him deeply. And although it was a beautiful thing to think the very idea of my loss could wound him so severely, I hated that that wound was there.

I just didn't know what to do about it.

So I did the only thing I knew to do. I pressed into him and smiled brightly.

Then I suggested, "How about this, *I* take *your xac* in *my lisa* when you get home tonight."

The intensity in his eyes shifted, then faded but returned in a different way, his arm curled around me, and he pulled me deeper.

"You just made me a promise, kah bahsah," he growled.

I pushed slightly up, and against his mouth, I whispered, "I won't renege, kah bahsan."

His eyes held mine for a heartbeat before his head slanted and he kissed me, deep and wet and I was really glad I used that twig.

When my toes had curled and my nipples had gone hard and I realized that I didn't feel at all like throwing up in his mouth, he released my lips, lifted up, kissed my forehead and then he maneuvered his big body over mine and out of the bed. I watched over my shoulder as his fabulous body with his seriously fine ass walked to the bathroom-ish style room.

When he disappeared, I rolled to my back and examined the state of my stomach.

I was fine.

I was about to call out to inform Lahn of this when a roil of nausea slid through.

Okay, so I wasn't fine. Therefore, I didn't call out to Lahn.

But I listened to him and watched him as he moved around in the other rooms and our bedroom. And as I listened and watched, I committed what I heard and saw to memory.

I also processed the last six weeks and I did this in an effort not to think about what the next six weeks (and longer) would bring.

We had stayed at our camp for two weeks after the attack. Lahn again mostly disappeared during this time as planning a war was obviously time consuming. But every day he woke me to say a very nice good morning then he'd be gone and I wouldn't see him until my next good morning.

As he ordered, a new cham replacing our old one was sheltering me in a week (actually, more like five days). This one was made with darker, thicker fabric and had a variety of new poles. Where the other one just had those holding up the roof, this one had four in a star shape between each support so that, even if a knife could cut through the fabric, there wasn't enough room for anyone to squeeze through unless they chopped their way through the wooden supports.

Lahn was clearly not taking any chances.

This felt nice. But, every time I saw those poles, it made me sad. I missed our old cham and I missed my Teetru as I knew her to be (not, obviously, who she ended up being).

I didn't dwell on the sad.

Our cham was also bigger, perhaps two feet all around but two feet added to the circumference of a circular tent was a lot. It seemed cavernous compared with our old one.

I would understand this added room when our long, narrow table was not returned and one just as long but three times as wide was set in its place with four chairs around it rather than just two at the ends. Also, another chair with a small ottoman were introduced to our décor (yes, an actual chair!). The chair was heavy on the wood, but the back and seat were cushioned and covered with rose velvet with a design cut into them.

These were spoils of raiding.

I didn't think of that.

I thought instead, my new furniture was perfect for girls' night in, and I used them for this purpose. Copiously.

I also had a new servant (more spoils of raiding). Her name was Quixa, she was older than Jacanda and Beetus, younger than Gaal and Packa and she was Korwahk.

Jacanda, who had naturally taken over as leader of the girls after we lost Teetru (a surprise, I would have guessed Gaal or maybe Packa, but Jacanda was really good at it, the girls took to her and settled very quickly), took Quixa under her wing and was delighted with the addition.

And she told me Quixa was delighted too. She also explained why.

"Quixa is born slave and her masters were kind. But when they were traveling through Keenhak, their party was set upon by Maroo and her masters were killed. She was taken by Maroo and *everyone* knows that the Maroo treat Maroo slaves one way, all slaves from other nations another and not in *good* ways. She is happy to be in service to a Dahksahna and she is *very* happy to be home. These last three years," she shook her head, "they have not been good for Quixa."

Okay, well, I had to admit that made me feel better about Lahn stealing her from someone else while out pillaging. Not a lot better but it was something.

For me, things were business as usual, outside of Lahn being absent most of the time and the fact that my personal guard swelled from two to six. Lahn added Bohtan, Feetak and Char and Vuntus's husbands Tark and

Yoonan (respectively) to their ranks. This was explained one morning when I'd asked about his choices and Lahn had the time to answer.

"You share a bond with their wives. Through that they are bonded to you more than you simply being their golden warrior queen. This intensifies loyalty. Their wives want no harm to come to you because you are their friend. And these warriors hold deep feelings for their wives, so they will make this so."

I thought that was a nice way to look at it.

It was nicer when he went on.

"And they all came to me separately, knowing I would be seeking more protection for my Dahksahna, and they volunteered for this service."

Definitely nicer.

I never went anywhere without at least two, but usually there were four of my guard with me, and after what happened, their presence was definitely welcome.

During these two weeks, I saw three of what Diandra told me were "raiders" or "raiding parties." In other words, groups of The Horde who went out marauding. They rode over the horizon to swell our ranks. In each raiding party there were about a hundred horses all together (warriors and wives) plus their convoy of wagons.

I also saw one "patrol" (again, this info gleaned from Diandra) that was a troop of The Horde that patrolled Korwahk to keep the civilians safe from other country's marauders or to be on the lookout for invasion. Korwahk did it themselves, but they did not countenance others doing it back. That said, it happened on more than the rare occasion, so these groups found action often. The patrol had what looked like a few hundred horses (plus wagons).

Lahn explained to me that these returning warriors were the groups that were closest in location to the Daxshee and would ride with us. We had been waiting for their arrival and the day after the patrol joined us, Lahn announced we would be packing up the Daxshee and meeting the rest of Suh Tunak in Korwahn.

Korwahn, by the way, was the largest city in Korwahk, where all the members of The Horde kept permanent residences even if they didn't spend much time in them.

It was a four-day ride to Korwahn, and the morning of the day we were to arrive, my girls gave me the business. I would not, Jacanda informed me, ride into Korwahn for the first time as Suh Rahna Tunakanahsa Dahksahna Hahla looking anything but head to toe queen.

I put my foot down about gold dust in my hair and my feathers (in other words, I did not intend to wear either). The Korwahk Horde rode as one. I wasn't going to shine like a beacon while everyone else had four days of dust on them.

But I did don a sarong made of pure gold silk, my belt of gold disks, a gold silk fold of material tied around my breasts with earrings that were simply long, thin gold chains with a gold ball at the bottom and a matching choker necklace of a bunch of the same chains with intermittent balls adorning them. I had peach tint on my cheeks, peach gloss on my lips, pearlescent peachy eye shadow, and I allowed them to dust around my temples and eyes with gold dust (because every girl knows, a little glitter was always okay, even if riding a dusty trail). I also allowed them to clip my curled, twisted hair in a fall in the back with a heavy, gold clip.

That was all, but I thought that was more than enough.

I should have listened to Jacanda.

When Korwahn came in sight, Bain's horse came back to mine and he plucked me off Zephyr, galloped us to Lahn, Lahn plucked me from Bain and planted me in front of him and away went Bain and Zephyr.

Apparently, I would ride into Korwahn at the lead with my Dax.

Lahn confirmed this with a squeeze of his arm and a murmur in my ear.

I didn't make a comment. I was too busy staring at the two, large, stark, cream stone plateaus jutting into the blue sky in front of me. They were at a forty-five-degree angle to each other with one slightly taller than the other, the shorter one jutting out further. And there was what looked like an enormous, jumbled, interconnected building made of cream mud and dark beams that rode up their faces and sprawled across the landscape.

It was phenomenal.

And that was from afar.

It got better up close.

The Dax's Horde had been seen and therefore people had time to prepare. We were greeted boisterously by men, women and children who had run out of the city to do so.

Therefore, when we reached what Lahn whispered in my ear was called the Avenue of the Gods, the podiums of the enormous statues that lined it were thick with people, all of them tossing petals at Lahn and me, crying out our titles and cheering.

Even if the colorful petals weren't drifting through the air, the Avenue of the Gods that led into Korwahn would be breathtaking.

Starting at the wide end of a sweep of statues that curved to (somewhat) narrow, were two cream stone podiums at least the height of a man and on each was an identical stone woman (the height of at least *three* men and we're talking Korwahk men) carved out of what looked like ivory marble. She was full-on pregnant, her big belly protruding over her sarong, her large breasts covered in a bandeau. One of her arms was curved under her belly, the other arm lifted, her hand held over her eyes as if blocking out the sun or peering into the distance to locate something (it was the latter, Lahn told me, the True Mother's eyes were peeled for the return of her warrior). Her hair was long and fell in carved marble curls and twists but was adorned with gold clips all around, these looking like they were made out of real gold and sparkling in the bright sun (and Lahn confirmed they were, indeed, real gold). There was also gold at her neck, her ears, her wrists and her biceps.

The next one in was a coiled snake, part of its long, thin body raised as if to strike. Its mouth was open, and its fangs and thin, forked, protruding tongue were gold. The diamond-shaped markings down his back the length of the coil were also gold.

The next was a jackal, standing at attention, the spots on its back and tip of its bushy tail both gold.

Then came a grand, stately, reclining lion, its entire mane gold.

Next was the horse, up on its hind legs, both front hooves clawing the air. Each hoof, its mane and tail all gold.

And finally, the tiger, carved on the prowl, its stripes gold.

They were fah-ree-king *amazing*.

Every.

Last.

One.

And I told Lahn so (after I pulled out a petal that had landed in my mouth).

It didn't get better than that, but it was still tremendously cool as Lahn and I rode a sedately walking Lahkan into the city.

And what a city.

It was a hustle and bustle of people. They were everywhere (as were the cheers and petal throwing).

And I was not wrong about it from far away. Everywhere you looked, there were windows covered with wrought iron crosses and there were tons of doors. There was one wide road trailing through the city, some less wide ones leading off it, but there were a bunch of narrow winding paths or steep, stone staircases that cut through the buildings.

Mostly, though, it was all a bunch of buildings clearly built with no city planning in mind. They rose one, two, three, even six stories up, dark wood beams visible jutting into the sky or out the sides from the roof. All of it made from what looked like a cream-colored adobe.

Everything, in fact, was cream. The dirt and stone of the roads (not paved, just natural), walkways, the steep steps and the buildings, all of it.

But there was color.

The wash lines that ran from building to building over roads or narrow pathways on which vibrant tops and sarongs hung.

There were window boxes and brightly colored pots on small balconies and at the sides of doors that were filled with vivid flowers and trailing greenery (I had to say, there weren't many of these, Korwahk clearly wasn't filled with green thumbs—but there was enough to break up the cream, add a splash of color and give your eyes a beautiful surprise).

The large squares that opened up off the main road were filled with market stalls that had colored tent tops over tables or striped awnings over stalls.

And, although most of the doors were bare wood, some were painted green, some red, some blue, some white, some black with blue, white and red stripes and some black (these were warriors' homes, Lahn whispered in my ear as we rode, their doors painted to match the paint they wore on their bodies).

The foot of each door held a small pile of blooms, a welcome home (again, whispered to me from Lahn), from the grateful citizens of Korwahn.

As we road with petals drifting, The Horde that followed broke off when they arrived home or needed to turn down a lane so they could make it home, so there were very few left at the top of the smaller plateau where Lahn stopped Lahkan at a double-arched door that was painted in black with a glimmering gold stripe painted across them both. The only one with such markings that I saw, and I was certain the only one with such markings in Korwahn.

Home.

At the sight of my gold and Lahn's black on our door, my heart warmed and my belly fluttered. I was nervous and excited. I couldn't wait to go through those doors, and for some bizarre reason, I was scared to death at the same time.

I didn't get a chance to puzzle through these emotions. Lahn dismounted, he pulled me off and then he took me inside.

It was cool inside. This was the first thing I noticed.

The second thing I noticed was that there was a courtyard in the middle that was exposed to the elements and in it, with a beautiful mosaic-tiled base, was a small, gurgling fountain. All around the fountain and courtyard were colorful pots filled with spiked or trailing green plants. There were two stories and every door opened out to a balcony that faced or looked down on the courtyard.

The third thing I noticed was there was an older, slightly stooped, short, round woman approaching us. She had an abundance of coarse, steel gray in her dark hair, lots of wrinkles on her face and a bustling but economical manner.

I knew this had to be Twinka, the housekeeper Lahn told me about who looked after his residence while he was away.

And she didn't like me.

This I knew instantly, and I wasn't sure she was all that hot on Lahn, for she gave me a nod, Lahn a slight bow, then she stormed right by us without a word to stand outside the doors, plant her hands at her hips and scowl in the direction of the wagons that were coming up the rear.

"She was with my mother and father. This was their home too. She has called this home longer than I have and has spent vast amounts more time here than I have. She thinks of it as her own," Lahn reminded me of something he'd told me the night before while we were lying under the stars on our hides.

"Mm-hmm," I muttered, staring at Twinka's straight back.

"She does anything you do not like, I'll whip her myself," Lahn muttered back in Korwahk. My eyes snapped to him and Twinka, whose elderly status obviously didn't affect her ears, harrumphed loudly.

I ignored the harrumph and hissed at Lahn in English, "You will not."

"Meena," Lahn said to me, then his eyes turned to Twinka and he finished firmly, "Kay jahkan."

He said, *Yes, I will.*

I pressed my lips together.

Lahn's eyes came back to me and he glared at my lips.

I unpressed them.

Lahn's glare melted and he grinned.

I rolled my eyes.

Lahn turned to Twinka, "Uvoo kah Dahksahna el cuun, boh. Lee aka lapan ansha bel fahkah yo na geenheeso." *Give my queen a tour, now. The others will be here soon enough for you to boss around.*

"Meena, kah Dax," she muttered, stomping back our way, "kay pahnsay yo nahna tahnhan." *Yes, my king, I live for your command.*

I couldn't help it, at her muttered, skating on insubordinate words, I pressed my lips together as my eyes grew big.

Lahn kept smiling at me.

"If you whip her," I said in English. "I won't speak to you for a week."

Lahn's smile faded before he replied in English, "If she does something to earn the tip of my lash, you will not do a thing."

Oh right.

I forgot.

"Right," I whispered. "I forgot."

Lahn looked at me a second, then he looked to the ceiling, likely for deliverance. Twinka made an impatient noise.

I took off for my tour.

Even if there was a lot of it, there wasn't much to it. Lots of rooms, not a lot of furniture.

Not that I could take too much in, Twinka was practically running, pointing at things, muttering words I barely caught, clearly thinking she had better things to do than give her new queen a tour and wanted to get this over with so she could boss around the girls when they arrived.

I did see they didn't really have furniture in Korwahn. Mostly lots of cushions and thick rugs over tiled floors. Even the dining room-ish room had a long, very low table with twelve big cushions set on the floor around it.

There was no room with a desk in it that would say "study." There were six bedrooms, and each had a bathroom-ish type room off it with a chamber pot behind a screen and basin with jug of water, and the master (I was guessing it was the master) had another room with a big, carved wood wardrobe and an actual chaise lounge. Each bedroom had real-ish beds. That was to say, the platform was two feet off the ground, the mattress was twice as thick as the one in our cham, there were twice as many pillows at the head, and it was covered in silk sheets (no hides) and intricately embroidered silk quilts. But no headboard or footboard.

The best of the lot in the house was the bathing room off the master suite that was really like a bathing *pool*, with cool blue and green mosaic tiles and blue and green pads on the edges. The bath was big enough to swim in and had a big window that opened to a balcony that looked out over Korwahn and the vista beyond it.

At my delighted intake of breath, Twinka grudgingly slid up a heavy, wooden door and a gush of steaming water flowed into the bath. I saw that the bottom of the bath had a slight decline and there were four narrow pieces of some gummy-type substance that plugged up drains at the opposite end to the water.

"We have," she stated haughtily in Korwahk, "a direct feed from the hot spring. We are," she went on snootily, "one of only *seven* houses in all of Korwahn who have such a blessing."

I nodded, thinking blessing was the word for it. The water gushing in (before she slammed the door down again), was clear and clean and steaming and I could not freaking *wait* to take a bath.

Twinka stomped out.

I followed her and we continued our tour

I noticed on the walls there were interesting paintings or sheets of copper or silver with designs pounded in the metal and even heavy, carved framed mirrors (and, seeing myself for the first time in months, I had to say, Korwahk sun, Jacanda painted face, love and pregnancy suited me—even I had to admit I looked freaking *great*).

It was all sparkling clean and clearly well taken care of by Twinka, who looked like she could keel over at any minute but moved like she was about twenty-three.

That was kind of it, except for the square roof (with the courtyard hole in it) which was absolutely freaking *awesome*. It had a bunch of colorful pots, huge to very small, filled with spiked greens, trailing plants and vibrant flowers. It also had an area with what looked like lounge chairs that had thick pads on them for lazing in and catching the sun. Another area with a round iron table ornate with curlicues and four matching chairs. And the last area was an abundance of thick mats and huge, brightly colored silk pillows.

Total oasis.

The best spot in the house, no doubt.

After the roof, it was downhill from there and Twinka rushed me through a kitchen at the back that had what looked like a fire-burning oven as well as a rudimentary stove and a long, battered table. Out the back door, through a small, tidy courtyard (with more potted plants) was where the servant quarters were. Four small rooms, two on top, two on bottom, each room had two twin-sized pallets on the floor, two-drawer wooden dressers beside each pallet with one, measly candleholder on each dresser.

Hmm.

I was going to have to do something about that.

Packa, I had learned from Jacanda, had served Lahn the longest and took care of his food and cham needs prior to my arrival. He had purchased the rest of them at an auction two days before the Hunt (where many soon-to-be husbands saw to the needs of their future wives).

From Oahsee (who asked Bain, who answered), I learned Lahn bought slaves prior to the other Hunts he attended but did not participate in as Dax then sold them immediately after when nothing struck his fancy.

Therefore, Packa was the only one who'd been there.

And by the time we arrived back in the courtyard area, Lahn was gone but my girls were there with trainee warriors lugging in our stuff from the wagon outside and the girls were looking around with awe.

The minute Twinka saw them, she opened her mouth to speak.

And the minute she did, I got there first.

See, I dug it that this was her place. I totally got that.

But these were *my* girls.

And no one bossed them around.

In Korwahk, I quickly introduced my girls to Twinka, Twinka to my girls, and then I announced, "These things can stay here for now. Twinka, please give my girls a tour of the house and then they'll need some time to bathe, put on clean clothes, rest for a bit after that ride and have some food. After that, these things can be unpacked."

Twinka squinted up at me with a mouth so tight it tripled the wrinkles surrounding it.

Then she muttered, "Gay na tahnay," *As you command*, glared through my girls, then raced off.

They all glanced at me as they raced off after her.

I pulled in a breath and let it go.

Then I went in search of Lahn and found him coming out of the bathroom-ish room and into the master suite.

"Hey," I said on a big smile. "I like your house. The roof is freaking *awesome*."

"Dohno," he muttered as he walked past me to the door.

I instantly deflated and I didn't even know I'd inflated.

I turned rather despondently to follow him with my eyes. I figured he had Horde and war things on his mind and was in king mode, so he was away to do king things.

But okay, so sure, he only lived here two months out of the year, so this probably wasn't an important place to him. And sure, he couldn't know that in my world a husband bringing his wife home for the first time was a big thing.

But still...

At the door, instead of walking through it, he grabbed it and threw it to.

He turned back to me.

I caught the look in his eye.

And I gave him another big smile as he stalked toward me. I let out a laughing cry when he got to me and caught me up in his strong arms.

We tested out the bed first.

It was huge, it was soft, and it was *sturdy*.

We tested out the bathing pool next.

It was *divine*.

LET'S just say Twinka didn't like Ghost.

Like, *at all*.

And we'll also say she didn't like the familiarity, consideration, caring and casualness with which I treated my girls and flatly refused to respond positively to me doing the same with her.

But I didn't care.

I was fucking queen.

I'd endured a Hunt. I'd witnessed a suicide-slash-execution. I'd watched a challenge for the Dax. I'd survived a bloody attack in my cham. I'd assisted in a minor medical procedure with only the most primitive of instruments at our disposal. I'd seen one of my girls beheaded. I had belatedly made one helluva match between a tiny, sweet, beautiful, timid Fleuridian girl and a dark, proud, taciturn Horde warrior.

I could create thunder, lightning, rain, flowers and rainbows.

And I'd made a savage brute fall in love with me in a month.

Hell, by his account, it was practically at first sight.

So she wasn't going to fuck with me.

Therefore, I ignored her and so did my girls.

It worked great.

ONCE SETTLED IN KORWAHN, life went on as normal. I spent time with my posse (on my roof, their roofs, in my dining room, their dining rooms, in my courtyard, their courtyards, you get the picture). I wandered the city with my protectors. I met my people. I shopped in the marketplace.

Lahn came home for dinner twice and before I went to bed three times. Other than that, my man was busy.

This stunk.

But I was queen, so I sucked it up.

WHEN THE MORNING SICKNESS CAME, I gave up Korwahk wine. Lahn questioned this when I stopped him from pouring me a chalice at dinner and I explained in my world pregnant women didn't drink alcoholic beverages as they'd noticed it affected growth in the womb.

His brows drew together at this, but he didn't question it further and he didn't pour my wine.

By the by, the arrival of morning sickness, thus confirmation I was carrying his child was taken in stride by Lahn. I was freaked out but happy. He already knew in his pahnsahna I was carrying his child.

Still, I made him celebrate.

With the way I chose to celebrate, Lahn didn't seem to mind.

WE WERE in Korwahn because Suh Tunak was amassing there before they rode on Maroo.

We were also in Korwahn because Lahn had sent another message out to his brethren and that was that he was building an elite squad to be left behind in Korwahn to guard his golden queen (an elite squad, how cool was that?). Any warrior who wished to put himself forward for this squad would need to compete for it and they had to arrive by a certain date.

I was not allowed to go to the competition, it was warriors only. This was, Seerim told Diandra, because it might turn my stomach, and Lahn knew firstly, I'd had enough of my stomach being turned, and secondly, my stomach was being turned every morning.

Thus, I was glad I wasn't allowed to go. Though I didn't much like the word "allowed," I didn't share this with Lahn.

Lahn did tell me my guard would number five hundred.

And he also told me fifteen thousand competed for these positions.

Yes. *Fifteen thousand.*

I was amazed and touched by this.

Then again, who wouldn't be?

I GOT to attend the Ceremony of the Paint where the queen's warriors painted each other with their new stripes (the Xacto, I'm sure, not there because of me and the other wives who attended).

I sat on my throne of horns in the massive clearing at the very top of the top plateau that was meant for official business, and I watched as the warriors were painted with three thin black strips that curved from a point at their shoulder blade, over their shoulder to a point at their pectoral. Three more were painted from that point and around their arm to the front. And one thick gold strip was painted in the middle around the tip of their shoulder.

They did not wear this paint for ceremonies. They wore it every day.

Lahn told me they did it with pride.

I was amazed and touched by this too.

So much, I burst into tears.

Lahn held me until I cried myself out.

When I was done, I explained it was hormones. Then I explained what hormones were.

He looked at me like I was crazy.

But wisely, he let it go.

Zahnin was their commander. Bain, Feetak, Bohtan, Tark and Yoonan his lieutenants.

Narinda told me Feetak, a young warrior who'd only made his first kill nine years ago (which meant at sixteen years of age, um...yikes!) was very pleased at this huge jump in rank.

It meant more sarongs for her, for Lahn was paying them all out of his own coin and it was more than they made raiding or warring (seriously, my man had to be loaded...I mean, five hundred warriors?).

It also made her happy.

So I was happy too.

YES. I was happy.

Korwahn was good. Life was good.

The only thing that wasn't good was morning sickness, but that only lasted until around ten.

Everything else was good.

And would be for one more day.

Then my husband went to war.

~

"KAH LAHNAHSAHNA, KAH LIPA," Lahn muttered, I blinked and looked up at him.

It was time to do his hair.

He sat on the bed beside me and planted his hand in it on my other side.

"Do you feel well enough to do it?" he asked, his eyes on my (probably pale) face.

I did, but I probably wouldn't once I sat up.

But there was no way I was giving up the chance to have my fingers in his beautiful hair. Not now. Not when the day after tomorrow brought Lahkan to our door, Lahn on Lahkan's back and my king riding off to war to avenge a wrong done me.

"Yeah," I whispered, sucked in breath, got up and walked to the small trunk that held his gold bands. "How do you want it?"

"Bunched," he stated.

I nodded, grabbed what I needed and returned to the bed.

He moved to sit cross-legged on the floor by the side of the bed. I sat on the bed cross-legged behind him, gathered his hair and memorized the feel of it as I bunched it.

When I'd put the last band in, I circled his shoulders with my arms and rested my chin on one.

"You know I love you," I whispered in his ear.

"I know," he whispered back, turned, I pulled my arms away and he got on his knees in front of me, his hands framing my face.

I looked in his dark eyes.

"Do you know how much?" I kept whispering.

"How much, baby?" Lahn kept whispering too.

I bent my forehead to his and told him the truth. "More than my world."

I watched his eyes smile. Then I felt his fingers press in my scalp. Finally, I felt the touch of his lips.

Then he gained his feet, and he was gone.

27

AFFAIRS OF STATE

I was lounging on the mats and cushions with Sabine and Narinda, watching the sun set over Korwahn. Ghost was lying on her belly on the mats by my feet, front legs stretched out before her, head up, blinking and sniffing the air.

From my vantage point, I could see the weakening rays of the sun striking deep pink, gold and vermillion through the sky, the last shimmers striking the gold on the statues of the Avenue of the Gods.

My eyes moved from the breathtaking view to slide across the roof where I saw my girls gathered around the table at the opposite corner. I saw the sun twinkling off the bangles at their wrists and their earrings.

Gaal was on her knees draping a bolt of fabric around a standing Quixa's hips. Vibrant swathes of different colored cuts of fabric were strewn everywhere around the table, the bolts of fabric I bought my girls in the marketplace that day.

I had decided some weeks ago that a queen's girls did not wander around in drab, threadbare sarongs and bandeaus, but they wore jewelry, makeup and brightly colored, fashionable clothing. To their delight, they each had received four pieces of fabric since the first one I bought so many weeks ago and a new piece today as well as their jewelry and pots of makeup for their own.

They also had more than one candlestick by their beds and each had mirrors in their rooms as well as small pieces of art and brightly colored quilts on their beds to break up the monotony of cream adobe in their quarters.

Movement caught my eye, I looked to the winding, black, wrought iron staircase that led to the roof, and I saw Twinka was arriving.

Twinka disapproved of me outfitting my girls and made this very clear nonverbally, as she was doing now with a tight-lipped look in their direction.

I ignored it and so did my girls, but I watched as she made her way to me.

She stopped two feet from our mats.

"Does my queen actually need a slave *to do something*?" she inquired.

We'd already had dinner and I looked down at the plate of carob drops, candied fruits, honeyed almonds, the jug of wine, the jug of mango juice and Sabine, Narinda and my silver chalices that were littering the mats, all of which my girls had brought to us before they'd settled with their fabric.

I looked up at Twinka and replied, "Me."

Her lips got tighter, and she inclined her head.

Then she turned and walked three feet away.

That was when I called, "Twinka?"

She sighed visibly, audibly and heavily and turned back then she lifted her brows.

"I bought three bolts of fabric for you today. Gaal will make you dresses," I told her, for she didn't wear sarongs around her hips and bandeaus or halter tops to cover her breasts but a long, wrap of material she crossed under her neck and tied at the back.

She had one. It was always clean but also threadbare.

"Your kindness is extraordinary, my queen," she lied about her opinion with obviousness. "But my clothing is fine."

"I disagree," I returned.

"The old Dahksahna gave me this fabric," she informed me.

"Well, the new Dahksahna is giving you more," I replied. She opened her mouth to retort, but I got there before her. "Fine, if you want to wear that in the house, that's your choice. You leave this house, you do it representing your Dax and Dahksahna and wear your new sarongs."

She glared at me a moment before she inclined her head, turned and moved quickly off the roof.

My girls watched her and waited before they emitted their low giggles, doing so only after she was well out of sight.

I smiled down at the mats, picked up my chalice of juice and took a sip.

"You're very hard on her," Narinda muttered.

I put my chalice down and looked at her in surprise.

"Sorry?" I asked and her eyes went from the top of the stairs to me.

"She is old, and she is stubborn, set in her ways. She has the running of this house for months and lives alone, clearly liking it that way," Narinda replied. "She is a slave, and this is rightfully your home with your husband, but you must understand the way she feels."

I made no response, for this was true.

Narinda carried on, "And my father taught me the best way to handle someone who is stubborn is to let them *be* stubborn and live with their decisions. If she wishes to wear shabby sarongs, then she denies herself kindness and beauty. That is her choice, Circe, and it is the wrong one, but it won't hurt *you* to allow her to live with it."

I still made no reply, for this was true too.

"You can't force kindness, my lovely," Narinda said softly.

And this was true too.

"All right, sweet Narinda," I replied, "I'll ask Gaal to make them, and I'll tell Twinka it's her choice whether or not she wishes to wear them."

Narinda smiled at me.

I smiled back, thinking it was good having wise friends.

"Your father was very wise," I said quietly.

She nodded and took a sip from her own chalice before her eyes drifted away and she said quietly back, "Indeed, he was."

She was smiling her small, weird smile so I left her to her thoughts and looked back at the view.

The pinks were disappearing, the gold was gone, and stripes of vermilion and midnight blue slashed the sky as stars started to come out. I heard one of my girls moving around, and as the roof illuminated, I knew she was lighting the torches that were stuck in holders around the edge of the roof.

I felt my leg nudged, looked down at it and saw that Narinda had given me a light prod with her toe. I looked at her to see she wasn't smiling small and weird but knowing and amused. Her eyes were on Sabine, who I noticed belatedly had been completely silent for at least the last ten minutes.

I looked to my friend who was lounging across the top of the mats at Narinda and my heads to see she was gazing at the vista as well, her face soft, her lips tipped up, her eyes, though, were heated.

Someone was thinking good thoughts.

I pressed my lips together and bugged my eyes out at Narinda.

She smiled big, tipped her head back and called in Korwahk, "Sabine? My lovely, are you with us?"

Sabine started and her head jerked to us. "Sorry, so sorry. I was miles away," she replied in Korwahk.

"No you weren't, you were in bed with your savage brute," I teased, watched her face flush then her eyes light. She scooted her cushions closer to us and asked, "Can I be forthright?"

This was familiar, and therefore was likely to get good, so Narinda and I closed into each other and Sabine as Narinda replied, "What you can do, my lovely, is not ask if you can be forthright every time you want to be forthright. I think you can take it as given you can be forthright."

I stifled a giggle, for this was true. Sabine always asked if she could be forthright before talking about what she got up to with Zahnin. And after breaking the seal on it the day I was attacked, she talked about this a lot. We never demurred, so she had to know she could tell it like it was.

Sabine nodded, leaned deeper into us and whispered, "Did you...did... erm, you know...did you know you can...*do it on top*?"

"On top?" Narinda asked mock innocently, and I nudged her shin with my foot as I stifled a giggle.

Sabine's eyes danced and her body gave a slight excited jump. "Oh yes, Narinda, *on top*. See, you know when...before, well, I told you how, after Zahnin got injured, I was hesitant to, you know...move things forward for before, erm...when we...um...when *he*...well, it seemed with all that grunting and groaning it took a lot of effort. I didn't want him to aggravate his wound."

"Yes, sweetheart, we know. You told us," I muttered not able to hide the amusement in my voice.

Sabine nodded again and went on, "So, as I told you, I didn't...erm... move things forward. But he, um...continued to use his hands in that way I like."

"We know that too," Narinda mumbled, and we did. She'd told us, sometimes in some detail, and it wasn't only his hands but his mouth that he used in ways Sabine liked.

Sabine kept talking. "But I was...well, something was, I don't know. I liked it, you know, quite a bit. Erm...*a lot*, really. But...something was missing."

I knew what was missing. Zahnin's savage brute sword was missing.

Narinda and I kept quiet.

Sabine kept talking. "I didn't know what but, it was good...I mean, *beautiful*, but I wanted *more*."

"Yes?" Narinda prompted.

"But I didn't know what," Sabine repeated.

I pushed closer to tell her what she wanted but she continued before I could.

"So, I asked Zahnin."

I blinked.

One could say that things were progressing—*slowly*—between Zahnin and Sabine. When he said he could be a patient teacher, he didn't lie. He had been very solicitous with her, and this included him doing things with his mouth and hands that she enjoyed very much but that he had to find very frustrating since she didn't return the favor.

There was a poetic justice in this, I felt, for Zahnin had twice the amount of time giving and not receiving after he took and didn't give. Not to mention his month of courting.

But I was beginning to feel sorry for Zahnin and that it might be time to intervene. At my request, the healer had long since visited his house to remove the stitches and even before that he was not wearing the bandages. The gash was still pink, but it was mostly healed.

That said, he was a warrior. He could survive a little somethin' somethin'. However, weeks had passed, and he was giving, a lot, but he wasn't getting anything.

And Sabine was still timid about it. I was shocked she'd asked him.

"You asked him?" I whispered, my voice filled with the shock I felt.

She nodded again.

"Yes, we were, I was...erm, *close*. But I made him stop and told him what I felt and that I was worried I would hurt him and then...then...*then*..." Her eyes got round and Narinda and I leaned in. "Then he rolled to his back, picking me up as he did so and planting me *astride him*." Her eyes drifted faraway, and before I could lift my hand and snap in her face to regain her attention since she was definitely in hot-sex la-la land, her body jerked and she came back to us. "He said that way, I could do all the work and he wouldn't get hurt."

He wasn't wrong.

I stifled another laugh and Narinda nudged my leg with her toe again as I heard her swallow a snort.

"But..." Sabine went on, totally missing all this. "I didn't...erm, do all the work. In the middle of it, he lifted up to sitting and used his arms and hands on me to make me go, um...*faster* and, erm...you know, *harder*. So, I... you know...*did*." She pressed her lips together before she burst out with, "After all he'd done before and how he felt inside me I couldn't stop myself!"

I bet she couldn't.

"Sabine—" I started but she cut me off.

"And it was fantastic. It was...it was *amazing*. And I think he liked it too."

I was sure he did.

"Sabine—" I tried again, but she kept talking.

"But I don't know...I'm worried. What if I hurt him? He seems strong and healthy, but I don't want..."

I tried and succeeded in not bursting out laughing thinking of tiny, sweet Sabine hurting big, strong Zahnin and decided it was time to be heard.

"Sabine," I called, reaching out to grab her hand. "Come back to the roof and out of your bedroom, my sweet friend."

Her eyes focused on me.

I squeezed her hand. "He's fine. Absolutely fine. Don't worry about him. You're taking care of him now in the way he needs. He's been trained since five to know what his body can and cannot do. Let him decide what he can take and just...uh..." I grinned. "Enjoy the ride."

Her eyes got wide, her face got so red I could see it in the torchlight and then she giggled.

When she did, I thought it was safe to giggle with her and Narinda joined in.

After another squeeze, I released her hand, and she looked back over the rooftop which now showed a sky that was mostly midnight blue and twinkling stars with hazy streaks of pink.

"My warrior husband is gentle and patient," she whispered to the night sky. "I never, ever would have thought..." she stopped, and her attention came back to us. "It started as a nightmare but now seems like the sweetest dream." Her head tipped to the side and a small, confused smile played at her lips when she whispered, "How can that be?"

"I don't know, sweetheart, but somehow these boys can pull it off," I answered with feeling.

"They sure can," Narinda agreed.

We all looked at each other and then we all giggled again.

That was when I heard a low, warning growl come from deep in Ghost's throat. I turned my head to her to see her head was turned to the top of the stairs. She gracefully gained her feet but in a watchful, guarded way that made me brace.

I looked to the stairs.

Bohtan and Bain were ascending them. I started to smile but caught the looks on their faces, felt the vibe and heard Ghost growl again, and I realized something was wrong.

I knew it definitely when Bain ordered my girls, "Prepare your queen to take her throne. Official business. Do it swiftly, we cannot delay." His eyes came to me. "We await you at the front with Zephyr."

He said no more before he turned and both warriors disappeared down the stairs.

What on earth?

"What's happening, Circe?" Sabine asked in a hushed, worried voice as I watched all five of my girls scurry to me, leaving their fabric where it lay.

I didn't know.

What I did know was that very soon I was going to find out.

And I was queen, so I needed to get my ass in gear.

Therefore, I rose to my feet and whispered, "All is well, I'm certain, but I must hurry."

And without a look back, I hurried.

"The beast remains here," Bain ordered, and I looked down at Ghost who was standing beside where I was mounted on Zephyr at the front of the house.

"I—" I started.

"Order it to the house," Bain commanded.

I started at his tone, one he'd never used on me. Then I nodded and looked down at Ghost.

"Ghost, go into the house, my baby."

She growled in a scary way that I heard as "me" or "no," but she didn't move.

"House, now, Ghost," I demanded.

She growled her denial again and still didn't move.

"We have no time for this, brother," Bohtan muttered.

"Very well," Bain muttered back, jerked his chin at Bohtan then jerked his reins and his horse turned. He took point. I moved Zephyr behind him, Ghost prowling at my side. Bohtan fell in at the rear.

"Bain, can you—?" I called.

"No talking, my golden queen," he ordered, and I bit my lip.

Something was wrong. Bain wasn't like this. Not with me.

Shit.

I rode to the top plateau with my guards and my tigress in silence. I was wearing a gold sarong shot with white, a white halter top, gold bands at biceps and forearms, gold hoop earrings, gold dust on cheekbones and around my temples and my gold crown of feathers.

Definitely, as always, the Golden Queen.

As we rounded the top of the plateau, however, I sucked in a very unqueenly breath.

This was because I could see from afar, well beyond the plateau on the rise leading up to it from behind Korwahn, there was a wide sea of riders, so many there would be no way to count. Thousands, maybe tens of thousands.

It was now full-on dark, but I still saw them as they carried torches and not a small amount of fires had been lit on the ground. I couldn't make them out, but I knew they weren't Korwahk for there were many flying pennants flowing in the light breeze that stirred the night air.

Korwahk warriors didn't bother with pennants, or at least, I'd never seen any.

And on top of the vast plateau in the official clearing there was a throng of Korwahk warriors, maybe two hundred, none painted except those who were in my guard.

They were all standing at what could only be described as loose attention and they were all fully armed.

As we rode along the side of the plateau, I saw Lahn sitting on his throne on the platform carved in stone into the jutting lip of the plateau, a platform that had five deep steps up. The Eunuch was by his side, my white throne of horns on his other. And as we made it to the front, I sucked in another breath when I saw there was a grand chair located about a foot from the bottom step of the platform.

In it was a man wearing a steel breastplate of armor with a black and red dragon painted on it. There was a helmet of armor by his booted foot that had a shock of black and red feathers shooting out of the top. But he wore breeches and boots, and on his head, a crown pulled low, almost to his forehead, made of gold inset with diamonds and rubies.

He was graying and jowly with ruddy cheeks and mean, beady eyes. He had a very big gut, which meant the breastplate had to be fashioned to contain it and it made him look ludicrous.

I did not laugh or even smile.

This was because his beady eyes were on me, and they blazed.

Beside him, my heart lurched to see, stood Geoffrey, looking much thinner, much paler but much cleaner.

His eyes were on me too and they also blazed.

I was thinking whatever this was, something I already sensed was not good, was actually even worse.

Last, there were eight, tall, armed men wearing full armor lined behind the man with the crown's chair.

Bohtan rode to my side and muttered, "You do not dismount. Swing your leg sidesaddle. Zahnin will deliver you to our king."

I gave a slight incline of my head and did as instructed when we stopped before Lahn who did not watch us dismount. His gaze never shifted from the man seated before him.

As Bohtan told me, Zahnin came forward and pulled me from Zephyr. He escorted me, with Ghost prowling close at my side, to my throne, and I vaguely realized all of his lieutenants had formed behind us as we walked.

Lahn didn't look at me as I moved in front of him, nor did he do so as I sat and my guards moved to flank the backs of our thrones, Zahnin standing beside mine, or next to Ghost who had settled on her belly, her head up, her eyes on the man in the chair, her demeanor watchful.

"You do not bow to your king?" the man in the chair said and my eyes shot to him. "My Circe grows a big head."

I blinked and realized several things at once.

One, The Xacme was translating for Lahn which I thought was weird since Lahn was mostly fluent in English. Two, this man in front of me thought he knew me, and I didn't think that was good. And three, I knew as a dangerous vibe slithered through the air that Lahn did not take kindly to this man calling me his Circe.

When no one said anything, I ventured in English, "Do I know you, sir?"

I felt that vibe coming from Lahn shift but only to get sharper, more alert, no less dangerous.

At my words, the man in front of me returned my blink.

"Do you know me?" he asked.

"Yes, do I know you?" I asked back.

"I would hope so, my dove, since you've been warming my bed since you were fourteen years of age," he replied, and I couldn't contain a sharp gasp nor could I hide the disgust in it.

Then I whispered, "What?"

His eyes narrowed. "Good question, sweet Circe, but the what I would wish to know is what do you expect to gain by playing this game?"

"Game?" I asked quietly, my mind reeling, trying to catch a thought.

"You know you are mine. You have been mine since you were six. You became *really* mine," he leaned forward suggestively, "when you were fourteen."

"That's absurd," I returned, not thinking and not including the words, "and sickening" because, seriously, fourteen? Not to mention, I'd never let this man touch me. He was old, for one. He was gross, for another.

His brows went up and he leaned back. "Absurd?"

"Absolutely. I've never seen you in my life," I replied.

He glared at me. Geoffrey shifted at his side. I tried to stop myself from hyperventilating.

His eyes moved to Lahn. "I tire of this. You know why we are here."

The Xacme translated (unnecessarily) and Lahn grunted, "Meena."

"Yes," The Xacme called.

"Then I will lay down our terms. You will see in front of you on your plain that with me I brought thirty thousand Middlelandian soldiers. I do know, of course, that your savages will cut through them with all due haste. I also know, before they do, they will ride into Korwahn and likely not be careful who *their* swords slash through...women, *wives*, future *warriors*."

I sucked in breath again at his heinous threat, but he continued.

"Not to mention the warriors of yours they will take in the process, on the eve of your riding on Maroo. This is, I would suspect, not what you would wish just prior to you leading your campaign."

I would suspect it too.

He kept speaking.

"In payment for you seizing my enchantress, and to stop us from riding on Korwahn, I will accept four trunks of Korwahk gold, four of your silver, four of your diamonds, the same of your rubies, emeralds and sapphires and..." He paused and looked up at Geoffrey then back at Lahn, "Another trunk of gold as payment for what you did to one of my most trusted ambassadors."

My eyes flew to Geoffrey who was staring at me with unconcealed hate. Then he leaned forward and opened his mouth wide. I leaned back instantly, for even in the light of the torches and fire pits, I saw he had no tongue.

Oh God.

Lahn had had him captured and his tongue cut out for speaking to me the day of the selection.

No wonder he was so thin and pale.

Oh *God.*

I tore my eyes away from Geoffrey and looked back at the man with the crown.

Lahn didn't reply.

So the man did. "You delay, which is unfortunate. You must know I can easily signal my troops to ride. I'm sure your men have been alerted and are preparing their defense. I will countenance no delays."

Lahn spoke then, in Korwahk, with The Eunuch translating. "You are on Korwahk land, King Baldur, be careful how you speak. You do not rule here."

So this was King Baldur.

Wow.

He was a jerk.

His chest puffed out. "And I'll remind you, you are not the only king in attendance."

"I am the only one that matters," Lahn replied in Korwahk after The Eunuch translated, and upon hearing it, King Baldur instantly lost it and slammed a fleshy fist into the arm of his chair.

"The gall!" King Baldur snapped. "You do not respect the crown I wear. You torture my emissary and steal my enchantress. You have no honor. I know you're primitives, but you cannot expect to behave like this in affairs of state without reprisal."

"Threats of intimidation, preposterous demands and righteous bluster may be how you conduct business in the Northlands, but you are no longer in the Northlands," Lahn replied (again in Korwahk).

King Baldur shifted angrily in his chair before he cried, "This is outrageous! The woman who sits beside you *belongs to me*!"

I tensed, but Lahn leaned forward, forearm to knee, not aggressively, just casually and returned, "My golden queen does not know you. How can she belong to you?"

"She lies!" King Baldur shouted with a hand pointed in my direction, and Ghost growled, pushing up on her front paws to sitting, her blue eyes not leaving the king.

"A caution, fat man," Lahn said in a low voice and King Baldur's face went red with fury when the words were translated. "Do not insult my queen."

He opened his mouth to retort, but Lahn kept speaking.

"This man at your side is no emissary. He is a spy. In the Southlands, these activities are dealt with harshly. He has been among us for many years. He knows our ways. His actions were foolish and his punishment swift. If he has run crying to you like a girl, then he should not have boarded the ship that would cross the Marhac Sea that would bring him to the dust and stone of Korwahk."

Okay, cutting someone's tongue out *was* harsh, but Lahn was not wrong. You know the rules, you play the game, you lose, you pay the price.

Still.

Yikes!

"Your actions are barbaric, *including* you seizing women and forcing them to be slaves to your cocks, one of these women being *mine* and she sits by your side. If you wish to keep her at your side, I will have restitution!" King Baldur yelled.

"Do you threaten to steal my queen?" Lahn asked.

"You do not pay, then you must be prepared for what happens, *all* that will happen, when my soldiers ride," King Baldur shot back, the armored men at his back straightened attentively and Lahn sat back.

What he didn't do was speak.

This silence lasted a long time and was clearly more than King Baldur could endure for his eyes flashed to me.

"Circe, come to your king this instant!" he ordered. "You serve *me*."

"I'm telling you, sir, I do not *know* you," I replied.

He jumped out of his seat, and the instant he did, Ghost gained all four of hers and started growling.

"Do not lie, you stupid *bitch*!" he boomed. "Come to your *king*!"

"Sit," Lahn ordered in English, and King Baldur's gaze snapped to him with both anger and obvious surprise at his use of Baldur's tongue.

"Do not, you stinking, savage animal, *dare* to command *me*!" King Baldur clipped.

"You sit or I'll force you to sit by cutting your legs off at the knees," Lahn told him in English again and I tensed because I knew he could do this and would. He was not armed but I suspected he could be, if he wanted, in less than a second.

"The insolence!" King Baldur shouted. "You cannot attack a king during a state visit!"

"You are in the Southlands, fat man, I can do what I wish. Now sit on your fat ass or your nation will lose its king. Your son, who is weak and prefers to have his cock stroked while he accepts his lover's through his ass, will succeed your throne. Which means, since he is weak, *his lover* will rule your nation."

King Baldur snapped his mouth shut, a telling sign that this was true. His eyes widening told the tale that he was surprised Lahn had this information.

"It is unfortunate," Lahn went on. "As there are many men who prefer this, that your son is not the kind who is strong. But you know, fat man, that he isn't, and his lover is greedy, manipulative and foolish. If your son sits on your throne and allows his lover to pull his strings, your own people will revolt to reunite with their sisterland of Lunwyn or Fleuridia or even Hawkvale as well as Prince Noctorno will ride on Middleland to seek vengeance for your years of gluttonous follies, and they will succeed. Middleland will cease to exist as they cut up pieces as their glory."

King Baldur glared at him then proclaimed, "We are done. We will ride," and he started to lift his hand, but Lahn warned, "I would not do that."

At Lahn's low, rumbling, severe tone, King Baldur's hand arrested in mid-air, and he continued to glare at Lahn.

When he did, Lahn shared, "You know of our plans to ride on Maroo. You know *when* we plan to ride on Maroo. I would hope you are not foolish enough to think you and your soldiers have crossed my land without my knowledge so you also know I would prepare to ride against you to defend Korwahn."

King Baldur said not a word, so I guessed Lahn was right. He came through Korwahk fully knowing Lahn knew he was coming which was a bizarre thing to do.

Lahn went on.

"What I know is, to have your tantrum and try your hand at taking our treasure, for, do not think, fat man, that I suspect for one moment you wish more to have your magical one back, but instead you wish to return to your throne with trunks of our riches. Your play centers around increasing the wealth of your throne, not your nation. Your throne. So you think that, if I were to refuse your demands, while I am otherwise engaged in defending my city, you will unleash a plot to kidnap my queen. This means you would sacrifice thirty thousand of your soldiers to my warrior's steel for a tantrum and for greed. Nevertheless, you undoubtedly have an escape plan so, as your warriors fall, *you* can safely return to your homeland and continue your tyranny at the same time demand ransom in return for my golden bride."

He paused.

King Baldur made no sound or move, and Lahn continued.

"What you do not know is that we have allied with Keenhak. They have sent forty thousand of their warriors to aid in our campaign against Maroo. And as you blustered before me, feeling safe in the knowledge that your soldiers are lined behind you, Keenhak warriors took formation behind *them*. You lift that hand, I lift mine, and your soldiers would be cut down before they took their first breath of Korwahn air, and I, fat man, nor my brethren, would have to lift a blade except to cut down the metal men at your back."

King Baldur's hand stayed lifted, his lips started to curl, and Lahn finished.

"And, you should know, your archers who took their positions an hour ago were dispatched before my queen reached Korwahn's Majestic Rim. Not one of them lives."

Geoffrey took a step back. King Baldur's face paled and his hand dropped. I tried hard not to smile. Ghost sat down on her ass.

"Now," Lahn went on, "you will leave with no trunks filled with Korwahk's bounty in your greedy, fat hands. What you *will* leave with is your life *and* the knowledge that if you *ever* carry forth a plot that threatens my golden queen, you will die choking on your own balls, and you'll do it while staring in my eyes."

King Baldur visibly swallowed. Geoffrey took another step back.

Lahn grew impatient. "I am savage so you must recognize I am being generous with this offer. Therefore, you also must know your continued presence is making me impatient."

Geoffrey shuffled back quickly, losing himself in the sea of Korwahk warriors behind him.

King Baldur gave Lahn one last, long glare then shifted his substantial bulk around and barked at the men behind him. "Bring me my mount!"

I sat silent beside a silent Lahn as his mount was brought to him and we watched as it took two tries for him to heft his substantial weight in the saddle while his armored soldiers deftly mounted their own steeds, and then, with some haste, they were away.

When I lost sight of them, I turned to Lahn to see his head tipped back and his eyes were on Zahnin.

"Take her to our rooms. Lock her in. She is attended by no slave and no wife and keep the animal from her. Do it now," Lahn ordered, stood and stalked down the steps while I blinked after him.

"Come, my golden queen, now," Zahnin demanded firmly and slowly.

Dazedly, my head turned to him.

His arm was extended to me.

I looked back where Lahn had disappeared, and I felt my chest rise and fall with my rapid, deep breaths.

Whatever was wrong wasn't over. And I had the distinct feeling, even as bad as that was, the worst was yet to come.

I stood without the aid of Zahnin, straightened my shoulders, kept my head held high and I walked to Zephyr.

28

THE REVEAL

I paced Lahn and my bedroom, my sarong flying behind me, and I did this for a long time. It could have been an hour, or it could have been five of them.

It felt like five.

I didn't even have Ghost with me, and as the time slid by, my adrenaline surged, as did my agitation. I was so freaking out, I was stuck in my head and I didn't cleanse my face or even take off my crown of feathers.

I just paced or walked to one of the four windows and tried to see what I could see in the torchlit streets.

I could see nothing.

So I paced more.

Lahn had locked me in our rooms.

Locked me in our rooms.

He didn't look at me. He didn't speak to me. In fact, although he said he believed me and made threats to defend me, he didn't look or speak to me at all during his confrontation with King Baldur.

He could do this, and had before, when he was in king mode. But with where I was now, I knew this was something else. Something not good.

In fact, so not good, it was bad.

And that King Baldur had known me. He'd said he'd known me since I was six.

What was *that* all about?

But I had a feeling I knew. I knew about pirate ships and kings.

It was all coming together.

I was in a parallel universe and there was another Circe here, one who looked just like me, one who was not here now.

And King Baldur had called her his enchantress.

So maybe she held magic, knew she did, could manipulate it and maybe it was *her* who had transported herself out of this world and to mine, sending me here.

If she knew how, after being seized by pirates and then Korwahk scouts, she would. If she knew of their practices in Korwahk and what awaited her while she waited in that corral, she'd do it. I knew it.

Sending me here.

Good God.

And knowing this, she'd never want to come back. She could have no clue that Lahn would be who and how he was. She would only think she'd escaped a nightmare.

Which meant, since my magic wasn't at my command but at the whims of my emotions, *I* couldn't get back to explain things to my father, my friends, to say good-bye and certainly there would be no visits back and forth.

I was stuck here forever, and now I wasn't certain that was good.

The door opened and Lahn walked in. It closed behind him, and I heard the bolt thrown home, just as it did when the silent Zahnin had escorted me in. Just as the doors to the bathing pool had been bolted seconds later. There were no doors that led to the balcony around the courtyard from our dressing room and bathroom-ish type room.

I'd been imprisoned.

"Lahn—" I began as I started toward him.

I stopped when he lifted a hand palm out and growled, "Do not near me, my queen."

Uh-oh.

My heart squeezed and my stomach clenched, and both hurt...a *lot*.

"Lahn," I whispered.

"I will fill you in on the parts you missed," Lahn stated, crossing his arms on his wide chest and planting his feet apart. "After my punishment was delivered on this Geoffrey for his insolence at attending a selection and talking to my queen without my leave, he returned with haste to his king. Once there, he reported that the Dax had installed his golden Dahksahna at his side, heralding the rise of The Golden Dynasty."

I nodded when he stopped, so he continued.

"Upon reading the description of my queen, King Baldur recognized her as his own personal sorceress. A woman who had been born displaying great powers, therefore as a child she was seized by Baldur so she could be at his command. A child who grew into great beauty. Therefore, he used her magic *and* her body at his whim."

Oh God.

Poor other Circe now in my world.

Lahn went on, cutting into my thoughts.

"Clearly, his sorceress did not enjoy his attentions or her forced service. Some time ago, she escaped. She sought to put distance between herself and her king, but her vessel was set upon by pirates in the Green Sea and she was later apprehended by Korwahk scouts. Nevertheless, when Baldur heard you were here, he spared not a second in amassing his soldiers and he moved on Korwahk."

He was calling her "she" which meant he knew she was not me.

"Lahn—" I started.

"Quiet," he whispered.

"But—"

"*Quiet!*" he thundered, leaning into me, his raw energy filling the room, and I instantly had trouble breathing.

I also got quiet.

He stared at me, and I held his stare. I did it fighting back the tremors that threatened to consume my frame, but I did it.

Finally, he spoke, and he did it quietly. "You are not she."

It took me a second to get the courage to shake my head, but I did.

He stared at me again.

Then he whispered, "I do not know *what* you are."

I held my breath as the pain sliced through me because he said that like not only did he not know what I was, he questioned whatever that was and he suspected he would abhor it when he found out.

I didn't hear it, my focus was in that room, but outside a light rain started to fall.

When he spoke again, the pain came back, tenfold.

"What I do know is that you are far more powerful than I suspected. You have bewitched me with your beauty. You have manipulated me through months of deception. You have tricked me with your skillful mouth and body to siring a child on you. *You*. A creature unknown. A changeling."

That hurt so much, I couldn't stop myself from whispering, "Lahn, baby, please listen to me."

He jerked his chin up. "You will be heard, but I will warn you, Circe, this will be your only opportunity to be heard, so you had better make whatever you say convincing." I stared at him when he finished by commanding, "And you will not speak your soft names to me when you do it."

I swallowed as I took that hit and my mind reeled.

He was the king of a primitive, savage horde and what I had to say to him would not go over well. I knew this. I knew.

Hell, if I told someone in *my* world what was going on they'd think I was crazy and be justified in that belief.

But I had no choice.

And I knew, looking at him, I should have told him well before now, of my own accord, not as his command. I didn't know if that would have gone down better, but I should have tried.

"I am not of this world," I whispered my admission.

"I am aware of that, Circe," he replied swiftly then asked, "Do you take this shape from another?" When I blinked at his question, he clarified, "What is your true form?"

I shook my head and held out my hands. "I don't take this shape. This is me. This has always been me."

His jaw went hard, and his stare started glittering.

He didn't believe me.

I sallied forth. "I-I woke up in the pen with the other women of the Hunt. I went to bed at home, in Seattle—"

"Seattle is a nation that does not exist, my queen," Lahn bit off. "Do you not think, when you told me this was your homeland that I would not confer with those who had traveled widely? None of them have heard of this Seattle."

"It exists in my world," I replied.

"*That*," he spat, "I will believe."

"Lahn—"

"Get on with it, Circe," he demanded impatiently.

"I...okay." I shook my head. "My world is different. Much different. It—"

"It has things called hormones," he interrupted to say. "And germs. And they do what you did to Bohtan's son to stop people choking. They do not allow their women to drink wine when pregnant. They sew the flesh of wounds together, before and after bathing it in spirit. They have a place called 'Mexico.' They say 'freaking out' to explain just about any emotion as long as it comes with shock or fear. They treat slaves like family. Their queens walk freely amongst their people. They do not hold themselves aloof as all queens should."

Wow.

He'd really paid attention.

Lahn kept speaking. "You have given me many indications you are not of this world, and I've been so drunk on your xaxsah, so bewitched by the spirit shining in your eyes, I ignored every one."

"That isn't how it was," I said softly.

"No?" he asked on a brow raise.

"No," I shook my head and lifted my hand. "Lahn...I...this place is very strange to me too, but I...well, I endured. I got over it. I adapted and I..." I hesitated, swallowed and whispered, "I fell in love with you."

The energy in the room went brutal. So brutal it pounded against my flesh.

"Do not *ever* speak those words to me again unless you wish to feel the back of my hand," he growled.

I stared at the wrath burning in his eyes.

He meant it.

Oh God.

Was this happening?

I kept staring into his furious, stony, beautiful face.

It was happening.

It was *happening*.

And with that thought it occurred to me that I was, again, blameless. I was innocent. The only thing I did was fall asleep. And I'd borne countless nightmares since that time, bouncing back from each stronger and stronger.

I had been a good queen. I had been a good wife. I had been a good lover. I had given him *everything*. My body, my world, my love, and I was carrying *our child*.

Fuck...

This!

I dropped my hand, squared my shoulders and locked eyes with my husband as outside, just above our house, without either of us seeing it, a bolt of lightning rent the air.

"I know it sounds unbelievable," I stated. "Because it *is* unbelievable. Fantastical. Extraordinary. *Bizarre*. But it...is..." I leaned forward, "*true*!"

He opened his mouth, but before he could speak, I carried on.

"Right here, right now, what you're feeling, *I* felt too, and it was probably a hundred times worse than what you're feeling now, Lahn, because in *my* world, they do not hunt women and rape them. In *my* world, if you do that, you go to jail for a long, long time. Everything, *everything*," I threw out my hands, "was different. Your clothes. Your language. The landscape. Your homes, food, furniture, shopping. And I don't mean a little different, like here warriors wear hides and up north, they wear armor. I mean *a lot* different. In my world, we don't ride horses, we drive cars. In my world, we don't have chamber pots, we have toilets. We don't have slaves. That was outlawed *years* ago. Most countries don't even have kings or queens!" I was now shouting, lightning striking fast and hot outside our windows. "And if they do, they hold no power but are only figureheads."

He glared at me.

It was scary but I didn't care. I was too far gone.

I just kept talking.

"I was *terrified* when I got here. I don't even know how I had it in me to breathe much less move or speak. This doesn't happen in my world, this changing of beings, me taking her place, her taking mine. But I suspect powerful sorceress Circe had had enough at men's hands, her king, those pirates, your scouts, and she knew what was about to befall her during your fucking *Hunt* as she stood in that pen, or she found out and therefore she got the fuck out of Dodge! And when she left her world, she changed places with *me*. I had no control, and I'll tell you, Lahn, so many times in the past months, I wished, I fucking *prayed* to go back home, because you and your people and your practices scared me and they *sickened* me."

"It is unfortunate for you, Circe, that just from your words, I cannot know this is true," he stated.

"Yes," I hissed. "It is. And guess what, big guy, even *I* don't know if it's true. The only thing I know is that I'm here and she's not. That's all I know. I'm just guessing."

"And I am guessing, because even as we stand here, you command the heavens, that you wield extraordinary power. You have not hid it. It is at your command, and since it is, I can only wonder what other power you have wielded for what other results."

"It isn't at my command, Lahn," I flashed and threw an arm toward the windows that now flared with lightning and roared with thunder as the rain pounded down. "That's happening and *everything* that has happened is because of what I was *feeling*. And you," I jabbed a finger at him, "fucking know it."

"I also know that you say you were sickened by my people's practices, but it didn't take long for me to win you, did it, wife? Three days you gave it before you were rubbing against my hand and rearing into my cock," he, unfortunately, stated the god's honest truth with that. "It has taken Zahnin's wife *months* to yield to his endeavors to win her. But not you," he threw an arm out toward me before locking it back across his chest. "No, not my golden bride, not only was she riding my cock, moaning while I drove it in her, she was offering to take it in her mouth if I gave up the Xacto, doing everything she could to keep me drunk on her charms while she manipulated me into capitulating to her whims."

"*That's insane!*" I screamed on an accompanying crash of thunder.

"I did not take free woman nor slave while I plundered, Circe, because *you* demanded it!" he shouted back.

"That's because it was important to me!" I returned, just as loud.

"Yes, keeping me bewitched is indeed, for whatever reason, important to you. This, at least, I believe is true."

I shook my head and went silent.

I couldn't believe this.

This was unbelievable.

It was also heartbreaking.

Nope, I was wrong about that.

It was soul destroying.

I breathed hard through my nose and looked away, trying to calm myself as the thunder and lightning stopped but the rain continued to drive down.

Then I sucked in a huge breath and looked at my husband again.

And when I spoke, I did it softly. "I gave up a world for you."

He glared at me, not giving me anything.

I kept right on going.

"I thought, perhaps, when I learned I had powers, I might be able to use them to go home."

His eyes flashed, but that was all I got so I kept on going.

"But not for good. My father isn't dead." Another flash. "He's alive and at home and living maybe with a fake Circe. He'll know the difference, though, I *know* it. He's out of his mind with worry, I know that too. He's wondering where I am and if I'm okay and how to get me back. I also know that. I know that and I know that my life there was good. I loved my life. I loved my home. I loved my job. I had a lot of people who loved me that I loved back." I sucked in breath and then whispered, "But as much as your world scared me, as much as our practices repulsed me, I still chose you."

His torso jerked. It was almost imperceptible, but I caught it.

I kept at him.

"I gave up my world for you, Lahn. I sat at your side through things people in my world would find loathsome and I did it with my head held high. I even felt *pride* that I could endure, that I could be a good queen to you. I didn't know how to be a queen, but every day I walked amongst your people giving them my time and my ear and my attention, hoping that was what I was supposed to do. Everything I did in this fucking place, even before I fell in love with you, was for...fucking...*you*."

After that, I was breathing heavily, and he said not a word, just continued to stare at me, stony-faced with fury.

I was not getting in. Not even a little bit.

Not even a little bit.

The rain outside stopped driving down and started to fall slower, softer, quieter as that knowledge settled in my soul.

"I gave up my world for you," I whispered. "And if you don't come to me right now, put your arms around me and tell me you believe me, I will stop at nothing to find my way back."

His answer was immediate. "I will not come to you, Circe. As of now, you are being sequestered, watched by guards with our most powerful witches in attendance to see you get up to no mischief. You will stay sequestered, alone, in this house, without slaves, friends or your pet, until the pregnancy culminates, and we see what creature you bear me. I am informed by those of our people who hold magic that you will not be able to hide it while birthing and it will not have the power to shield its true form while being born."

Oh my God.

That was when he delivered the killing blow.

"Only then will I come to you to deliver my judgment or allow you back into my bed."

That was it.

I was done.

Just as he had with the claiming chain Dortak had hooked to me, with those words, Lahn severed our connection just...like...*that*.

"I've left you," I whispered, and his head jerked.

"What?"

"I'm standing right here, but I promise you, even if it is simply in my mind, I've left you. I'm gone. You've lost me forever."

He planted his hands on his hips. "You birth a warrior or a golden girl, we shall see."

I shook my head.

"No," I swallowed back the tears. "No. This is it. You've gone too far. We're done. I'm gone. You'll never get me back, Lahn. Never."

"If what you say is true, I have won you before, Circe. And if you are what you say you are, I will do it again."

I stared into his dark, beloved eyes as mine filled with wet, and unbeknownst to me, the shining, golden swirl of spirit that always was so close to the surface for Lahn to see twinkled brightly then extinguished completely.

Then I whispered, "No. You won't."

I turned from him, missing the quickly hidden flash of alarm that slashed across his features.

I moved to the windows and stared out, my arms crossed protectively on my belly, the tatters of my heart dripping blood, my lungs feeling empty as silent tears slid down my face.

"Circe," Lahn called, but I didn't look.

I couldn't look.

And I knew even if I saw him again, I would never see him the same.

I knew it was crazy, all I said, but I also knew I was *me*. And I'd only been me for months.

And he'd fallen in love with me.

But he needed to believe in me in the good times and bad.

Like I did with him.

Sometimes it was a struggle.

But I fucking did it.

And he didn't.

I'd had enough. Hell, I'd had *more* than enough.

I was done.

"Circe, look at me," he ordered.

I stared at the rain, and I did this for a long time before he spoke again.

"It will be reported to me if you do not care for yourself and the creature you carry."

The creature I carry.

Nice.

When he received no response, he continued, "And Circe, if this is the case, they will have orders to make certain you care for yourself and what is in your womb."

"I will not...*ever,*" I whispered fiercely to the rain, "do anything to harm *my* child."

Lahn fell silent.

I kept my eyes on the soft rain as corresponding tears slid down my cheeks.

His voice came at me again, this time it was softer, nearly sweet, almost, but not quite, my Lahn.

"Circe—"

I cut him off, my voice flat, dead and nothing like anything he'd ever heard from me.

"Good-bye, Lahn."

I heard nothing for some time before I heard the pound of fist on door, the bolt slide, the door open, then it closed, and the bolt was thrown home to lock me in.

I closed my eyes and fresh tears surged down my cheeks.

I waited, and when I felt that his energy had indeed left the room, I looked to the door.

I was alone.

I tore off my crown of feathers, ripped it in half, ripped it in quarters, ripped it until it was nothing but shreds.

I threw its remains away from me and sank to my ass on the tiled floor, knees to chest, face to knees, my arms tight around my calves and my sobs pierced the room as the rain outside no longer came softly but hit the city in unrelenting sheets.

And I rocked back and forth, whispering brokenly to my thighs, "Take me home, take me home, take me home, I *need* to go home. Please, please, whatever magic is out there for me, let it be at my command to *take me home.*"

I did not go home.

No, I fell asleep curled on the tile, exhausted from my tears, the rain still pounding down, unremitting, outside.

Then it stopped.

And when it did, it did this abruptly.

THE RAIN STOPPED SO ABRUPTLY, Dax Lahn heard it.

All night, listening to his queen's sorrow driving its wet into the city, feeling that wet as if it was pounding against his skin causing emotions he didn't understand to war in his gut, emotions he would not know until later were doubt and guilt, not sleeping or having slept, he shot from his bed, tore down the hall and ignored Bohtan and Feetak who were standing outside Circe's bolted door.

He threw back the bolt, threw open the door and saw the room empty.

After searching, every room was empty, not just the rooms he shared with his wife but throughout their home.

Nothing was left of her except his queen's tattered feathers lying on the tiled floor.

The iron crosses outside the windows were in place, they had not been tampered with and Lahn knew even his little Circe could not force herself through the space that a small child could not get through.

And even if she could, the house butted the side of the plateau, there was nothing to catch her should she jump and the fall was so deep, it would kill her.

Even so, Dax Lahn ordered warriors to search the bottom of the plateau.

They returned with no sightings of Circe, dead or alive. Not even a footprint should her magic have saved her so she could run away.

His wife was gone.

I gave up my world for you.

As this news processed through his system, Dax Lahn, the commander of Suh Tunak, the King of all Korwahk threw back his head and roared.

29
HOME

I heard my name being called, and, weirdly, it sounded like *me* who was calling it.

My eyes fluttered open, and I looked into a mirror.

"You are fine, my sweet twin," my reflection, which appeared to be leaning over me in a bed, said to me, and I felt my hand squeezed tightly. "Do not be alarmed at the fatigue. The magic takes it all out of you. It will be a few days. We will care for you. Rest, my sweet."

My eyelids drifted closed because I was right with what I told me. I was fatigued. So freaking tired, it was unbelievable. I'd never felt that fucking tired in all my life.

But I forced them back open and saw me still leaned into me.

I smiled at myself, but it wasn't *me* smiling.

Then I whispered (but it wasn't my whispering), "You are safe, sweet Circe, you are *home*."

My eyes drifted back to closed.

And those actually were mine.

"She will be like this for a day, Harold, maybe two."

I tried to force my eyes open as words in my voice but not said by my lips were whispered close.

Harold.

My pop.

"She's okay?"

Oh God.

Yes.

My pop!

I tried to open my eyes and turn toward his voice, a voice I never thought I'd hear again, but I just could not fight off the sleep.

"She is..." a hesitation, "fine."

"Circe, darlin', if you haven't got that you can't hold back with me..." Pop's warning trailed off and I heard a sigh.

"I'm sorry, my beloved father, they are weak, but my senses tell me she's with child."

I heard my father suck in a hard, rough breath.

Then I was out.

~

"Are you with me, my love?"

My eyes slowly opened, and I saw my bed, and beyond that, my bedroom.

In Seattle.

Holy crap!

I turned to my back and looked to the side of the bed. Sitting in one of my dining room table chairs was me.

Or...the other me.

"Circe?" I whispered, and she smiled.

"Sit up, my twin," she whispered back. Moving off the chair bent toward me, she helped me pull myself up and arranged pillows behind me.

I stared at her in shock.

Totally me. The spitting image. Wearing my clothes but having had a haircut in the last few months.

She sat back down and scooted a bit forward taking my hand.

"You know I am not you?" she inquired.

I nodded.

"You know who I am?" she continued.

I nodded again and she smiled.

"You worked out what happened," she whispered.

I nodded yet again, and she nodded back.

"How are you?" she asked.

Flipped out was how I was. Totally.

"Um..."

"Still tired?" she went on.

I nodded.

"Are you thirsty, hungry?"

I shook my head, though I was. I was both.

"How...?" I started, and she shook her head this time.

"I do not know. Though you clearly have powers, like me. That said, Harold tells me you never did, and indeed, he told me *no one* in this world does. But he is wrong. Those holding power here are smarter than we at home. They keep it guarded, the most guarded secret. This is wise. Nevertheless, it is clear from your extreme exhaustion that you discovered how to spirit yourself out of that world to your home. I felt the same when I..." she hesitated, her face going soft yet cautious, "spirited myself."

I knew it.

She totally bailed.

Good for her.

Way bad for me.

"We have been searching," she continued, "to find a way to bring you home. My magic is depleted. I did not know, though had been warned, but it takes much power to move between worlds, vast amounts. I feel it growing inside me, but it is feeble and it may take years, even decades, for it to replenish. But we have located a witch in this world who we thought could help. Before we could try, you returned." She smiled a small smile. "This is good and has caused our father great relief."

"*Our* father?" I whispered, and she gave a small, wary shrug, still smiling.

"He has forgiven me for what I've done to you, especially since I have worked so hard to locate this witch at the same time trying to find ways to rebuild my own powers to bring you home. My father was murdered by my king when I was very young so that he could um...well..." She stopped then went on, "I have talked much with your father. I have explained things and we have grown close." Her eyes grew warm. "He is a fine man and has a big heart. He says, since my father looked exactly like him, but of course through memory, much younger, then he is really my father anyway, in a way." She smiled again. "But I still call him Harold."

I stared at her. Or, more to the point, at *me*.

Her smile faded and her gaze grew intense before she whispered, "Now

I must ask the same of you, if you could find it in your heart to give it to me."

"The same what?" I whispered back.

"Forgiveness."

I stared again, and she leaned closer, squeezing my hand.

"I knew. I knew you existed," she said softly, closed her eyes tight and opened them before she continued. "I knew what I would...what I was doing to you in an effort to protect myself, but...but..." She pressed her lips together and released them before she said so quietly it was an effort to hear her, "I could bear no more."

I knew it. I knew that.

Shit, I knew it.

"Circe," I whispered.

"For years," she whispered back, "my king..." She shook her head. "Then those pirates taking turns. Then those scouts apprehending me. I knew about Korwahk. I knew about the Hunt. I'm so sorry, my sweet twin." Her hand squeezed mine hard as tears filled her light-brown eyes that looked, I noticed for the first time on her but never noticed on me, golden. "I could bear no more. I knew of the spell. I had heard of it and considered it often. But the only spell I knew was to change places. Not to move between worlds on my own, but to switch me with you. I couldn't live with myself if I did that to the unknown you. But standing in that pen, having been prepared for the Hunt, I had no more strength to do the honorable thing and instead I did the selfish thing. So I changed places with you and I know why I did it. I know why. But learning of you, living your life, being with those you love, you must know I regret it."

I squeezed her hand back. "Don't."

She blinked at me in surprise. "What?"

"I met Baldur." Her eyes widened and I nodded, continuing, "I heard about the pirates. I put it together and I know why you did it," I said gently. "I get it. Boy..." I smiled as best I could at her, "do I know."

She nodded and her eyes moved to my belly then back to me. "I know you do. Oh Circe, the horrors you must have endured because of me."

"Don't do that either." I squeezed her hand again. "It's over."

She nodded. "That it is."

Yep, that it was.

"What has been, has been," I whispered. "And what will be..." I trailed off, my eyes filled with tears, and unlike the other me, I could not hold them back.

"Oh, my twin," she whispered, pulled me into her arms, sat on the bed at my hip and held me while I cried.

My arms wrapping around her, I shoved my face in her neck and sobbed.

And I sobbed for my lost kingdom. For my lost Ghost. For my lost Diandra, Narinda, my girls and my posse. For my lost guard.

And for my lost king.

This meant I cried hard, and I did it for a long fucking time.

And when I stopped, my twin settled me back in the bed, brought me a box of tissues then moved my hair away from my face as I wiped my eyes and cheeks and blew my nose.

"I will bring you coffee and breakfast. Yes?" she offered.

I nodded.

"And I will phone your father."

That was when I nodded and gave her a shaky smile.

She nodded back, murmuring, "I will do the second first."

She grabbed my hand and gave one last squeeze before she let me go and moved from the room.

I stared at her back.

Yep, she was wearing my clothes. It was good to see I wasn't wrong when I bought them. Those jeans looked great on me.

I wondered if I'd miss my sarongs.

Or the sun.

Or the dirt, sand and stone.

I knew I wouldn't miss chamber pots.

The rest of it, fuck me, I was going to miss.

I pushed back down in bed, curled into a ball and deep breathed.

No more crying.

That was done.

Now, I had to suck it up.

I was home.

30
BACK

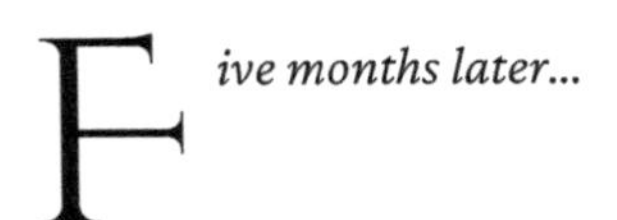

F*ive months later...*

The lights over the fleet (fleet, as in, four of them) of moving trucks in the garage went out panel by panel, the only one staying illuminated being the one by the front door, and I knew Pop was closing down for the night.

In my office at the back, I shoved the last invoice in an envelope, checked that the address could be seen in the window and licked it closed.

Pop moved through the doorway, and I smiled at him.

"Just need to stamp this then I'm off home to change. I'll meet you at the party."

The other Circe was leaving and we were having a going away party. She was taking the money Pop had given her, I had given her and the boys had collected for her (with a little training, she'd taken over the office for me while I was gone, she was good at it and the place was not the mess I'd worried it would be) and she was going to New Orleans.

She was going there because she'd read about it and wanted to see it. In fact, when not searching for ways to get me home and working in the office, she read about a lot of her new world, and she wanted to explore as much of it as she could see.

New Orleans was a good choice, seeing as she'd see a whole heckuva lot of the country driving there from Seattle (Pop, by the by, taught her to drive).

And she was also going there because an old buddy of Pop's had a job opening in his office at his tow truck company. Pop recommended her (or, kinda, me) and called in a favor to get her hired.

Unfortunately, I'd met this old buddy of Pop's a couple of times when I was young so he was going to get a surprise when I walked in (but didn't walk in) to meet him for the first time and he would have a Circe who wasn't Circe.

Pop said he would explain things after it happened and his friend Buster got to know Circe. He thought this was wise. My twin agreed.

I didn't bother arguing. Those two were two peas in a pod and ganged up on me frequently, and frankly, I didn't have it in me anymore to give any lip.

They wanted to give Buster a heart attack?

I wasn't going to stop them.

I put the stamp on the envelope, grabbed the other four I'd done and put them in my out tray, which wasn't really an out tray as such, since it would be my (now) fat ass that would waddle out of the garage and put them in the mailbox at the end of the block tomorrow. Still, I liked my outbox even if it was me who dealt with the out as well as the in.

I started to switch off my computer but saw Pop had settled in one of the two cracked, vinyl seats in front of me.

"Darlin', we gotta talk," he declared.

Oh shit.

I didn't want to do this. In fact, I'd successfully avoided doing this for five months. I was hoping to hold out for five more months, or maybe fifty years.

"Not now, we'll be late," I told him, hitting the button on my mouse to click the shut down on my machine.

"Now, Circe, uh...the other Circe'll understand."

Seriously, it was weird there being two mes.

I looked at him and I took in his look. It was his determined look.

Then *I* determined we weren't going to talk, now or ever.

"Pop—"

Like it was since I was a child, Pop's determination when it came to him saying what he had to say *and* hearing what *I* had to say was a lot more determined than mine could ever be.

"Circe, darlin', what gives?" he leaned toward me. "You ain't right."

I switched off my monitor and declared. "I'm fine."

I started to get out of my chair when Pop's words arrested me.

"Girl, do you *not* think I know heartache when I see it? Damn, darlin', I've seen it every day of my life for twenty-five years starin' back at me right in the mirror."

My (now) fat ass plonked back into the chair, and I looked at Pop.

"And now," he went on, "I see it every time I look at you." He lifted a hand and knocked his knuckles on my desk before sitting back and demanding, "So, no more foolin'. What...*gives?*"

"Pop," I whispered.

"Circe," Pop stated firmly.

"Pop!" I snapped.

"Circe!" Pop clipped back.

Shit!

I stared at him. He took my stare and raised it with an eyebrow lift.

I shook my head. "I don't—"

Pop cut in, "You love that asshole."

I blinked, the pain knifed through me, and I looked away.

After a moment, Pop muttered, "Shee-it. You do. You love that asshole."

I looked back at him.

He knew.

Yeah, he knew.

We'd never discussed it. The other Circe had told me her story in total (and it was worse than I imagined, and I imagined it being bad).

I had not shared mine.

She didn't pry. But she knew the Korwahk and their practices, and she watched me like a hawk, like my father did since I figured she'd shared (not to mention I'd disappeared for months so he was gun shy). But she didn't pry. I'd seen those two with their heads together, starting a few times in the beginning when I came home. But it was growing more and more frequently lately.

They'd orchestrated this. It was a wonder she wasn't there browbeating me right along with Pop.

By the way, the other me could be annoying. She was sweet and she was funny, but she was also seriously annoying.

"Circe, start talkin' or I'll talk for you," Pop warned.

"Yeah?" I asked sharply. "You and Circe, you both think you've got it figured out, do you?"

"What I got figured out, child, is that is the first time I've seen you spit fire at me in five fuckin' months. And *my* Circe could spit fire when she had tonsillitis. She could spit fire at Larry, who was six foot five, weighed three hundred pounds and had a meaty fist bigger than her head. She could handle my crew of twelve guys without them knowin' they were bein' handled. That fire, girl, it's been gone and Circe and me, your friend Marlene, we thought it was because..." He stopped, his jaw flexed at the thought of me being violated, then he started again, "But it ain't. It ain't that. I don't see pain in your eyes from memories that are torturin' you. I see a different kinda pain, darlin', one I recognize. One I know. One that *lives in me*."

"Can we not talk about this?" I asked quietly.

"No, we been *not* talkin' about this for five months and you ain't snappin' outta it. Now tell me, girl, did you fall in love with him?"

I licked my lips. Then I closed my eyes.

I opened them and whispered, "Yes."

He tipped his head to look at the ceiling, muttering, "Shee-it. Circe warned me this crap happened."

"Pop—" I started, but he tipped his head back to me.

"So why the fuck you come home?"

I blinked. "What?"

"You went to the doc, there was time. You coulda had that kid you're carryin' taken care of..." I knew my eyes flashed at the very mention of abortion when he pointed right at me. "That. That right there. You *want* this kid. That asshole didn't force that child on you. You're carrying it *for* him. You made that baby and you liked doin' it. Am I wrong?"

Oh God.

Seriously.

With my pop, I didn't want to go there.

"Pop—"

"Answer me, am I wrong?"

"No," I bit off.

"I fuckin' knew it," he clipped.

"Pop—"

He interrupted me again. "So why'd you come back?"

"It doesn't matter why," I returned swiftly.

"It sure as fuck does 'cause you, Circe, girl, you...*you* are the product of your mother and me. I didn't love that one before death and all this time after it for foolish reasons. I did it 'cause you got a love like that it does...

not...*die*. And I'm tellin' you, darlin', I took that bullet instead a' her, she would be lookin' at you with that same dead in her eyes as I'm lookin' at you with now. The same dead that's in *your* eyes as you're lookin' at me. We Quinns, we don't fall in love. We fall *in love*. And you, girl, you're *in love*, so what I wanna know is, why the fuck you used up all your magical power, pixie dust and shit and came home when you got his baby inside you, and you couldn't know that you'd ever get back?"

I couldn't hold up against his words, so I didn't. I just told him because I might as well get it over with.

"He found out I wasn't from his world."

"So?"

"He thought I was...wrong. A changeling. He thought I bewitched him. They're different, primitive. But even here...it's only because you're you and you're my pop and you love the way you love that you got it with Circe and what happened with me. Any other man, the Circe that came here would be screwed. Not you. She was lucky. I..." I sucked in breath and finished, "was not so lucky."

"So he don't listen?"

"He listened. He just didn't believe me."

"So you told him and then what?" Pop asked.

"I...well, I guess I spirited myself away."

"Right then?" Pop pushed, and I blinked again.

"No, um...maybe a few hours later."

He shook his head. "Right, well, gotta say, girl, as much as I don't wanna give that asshole nothin', *this* I can see. This shit...it's fuckin' nuts. Took me a few days to sort my head out when Circe told me what was goin' on. Thought you'd gone 'round the bend. You think for a second to give that asshole a day or two to come to terms with this shit before you hightailed your...*pregnant*, I might add...ass outta there?"

I stared at him, and I did this because, no.

No, I had not.

He shook his head, but his attention never left me. "No, you didn't. Not my Circe." He looked to the ceiling and said, "Shee-it," again before his gaze came back to me. "You'll never change. Always leadin' with your heart, lettin' your emotions get the better of you and not thinkin' with your head."

I'd heard *that* before.

"Pop—"

He leaned forward again. "Girl, you listen to your father."

Oh shit.

He was worse than Diandra when he had something to say.

He kept at me.

"I do not want to lose you. I'll tell you that right now. You go again it would break my heart. But you go, I would know you went and that grand-baby of mine would have his daddy and you...*you* would have him too. And I can see by that dead in your eyes that if you went back, you'd have what I had. What I've held precious all these years. What I had with your mother before she was lost to us. And I know this, darlin', I had to go to a whole other fuckin' world where primitive people lived and I had to piss in the trees and take a shit by a river, I do not fuckin' care. Your mother was there, *that* is where I'd fuckin' be."

My eyes filled with tears, and I whispered, "Pop."

"And I'll go on to tell you this. It would be a hard drive, the hardest in my life, but you want me to take you, I'll drive you to that witch and I'll hug you hard before you go, but you'll go knowin' that, even though I'll miss you, I'll be happy for you, knowin' you had what I lost."

I closed my eyes, looked away and said to the wall, "You don't get it. He...it was...the whole thing was hard, being with him, adapting to that world, but I stuck by him."

I looked back at Pop and kept sharing.

"I stuck by him with every trial thrown at me, and when I say that, Pop, I mean I watched women plunging knives in their stomachs and men having their legs cut off and heads sliced clean from their bodies."

Pop's eyes got big, but I kept going.

"And I took a man's life...well, one and half men actually, but...whatever. I stuck by it. I stuck by Lahn. Through everything that world and *he* threw at me. He had one trial, Pop. *One*. And he didn't have to witness anything that turned his stomach. He didn't take his first life. He didn't get betrayed by someone he cared about and nearly lose his life because of it. He just had to believe in me. Simple. Just believe in me. He didn't. *He* killed what I felt for him. He killed it *dead*. I don't have the power to go back, and Circe doesn't have the power to send me. And I'm not going to that witch, Pop. I'm never going back. I'll miss it. I made friends. I had a pet tigress who could talk to me, and I was a fucking *queen* for God's sake. Life was strange and it was insane, but it was also good. But I'm not going back. Ever. If what he killed in me never comes alive again, so be it. I'll have what you had and I'll make do. I'll have his child and just like you, that's going to be good enough for me."

Pop stared at me, and I held his eyes.

Then he came to the realization he'd come to often in my life, and that was the fact that, when I made up my mind about something, when my heart led me down the path I was determined to take, he wasn't going to be able to sway me.

I knew this when he asked, "You were a queen?"

I closed my eyes, sucked in breath then opened them. "Yes, the true, golden warrior queen of the Korwahk nation."

He blinked and muttered, "Holy fuck."

"Damn straight," I muttered back, and fuck me, I did it proudly.

He kept staring at me a few seconds before he asked, "Girl, how do you kill half a man? They got half men there?"

I relaxed and I grinned as I said, "Pick me up for Circe's party, I'll tell you stories on the way there."

He shook his head as he stood, muttering, "Not sure I wanna know."

This was probably wise.

His eyes came to me.

"But I'm gonna listen," he said softly.

Yep, that was Pop. He'd always listen.

"Then I'll tell you," I said softly back.

He nodded. Then, "His name was Lahn?"

I clenched my teeth to battle the pain.

When I had it in check, I nodded. "Dax Lahn, king of Korwahk and the mightiest warrior of the Korwahk Horde."

Pop's lips twitched as he noted, "Girl, you aimed high. Proud a' you, catchin' the eye of a king."

I rolled my eyes.

Pop moved to the door, and I opened the drawer with my purse in it. As I was standing, I noticed he hadn't moved through, and I stopped and looked at him.

"You sure, darlin'?" he whispered.

I nodded.

I was sure. Very sure.

It hurt every day, *all* day.

But I was sure.

He nodded back. "Pick you up in an hour," he muttered and moved away.

I waddled out behind him.

Truth be told, I wasn't *that* fat. I was doing yoga and taking walks every day and eating right because I might have a six-foot seven (in future) warrior growing inside me and he needed the proper nutrients.

Just as a golden girl would need.

So I took care of myself.

I hadn't learned the sex. I refused to know. I hadn't even glanced at the ultrasound and flatly refused to hear any news except to learn if the baby was growing healthy or not (he or she was).

I wasn't admitting to myself why, but I knew I did it because, if I was still in Korwahk, Lahn and I wouldn't know until the golden moment.

So here, I didn't want to know either.

I moved to the door, turned out the lights in my office and met my father at the front door he was holding open for me.

Then I went home to put on my new pregnancy dress and say good-bye to the other me as she started her life in her new world.

I LOOKED out the window at the rain as my best friend Marlene deep breathed in front of me.

"No kidding?" she asked.

My eyes went to her, and I shook my head.

I'd just told her what I'd told Pop about loving Lahn and why I left anyway. This included the stories I'd shared with him on the ride there (and through his first three beers at the party), stories of Ghost, Diandra, Narinda, Zahnin and Sabine, challenges for the Dax and bloody fights in a tent.

Amongst other things.

Marlene was freaking out and binge drinking.

I was deciding that my tactic of talking about it didn't make me feel any better and also deciding I was her ride home (as well as Pop's, I'd already confiscated his keys, they were in my purse).

"Wow," Marlene breathed. "So...he was hot?"

I looked out the window. "Very hot."

"And he was good in—" she started.

I cut her off not looking at her. "*Very.*"

"Girl," she drawled out so the one-word syllable had seven.

I sighed.

Her hand touched my arm and I felt her get close, so I looked to her to see her face had grown soft.

God, I loved Marlene.

"Honey, are you sure you don't want to go to that witch?" she asked quietly.

Except, right then, I didn't love her so much.

"I told you. No."

"Circe, really, I don't know. You have a baby on the way."

"I know and it's still no."

Her eyebrows went up. "But maybe he's back there pining for you, kicking himself that he screwed things up, wanting you home. Maybe he's worried about you, where you are, where his baby is, wondering if you're both all right. Did you think of that?"

No, I hadn't.

Though Lahn pining for me was a joke. He was probably raping and pillaging and cutting people up with his sword.

And he had the Xacto to turn to.

"I don't care," I replied. "But no. In truth, I haven't thought of that, but Lahn is not the kind of man who *pines*. He can get what he needs from a variety of women, and he can have another wife in a less than a year and a half. And most of the women he could choose from would be panting to have him. He'll be just fine."

"Cir—"

I pulled my arm from her hold but grabbed her hand and squeezed. "Really, honestly, honey, like I said...*no*. He'll be fine, I'll be fine, and *my* baby will be fine. No witch. No going back. And I want another baby shower *after* I have this kid and at that one..." I grinned, "you serve alcohol."

She stared at me before she grinned back.

Marlene was over the moon she was giving me my shower. She'd been planning it since she found out I was keeping the baby, which was the day she first saw me back and learned I was pregnant. Half of Seattle was attending. She'd asked my friends, her friends, her friends' friends and had probably put an announcement in the paper with an open invitation (just as long as they brought gifts).

When I'd registered at the baby store, she'd jerked the scanner thing out of my hand, made my selections, and I could swear I saw drool on her lip once, she was so rabid. She was baby bonkers. She couldn't wait for me to have this kid.

Okay, I was back to loving Marlene.

Therefore, I let her hand go, pulled her in my arms and hugged her.

"Love you, baby," I whispered in her ear.

She gave me a squeeze and whispered the same words back.

I pulled away and turned my head when I heard my father shout, "Time for fuckin' cake!" and I saw him walk out of Ernie's kitchen.

Ernie was one of Pop's best friends. Pop and his boys ate lunch at Ernie's greasy spoon practically every day if their move was even a little close to it, and therefore Circe's party was at Ernie's.

He had a big rectangular cake in his hands, the kind with white frosting, thick frosting swirls around the edges and massive frosting flowers, these yellow. His face was brightly illuminated by the candles burning on the cake and his eyes were brightly lit at the thought he'd soon be eating birthday cake.

Seriously, my pop was birthday cake mad. He'd serve birthday cake *with* candles if a new day dawned if he could.

He walked toward Circe, and he was, for some reason, starting a chorus of "For She's a Jolly Good Fellow."

I looked to Circe who was beaming.

She was happy, no doubt about it. She was safe in this world, my friends and family had accepted her (and our story, weirdly) without qualm (well, by the time I got there, they had).

She was no longer the toy of a tyrant or the plaything of a ship full of pirates.

She was free.

This was good.

Very good.

Two good things came out of this. Circe was smiling, her eyes alight, and I had a life I knew I'd hold precious currently kicking in my belly.

I smiled.

"Circe?" Marlene called, and I turned to look at her.

She looked alarmed.

"*Circe!*" she shrieked.

I opened my mouth to speak, but I couldn't get words to come out and everything—Marlene, the restaurant behind her, the booths—everything was...it was...

It was *melting*!

Oh fuck!

My head snapped to my father.

"*Pop!*" I screamed, but nothing came out even as I saw the wavy vision of him drop the cake to the ground and start running my way.

He didn't make it.

All had gone black.

Suddenly, it went bright with sparkling shots of pure gold.

Then I was standing in the middle of a cham, a fire burning behind me and a woman with wild, ratty-assed hair wearing a rough sarong tied around her neck fell in a dead faint to the stone at my feet.

I saw movement in the shadows.

It came toward me.

I looked up as it formed into a man's body, and when I did, I looked into Lahn's dark eyes.

"No," I whispered as he kept coming at me.

I lifted a shaky hand, palm up toward him as my eyes drifted down to the woman at my feet.

She was out like a light.

She'd depleted her magic bringing me back.

My eyes went back to Lahn to see he was upon me, the hard muscle of his chest at my palm.

I took a step back.

He moved fast as lightning, and I was lifted in his arms.

I arched my back and screamed, "*No!*"

"Rayloo, kah rahna fauna," he whispered, his arms going tight and strong as iron.

I closed my eyes hard and my body went slack in his arms.

"No," I whispered.

Then we were out of the cham, my ass was on a horse, and I felt Lahn immediately swing up behind me.

I opened my eyes to see the Avenue of the Gods in front of me and feel Lahkan under me.

Lahn's arm got tight around my protruding ribs. He bent me low to Lahkan's back, buried his heels in his steed and we shot down the avenue toward Korwahn.

Fuck.

31
THE SEARCH

Six weeks later...

TIGRESSES PURRED.

I knew this because my now full grown one was lying on her side in bed with me. I had my big belly pressed against her back, my hand was sifting through her soft, thick fur, and she was purring.

She was glad her Loolah was home. I knew this not only because of the purring, but because she told me.

Suddenly her head came up sharply and she moved quickly to her belly, looking down her body to the door, the purr gone, a low growl in her throat.

I closed my eyes.

Lahn was there.

"Off, beast," he ordered. She growled a bit more and he clipped, "*Off.*"

She let out another growl and turned her head to look at me. I smiled at her. She blinked her blue eyes and only then did she get up and prowl gracefully off the bed.

I closed my eyes and waited for it.

I didn't wait long.

I never did.

Lahn joined me in bed then he pulled me to his side, shoving his arm under me and holding me close as he reclined on the pillows.

I had no choice but to rest my head on his shoulder, so I did. I kept my eyes closed. Then I opened them because his fingers were drawing random patterns on my hip over the silk of my nightgown and that felt better with my eyes closed.

The problem was, I could see his chest when my eyes were open.

So I was screwed either way.

"Kah Lahnahsahna, nahna rahna linas, shalah," he murmured. *My tigress, your golden eyes, please.*

I sighed softly, pushed up to my elbow and looked at him.

God, he was gorgeous and I freaking hated that.

He stared in my eyes and said not a word. Then his gaze moved over my face before he stared in my eyes again.

Same drill. Every morning. Every single morning, every freaking day for six weeks.

"She keeps it locked from me," he muttered, and I blinked.

Hmm.

That was new.

And that's also when I understood. I finally understood what he was doing.

He was looking for my spirit.

Well, that was gone. He'd broken it.

I looked away.

His hand came up and curled around my jaw, gently moving my face so I was looking back at him.

"I lost your eyes for five months, my doe, and I missed them. Even having them back without your spirit shining in them, I don't like them turned away."

Yep, same drill.

He was being sweet.

I held his eyes. I did not stare. I did not glare. I waited for this to be done.

Sometimes, it took longer than others. Today, I had a feeling he was in for the long haul.

Then he did something else new. He rolled me to my back and loomed over me but close, and his hand moved to my big, swollen belly, its warmth penetrating the silk.

"He comes soon," he murmured.

This was true. It was getting close. Any day now.

And Lahn, I also knew, had given up on his golden girl.

I knew this because he told me one time in the dead of night when my kid kicked me so hard, he woke me. And Lahn, who had his hand on my belly, woke too. It sucked, but I had to admit when I saw his eyes in the moonlight shining bright with wonder, his spirit exposed for me to see, his delight at feeling his child move for the first time not even close to hidden, I liked it.

All of it.

It was the most beautiful thing I'd ever seen.

And he had murmured, pressing his hand gently into my belly, "*That* is a warrior, my golden doe."

I figured he wasn't wrong. The kid could freaking kick and he was a mover. It was like he was swimming in there, flips, breaststroke, the whole enchilada. And he was peeved he didn't have more room to move and told me so frequently by kicking the crap out of me.

Lahn took me out of my thoughts when he informed me, "I know you don't wish it, but I will be in the bath with you and the healer."

I sighed again.

I'd guessed that.

Lahn had, by the way, sometime in the last five months, decided to believe me. He was looking forward to this kid again if him sleeping with his hand on my belly or coming up behind me whenever he came upon me standing, wrapping his arms around me and putting both hands on it were anything to go by.

The good news was I was to have the healer with me. The bad news was I was giving birth in the bathing pool. I was thinking this would be okay, normally, but the water came from a hot spring, and I wasn't big on my kid being boiled alive before it took its first breath.

But I said not a word.

And anyway, maybe I was being dramatic about the water. It wasn't that hot. *I* bathed in it.

I didn't reply to Lahn's comment, and it was his turn to sigh.

"Your friends, I am told, come daily to see you, Circe," he told me quietly and my eyes slid away. "Linas, shalah," he whispered, and my eyes went back.

I'd been avoiding the girls. I hadn't seen any of them since I returned.

Not even Diandra.

This was rude, but I was in a state. I didn't want to be here, and I didn't intend to stay here, therefore I didn't want to continue to build our friendships because I'd missed them enough the first time.

I was going to go home.

How I was going to do that, I didn't know, because now I really had no way of getting home unless I could get out from under Lahn's thumb and somehow find another witch who didn't mind being out of it for a day or two, losing all of her power for a decade and sending me home.

I did not think this kind of search would prove fruitful.

But I had hope.

Every day, I hoped my father was working with that witch and Korwahn would melt, and I'd be back home. Then I was finding a protection spell to root me there. I didn't care if that meant I had to tattoo weird shit on every inch of my body. I was *never* leaving.

"They are missing you, my queen," Lahn kept talking and I focused again on him. "They are concerned for you, the child you carry. They wish to see you."

"I don't wish to see them," I said quietly.

His eyes got soft. "Circe—"

I shook my head. "I can't build strong ties here. My father knows of a witch at home who can take me back. I'm sure she's gearing up. I'll be leaving soon."

Wrong thing to say.

His face got hard, and his hand slid down my belly, up my side and then his arm tightened, locking my other side to his front as his face got close.

"You will not leave again," he growled.

"I'm afraid you don't have any choice in that, Lahn."

"I know at this time this will upset you, kah Lahnahsahna, but I do. Did you not think, when I crushed your spirit, that, when I got you back, I would not know you would again try to leave? The spell cast to guide you to your *true* home also tethered you to this world, Circe, *our* world. You're never going back."

I stared at him.

He wasn't serious.

Was he?

He kept talking. "It also anchors you to me, so even if you were to try to escape me in this world, I would sense you and could seek you out. You couldn't cloak yourself. You'd always somehow be visible to me."

I kept staring at him.

Seriously, he could not freaking be serious!

"You didn't," I breathed.

"I did," he returned.

"You didn't," I repeated on a breath and his face got closer.

"I...*fucking*...did," he growled. "You promised never to leave me, and you left me. I've seen to it that will not fucking happen again."

I knew my lips had parted and I felt the sting of tears in my nose.

Then I whispered, "I can't believe you did that."

"You gave me you of your free will, you are mine. And I gave you me, I am yours. I will do anything to keep you, my queen, believe *that*."

"That's like...stalker psycho." I was still whispering.

"I have no idea what that means, and I do not care. It is the way it is. And Circe," his face got closer, his hand sliding up my side, over my chest, up my neck to cup my jaw where his thumb swept my cheekbone as he finished softly, "I will resurrect your spirit inside you. I will stop at nothing to do it. It will shine for me again. You can believe that too."

Before I could stop him, his thumb swept over my lips, locked around my jaw and he held my head steady as his dipped down and his lips touched mine.

My belly clenched.

He lifted his head and looked deep in my eyes before his thumb swept back over my lips, he lifted up and kissed my forehead then he rolled off the bed and stalked across the room.

I got up on my elbows to watch him open the door and saw Twinka was there holding some bath cloths.

"Her warrior wives visit, you do not send them away. You let them in. If they do not, you send one of her girls to go get them. This is a command from their king, and if one of them disobeys, any of them, wife or slave, they answer to me. Am I understood?" Lahn asked firmly.

Twinka looked at me and smiled huge.

"Meena, kah Dax," she muttered, as she would because she knew this would piss me off and/or upset me and she was all for anything that did that.

"Dohno," Lahn muttered and then he was gone.

I collapsed back on the bed and stared at the ceiling.

Twinka hummed happily as she took the cloths to the bathroom-type room.

~

I SAT on a lounge chair on the roof, stared into the distance at the sun sparking off the gold on the Avenue of the Gods and I pulled the intricately knit, loose-woven shawl closer around me while wondering if there was some troop of slaves who went out every day and polished that gold. It always sparkled even mostly surrounded by sand and dust.

I figured there was.

Ghost, as always since I got home, was at my side, now lying on her front, jaws to paws.

I stroked her absently and unfortunately my thoughts drifted from statue slaves to other matters that I didn't want to think about but couldn't stop myself.

When I'd been gone, Lahn had had a busy five months. Although I hadn't seen my posse, I could not avoid my girls, and they had told me all they knew.

Firstly, Lahn, Suh Tunak and the Keenhak warriors had ridden on Maroo as planned. Maroo had had their grisly message that vengeance would be sought by the Dax so they had planned for the invasion, but they had no clue they'd also be facing the additional challenge by neighboring Keenhak.

Gaal, with bright eyes and scary excitement at telling her macabre tales, informed me that Suh Tunak and Keenhak had trounced Maroo, and, in telling me this, she unfortunately went into some detail.

Vengeance was sought and found and Maroo would not soon forget the lesson they learned.

"Not," Gaal leaned forward, eyes wide and joyous, "*for generations*."

If her stories were anything to go by, I believed this to be true. In a *serious* way.

Apparently, Lahn and his boys didn't fuck around exacting vengeance.

Yikes.

This took all of about three months and Suh Tunak rode back into Korwahn bearing a shitload of Maroo booty.

The people of Korwahn rejoiced. As these riches rained down on them, they felt it was irrefutable proof The Golden Dynasty had begun.

Lahn and Suh Tunak had shared in a week's worth of celebrations for their victory and then they rode off in their parties to wreak havoc or patrol, this including the Daxshee packing up and going on their way.

My disappearance and my not traveling with the Daxshee had been explained by the fierce storm that had struck the city prior to me going back home. Jacanda told me that word was spread that the storm was a result of me having a very bad turn and developments in my pregnancy that night meant I had to keep to my bed throughout it.

This was accepted readily.

But my girls and my girl posse knew I had disappeared because my girls had been ordered to search for me in the house the day I disappeared, and my posse had been told by their husbands. They had been sworn to silence about this information (with threats of their tongues being cut out, which would do the trick for anyone). But Beetus explained that singly, in pairs, in trios or sometimes all of my girl posse visited every day prior to the Daxshee leaving and them going with it and they did this in order to ascertain if there was news.

This was nice.

Also, the people of Korwahn or travelers who had heard the news of my enforced rest who were passing through Korwahn put flowers on our doorstep in hopes of me safely delivering the heir to The Golden Dynasty.

This was nice too.

The Daxshee drifted until it was time to return to Korwahn to settle in for the winter and for the Dax to be close to his Dahksahna for her delivery.

I had decided that Korwahk was likely south of the equator in this world because winter for them was summer for Seattle.

Their winters were as different as everything in my world. The days did dawn later, and dusk came earlier but only a little bit. And there were some gray days and occasional sprinkling rain that did not happen due to my moods (or I didn't think so). Not many, maybe one a week. The air was slightly chillier, more so on the gray days. And the evenings were definitely chillier. Lahn and I now had a soft, fluffy, brightly colored woolen blanket covering the silk quilt of our bed which worked wonders keeping the heat in, and with Lahn's warm body thrown in, I never caught a chill.

When Lahn decided to believe me, I did not know, and obviously my girls couldn't know.

That said, his going off to war and then traveling with the Daxshee pretty much told that tale.

In other words, it was business as usual for Dax Lahn, disappeared queen or not.

But Jacanda had shared that every single day, all day and all night while I was away, one of the girls was assigned to sit in my room in case I returned there (only Packa went with Lahn and the Daxshee) and there were four of my guard assigned to the house at all times. A witch had also moved in. This was so the girls could alert the guard, and if I returned, they would physically detain me, the witch magically detaining me, and orders were given that Lahn was immediately informed (or as immediately as a messenger could ride to wherever he was).

Whether this was because Lahn was taking no chances, especially when I might be carrying his true child and not a monster, or because he believed me and wanted me back, I had no clue.

And I didn't care.

I was back to needing to find a way to live in a world I wanted no part of. And I was back to Lahn giving me no choice about my own life.

What I wasn't back to was finding it in me to give much of a shit.

All the fight had left me, and I had no energy to find it.

So what has been has been and what will be was what I would make of it.

I just needed to figure out what I was going to make of it.

I felt a weird pain tighten in my belly and my brows drew together as my hand went there.

That was new.

I looked down at my stomach. I now wore sarongs wrapped around my body and tied at the back of my neck like Twinka did. Jacanda told me that this was unusual for a pregnant woman in Korwahk. They wore their sarongs and tops as normal, their bellies protruding over their belts.

I could dig that for the Korwahk. They were the Korwahk. They did crazy shit all the time. But no way *in hell* was I wandering around with my giganto stomach on display. I had managed to contain a bunch of extra weight being gained, but my stomach was enormous. The kid had to be huge.

"What are you up to now, kah teenkah tunakan?" I whispered as I slid my hand to wrap around the bottom of the enormous swell and hold him close.

Ghost's head came up and she looked to the top of the stairs. I followed her gaze, and I held my breath when I saw Diandra alight at the top. Then I let it out in a gush when I saw The Eunuch follow her.

My gaze shot back to Diandra, and I kept my silence. Her eyes were warm as they traveled over me, but her face was expressionless.

I got that.

I had been rude, insufferably and unforgivably rude to a good friend who had stood by my side through some serious thick and some anorexic-style thin. I was going to have to find the words to explain it to her, and what was good, and made me feel guilt at the same time, was that I knew she would understand and forgive me.

Something I wasn't sure I deserved.

But now, the presence of The Eunuch, with Diandra of all people, made me keep my silence, slap up my guard and brace.

His eyes slid over my face then he walked to the table and chairs. Grabbing two, he picked them up, brought them over and set them at the foot of my lounge chair. He held the back for Diandra until she sat and arranged her two layered sarongs over her legs (good idea that, two matching sarongs to ward out the chill, I'd have to remember that) and pull her own shawl closer around her upper body that was not covered in a bandeau or short halter top but what looked like a short-sleeved, tight fitting t-shirt made of thin weave, soft wool that covered her to her belly.

Only when Diandra had settled did The Eunuch sit facing me.

Both their eyes were on me.

I said not a word.

Finally, The Eunuch spoke in Korwahk. "I trust you are well, my true, golden queen?"

I blinked.

His voice was quiet, there was a thread of concern in it, and he'd called me his true, golden queen. Not just his queen.

Hmm.

"I am fine," I replied.

He nodded his head once and informed me, "Our king speaks true. Your beauty blooms magnificently having grown heavy with his child."

Really, I wished Lahn would quit being sweet. Not only to me but now hearing he was wandering around complimenting me. It was getting on my nerves.

"Shahsha," I muttered, my eyes slid to Diandra to see her head tipped slightly to the side, concern she wasn't quite able to hide now on her features.

Shit.

"It has come to my attention you do not allow your women to attend you," The Eunuch stated, and I looked back at him.

"I have been...not myself for some time," I replied.

He inclined his head.

Then he said softly, "You grieve your lost world."

I blinked at him.

He knew.

That was a surprise.

Well, whatever. If Lahn was stupid enough to trust this guy, so be it. It wasn't any of my business.

I decided not to answer.

"There is only one person in Korwahk who calls me Karrim," he stated bizarrely, changing the subject, and I spoke not a word but didn't take my eyes from him. "My king," he finished quietly.

I braced again.

Ghost shifted so her sleek bulk rested against my lounge chair, a show of support.

My hand went from my belly back to her fur and I stroked.

What I didn't do was speak.

"After..." he paused a moment before going on, "what happened to me, it was not my manhood I missed."

He waited, and when I made no reply (though I had to say I was pretty surprised at this news), he went on.

"It was my Horde. Since I could remember, my father spoke to me about my future as warrior, and since I could move my limbs at my command, he started training me to *be* warrior. He was warrior. It was in his blood, passed down to me. There was no day more beautiful to me than when the Dax pressed his palm to the earth, and at five years of age, I took my knee for the first time in service to The Horde."

Wow.

Interesting.

He kept speaking. "Therefore, there was no day worse for me than when I was cast out of it."

"I'm sorry," I whispered, because, really, I needed to be cautious with this guy, but I felt I had to say something mainly because his voice shook with emotion I could not believe was fake.

He inclined his head again. "So, I would hope you could imagine my joy when the new Dax sought me out and requested my service to return to my brethren. I was not able to fight. My strength was not the same. But I could be of service using other skills. This new Dax was the mightiest I ever saw, but mightier because he used more than his muscle to command. He knew the strength of any warrior was not in their steel but elsewhere. And he allowed me to use that...a power I could wield that was still at my command and strong as ever...to provide service to my nation. He asked for me not only to provide service for the Hunt, the selections and the Daxshee, but to be his eyes and ears and to act for him in matters of crucial import.

And this I was, I am, I did, and I do, serving my Horde proudly, but more, serving the mighty Dax who begins The Golden Dynasty."

I nodded when he stopped talking.

He continued.

"It is my duty to know all and see all. It is my duty to protect Suh Tunak, my Dax and doing thus, my Korwahk. And therefore, after she was claimed, it was my duty to watch and then seek out my queen, a foreigner, and put her to the test." He paused then smiled a small smile. "She asked me my name, a name only her husband calls me, and even though our ways were strange to her, she held firm and true to her husband." His eyes held mine and he whispered, "She passed the test."

I blinked at him.

Oh my God!

Karrim didn't give me time to freak out, he kept speaking.

"And therefore, I now have grave concerns of news that she, our warrior queen, the golden one, has had her spirit broken. She hides her glory from her husband. She sheathes her claws that he enjoys challenging with his steel."

Oh man.

I kept quiet and kept my eyes glued to him even as Diandra shifted.

I knew what that shift meant. It meant my girls were talking, Diandra was listening and now she was meddling.

Shit.

"His roar of grief was heard far in Korwahn that day you disappeared," Karrim said softly, and I felt my body go completely still. "With the violence of the storm, its abrupt halt, all knew you commanded it, and many thought he had lost his child, and, the sound was so tortured, perhaps even you. All were pleased to hear you had simply taken a turn, you were well but resting."

I pressed my lips together to deny his words bouncing around in my brain.

Good words.

Great words.

Dangerous words.

Dangerous to my peace of mind and my heart.

"And that day, I was summoned," Karrim pressed on. "The Horde was off to war, and I usually attended my king, made certain his messages and commands were sent and received to and from warriors who fought on different fronts. But he ordered that I would not ride with The Horde when they rode on Maroo. He told me under strictest confidence that there was another world, you, his goddess, had come to him from it, and in the night, he had lost you as you had returned to it. And then he ordered me to search this earth to find a witch who could bring you home and bind you here. He commanded that no expense was to be spared. If I had to scour the icy depths of Lunwyn, I would do so. If I had to cross the entirety of the Green Sea to search faraway lands, I would do so. I would not stop until I found the magic to bring you back home and *keep you here.*" He nodded once. "And this I did."

I was now breathing heavily.

Lahn had done this the day I disappeared.

Lahn had ordered this instantly.

Lahn hadn't decided to believe me sometime in the last five months and Lahn hadn't gone about his business.

Lahn had immediately launched plans to bring me back.

Oh *God.*

"Fortunately, I was able to provide this service to my king. I rode hard, lathered many horses, exchanged many riches. And I not only found the witch who brought you back, but I also found a frost-haired princess of the north who graces her Raider husband's ship, where I discovered her. A ship she dwells on when she is not gracing one of his wintry homes in Lunwyn. And she confided in me that she, too, comes from your world."

Holy crap!

"Really?" I whispered, leaning forward.

He nodded and again smiled. "Really. She and her husband are very interested in you, for she has never heard of another like her. They requested no payment for the long conversations she had with me, telling me of your world, asking about you. They only requested that I send a messenger to find them when you returned. They travel widely and I have no idea when my message will be received, but when it is, she intends to visit you, my golden queen."

Wow. Wow. *Wow.*

"*Wow,*" I breathed, his smile widened, and I heard Diandra stifle a laugh, so I looked to her. Forgetting I had been a total bitch, I smiled at her and asked, "Diandra, sweetheart, isn't that *cool*?"

Her mouth went soft, her eyes grew bright, and she whispered, "Indeed it is, my love, very...*cool.*"

I held her gaze and felt my eyes grow bright too.

Then I felt another tight pain in my belly, my brows drew together, and I looked down at it, but Karrim again spoke.

"I tell you all this, my true, golden queen, because I cannot know what happened with you and our Dax to understand why this rift continues. But I wish you to know—"

He stopped talking when I groaned as the pain came back, tighter, deeper, and I bent forward reflexively, taking my hand from Ghost and wrapping it around my swollen stomach.

"Circe?" Diandra called.

I stopped clenching my teeth as the pain faded away.

I pulled in a breath and let it out through my lips that I formed in a tight "O."

Then I looked at my friend. "I'm okay, it's just a—"

I stopped talking and Karrim shot out of his chair, Ghost shot to her four paws and Diandra shot toward me.

This was because my water broke.

Oh man.

I looked at Diandra and finished. "I'm okay. It's just that I'm having a baby."

She smiled into my face.

Karrim rushed to the steps and shouted down, "Call the Dax immediately! His child comes!"

Great.

Karrim had a big mouth.

Diandra pulled me carefully out of the lounge chair, murmuring, "Let's get you down those stairs while we still can."

This, I thought, was a good idea. So I followed her after I got to my feet and Karrim rushed back to us. They walked me to the stairs, one on each side holding my arms tightly like I was an invalid, not just pregnant.

I ignored this and turned to Diandra. "We must talk."

"Yes, my dear," she nodded. "But perhaps not now."

We made it to the top of the stairs. "I need to explain."

"I'm sure you do." She let me go, took a step down then turned and grabbed my hand, starting to lead me down as Karrim spotted me from behind. "But later."

"There was a reason I was—" I started.

She stopped halfway down the stairs and gripped my hand tight.

"Circe, can you please concentrate on getting down the stairs, successfully delivering the warrior who will succeed the Dax and *then* we'll chat about why you locked yourself away to lick your wounds, grieve your lost world, consider your future...all of which I, and all your friends, already *understand*. Does that sound good to you?"

I grinned. "Yeah, sweetheart, that sounds good to me."

She nodded smartly, muttered, "Dohno," and she and Karrim finished leading me down the stairs where all my girls, save Twinka, were waiting, bouncing on their toes with ill-concealed excitement.

Shit.

32
THE GOD AND GODDESS

"Push, my golden queen," the healer, standing behind me in the bathing pool supporting my torso with her arms wrapped under my armpits, hands curled around my shoulders, urged in my ear.

My eyes stayed locked to Lahn's as I breathed, "Right."

It was official. I was never having another child. And I wasn't because this shit hurt like *a mother*.

And I wasn't all fired up about how the Korwahk delivered babies.

That was, me in a Korwahk-style nightgown in the pool, the healer holding me up at my back, one of her (three! like I needed that much fucking company!) assistants holding me on one side, another on the other, the third outside the pool for some reason I did not ask, and best of all (not!), my ankles resting on Lahn's broad shoulders. This was, by the way, a Lahn who was in his hides, kneeling in the pool ready to catch the kid should he ever deign to make an appearance.

Apparently, I was wrong. Kah teenkah tunakan wasn't peeved he didn't have enough room to move.

He liked it in there and he was staying.

My body just was done with him being there.

The problem was, as hard as I tried, as deep as I pushed, I couldn't get the kid out.

And this had been going on a long time.

Too long.

I was worn right the fuck out.

I pushed with all I had left, which really wasn't a lot, then gave up, my head falling back on the healer's shoulder because I couldn't hold it up anymore, my eyes losing contact with Lahn's for the first time since this shit started (except, of course, when I closed them to push).

"Circe, my dear, please, please, *push,*" Diandra encouraged.

She was wandering the edge of the bathing pool with Ghost prowling at her side, watching, wringing her hands, and as the minutes passed, visibly moving from excitement, to minor freakout, to major freakout, and now she was not hiding out-and-out panic.

"I can't," I whispered, the pain ripping through me. I couldn't push and fight the pain at the same time. It just wasn't happening.

"I must cut, my Dax," the healer said quietly.

"Me," Lahn growled fiercely.

"He is not coming," the healer continued quietly, stating the obvious.

"*Me!*" Lahn barked and her arms tightened around me.

"My queen, please, you must *push,*" she whispered in my ear.

I nodded weakly, lifted my head and tried again. I had little left, I gave it all I could, squeezing my eyes tight and digging my heels in Lahn's shoulders but nothing doing.

I collapsed back into the arms supporting me.

"My Dax," the healer hissed urgently. "I must *cut.*"

"You cut, I lose my queen," Lahn growled, and I closed my already-closed eyes tighter.

"Maybe I can sew her together, like she did the warrior," the healer suggested.

Oh man. Primitive experimental surgery.

Fucking great.

"You will *not cut,*" Lahn growled again, and I felt his fingers wrap tight around my ankles. "My doe," he called, his voice soft. "Give me your eyes."

I fought the pain, pulled in breath, and with effort, lifted my head.

Then I stared at what I saw. It was a hazy stare, but I saw it.

Yes, I definitely saw it. Clear and unhidden.

Lahn was scared.

"My tigress does not admit defeat," he told me, his fingers tightening around my ankles. "My golden warrior never admits defeat." My eyes closed slowly, and his fingers gave me a squeeze, so I opened them. "Push, baby," he whispered.

He held my gaze, and just like that day in our cham, something came over me. Something I didn't know I had. It surged through me, taking over, and I gritted my teeth, nodded my head, closed my eyes, dug my heels in my husband's shoulders, and I pushed.

Hard.

Then again.

And again.

And a-fucking-gain.

"He crowns," an assistant whispered.

"Praise the True Mother," the healer breathed.

Then I pushed again.

And again.

"That's it, my Circe," Lahn encouraged, his fingers not curled around my ankles anymore but stroking deep into the flesh of my inner thighs, his arms wrapped around to do it.

I pushed again and Lahn's hands moved from me to between my legs as I felt him come.

"Oh, Circe!" Diandra cried with delight.

"The king's blade!" the healer called quickly.

I collapsed into my supporting arms as water splashed around me.

Hallelujah.

He was *out*!

I licked my lips and rolled my head on the healer's shoulder to see the last assistant was now in the water too and working with Lahn between my legs.

Then I heard his deep, now thick voice call, "My Circe," and I rolled my head back to see him holding up a perfect, tiny, black-fuzzy-headed baby boy.

And he was *perfect*. Absolutely. From the top of his fuzzy head to the tips of his baby toes.

He was also bawling his brains out.

I lost sight of my baby when the tears filled my eyes.

But suddenly my body jerked, and my scream pierced the air when new pain tore through my belly.

"Take the child!" the healer yelled, and my body bucked then convulsed as pain washed anew, water splashed around me, people switched places, and Lahn barked, "What is happening?"

After a few moments when my belly was prodded as was between my legs, the healer answered happily, "There comes another. Push my queen, *push*."

Another?

I twisted my head to look at her as she positioned herself again behind me.

"Another? Another what?"

"You carry twins," she told me. "Push, my true golden queen."

Twins?

My eyes shot to Lahn, and I snapped, "Do you have twins in your family?"

He stared at me and ordered, "Circe, push."

"*Tell me!*" I shrieked.

"Yes!" he clipped. "My father was birthed before his sister who shared his womb."

Oh. My. *God!*

"*And you didn't think to tell me?*" I screeched.

"Circe, my love, *push*!" Diandra cried.

I glared at Lahn.

Then I gritted my teeth, closed my eyes, dug my heels into my king's shoulders (*hard*), and I pushed.

My daughter slid out easily.

She had golden fuzz on her head.

I FELT the bed move and my eyes drifted open about the time Lahn had settled tight to my side.

I saw his head was up and he was nodding at someone, so I turned my head and saw Diandra and the healer beside the bed, each holding a swaddled bundle.

Diandra bent first with my dark-headed son and rested him on my chest. The healer came second, laying my golden-headed daughter close, next to her brother. At the same time, Lahn's arm closed around his newborn children as well as me and mine moved around my babies.

Diandra and the healer moved silently away, the door closing behind them.

My eyes went to Lahn when I felt his lips brush my temple then the bed moved as he shifted, and I watched as he touched his lips to each fuzzy head.

And, incidentally, with each touch of his lips, my heart melted.

His head came up and his face came close to mine.

Then he declared in his soft, sweet voice, "I name him Tunahn, the horse. As my father named me after the tiger god, proud, fierce and cunning, I name our warrior after the horse god, strong, clever and loyal."

There it was.

That was Dax Lahn, naming our kid without even asking what I thought.

Though, I kind of liked "Tunahn" and I definitely liked the reasons he chose it.

"Now, kah teenkah tunakanahsa," he whispered. "What do you name our daughter?"

Oh.

We were taking turns.

Okay, I could dig that.

"Isis," I blurted for reasons unknown to me. It just came out.

"Isis," he whispered, his eyes drifting to her golden head, and the way he said those two syllables, I decided that was it. My girl was Isis. Then his gaze came to me. "Why do you name our golden princess this?"

I tilted my head a little as it hit me for the first time that my husband and I shared something weird and pretty freaking cool.

So I replied quietly, "Your parents named you after a god and my parents named me after a goddess. Circe was the goddess of magic. Isis, too, is a goddess. She's the goddess of motherhood and magic."

Lahn grinned a grin I liked a whole lot.

"This pleases me," he whispered.

It pleased me too, and damn it all, it pleased me that it pleased him.

I stared into his eyes and whispered back, "Dohno."

His long, strong arm tightened around his family and his eyes dropped to my mouth. My warmed heart warmed more as my breath caught and my eyes dropped to his. It was coming toward mine. And when our lips touched, his opened and mine didn't hesitate to do the same, nor did the tip of my tongue hesitate moving to touch the sweetness of his. At that touch, warmth rushed through me, strong and unbelievably sweet.

He lifted his head, and I knew with one look in his eyes, he'd felt the same.

"I am very proud of you, my golden doe," he whispered.

"Shahsha," I whispered back.

"Though," his lips twitched, "I think the last time you dug your heels in my shoulders it was less an effort to bring our daughter into this world than it was something else."

He wasn't wrong about that.

My eyes slid away.

"Circe," he called, my eyes slid back, and he shared gently, "There has been only one moment in my life when I have been happier than I am in this one and that was sharing the beauty your magic created while you told me you loved me." His arm gave us another squeeze. "Thank you, baby."

I bit my lip as that slid through me warm and sweet as well.

Okay, I was in trouble.

I wasn't going to be able to hold up against this kind of sweet.

Still, the moment warranted it so I couldn't help but whisper, "You're welcome, Lahn."

His eyes warmed further then his head descended so he could brush his lips against my forehead, my temple and then my lips.

He settled at my side and urged quietly in my ear, "Rest, my doe. I will hold you and our family safe as you sleep."

Okay, shit.

Shit, shit, shit.

This was beyond sweet.

This was beautiful.

"Okay," I whispered.

My arm going tight around the tiny bundles sleeping on my chest, I pulled in a soft breath, let it out on a light sigh and closed my eyes.

A few minutes later, me and my family slept safe in my husband's strong arm.

I HEARD HIS ROAR, it wasn't exactly close, but it wasn't far away, and my eyes opened.

Soft candlelight lit our room from the four, tall iron holders around the head of our bed.

The rest of the room was in darkness, but as the shouted words came at me, my eyes drifted over my two swaddled babies resting on their backs in the bed, tucked close to the curve of my body, and I tipped my head back on the pillows.

Looking through our room and the opened doors to the bathing room, I saw my husband standing on the balcony, backlit by the bright lights of many torches coming up from the street.

"Your golden warrior queen proves again my claiming her beauty heralds The Golden Dynasty!" Lahn was shouting. "She battled mightily and refused to taste defeat when the fruit of our union, the future of our empire challenged her. As my golden queen always does, she triumphed, bringing forth not one but *two* heirs planted from my seed in her golden womb!"

An excited, shocked cheer rang out, but Lahn spoke over it.

"A strong, warrior prince who will be your future Dax and a beautiful golden princess who will rain beauty and bounty on all Korwahk!"

Another boisterous cheer, but again Lahn kept talking right through it.

"Prince Tunahn and Princess Isis sleep in the web of safety woven from my golden queen's magic and my might, they will grow and flourish until they carry forth our Dynasty for all our people!"

Another cheer and more from Lahn right over it.

"Hail Prince Tunahn! Hail Princess Isis! And hail your golden Queen Circe!"

These cheers rang out, hailing my kids and me, but I knew Lahn was done. As usual, he didn't bask in the frenzy he created. He turned and walked to me.

I watched him move thinking that was laying it on a bit thick, but I couldn't help but like it.

I felt my precious bundles shift and tore my eyes from Lahn to see both my babies were awake and moving in their tight wraps. Tunahn's movements seemed agitated, even demanding. Isis's seemed exploratory, her unseeing eyes blinking. She was awake but appeared content.

Lahn's weight hit the bed even as the cheers continued to ring out, and he whispered, "They wish to suckle, kah rahna fauna."

Oh man.

I nodded, thinking I'd have to get used to this so I might as well start now, and, wincing, I shifted up to sitting.

Lahn carefully picked up Isis and handed her to me after I pulled the drawstring loose over my breasts.

"Our princess first," he murmured as I cautiously took her.

I was positioning her, feeling a little weird and a lot embarrassed as I offered my nipple to my daughter and Lahn picked up the fussing Tunahn.

Then, with Tunahn snug in the crook of Lahn's arm, his other one snaked out, wrapped around my waist, and he gently turned me and pulled me and Isis back so we were resting against his solid bulk.

Once there, instantly Isis latched on and started to suck.

I closed my eyes as my milk flowed, nourishing my child with my husband's strength supporting me, and all this slid through me like silk.

I relaxed and cradled my daughter to me. Lahn's fingers stroked my side soothingly. Tunahn continued to fret.

"Our son will be greedy," Lahn murmured

I smiled.

Like father like son.

"Maybe, in future, Tunahn should go first. Isis seemed content to wait," I suggested.

"Me," Lahn replied. "He took more of your womb and pushed out first. He must now learn patience and sharing."

This was true, the taking more of my womb part. Tunahn was a healthy little bugger. Isis was dainty in comparison to her brother.

"Okay, Lahn," I said softly. "You know how to build a warrior."

"Mm," he murmured and that slid through me like silk too. "And I look forward to learning how to spoil a princess."

Man, oh man.

Oh *man*.

I couldn't stop it and didn't try. I rested my head on his shoulder and turned it so I could press my temple against his neck.

At this, Lahn held on tighter.

When Isis was done, it was Lahn who executed the impossible maneuver of exchanging babies and held Isis and me again while Tunahn fed (he latched on immediately and sucked hard—definitely greedy and knowing what he wanted—therefore definitely his father's son).

I fell asleep in the middle of it, temple to my husband's neck, son in my arms, and woke up later to a dark room, my nightdress tied over my breasts, my body sheltered against the chill under the strong safety of my king's.

"Sleep, my Circe," he murmured, his arm around me tightening. "You must regain your strength."

"Where are the children?" I asked in a drowsy voice, my eyelids drifting up and down, wanting to adhere to his command at the same I wanted an answer.

"In their beds, where they will always sleep. This is our bed, my golden queen," Lahn replied. My eyes drifted closed, but before I drifted away, I heard him finish on a murmured afterthought, "Unless my golden Isis is troubled. Then she will have her father."

I floated away thinking, *oh man.*

33
THE RESURRECTION

S*ix weeks later...*

"CIRCE! I just don't know what to do with you!" Diandra cried, staring at me with unconcealed impatience, and I lifted my hand to cup the dark head on top of the tiny sleeping body strapped to my chest.

"Diandra!" I hissed, "Shush!" My eyes slid side to side around the bustling marketplace me and my posse were wandering through. "You'll wake Tunahn or people might hear."

I heard a slight giggle and my eyes moved to Sabine who was standing very close to Zahnin and also by Narinda who had Isis strapped to her chest over her own little baby bump.

Then my gaze moved through Claudine, Nahka, Anastasie, Oahsee, Char and Vuntus, who quickly looked away, pressing their lips together, turning their dancing eyes and feigning avid interest at a stall that held a variety of leather straps men could wear across their chests.

Diandra got close to me and laid her hand on mine on Tunahn's head, and she hissed back, "I do not want to disturb your little warrior, but I do not care if people hear! This cannot go on."

At Diandra's not-so-gentle questioning, I had hesitantly just shared with her (and my posse) that, even after the touching scenes after our children were born, things had not changed between Lahn and me.

This was mostly because I was caught up in suddenly being a mother of two in a primitive world and deciding, even if I had servants who could not wait to get their mitts on my babies, this would be hands on.

Not to mention, considering I was nursing them both, and Tunahn seemed to want to feed continuously, I had no choice for it to be hands on.

Therefore, I was exhausted, constantly running around and had one or two children in my arms (or attached to my body) almost all the time. Even half the night. And when this wasn't happening, I was trying to catch up on sleep or bolting down food because nursing made you ravenous.

So I didn't see my husband a lot. Partly because I was busy. And partly because I was doing my all to avoid him (thus wandering the marketplace with my posse and the many walks I would take with my kids to be amongst my people and to work off my baby weight). Because when *he* was with our kids, especially Isis, the way he doted on her (and both of them, really, but early warning signs showed Princess Isis was going to be Daddy's Little Girl) sent that warm sweetness through me so strong, sometimes it was a wonder I kept my feet.

And this didn't take into account the way he doted on *me*.

Dax Lahn was proud of his family, and he made no bones about it. As he would be, mostly because I dug my heels in his shoulders as payback in the heat of the moment. I'd forgotten that my mom's mom had been a twin and I'd researched this ages ago to discover what it might mean to my future and found it was the woman who was genetically predisposed to carrying twins.

So it was my fault-ish.

Or, more accurately, my boon.

I did not share this information with anyone and therefore everyone was crowing their Dax was not only the mightiest but also the most virile, seeing as his *other* powerful sword sired two children on me. They had no idea it was me who was predisposed to it and released two eggs his swimming warriors could fertilize. They wouldn't get it even if I tried to explain, and it must be said, Lahn himself seemed pretty freaking pleased with the results of our union, so I didn't have the heart to explain.

This was all also, I was *not* admitting to myself, my defense mechanism against a husband who had injured me deeply but whose unrelenting sweetness was healing a wound I had stubbornly refused to allow to heal.

But now, I had forgiven him, and I just didn't know how to tell him that.

And the tables were turning.

The longer I procrastinated, the more it was becoming less a matter of me telling him I forgave him and more me needing to be forgiven for my delay in letting my savage brute off the hook.

Why did I always do this?

God, I was so freaking stupid!

And now, because I was stupid, about three weeks ago Lahn's sweetness started to hold an edge of impatience. That edge grew, spread, built and honed, and now it was long and very sharp, like the side of his sword.

Yes.

So. Freaking. *Stupid*.

"The Dax is in a foul mood," Diandra snapped, pulling my attention from me being stupid back to her pointing out the results of my stupidity. "And this foul mood might come home with him, but it also spreads, and being the Dax, when it spreads, it spreads *far* and it spreads *wide*. I can assure you that, if he shares his frustration with you at home, you can take this a hundredfold at how he shares it with his warriors and anyone close enough to receive the lash of his tongue." She leaned into me. "I can assure you of this because *Seerim told me* that King Lahn is surrounded by an aura of black, and everyone, be they warrior, trainee, free man or slave, is giving him *and* his aura a *very wide berth*."

Oh man.

Being Diandra, she kept at me.

"And, I would say, that Dax being *Dax Lahn* it is a good possibility that lash might graduate to the tip of a whip or the edge of steel should you carry on much longer holding your grudge and *withholding your charms*. The man is practically begging for a challenge or *some* reason to unleash some of his impatience on *someone*, and the only thing I know is that someone will *not* be *you*."

Oh man!

Before I could even open my mouth, she kept right on going.

"What I'd like to know is, are you willing to be responsible for one of the trainee warriors not buffing his saddle to a deep enough shine and having his back opened up for this perceived mistake?"

No.

One could say I didn't want that, like, not at all.

Though I was surprised Lahn had his saddle buffed. I didn't think a savage brute would care about something like that.

"No, Diandra," I whispered and my hand curled tighter on my son's head because, really, I was so...*fucking*...stupid!

Her hand dropped but she didn't move out of my space.

"I understand, my dear, after you told me how he reacted to your being who you are and where you're from...the words he said, how this would mark you. Words make marks deeper than fists. They last longer and sometimes never go away. But The Eunuch *told you* Dax Lahn stopped at nothing to bring you home, and when he got you here, to keep you at his side. And I saw the fear..."

Her eyes narrowed on my face when mine widened, but she kept talking.

"Oh yes, my dear, I didn't miss it when you were delivering upon him your children and he thought you would be lost to him in a way no magic could bring you back."

She sucked in breath then kept right on going.

"I love you, my beautiful friend, my golden queen, you know I love you dearly, but this has gone far enough. I know with the instances you and I have shared that you find it difficult to speak to those you love when you feel you have done them wrong..." Jeez, freak me out, she *totally* knew me. "But I also know that you are our warrior queen, your heart is as fierce as it is warm, and that you can pull up the strength to find the words to mend wounds and find forgiveness."

Her hand came back to mine at Tunahn's head, and her eyes looked deeply into my own.

"Find words, Circe," she urged gently. "Mend the wounds in your marriage, forgive your husband and let him forgive you. Do it for you, for him, for your wee ones and, by the gods, for us *all*."

I bit my lip and looked through my posse.

Then my eyes lifted and, one by one, caught Zahnin and Bain's.

Zahnin tipped his chin up. He'd heard. He agreed with Diandra.

No surprise there.

Bain grinned. He'd heard. His thoughts were already beyond the hard part and getting to the good stuff.

And one could definitely say I missed the good stuff.

So no surprise from Bain either.

I shook my head at Bain then dropped it and Diandra took her hand away as I rested my lips against my son's fuzzy head.

I heard a flurry of movement, my head came up and my hand left

Tunahn's head to wrap an arm protectively around him as I saw Zahnin detaining a young boy with his big hand wrapped tight on his shoulder.

"The Dax commands his golden queen's attendance. It is urgent. She is ordered not to delay," the boy, out of breath from his run, rushed the words out.

Oh shit.

My attention went to Zahnin to see him jerk his chin at me and then he moved as commanded, that was to say, without delay. My posse fell in and Zahnin took point, Bain took rear as we hurried through the marketplace and the streets of Korwahn up to Lahn and my house.

We all barely crowded through the door before I stopped, shocked to see Lahn standing, arms crossed, legs planted, face set in granite, in the courtyard.

Beside him stood a woman who had to be older than time. Her hair was all gray, wiry and there was a lot of it shooting everywhere around her head, down her shoulders and chest. She was even more stooped and wrinkled than Twinka, who stood just behind her and Jacanda stood behind Twinka.

"Take the children, now," Lahn barked.

My body started at his tone and Twinka and Jacanda jumped forward.

Twinka, by the by, still did not like me and still did not hide it, but she freaking *adored* my kids. So much I had to keep an eye on her because I swear, the crazy woman would spirit them away in the night if I didn't.

Twinka went to Narinda and Jacanda came to me, both moving to untie our wraps and take the children as Lahn kept issuing curt orders.

"The rest, go. Now. I want no ears." His eyes sliced to Twinka. "The children will be cared for in your quarters. Do not enter this house until you have my leave." He jerked his head at Twinka, who nodded and rushed away with Isis, Jacanda with Tunahn on her heels. "Zahnin," Lahn finished, "you stay to escort the witch out when she is through."

I blinked at the crazy-haired, stooped woman to see she was studying me, and she had the skin and probably used to have the hair of a Korwahk but her eyes were bright blue.

Weird.

And she was a witch.

Weirder.

I didn't know what to do with that. What I did know was that whatever she was doing here, Lahn did not like.

I didn't think this was good.

My posse filed out. Zahnin took his place inside the front doors. And Jacanda and Twinka were long gone with Tunahn and Isis when Lahn dropped his arms and stalked into one of the rooms on the bottom floor, which was kind of a living room, but then again, they all were, seeing as they all mostly just had rugs and cushions, except the room that had a dining table.

When the witch and I followed, he slammed the door after we entered the room and wasted no time turning, planting his legs, crossing his arms and barking, "Deliver your message to my queen."

My head jerked and I looked from my husband to the witch.

"You are Circe Kaye Quinn?" the woman asked in Korwahk.

I opened my mouth to answer, but Lahn got there before me to bite off, "She is Dahksahna Circe, the true, golden warrior queen of Korwahk."

The witch nodded to Lahn, a small smile tipped her lips, and her eyes came back to me.

She lifted her hand, reached into a pleat in her sarong and pulled out a folded piece of rough-edged, brownish-yellow parchment.

My heart leaped and my head got light when she announced, "One week ago, I fell into a trance and a message was delivered upon me by your father."

"Oh my God," I whispered, my hands clasping and coming up to my chest as my eyes stayed glued to her.

"It is in a tongue I do not understand. I wrote it down as I heard it, and I will share it with you that same way. He expects a response and I have moved quickly through Korwahk to give this message to you for his spell has bound me and I am not at my own free will until I provide your reply."

"What did he say?" I asked.

She nodded, unfolded the parchment and started speaking in halting English.

"Circe, girl, this is your father. I'm guessin' you're gettin' that I'm leavin' you there for your own good and the good of my grandbaby. That asshole ain't treatin' you right, you tell whoever gives you this message and we'll move heaven and earth to find a way to bring you all home. He is, you tell her that too, and I wanna know my grandchild's name. And he isn't, you tell him I'm gonna find a magical way to kick his warrior ass. But I got all the hope in the world that you're happy, darlin'. I love you, Circe girl, and I always will."

I clenched my teeth and swallowed as I closed my eyes.

"I can assume I know what 'asshole' means," Lahn remarked tersely, and my eyes flew open.

He'd heard the message before, he'd understood it, and that was why he was pissed.

Shit!

I opened my mouth to say something, but Lahn got there before me, barking at the witch, "Leave now. My wife will give you her reply tomorrow. Come back after the sun begins its descent."

She nodded, reading his mood (which was hard to miss) and got the hell out of there.

The door barely closed on her when I started, "Lahn—"

But I didn't finish. This was because he lunged toward me, grabbed my hand in a tight grip and dragged me out of the room.

I was running to keep up with his long, angry strides, and he was already at the stairs before I got myself together to cry, "Lahn! What on earth?"

"Quiet," he growled.

Uh-oh.

Perhaps Diandra was wrong. Perhaps Lahn wasn't going to find someone else to receive the sharp edge of his impatience. Perhaps that someone was going to be *me*.

He went straight to our room, pulled me in so hard I went flying in five steps when he released me. He came in after me and slammed the door behind him.

Uh-oh again.

I lifted a hand and started retreating as he started advancing.

"Lahn—" I whispered.

"Eight months," he clipped, and I blinked.

"Wh-what?" I stammered as I kept backing up and Lahn kept advancing.

"Eight months, my queen, I have not taken a woman."

Oh my God!

I blinked again, and in the nanosecond of that blink, this news hit me like a shot.

Oh...my...*God*!

My eyes stayed glued to him as my heart started beating fast.

I hit bed, skirted it and kept retreating.

Then I whispered, "Really?" and he jerked his chin up.

"*Really*," he spat.

Oh man.

"Uh..." I mumbled, liking this, hating this (mainly because I wasn't giving it up to him as I should as his wife and the woman who loved him), being thrilled by it and feeling massive guilt at the same time.

I hit wall and slid to the side, hitting corner and sliding down a new wall as he stopped and slowly turned his big body to keep facing me.

"My Circe told me it was important to her..." he leaned in and his eyes narrowed, "*crucial*," he hissed, "that I use my body on no one but her. So I have *used my body on no one but her*."

Oh...*man*.

My heart stopped beating fast and started thumping *faster*.

"Lahn—" I whispered.

"But she withholds from me."

Oh shit.

When I'd cleared him, I came away from the wall and started to back toward the door.

Lahn came at me again. "She withholds her xaxsah. She withholds her golden honey. She withholds her claws. She withholds her spirit. And, since she bore my children, she withholds even her *time*."

"Uh..." I mumbled again.

I hit door and didn't even get close to finding the knob. Lahn moved fast, I was up, across the room and on my back in the bed, Lahn on top of me. I was winded, his face was in my face, and he was beyond furious. He was seriously fucking *pissed*, him *and* the brutal, golden spirit that was shining in his eyes.

And he was something else. Something I didn't get. Something I couldn't read. Something that didn't belong in his eyes.

It was wrong there.

Cataclysmically wrong.

"I will not take you by force for I know you will use it as well as reason never to forgive me. And now I know it to be true, from the name your father called me, that you never will."

"Lahn—" I whispered again as what I saw in his eyes, held by his spirit, started to dawn.

He talked over me.

"But you should know before I leave you to be my queen only for our people, my wife only to be mother to Tunahn and Isis, and I let you go, that I suffered for my mistake. I suffered for it greatly when I found you left me."

My heart thumped harder just as my belly melted.

Yes, I knew what that was in his eyes.

Defeat.

Oh God.

I had to stop this.

Now.

"Honey—" I tried speaking softly, using an endearment he liked as I gently put my hands on him, but I failed to break through.

"I spent five months agonizing that I had lost you forever. Haunted in sleep and in wake with the vision of your spirit fading to nothing in your eyes, knowing *I'd* crushed it to death, and *I'd* forced you to escape me. Me, your king, your warrior, your Lahn, *yours,* in the end being no better than Dortak."

Oh *God.*

"Lahn—" I started as my body softened under his and my arms wrapped around him.

"And knowing with every day that passed when you didn't return to me, *you* were never going to find your way back to me. And despairing as each day moved into the next with no word from Karrim that *I* wouldn't find a way to bring you home."

I slid my hands to his front and up to curl them light around his neck. "Baby, listen to—"

"My golden doe, gone. My child with her. Never to see her heavy with my seed, never to look upon my warrior or golden daughter, never again to feel her body at sleep in our bed next to mine."

"Lahn, seriously, honey, please listen—"

"Then Karrim finds a witch to bring you home to me, we give her trunks of gold only for you to come back broken."

God!

He needed to *shut the fuck up* so I could *fucking talk*!

"Lahn!" I snapped urgently, my fingers digging into his neck, but I *still* didn't break through.

"And *I* did that. *I* broke you and the only hint you gift me with that there is a possibility my golden goddess lives on somewhere inside is when you found the strength to deliver upon me our children."

Jeez, when my man got on a tangent, there was no shutting him the fuck up!

"Lahn, damn it—!" I shouted in his face, but it was like I didn't make a noise as he kept talking over me.

"But still, you remain lost, never to come back to me."

And that was it. I'd had enough.

And to communicate that, with a mighty heave, I planted my feet in the bed, arched my back and shoved his shoulders, pushing him to his back but going with him so I was straddling his hips, my fingers curled into his shoulders, my torso pressed to his and my face an inch away.

"Will you...*shut...up*?" I yelled, his mouth closed, and he scowled up at me. "Jeez!" I cried, looking over his head before I looked back at him. "The drama. God!"

"Circe—" he growled.

But I snapped, "Quiet, Lahn, I'm talking now."

He closed his mouth and scowled again.

I glared.

Then I spoke. "You upset me, broke my heart, okay, I think you get that. That's coming through loud and clear, big guy. You hurt me. But seriously, I mean, the shit I was telling you, it was whacked. Totally unbelievable. So I get that too. But *I'm* an idiot and I lead with my heart and do stupid shit *all the freaking time*. And I got so upset because I loved you so much it hurt so badly, what you said, that I did it again. I acted before I thought. I followed my heart, which hurt, and I did something really freaking stupid. So, okay, Pop calls you an asshole because he knows things didn't start too great, but...clue in, Lahn. He *left* me here. He knows I love you and he wants me to be happy. Yeesh!" I sat up, tipped my head back and looked at the ceiling. "For someone as unbelievably clev—"

I didn't finish because I was on my back and my body was jolted violently because my sarong was yanked clean off.

Oh man.

I focused on his heated eyes just in time for my undies to be torn away... yep, *torn away*, my body jerking again as they went.

Oh *man*.

"Lahn," I breathed as he rolled on top of me.

I was already turned on because I suddenly found myself naked under my king's fantastic, heavy, warm body *and* from the hot look in his eyes.

His big hands trailed swiftly down the backs of my thighs then they yanked up.

"You forgive me," he growled.

"Uh...yeah, a while ago. I'm just a—"

I didn't finish because his mouth took mine in a searing kiss, a wet one, a deep one, a long one and a very, *very* hot one.

Oh yeah.

Yeah, yeah, *yeah.*

He tore his mouth from mine, and I finished my sentence on a dazed, breathless, "*Dork.*"

"I do not know what that is, my doe, but I do not care," he whispered against my lips as his fingers slid through the wetness gathering between my legs, and then his lips slid to my ear. "I will try to be gentle, but since I took my first at the age of twelve, I have never waited this long. Nowhere near. I do not think I can."

I pressed into his hand, tugged at the ties on his hides, turned my head and whispered in his ear, "Don't bother with gentle, honey, I just want to feel you again."

He didn't wait to be asked twice and there he was.

Oh yeah.

God, I *loved* the feel of my husband.

"Yes," I whispered and that was all I could say.

His mouth came back to mine, his hips drove in, hard, fast, uncontrolled, my thighs pressed tight to his sides as one arm held fast around his muscled back and the other hand pulled out his plait and slid into his gorgeous hair.

I knew he struggled. I felt it, but my Lahn, like always, held on until it hit me, hot, hard and piercing, and I cried out into his mouth, my limbs tightening, then he let go, his growled release mingling with mine.

Oh *yeah.*

I was right there, right where I needed to be.

I was home.

After we both recovered, Lahn stayed planted deep as his mouth trailed to my ear.

"You love me," he whispered there, and my limbs tightened.

"Yeah," I whispered back.

"Say it," he growled, and I closed my eyes and turned my head so my lips were at his ear.

"I love you, baby."

I barely got the words out before his head came up and his mouth came back down on mine. This kiss was slow, gentle and sweet as well as wet and deep.

When he broke the connection of our mouths, he rested his forehead on mine and my hand slid from his hair to cup his bearded jaw.

"I'm sorry, honey," I said quietly. He closed his eyes, the pads of my fingers dug in and he opened them again. "I left it too long and the longer I left it, the harder—"

"Okay, my Circe," he cut me off and tipped his chin to touch his mouth to mine. He rolled to his back so I was on top and his arms were tight around me. "Okay," he whispered in my ear.

Okay.

Man, I loved it when he said that.

Yep, I was a dork.

But I could not let it go at that. He was my Lahn and he deserved more so I lifted my head and one of his hands came up to pull my hair back and hold it bunched at the back of my head.

"I'm glad you think it's okay, baby, but I need to know you understand I'm sorry," I said softly.

"I understand," Lahn returned, his voice as gentle as his handsome face.

I licked my lips and shared, "I missed you." I closed my eyes, tipped my head and dropped it so my forehead was on his and then I opened them, saw the warm softness in his dark ones and continued, "I missed you when I was gone, and I missed you when you brought me back."

Lahn didn't reply but his arm around me squeezed.

My hand still at his jaw, I swept my thumb over his beautiful lips as I said quietly, "I don't want to be anywhere but here."

His eyes closed slowly and his hand in my hair tipped my face so I would touch my mouth against his then he released me, and I lifted my head away just an inch.

"Are we good?" I whispered.

"Yes, Circe, good," he whispered back.

My thumb swept his lips again and then moved back over his cheekbone as my eyes watched.

"Linas, kah Lahnahsahna," Lahn demanded quietly, and my gaze shifted back to his. His eyes were warm, his mouth soft and his voice softer when his hand in my hair slid around to my face and his thumb pressed lightly under my eye. "There she is."

I felt my smile wobble as my lungs squeezed and my eyes got wet.

"Did my Lahn resurrect her?" I asked softly and his fingers slid back into my hair, pulling me down for another lip touch before letting me move away an inch.

And that was when I saw *his* brutal, fierce golden spirit burning bright in his eyes for me to see and I knew his answer before he gave it to me.

"Yes, my Circe, she burns bright again for me."

"Dohno," I whispered then kept whispering, "Now I know what I suspected to be true. My husband *is* a god. He can do *anything*."

I caught his grin before he rolled me to my back.

Then he muttered in my ear, "Let us see if this is true."

"Okay," I agreed readily and listened to his chuckle as it rumbled against my skin.

Oh yeah.

I was home.

I WATCHED Lahn walk back into our room after putting down Tunahn who I'd just fed.

Night had fallen but candlelight lit the room softly. If I was lucky and fell asleep quickly, I could maybe get four hours in.

Lahn got under the covers, stretched out beside me, shoved an arm under me and curled me to his long, warm, hard side.

Okay, fuck that.

No way I was sleeping.

I lifted up on an elbow, rested my hand on his chest and looked into his dark, beloved eyes.

"Do you make trainee warriors buff your saddle?" I asked.

He blinked. "What?"

"Trainee warriors. Do you make them buff your saddle?"

His mouth twitched. "Warriors in training learn and do many things, kah Lahnahsahna. Buffing saddles is not one of them."

My eyes drifted to his shoulder, and I muttered, "Oh."

"Something they *do* learn," he went on and my eyes moved back to his, "is not to waste time performing deeds that are not worth performing. Like buffing saddles."

I started giggling. Lahn's arm gave me a squeeze as his lips tipped up into a smile.

I rested my chest into his, my arm curving around him, my face getting closer.

"Did you really lose your virginity when you were twelve?" I whispered and his eyes immediately shuttered so I shook his body with my arm. "Lahn."

"Meena," he said shortly.

"No joke?" I asked, eyes wide with surprise.

He studied me then he shook his head. "No joke."

"Wow," I breathed. "That's kinda young isn't it?"

He kept studying me.

Then he stated, "A warrior's trainer will decide when a warrior is ready to advance through all facets of his training. My trainer decided I was ready to take a woman at twelve. So I took a Xacto at twelve."

I felt his gaze sharpen on my face when he said the word "Xacto" so I told him quickly, "Baby, I know you're not going to step out on me. If a guy like you who needs it as often as you do and the *way* you do can hang on for eight months for me, I have no worries about you going to the Xacto."

"No, my Circe, you have no worries about me going to the Xacto," he said quietly.

I smiled at him.

Lahn smiled back.

Then he asked, "What is a...*dork*?"

I giggled again before I explained, "A kind of, I don't know, it's hard to explain. A person that does stupid shit, kinda klutzy, kinda bonkers, kinda foolish, not enough of any of those to be really stupid or harm anyone, just, I don't know, a dork or..." I tipped my head to the side and grinned. "*Me*."

Lahn wasn't grinning.

"My golden queen is not a dork," he declared.

I slid in closer and said, still grinning, "Big guy, I lost it and spirited my pregnant ass home for five months, leaving you behind when I promised never to leave you *at all*. Then my pop gave me a big lecture about leaving the man I was in love with, I got back, forgave you weeks before I told you I did, which was about the time Karrim told me you never gave up on me, then got myself caught up in procrastination, which by the way, Pop also used to lecture me about all the time. So it got harder and harder to talk to you about it to the point where I pissed you off and made you give up on me. Calling myself a dork is being nice. I was *way* beyond a dork."

"This is true," he agreed so swiftly I blinked.

Then I stared.

Then I burst out laughing.

And I didn't stop when I was pulled full on top of my husband, he rolled me to my back, covered my body with his, shoved his face in my neck and I heard his deep laughter rumbling against my skin as I felt it shaking my body.

And passersby, spies and those who were just plain nosy who were paying attention outside our house heard the mighty Dax and his rahna

Dahksahna's mirth, and about forty-five minutes later, they heard something else entirely.

And all they heard was all over Korwahn the next morning.

THE SUN WAS TOUCHING the sky when something woke me. I felt disconcerted before it hit me.

I was not sleeping under Lahn's warm body. I was pressed to the side of it, his arm around me, my cheek to his shoulder, my arm around his abs.

My eyes opened and I stared at my daughter, her rosy, chubby cheek pressed to her father's brown, muscled chest, her eyes closed, her pink lips pursed in a cute, little baby pout, her sweet little fist resting light on his smooth, dark skin.

I felt my lips turn up and I slid my arm from my husband's stomach so I could rest my hand on my daughter's fat rump.

Then carefully, I tipped my head back to see my handsome husband's sleeping profile.

I hadn't heard her, and this meant she'd probably woken, and as Isis was content to do, she just quietly took things in.

But my husband's sensed her awake and went to go get his daughter.

That made my lips turn up deeper.

He either felt the slight movement of my mouth or sensed my eyes on him, his opened and his head turned to me. When I looked into their dark depths, I saw they were somnolent and sexy and all the love he felt for me was warm, sweet and openly read in the depths of them.

Yes, oh yes.

I was home.

I pressed against Isis's bottom.

"We're going to have to talk about this," I whispered.

I watched with fascination as he grinned.

I let that process through me as I grinned back.

Then I sighed.

I tipped my chin down and closed my eyes, deciding we'd talk about it later.

Tunahn would be hungry soon.

I needed to get my rest.

Harold Quinn listened as he watched the old woman in a trance, her voice saying his daughter's words, his heart breaking a little and mending a little more.

"Hey, Pop. Get this! You've got *two* grandbabies. Twins! Can you believe that? Tunahn is our boy, and his name means horse. They have a bunch of different gods here and the horse god is one. Lahn's name means tiger and that's a god too. He named Tunahn after the horse god because horses are strong, clever and loyal. Our other baby is a little girl. She has fuzzy, golden hair that I'm pretty sure is going to be just like Mom's and mine. Tunahn, I forgot to tell you, has black hair like his dad. Her name is Isis. I named her like you and Mom named me. Tunahn is already strong as an ox, no joke. He also bawls a lot, but that's because he's a greedy, little monster and cannot seem to get enough milk. But he doesn't have to bawl long. I can't keep my hands off him. He's my little warrior. He's growing leaps and bounds. Isis is my golden baby. She rarely cries and is super sweet. Her dad freaking *adores* her. If Tunahn wakes in the night, Lahn is cool with me getting up and feeding, but he's firm about Tunahn going back to his bed. If Isis does, Lahn's all over letting her sleep with us. Don't worry, I've nipped *that* in the bud. Well, kind of."

The witch sucked in a huge breath and then kept talking, just like his Circe could do.

"You were right, as usual. I guess it sucks that I've learned that now, when you're a world away. The witch says that we can try to send these messages, but they can't be certain to reach their target. Though I hope we can, even if it's only random. I'll promise to keep trying and I hope you do too. But, like I said, you were right. Lahn and I worked things out. He worked hard at it and maybe I made him work *too* hard. But I love him, and I forgave him and now I'm happy. You don't have to worry. It's all good. He loves me a lot, Pop, and shows me he does. I'm happy, honestly, very happy. He's a good guy, and if you met him, it might take a while, but you'd like him." A pause then, "Oh, by the way, if you could do me a favor and not call him an asshole in your next message, that would be cool. I taught him English, and he figured out what that meant, and he didn't much like it."

Harold Quinn grinned.

The witch went on.

"If I don't hear from you, or you don't hear from me, I want you to know I miss you and I love you and I always will. Always, Pop. You're the best pop a girl could have. The...*absolute*...*best*."

Oh yeah.

There it was.

That was his girl.

The witch kept talking. "Tell the guys I said Hey and give Marlene a hug for me and let her and Circe know I'm all right."

Another sucked in breath and then the witch went on.

"And I promise I'm all right, Pop. Promise. I'm...well, Daddy, what can I say? I'm home."

The woman's shoulders slumped, her head dropped then it shot up and she blinked, her blind eyes focusing on nothing but no longer hazed by her trance.

"Did it work?" she asked, face alight.

When Harold Quinn answered, his voice was gruff, "Yeah."

The old woman paused as if attempting to sense his mood, the brightness in her face faded when she succeeded in this endeavor and she nodded.

Quietly, she said, "We're lucky it worked."

He nodded back, though she couldn't see him. He'd heard her. Communication with that world was difficult. Messages were received only randomly, messages sent might never be known if they were heard.

Tunahn and Isis and his Circe happy with her king.

Yeah, he was lucky it worked.

"If you want to try again..." she trailed off, and he nodded again even though she couldn't see him, somehow he knew she sensed this too.

Harold was right for she smiled a gentle smile.

Then she reached out blindly, touched his arm and whispered, "I'll never be far, father of the golden Circes."

With that, she turned and walked quietly out of his garage, her cane clicking on the floor as she went.

Harold watched the door close behind her before he walked into his daughter's office and settled in her chair behind her desk after pulling out his wallet. He flipped it open, gently tugged out the oft-touched photo and looked into a pair of familiar golden eyes.

"She's happy, Andie," he whispered to his wife.

Andromeda Quinn did what she always did.

She smiled back at him, her beautiful eyes lit with that bright, golden light Harold Quinn loved so fucking much.

The End

KORWAHK/ENGLISH DICTIONARY

Words, phrases and conjugations

Ahno—(v) To like
Aka—(pro) Others
Ana—(adv) Then
Anah—(n/adv) Tonight
Anka—(n/adv) Tomorrow
Anla—(n/adv) Today
Ansha—(adv/exc) Here
Ato—(v) To bow
Bahsah—(n) Wife
Bahsan (n) Husband
Bel—(adv) Soon
Boh—(adv) Now
Boonahn—(adj/adv/n) Better
Chah—(adv/pro) A lot
Cham—(n) Tent
Cuun—(n) Tour
Dahksahna—(n/title) Queen [of the Korwahk Nation]
Dahno—(v) To wake

Danho—(v) To forget

Dax—(n/title) King [of the Korwahk Nation]

Daxshee—(n/place)—The traveling encampment of the Dax [king] of the Korwahk Nation

Dohno—(adj) Good

El—(determiner) A; an

Et—(conj) If

Fahnahsan—(adj) Happy

Fahno—(v) To smile

Fahkah—(adv) Enough

Fahzah—(adv) Always

Farzah—(adv) Never

Fauna—(n) Doe [also used as endearment]

Gay—(adv/prep) As

Gahn—(conj) But

Gahsee—(adj) Hungry

Gahso—(v) To be hungry

Geenheeso—(v) To boss (around) [different than order or command, not formal or official]

Gingo—(v) To drink

Goyah—(expression) Good-bye/Farewell

Hahla—(adj) Pure; true

Hahnee—(adj) Liquid

Hansahnalo—(v) To love

Jahnjee—(n) Protector

Jahko—(v) To do

Jahno—(v) To have

Jak—(adv/pro/determiner)—All

Juno—(v) To play

Kay—(pro) I; me

Kay tingay—(expression) I'm sorry/I apologize

Kah—(possessive) My

Kahna—(possessive) Mine

Keeta—(n) Things

Kut—(n) [slang] Bitch

Kuvo—(v) To understand

Lahn—(n) Tiger

Lahnahsahna—(n) Tigress [female tiger]

Lapo—(v) To be

Lee—(determiner) The (not used with a title)
Leeka—(n) Skin
Leenyahso—(adj) Skilled
Linas (n) Eyes
Lino—(v) To see
Lipa—(n) Hair
Liros—(n) Legs
Lisa—(n) Mouth
Loh—(prep) on
Loolah—(n) [familiar] Mama
Loot—(conj) And
Lornya—(n) Robe
Luh—(prep) To
Luna—(n) Body
Luto—(v) To sit
Marko—(v) To allow
Mayo—(v) To go fast
Me—(excl) No
Meera—(adv/prep) Between
Meena—(excl) Yes
Na—(pro) You
Nahna—(possessive) Your
Nahrahka—(expression) You're welcome
Nayeeso—(v) To own
Neenkah—(adj/adv/n/prep) Inside
Neeso—(v) To rest
Pahk—(n) Fire
Pahkah—(n) Firepit
Pahkan—(n) Torch
Pahnsahna—(n) Spirit [Soul]
Pahnsahnak—(n) God [Mythical not Biblical]
Pahnsahnalla—(n) Goddess
Pahnso—(v) To live
Poyah—(expression) Hello
Punto—(v) To end
Quaxi—(n) Paint
Rah—(n) Gold
Rahna—(adj) Golden
Raylo—(v) To be quiet

Ruhno—(v) To take

Sah—(pro) This

Sahka—(adj) Healthy; well

Sahna—(adj) Beautiful

Sahnahso—(v) To let

See—(pro) That

Shahsha—(expression) Thank you

Shalah—(expression) Please

Suh—(determiner) The (used only with official titles i.e.; Suh Tunak; Suh Xacme)

Suh Tunak—The Korwahk Horde

Ta—(pro) We

Tahko—(v) To leave

Tahna—(possessive) Our

Tahnhan—(n) Command

Tahno—(v) To command

Tan—(pro) Us

Tee—(pro) It

Teenkah—(adj) Little

Tela—(adv) What

Tera—(adv) How

Tooka—(adv) Again

Tooyo—(v) To fuck

Tooyo—[As expletive]—Fuck you!

Trahyo—(v) To sleep

Trooya—(n) Name

Tunahn—(n) Horse

Tunakan—(n) Warrior

Tunakanahsa—(n) Female warrior

Tuno—(v) To ride

Unahyo—(v) To melt

Uvo—(v) To give

Vato—(v) To win

Vayo—(v) To come

Veeyo—(v) To go

Wahlo—(v) To start

Weyko—(v) To promise

Xac—(n) [slang] Cock (penis)

Xacme (n) Eunuch

Xaxsah—(n) [slang] Cunt (vagina)

Xacto—(n) Group of female slaves that are owned by the Korwahk Horde and serve only warriors.

Yahka—(adj) Well; good; fine

Yo—(prep) For

Zah—(pro/possessive) Her

Zak—(possessive) His

Zakah—(n) Raw, distilled spirit (alcoholic beverage akin to inferior/rough whiskey)

Zan—(pro) Him

Zo—(prep) From

Zooko—(v) To want

Zut—(prep) With

Verb Conjunctions

oo—imperative/command

al— imperative with "must"

ay—present tense

an—future tense with "will"

ee—future tense with "to be"

un—past tense

GLOSSARY OF PARALLEL UNIVERSE

PLACES, SEAS, REGIONS IN THE KRISTEN ASHLEY'S FANTASYLAND SERIES

Bellebryn—(place) Small, peaceful, city-sized princedom located in the Northlands and fully within the boundaries of Hawkvale and the Green Sea (west)

Fleuridia—(place) Somewhat advanced, peaceful nation located in the Northlands; boundaries to Hawkvale (north and west) and the Marhac Sea (south)

Green Sea—(body of water) Ocean-like body of water with coastlines abutting Bellebryn, Hawkvale, Lunwyn and Middleland

Hawkvale—(place) Somewhat advanced, peaceful nation located in the Northlands; boundaries with Middleland (north), Fleuridia (south and east) and the Green Sea (west) and Marhac Sea (south)

Keenhak—(place) Primitive, warring nation located in the Southlands; boundaries with Korwahk (north) and Maroo (west)

Korwahk—(place) Primitive, warring nation located in the Southlands; boundaries with the Marhac Sea (north) and the nations of Keenhak (southeast) and Maroo (southwest)

Korwahn—(place) Large capital city of Korwahk

Lunwyn—(place) Somewhat advanced, peaceful nation in the farthest reaches of the Northlands; boundaries to Middleland (south), the Green Sea (west) and the Winter Sea (north)

Marhac Sea—(large body of water) Separates Korwahk and Hawkvale and Fleuridia

Maroo—(place) Primitive, warring nation located in the Southlands; boundaries to Korwahk (north) and Keenhak (east)

Middleland—(place) Somewhat advanced nation with tyrant king located in the Northlands; boundaries to Hawkvale (south), Fleuridia (south), Lunwyn (north) and the Green Sea (west)

[The] Northlands—(region) The region north of the equator on the alternate earth

[The] Southlands—(region) The region south of the equator on the alternate earth

Winter Sea—(large body of water) Arctic body of water that forms the northern coast of Lunwyn, filled with large glaciers

KEEP READING FOR MORE FANTASYLAND

Fantastical

Cora Goode has woken up in a fairytale world where she can understand what birds are saying, men ride horses and have fluffy feathers in their hats and furniture zigs, zags and whirls in miracles of construction.

The problem is, she thinks she's in a dream, but she's actually taken the place of the parallel universe Cora. Without realizing it, our Cora does something that starts a centuries-old curse that will sweep the land if she gets captured by the evil Minerva.

At this point, her dream world becomes a nightmare.

Luckily, hot guy, fantasyland Noctorno is there to save her from the clutches of the grotesque vickrants sent by Minerva to capture her.

Unfortunately, hot guy, fantasyland Noctorno doesn't like the Cora of his world all that much (to say the least) and he thinks our Cora is her. And no matter what our Cora says or does to try to convince him, he won't be convinced.

But Cora needs Tor to keep her safe and guide her through this fantastical world as she hopes one day to wake up in her not-so-great apartment in her not-so-great life in her world.

The problem is, the more time she spends with the gorgeous warrior Tor, the faster she falls in love with him.

FANTASTICAL
CHAPTER ONE

Holy Crap

I heard birds.

They were singing. Not chirping. Singing. It wasn't birdsong. It was just plain old song but in chirps. It was hard to describe, but there it was.

A lot of it.

It made me open my eyes.

Then I blinked and felt it.

I was lying in a bed but not my bed. The mattress was strange, very soft, very plush. I wasn't on it. I was *in* it. It partially enveloped my body like a warm, comfortable, squashy cloud.

What on earth?

I stared at the sun-washed walls, felt the bed and heard the strange birdsong.

One thing I knew for certain: I was not home.

I shot straight to sitting in the bed and looked around the room.

I was in a four-poster bed, gossamer, pale-lilac curtains all around, a fluffy pale-lilac-covered duvet on top. The walls of the room were an even paler lilac, and I took in the bizarre white furniture.

A big wardrobe with scrolled feet, the sides bowed in, the top an arch. It was bulky and yet delicate. A miracle of construction. There was no way that wardrobe could stand on those flimsy, curled feet, but it was.

Two tall dressers. One that zigged at the top, zagged in the middle and zigged again at the bottom. Another whose drawers went up like steps on one side, a different miracle of construction for it appeared to be teetering yet stood true.

Then there was a dressing table with a big oval mirror on the top and two smaller ones to its side. The dressing table was also delicate with curly whirls for legs, around the mirrors and carved into the three drawers down either side. It was covered in fragile, intricate glass bottles, all of them in various shades of purple.

"Holy crap, I'm dreaming," I whispered.

That had to be it. I was dreaming. Dreaming the most freaking real dream I'd ever had in my life.

Suddenly, the door flew open.

I jumped and looked to my right to see a blonde woman dance into the room wearing an old-fashioned, blinding-white nightgown, the voluminous kind that had a string at the neckline and gathers all around.

Yeesh, how did she get that nightgown so white? I was never good at keeping whites white. They always grayed out.

It had to be new.

Oh wait, this was a dream. Of course it would be that white.

"Cora!" she cried my name, whirling into the room. "Cora, Cora, Cora! Today is the best day *of my life*!"

She stopped at the foot of the bed, shoved a diaphanous curtain aside and smiled down at me while I stared up at her.

Whoa.

Seriously.

She was gorgeous. Bright-blue eyes. Thick blonde hair. Delicate features. Petite. A stunner.

"Can you believe it?" she asked then clapped her hands. "I'm getting married today!"

"Uh..." I started, but she rocked swiftly up to her toes and then danced gracefully on them to one of the two sets of French doors that were on either side of the dressing table.

She flung them open, the birdsong stopped, she stepped out on a Juliet balcony and threw her arms up and out to the sides.

In position, she let out two beautiful, perfect notes in a gorgeous soprano. The birdsong started again, in earnest this time (and I thought it was earnest before), and I blinked through the sheer curtains as I saw a tiny colorful bird (and I knew there were colorful birds in the world but there weren't birds *that* colorful) alight on her outstretched hand.

She brought the bird to her face and the bird chirped gaily at her instead of flying away.

"I'm getting married to the man I love today, Aggie! Isn't that *marvelous?*" she told the bird.

The bird chirped happily at her and then pecked her nose. Not like a peck, more like a kiss.

She giggled and it, too, sounded like a happy song.

Whoa!

I blinked.

That was when I knew.

I was dreaming I was in one of those animated movies.

Wow.

Cool! What an awesome dream!

She turned and the bird hopped up to her shoulder and somehow kept its place as she danced on her toes back to the bed with more grace than any human I'd ever seen. Then again, seeing as she was part of a dream, she could be as graceful as any character in an animated movie that my mind could make up.

She threw the side curtains aside and ordered merrily, "Get up, silly! We have to get ready! So much to do, so much to do! Tra la! Tra la, la, la, la! Tra, la, la, *la, la*!"

She emitted the tra las in her gorgeous voice while whirling toward the door and the bird fluttered off her shoulder onto the bed as she did so. Then it hopped to me, looked in my eyes and chirped.

God, I swear I knew that the bird was saying, "Heya."

Holy crap.

"Heya," I whispered to the bird.

That was when I could swear the bird's eyes lit up with a smile.

Holy crap!

"Up, Cora, you can't be lazy today! I stayed with you to make certain you got up and got ready in plenty of time. As my matron of honor, you have to be nearly as beautiful as me!" the girl called from the door then threw her shining, golden-blonde mane back and laughed a sing-song laugh before she tipped her head back down and smiled a stunning smile at me. "Not that *that* will be hard, my exquisite sister."

She clapped her hands with delight again and exited the door, closing it behind her.

I stared at the door. Then I looked back down at the bird who was still looking up at me.

"This is a way cool dream," I told the bird, and it tipped its head to the side like my words were confusing.

It took two hops so it was sitting on my thigh.

Awesome!

Then it said, "Chirp chirp," which I took to mean, "You aren't dreaming."

"I am so totally dreaming," I told the bird.

The bird replied, "Chirp, chirp, chirpity, chirp," which came to me as chirps, but I knew meant, "No, really, this isn't a dream, Cora."

"It's a dream, bird. I know this first off because people don't talk to birds, or at least know what they're saying. Unless, of course, they're bonkers," I returned.

The bird tilted its head again and then chirped, "Chirp, chirp, chirp, chirp," (with a bunch more chirps) which meant, "Are you ill? Of course people talk to birds. And bunnies. And deer. And mice. And my name is Agglethorpe. You and everyone call me Aggie."

"There it is," I told the bird. "Your name is Agglethorpe. That's a perfectly ludicrous name that only could be given to a bird in a dream or a Disney movie."

That was when the bird hopped forward and pecked my hand, which kind of hurt, and then looked up at me and chirped what I took to mean, "My name isn't ludicrous! I know this because *you* gave it to me!"

But I was staring at my hand where the bird, or Aggie, had pecked.

That peck had kind of hurt.

What?

You weren't supposed to feel pain in dreams, were you?

At that point I heard a noise I'd never heard in real life before. The kind of noise you hear in movies when horse's hooves are beating on cobblestones, or the members of Monty Python were cracking together coconuts. Aggie flew up and to the window to alight on the balustrade of the Juliet balcony.

It looked down then it started hopping up and down as it turned its head toward me and started chirping madly, telling me, "Come quick, Cora! Oh no! Come quick! Dashiell is here! With Orlando and..." the bird looked back down then urgently to me, chirping in a dire chirp (yes, seriously, a *dire* chirp), "*Noctorno!*"

About the Author

Kristen Ashley is the *New York Times* bestselling author of over eighty romance novels including the *Rock Chick, Colorado Mountain, Dream Man, Chaos, Unfinished Heroes, The 'Burg, Magdalene, Fantasyland, The Three, Ghost and Reincarnation, The Rising, Dream Team, Moonlight and Motor Oil, River Rain, Wild West MC, Misted Pines* and *Honey* series along with several stand-alone novels. She's a hybrid author, publishing titles both independently and traditionally, her books have been translated in fourteen languages and she's sold over five million books.

Kristen's novel, *Law Man*, won the *RT Book Reviews* Reviewer's Choice Award for best Romantic Suspense, her independently published title *Hold On* was nominated for *RT Book Reviews* best Independent Contemporary Romance and her traditionally published title *Breathe* was nominated for best Contemporary Romance. Kristen's titles *Motorcycle Man, The Will*, and *Ride Steady* (which won the Reader's Choice award from *Romance Reviews*) all made the final rounds for Goodreads Choice Awards in the Romance category.

Kristen, born in Gary and raised in Brownsburg, Indiana, is a fourth-generation graduate of Purdue University. Since, she's lived in Denver, the West Country of England, and she now resides in Phoenix. She worked as a charity executive for eighteen years prior to beginning her independent publishing career. She now writes full-time.

Although romance is her genre, the prevailing themes running through all of Kristen's novels are friendship, family and a strong sisterhood. To this end, and as a way to thank her readers for their support, Kristen has created the Rock Chick Nation, a series of programs that are designed to give back to her readers and promote a strong female community.

The mission of the Rock Chick Nation is to live your best life, be true to your true self, recognize your beauty, and take your sister's back whether they're at your side as friends and family or if they're thousands of miles away and you don't know who they are.

The programs of the RC Nation include Rock Chick Rendezvous, weekends Kristen organizes full of parties and get-togethers to bring the sisterhood together, Rock Chick Recharges, evenings Kristen arranges for women who have been nominated to receive a special night, and Rock Chick Rewards, an ongoing program that raises funds for nonprofit women's organizations Kristen's readers nominate. Kristen's Rock Chick Rewards have donated hundreds of thousands of dollars to charity and this number continues to rise.

You can read more about Kristen, her titles and the Rock Chick Nation at KristenAshley.net.

facebook.com/kristenashleybooks
twitter.com/KristenAshley68
instagram.com/kristenashleybooks
pinterest.com/KristenAshleyBooks
goodreads.com/kristenashleybooks
bookbub.com/authors/kristen-ashley

Also by Kristen Ashley

Rock Chick Series:

Rock Chick

Rock Chick Rescue

Rock Chick Redemption

Rock Chick Renegade

Rock Chick Revenge

Rock Chick Reckoning

Rock Chick Regret

Rock Chick Revolution

Rock Chick Reawakening

Rock Chick Reborn

The 'Burg Series:

For You

At Peace

Golden Trail

Games of the Heart

The Promise

Hold On

The Chaos Series:

Own the Wind

Fire Inside

Ride Steady

Walk Through Fire

A Christmas to Remember

Rough Ride

Wild Like the Wind

Free

Wild Fire

Wild Wind

The Colorado Mountain Series:

The Gamble

Sweet Dreams

Lady Luck

Breathe

Jagged

Kaleidoscope

Bounty

Dream Man Series:

Mystery Man

Wild Man

Law Man

Motorcycle Man

Quiet Man

Dream Team Series:

Dream Maker

Dream Chaser

Dream Bites Cookbook

Dream Spinner

Dream Keeper

The Fantasyland Series:

Wildest Dreams

The Golden Dynasty

Fantastical

Broken Dove

Midnight Soul

Gossamer in the Darkness

Ghosts and Reincarnation Series:

Sommersgate House

Lacybourne Manor

Penmort Castle

Fairytale Come Alive

Lucky Stars

The Honey Series:

The Deep End

The Farthest Edge

The Greatest Risk

The Magdalene Series:

The Will

Soaring

The Time in Between

Mathilda, SuperWitch:

Mathilda's Book of Shadows

Mathilda The Rise of the Dark Lord

Misted Pines Series

The Girl in the Mist

The Girl in the Woods

Moonlight and Motor Oil Series:

The Hookup

The Slow Burn

The Rising Series:

The Beginning of Everything

The Plan Commences

The Dawn of the End

The Rising

The River Rain Series:

After the Climb

After the Climb Special Edition

Chasing Serenity

Taking the Leap

Making the Match

The Three Series:

Until the Sun Falls from the Sky

With Everything I Am

Wild and Free

The Unfinished Hero Series:

Knight

Creed

Raid

Deacon

Sebring

Wild West MC Series:

Still Standing

Smoke and Steel

Other Titles by Kristen Ashley:

Heaven and Hell

Play It Safe

Three Wishes

Complicated

Loose Ends

Fast Lane

Perfect Together (Summer 2023)

Milton Keynes UK
Ingram Content Group UK Ltd.
UKHW011412010424
440427UK00001B/108